I0659675

Six earth days, two mismatched matchmakers,
and one pair of stubborn soul mates.

SOULS ADRIFT
in the
WINDY CITY

A Novel

JoAnn Hornak

VERPAZZA
PUBLISHING

This is a work of fiction. Names, characters, places and incidents either are the product of the author's imagination or are used factiously. Any resemblance to actual persons, living or dead, is entirely coincidental.

Books by JoAnn Hornak

Adventures of a Salsa Goddess

A Delicate Bond

For my mother

"In order to live free and happily,
you must sacrifice
boredom.

It is not always an easy
sacrifice."

—Richard Bach

"A life lived in fear is a life half lived."
—Spanish proverb

Prologue

Nimbus clouds hung low over the Chicago sky; flashes of lightning briefly brightened the night followed by a low trill of thunder sounding in the distance. But the heavens had yet to release a single drop of cooling rain on the summer evening that Zeke Nomad fell in love. The faint breeze blowing off Lake Michigan could not move the thick, spongy air, but Zeke didn't notice the heat as he stepped up to the open-air dance floor in Grant Park. Waves of anticipation washed through him; he could feel the energy all around him. With a strange certainty that he could not explain, Zeke knew something extraordinary was about to happen.

Sweat poured down the faces of the musicians in the twelve-piece Latin band on stage. As their music filled the park, the pulsing melody energized Zeke. A pretty Latina, spilling out of the top of her tight red dress, sang Quimbara, doing a passable Celia Cruz imitation, as she swiveled her hips in time with the contagious rhythm. Without noticing, Zeke began tapping his foot to the beat. Hoping to find a partner, he turned his attention to the dance floor.

Couples of all ages and sizes twirled and glided across the floor as though it were as smooth as glass. His gaze fell upon a woman who was in the midst of sliding her slender leg between the two outstretched legs of her partner. She pulled herself up, dangled her foot in the air like an appetizer, and then seductively rubbed it up and down his calf. As her partner twirled her, her short black skirt flared out like a halo along with her shoulder-length ginger curls. On the very last beat of the song, he dipped her backwards over his arm where she lay draped like a string of pearls.

She straightened, nodded to him with a big grin, and then retreated to the sidelines where she joined another woman. Zeke could not take his eyes off her.

Across the dance floor, Inez Paris's heartbeats slowed to normal, but the intense high she'd felt during the last dance still coursed through her body, making her feel much lighter than the heavy, humid air. After years of dancing, she was able to follow any man's lead—no easy feat since each partner had a different style. The last guy's lead had been super heavy, sort of like dancing with a cement mixer, but she'd still enjoyed it, especially at the end when he'd let her show off.

"You're doing it again, Izzy," said her sister Rachel when Inez reached her at the edge of the dance floor.

"What?"

"Smiling like you swallowed a rainbow or something."

Inez laughed. "I can't help it. Salsa is like the best. It's like heaven!"

Rachel rolled her eyes. "Whatever."

Inez couldn't understand why Latin dancing had failed to captivate her sister—and everyone else on the planet for that matter. Joy just bubbled through her body whenever she heard the music. Her feet moved to the throbbing pulse as if she had no will of her own. Nothing made her feel the way salsa did, except perhaps thunderstorms.

The wildness and strength of storms thrilled Inez, making her feel at the same time both smaller and larger than life. She could smell the rain in the air and feel the current that flowed through it. Every cell in her body tingled. Inez knew—without understanding how she knew—that something special was about to happen.

"Close your mouth," said Mike Knight, with a nudge to Zeke's arm.

"What?"

"The redhead you're gawking at," Mike replied. "She's cute."

"Cute? Are you blind?" said Zeke. "She's gorgeous!"

Mike shrugged. "Good thing we like different types. Speaking of, get a load of that blonde over there."

"What about Karen?" asked Zeke, referring to the woman Mike had been dating for the past few weeks.

Mike rubbed his hands together and winked. "Karen who?"

Zeke shook his head. His roommate had been with more women during their first two years at DePaul University, than all of the men in their dorm put together. Zeke was happy to be a one-woman man and had been, up until his break-up with Patty at the end of last semester. Patty, a pretty girl with a heart-shaped face who'd grown up on a farm in Iowa, was sweet, but they'd run out of things to talk about over the last six months. She had no interest in the Latin culture or salsa dancing or traveling abroad—all of the things Zeke loved. No one understood his newfound passion—everyone Zeke had grown up with thought salsa was something that came in a jar at the grocery store.

Zeke tried not to stare, but his gaze returned to her again. A frisson shot through his body. There was something about her—it was almost as if he recognized her, as if he already knew her. The voice from inside urged him toward her.

Inez noticed Rachel staring at someone on the opposite side of the dance floor.

"You see that cute guy over there with the wavy hair," Rachel said. "He's been staring at you, like a lot."

Inez looked. Their eyes met and held for an extra long second until Inez broke off her gaze. With her peripheral vision, she saw him coming her way, and her heart did a little flip.

Zeke felt as if he were being physically pulled across the dance floor by an invisible rope. His heart tumbled in circles as he approached her, trying not to stare. Her cinnamon-colored eyes sparkled with humor, as if she'd just heard a funny story. A dash of freckles splashed across the bridge of her slightly askew nose, and her friendly grin gave her a girlish quality he found irresistible. He reminded himself to breathe and then asked her to dance.

He took her hand and led her to the center of the dance floor just as the band struck up his favorite salsa song, Mambo Yo Yo. The fast-paced beat of the song challenged all of his skills, but he managed to lead her into several clockwise triple twirls, followed by two counterclockwise twirls. She responded to the slightest pressure of his hand, following his lead perfectly, with no hesitation. Nearing the end of the song, he spun her a dozen times in a row, and on the very last beat, Zeke dipped her so low the top of her head just skimmed the ground.

Inez smiled broadly as he pulled her up. Now this guy knew how to dance! He'd barely touched her hand, but she'd known exactly what he wanted her to do, almost as if she could read his mind.

"Wow!" Inez exclaimed. "That was so fun!"

"Did I spin you too many times?" he asked.

"There is no such thing as too many times." Inez was dizzy but not from being spun, that dip had sent her heart soaring.

They stood for a moment, not speaking. She found it difficult to look into the deep brown eyes that hadn't left her face. Rachel was right, he was cute, and she sensed a strength about him that was very appealing.

"Would you like something to drink?" he asked.

Inez glanced in Rachel's direction and saw her talking with a lanky boy about her age.

"Looks like your friend is busy," said Zeke, following her eyes to a much taller, dark-haired woman.

"That's my sister Rachel," Inez responded. "She's going to be a junior in high school."

Zeke bought two bottled waters at the concession stand, and they sat on a nearby bench. He opened one of the bottles and handed it to her.

"Where did you learn to dance?" Inez asked.

"A friend in my Spanish class took me to a club one night, and I was hooked from the first dance," he said. "I go to DePaul, how about you?"

"I'm at U of I Urbana-Champaign," she said, wishing again that she had gone to college in the city. She managed to get home only once a month during the school year because her schedule was so full. She missed her family and also missed living in Chicago. There wasn't a lot to do in rural Illinois but cow-tipping and getting drunk.

"What's your major?" Inez asked.

"Political Science and Spanish," Zeke replied. "And you?"

"I have a double major, too. International Relations and Spanish."

Zeke didn't want to stare, but her face was alive and full of passion, unlike so many of the girls in his classes who always seemed bored, as if college were a burden to get through until their real lives could begin.

"I like my Spanish classes a lot more than poli sci," Zeke said, "but I want to go to law school, after I go into the Peace Corps."

"Me too!" Inez said. "I mean, not law school, but I'm going into the Peace Corps too. I just applied."

"I sent my application in last month," he said. Her enthusiasm worked its way into his bloodstream. Zeke was drawn to her in a way he'd never felt with anyone before. "Where do you want to go?"

"Central or South America."

"Me too." Zeke said. "Wouldn't it be cool if we ended up in the same country?"

Inez agreed. Why weren't there any guys like him at school? During her first two years of college, she had dated steadily, but no one seriously. The guys in her classes were so immature, especially the frat boys. All they wanted to do was get drunk every weekend and score with as many girls as possible. She had so much in common with this guy. Too bad the timing of their meeting was so bad.

"Is something wrong?" he asked her, noticing a furrow form between her eyes.

"No, it's nothing," she said. "Are you going to be the kind of lawyer that argues in front of juries?"

"I hope so. I want to work at the Legal Aid Society," Zeke replied. "When I get back from the Peace Corps I'll be fluent in Spanish, so I plan to work in the Latino community. What do you want to do?"

"I'm going to get a job with the U.S. Agency for International Development in the Caribbean, maybe the Dominican Republic. Then somewhere in Central America or South America."

"It sounds like you have your whole life planned out."

"I do," Inez replied. "And guess what? I'm leaving for Madrid next week for my junior year abroad. It's my first time to Europe!"

Zeke's heart fell. Talk about bad timing. At last he'd met someone he could really talk to, but she was going to be halfway across the world for the next year.

"Hey, let's dance again," she suggested, noticing his frown.

Zeke smiled and took her hand. Their second salsa dance was even better than the first. As their bodies found their own unique rhythm together, their movements became more fluid and intense. When the band switched to a Merengue, a simple two-step dance, Zeke started by holding her away from his body, but as the song went on, they moved closer and closer until he held her tight against him, as if they were slow dancing. She felt so good in his arms, and as they swayed together, everything else fell away. Zeke barely noticed when the first drops of rain began falling. She didn't seem to notice either. They kept dancing as if time were suspended.

And then the sky broke open. Within seconds they were drenched. They pulled apart and simultaneously burst out laughing. Auburn hairs darkened by the rain clung to her ivory cheek. Without thinking, Zeke brushed the hair aside with his fingers. Their eyes met and held. Zeke wanted to kiss her, but held back.

Inez looked into his eyes. It seemed like he might kiss her. Would he? And then, just as he began moving his mouth toward hers she felt a tug on her arm, breaking the spell.

"Come on!" her sister cried, yanking at her wrist. "Let's go."

"Wait!" Zeke shouted over the thunderous downpour. "What's your name?"

"Inez."

"I'm Zeke."

They didn't move. In the long moment that followed, Zeke memorized every detail of Inez's face.

"I'm soaked, let's go!" yelled Rachel, pulling Inez away.

"Wait, Inez!" he shouted, sprinting after them. "What's your last name?"

A crack of thunder exploded, drowning out his words. He watched Inez until she rounded a corner and was gone.

"What the hell is wrong with you?" Mike yelled a minute later, startling Zeke out of his trance. "Come on!"

Zeke turned slowly and then followed Mike to the car. They got into Mike's beat up Chevy Impala, both of them soaked, their clothes clinging to their skin. Mike started the car, which sputtered and then roared to life.

As they drove, Mike began rambling about the blonde who'd given him her phone number. But Zeke's thoughts drifted to the story his mother had recounted so often—of the night she'd met his father at a dance at the VFW and had fallen in love at first sight. Zeke always assumed that his mother had been exaggerating. He'd never believed it was possible, until tonight.

Y ou called for me, Sir? I believe this is about the necrotic ring spot virus ravaging the evergreen rhododendron in the Midwestern sector of North America. I feel so terrible. I'm doing my best to stop this plague, but due to circumstances beyond...

NO, HERODIUS, THIS HAS NOTHING TO DO WITH YOUR CURRENT ASSIGNMENT. WE NEED YOU TO COME BACK FOR ONE SPECIAL CASE.

Sir please, you can't ask me to do this, especially at a time like this. My rhododendrons need me.

I KNOW WE PROMISED YOU, HERODIUS, BUT WE BELIEVE YOU ARE THE ONLY ONE WHO MIGHT SUCCEED WHERE BALTHAZAR HAS FAILED.

Sir, with all due respect, I have been called away from my current assignment too many times to repair the mistakes he has made since he replaced me. I do not believe that match-making is Balthazar's true gift.

WE AGREE. BALTHAZAR HAS BEEN PERMANENTLY TRANSFERRED TO SLUGS.

Slugs have their own department?

NO, TECHNICALLY HE IS ASSIGNED TO THE CRUSTACEAN AND MOLLUSK DEPARTMENT, BUT FRANKLY, ALL WE CAN TRUST HIM WITH ARE SLUGS. NOW HERODIUS, AS FOR THE REASON WE NEED YOUR HELP, THIS COUPLE WAS SUPPOSED TO MEET

AFTER COLLEGE GRADUATION IN COSTA RICA, ELEVEN EARTH YEARS AGO, FALL IN LOVE, AND MARRY. THAT NEVER HAPPENED. THEY HAVE STRAYED SO FAR OFF THEIR INTENDED PATHS THAT I AM NOT HOPEFUL THEY CAN BE BROUGHT TOGETHER.

Sir, you cannot mean that. To lose faith is to lose everything.

THERE ARE ONLY SIX EARTH DAYS LEFT TO JOIN THIS COUPLE BEFORE IT IS TOO LATE FOR THIS LIFETIME.

Six earth days? That would take a miracle.

PRECISELY, HERODIUS. THAT IS WHY WE NEED YOU.

I have a question, if I may? You said this couple was supposed to meet eleven years ago in Costa Rica, but has Balthazar made any attempts to get them together since then?

NUMEROUS. BUT THEY'VE BEEN MISSING ONE ANOTHER FOR YEARS—AT SALSA CLUBS, BOOKSTORES, MUSEUMS, RESTAURANTS, AND CONCERTS—AND ALWAYS BY TEN EARTH MINUTES OR LESS.

Why did they fail to go to Costa Rica?

IT IS A CLASSIC CASE OF FEAR HOLDING BACK PASSIONS AND DREAMS. NOW, WILL YOU ACCEPT THIS ASSIGNMENT, HERODIUS?

Will I be able to return to my department when this is completed?

OF COURSE. AND ONE MORE THING, I'M GIVING YOU SOME HELP. SERENA HAS ONLY BEEN WITH US FOR A SHORT TIME, BUT SHE HAS SPECIAL SKILLS THAT WE BELIEVE WILL BE OF SOME ASSISTANCE TO YOU. AH, HERE SHE IS NOW. WE'RE COUNTING ON BOTH OF YOU.

Thank you, Sir. I will do my best.

Howdy, Mr. Herodius. Well aren't you just as cute as a bug's kneecap. I'm Serena Darling. Well, that's what I was called on Earth. I still find it hard to believe I'm actually among the deceased. Guess these things take some getting used to.

It is a pleasure to meet you, Serena.

Now, no autographs please. I'm afraid it won't do you much good up here anyway.

Autograph? I am not certain I understand.

Doesn't the name Serena Darling mean anything to you?

No.

You've never heard of me?

I am sorry, no.

You've never heard of Serena Darling, author of seventy-two internationally acclaimed romance novels, twenty-six novellas, and three-time winner of the highly coveted *RITA* Award?

I do not read.

You don't read? Why don't you just stab a skewer through my heart and serve me up for barbeque.

Oh, I would never do that Serena, you seem very nice.

That was a joke. Now, what's your story, honey?

My story?

Did you sprout in a lima bean patch yesterday,

Herodius? Where are you from? How long have you been here? How'd you get involved in this messed up case?

I worked in this department for nearly two millennia before I retired from matchmaking. On occasion, I am called in to assist with the most difficult cases. Perhaps you have heard of my most famous case? I brought Liz and Dick together.

Oh my Lord! Elizabeth Taylor and Richard Burton?

No, Liz and Dick Kowalski from Mount Horeb, Wisconsin. Liz and Dick were high school sweethearts. They had been dating for twenty-three years when I took over their case. Within one earth month Dick proposed to Liz and since then... Well, this is embarrassing. I would rather not say.

Confidences are my specialty, honey. I'd sooner rip a hole in my best pair of fishnet stockings than ever breathe a word of what you tell me.

I am known as the Miracle Maker.

The Miracle Maker? Well, from what I know about this case it'll take a miracle to get these two together. What's your usual assignment?

I am an Ericaceae specialist in the Flora and Fauna Department.

Will you please translate that into English?

I specialize in flowering shrubs such as rhododendrons and azaleas.

Plants? You're pulling my leg, Herodius.

You do not have legs, Serena; at least, not anymore.

Honey, it's an expression. Pulling my leg means you're teasing me.

Oh no, I am quite serious.

Dear God in the morning! We're starting off here like a herd of sleepy turtles. First, Balthazar drops the ball on this case. Can you believe that in eleven earth years he couldn't manage to get this couple within spitting distance of one another? And now I'm paired up with a weed whacker! Well, we don't have much time so we might as well get started. Where do we go from here?

It is time for you to meet Zeke and Inez.

Sunday

1

Zeke Nomad stroked the dark stubble on his chin as he pondered the file on his desk. He tried not to picture the human beings whose stories were contained in the boxes of documents piled high in his office, because it always made his job more difficult. But the picture always formed. The plaintiff he would depose on Friday—Joseph Pulaski, seventy-three, a retired baggage handler at Midway Airport, with a tenth grade education—could be his father. Andrew Nomad would have turned seventy this year if he hadn't passed away suddenly, one month after Zeke's college graduation, eleven years ago.

Zeke's phone rang. He saw his mother's cell phone number on the caller I.D. and felt a small jab of fear. He could recall only two times in the past five years that she'd used the cell phone that he'd purchased for her, the one that she never took with her when she left the house.

"Honey, what are you doing at work on a Sunday?" she said. "Why aren't you outside having fun?"

He'd been wondering the same thing himself. There wasn't a cloud in the sky, and it was in the eighties for the first time this year. Throngs of people had flocked to Lake Michigan, but this was to be expected. It was June and after the long cold winter, the moment the thermometer hit fifty, the bikinis, shorts, and sunscreen came out, as though everyone in Chicago had been cast as an extra in *Beach Blanket Bingo*.

The fact that he could see the lakefront from his hermetically-sealed office—if he angled his head just right—was both a blessing and a curse. He had spent more time gazing out his window, wishing he could go rollerblading, than doing much actual work this weekend. But he kept telling himself that all of the weekends he'd given up over the years would be worth it on Friday when the announcement was made that he was promoted to a partnership.

"I've got a big deposition on Friday, Mom" he said. He'd handled over one hundred depositions in the Xanadu Pharmaceuticals litigation, but the Pulaski case was different. It would be his first case involving a plaintiff who claimed to have suffered a stroke as a result of taking his client's drug. He'd have to put in fourteen-hour days this week to be ready for it.

"I hate to bother you at work, but I've got a little problem," his mother said in a strangely muffled voice. A little problem could be anything from having a squirrel in her attic to needing emergency brain surgery. She tended to either vastly underestimate or overestimate the nature of any crisis. "Those men are back, the ones you told me not to talk to."

"Are they the same ones who came before?"

"I don't know," she replied. "They're wearing dark suits and ties."

That could be anyone from the CIA to the *Men in Black*, he thought. But Zeke believed they might be a new brand of crooks he'd recently read about in the *Chicago Tribune*, who targeted poor, largely uneducated communities, posing as door-to-door salesmen attempting to trick people into buying long-term health insurance policies from non-existent companies. He'd tried countless times to convince his mother to move out of his childhood home and move into a secure retirement community in the city. But she refused to leave the home she and his father had purchased thirty-six years ago as a newly married couple.

"Where are you now, Mom?"

"I'm hiding in my pantry."

"Mom, if you're in the pantry, then they don't know you're home."

"Honey, they keep ringing the doorbell."

Zeke looked at his watch. He could be there in twenty to thirty minutes, assuming there wasn't an accident, which could tie up the freeway for hours. He told his mother to stay put until he arrived.

Twenty minutes later, Zeke jumped from the back seat of a taxicab and sprinted up the cracked sidewalk leading to a two-bedroom brick ranch home. He noticed with irritation the sea of dandelions carpeting the lawn and made a mental note to talk to the neighbor kid he'd hired about mowing more often. Throwing open the unlocked front door, he found his mother serving tea and cookies to two Jehovah's Witnesses. Zeke breathed a sigh of relief. His mother was too nice for her own good. She would invite the head of the mafia in for coffee, if he happened by.

"Oh honey, how nice to see you," his mother greeted him, as if she weren't expecting him. "Please join us."

Zeke reluctantly took a seat on the sagging, flowered-print chair, across from the Jehovah's Witnesses, who had taken over the couch. Their opened black briefcases, on the carpet next to their feet, were stuffed to overflowing with pamphlets.

"This is my son, Zeke," his mother said, with a wave in his direction. "He's still single and almost thirty-four years old."

"Oh my," said the older man. He turned to his younger associate, whispered something, and then reached down to his briefcase, returning with a pamphlet titled: "How to Find God's Ordained Spouse," which he handed to Zeke.

"Son, are you feeling unloved?" asked the older man, who resembled a nocturnal creature, somewhere between a hedgehog and an anteater. He had hair sprouting off the tip of his pointed nose and his knuckles were so hairy they weren't visible to the naked eye. Zeke watched as he inhaled one of his mother's cookies in a single bite and reached for another.

"Honey, it's okay," said his mother. "You can tell them that you never date."

"Oh my," repeated the older Jehovah's Witness.

Zeke hadn't bothered to tell his mother about Pamela, the woman he was currently dating, or about the dozen or so other women he'd gone out with since his graduation from law school eight years ago. None of those relationships had lasted more than six months. He hadn't wanted to get his mother's hopes up, but he realized now that this might have been a mistake.

"Brother," began the younger man, addressing Zeke, "Jehovah knows your pain. You can take comfort from the fact that in the new world promised by the Scriptures, no one will feel unloved. Instead, true love will flood our society."

"That is very comforting," Zeke replied.

He tuned out the rest of the man's sermon as he sipped tea from the non-chipped side of his mother's china cup. He leaned an elbow on the arm of the chair covered with one of his mother's hand-crocheted white doilies, which had been carefully positioned to hide the worn patches beneath.

Although it had been a month since Zeke's last visit, everything looked the same, including what he'd always thought of as the: "Shrine to the Only Beloved Son." On the wall opposite Zeke hung a dozen photographs of him, in dollar store frames—sucking on a pacifier dressed only in a diaper, kneeling as he received his first communion, in his softball uniform clutching a leather glove, at his high school prom wearing a brown suit with fat lapels and a tie thick enough to double as a bib, and with his arm around his law school girlfriend Susan, in front of the Laird Bell law quadrangle at the University of Chicago. On a table below stood all of the sports trophies Zeke had won over the years.

On the end table next to him, in a small metal frame, was a yellowed *Chicago Tribune* photograph of his best friend Mike Knight and himself, from their sophomore year of college. During his freshman year, Zeke had started a newsletter called "Unite!" which chronicled all of the activist events happening in Chicago. The newsletter had caught the attention of the *Tribune*, when Zeke had written a story about a group petitioning the mayor to provide more housing for the homeless after a four-year-old girl froze to death on Christmas Eve.

When the article came out, Zeke remembered waiting anxiously for some sort of response from his father who read the *Tribune* cover-to-cover each day. But to Zeke's disappointment, he'd never said a word. His mother, however, had clipped and framed this photograph, which thirteen years later was still displayed in the same spot.

Knowing it would make his mother happy, Zeke leaned over and grabbed one of her peanut butter cookies pressed flat with a crisscrossed fork pattern. It was so soft and crumbly it practically melted in his mouth. He'd forgotten how delicious his mother's cookies were. As a kid, Zeke and his buddies would head straight to his house after baseball or football practice to gorge themselves on her cookies, which always seemed to have just left the oven. Zeke hadn't tasted store-bought cookies until college.

"You might want to read these," said the younger Jehovah's Witness with a wave toward the pamphlets spread out over the coffee table. Zeke glanced at the titles on dating and singles, the joys of celibacy, and the sanctity of marriage.

At the first lull in conversation, Zeke seized the moment and escorted the two men to the front door, swinging it shut in their flabbergasted faces with a smile and a firm good-bye.

"They were so polite and interesting," said his mother. "Look at what they left me." She held up a pamphlet titled, "Deliverance Is at Hand!"

"Mom, I'm not gay," Zeke said, "just in case you were wondering."

"I know that, honey," she replied. "But I don't like it that you're still alone, eating those horrible TV dinners for one. It just isn't natural."

He supposed he should be happy his mother did not believe that one of his major functions in life was to produce grandchildren. In fact, she had once told him she could take grandchildren or leave them. Still, it was irritating his mother assumed that unless he got married, he would never be happy, although the truth was he often felt the same way, especially lately.

Zeke watched his mother as she carefully collected her rose-patterned china teacups and plates, which had been a wedding gift to her and his father. Unlike so many people who only used their china for special occasions, his mother brought hers out every time anyone showed up at the house, for any reason, which explained why nearly every piece was chipped and cracked. For some reason, the sight of this damaged porcelain made him sad; it reminded him of happier days when his mother was still young and strong. Standing just five-feet-two inches tall, her back rounded with age, she seemed as fragile as her china. Her waist-length hair was dyed a blondish color that didn't quite cover the gray and was tucked neatly up into its usual chignon at the nape of her long neck, exactly the way his father had loved it.

"I worry about you, Mom."

"Oh honey, I'm just fine."

Although his mother was spry and fiercely independent, Zeke had noticed the slow, inevitable role reversal that happened when the offspring became the parent and the parent became the child. There were so many things she couldn't do for herself anymore, including keeping up the house and yard work. Recently, her license was taken away when she'd driven into an automatic teller machine in downtown Bellwood in her boat-sized, fifteen-year-old Cadillac Fleetwood. Arthritis had stopped her daily walk around the neighborhood over the last few months, but that was a blessing in disguise.

His childhood neighborhood had changed so much in the last decade it was nearly unrecognizable from the idyllic *Leave It to Beaver* suburb of his childhood memories. Zeke could easily imagine himself back in those days, the feeling of absolute freedom when school would let out each summer, the smell of fresh-cut grass, playing with the dozens of neighborhood kids who were all about the same age, and his favorite pastime, pretending to shoot down enemy planes carrying innocent passengers from Midway Airport, just a mile away, on their way to destinations his family had never visited.

As he'd grown older Zeke realized it was the patina of youthful ignorance, which made his neighborhood seem perfect in his memories. It wasn't until college that he was able to see Bellwood for what it actually was: a blue collar community made-up of honest, hardworking folks who took pride in their small, humble homes and had few expectations for their lives beyond backyard barbeques, family camping trips, and the hope for healthy children and grandchildren.

But today, en route to his mother's house, as the taxi drove him down Bellwood's main street, he was shocked to see that this former safe, working-class suburb had deteriorated to the kind of hopeless poverty of the slums. There were boarded-up buildings covered with gang graffiti and too many working-aged men milling around on the street corners, wearing the bleak expressions of the chronically unemployed. And it seemed that every week his mother was mentioning another burglary or robbery in the neighborhood. Although Bellwood and his law office were less than fifteen miles apart, whenever Zeke traveled here directly from the Loop, it felt like taking a trip to a different country.

"Mom, let's sit down for a minute, okay?"

His mother took a seat beside him on the couch. He grasped one of her cool, bony hands, holding it carefully as if it might break with too much pressure.

"Remember the retirement home we visited in the city?"

She nodded, her head wobbling more than usual. On every visit she seemed to have become frailer. "The one with the nice pool."

"Yes, that's the one. I want you to re-consider moving there. I could visit you a lot more often. And you'd have so many people to do things with."

The Towering Oaks Assisted Living Center, in the heart of Lincoln Park, was just a quick cab ride from Zeke's condo. It had everything—private units, a twenty-four-hour staff, a workout facility, a library, organized activities, common living areas and transportation to doctor's appointments. It was perfect. For Zeke.

"I'm so proud of you, Zeke," she said, staring into his eyes with such love it nearly knocked him off the couch. "To think, a lawyer in our family!" she added proudly, for perhaps the one millionth time. "But I can't leave here. I've lived in this neighborhood my whole life, and all of my memories of your father are here."

In honor of his father, his mother had changed nothing in their home since his death. Although Zeke had offered many times to buy her new things, every piece of furniture was the same—from the burnt orange sofa to the scratched, badly nicked hutch displaying his father's bowling trophies, which she still dusted each day, just as she had done throughout their marriage. The house even smelled the same—of fresh-baked bread and cookies, his mother's rose-scented perfume, and mildew from the basement that flooded each spring.

"I'm happy here, Zeke," she said, looking around the living room as though it had just been featured in this month's *Better Homes & Gardens*. Zeke wished he could see it the way his mother did, but all he saw were the cracked walls and ceilings, marred paint, frayed carpeting, and furniture so dilapidated the average college student would refuse it.

His mother's watery blue eyes fixed on a vision from the past. The smile on her face told him she was thinking about his father. Whenever he made unexpected visits home, letting himself in with his key, he'd often catch his mother sitting in the rocking chair, wearing the same expression as she stared at their framed wedding photo.

"I can't keep an eye on you here, Mom."

"Oh, don't be silly, I'm fine," she said, popping up from the couch and continuing to clear away the dishes. Knowing it was pointless to persist, Zeke helped her carry everything into the kitchen.

"Will you bring Susan for dinner this Sunday?" she asked.

Alarm gripped hold of Zeke's insides. This was the third time in the last few weeks that she'd mentioned his old law school girlfriend, a woman he hadn't set eyes on in years. Zeke dated Susan, who was in the same class with him at the University of Chicago Law School, their last two years of school. The relationship had ended just after graduation when she got her dream job, a clerkship with the U.S Supreme Court. Zeke had heard that she was living in the Netherlands, working for The Hague, and was married to an Italian diplomat. It was strange to think he'd once been certain he would marry her.

"I can come on Sunday, Mom."

"What about Susan?" she persisted. "You haven't broken up with her, have you?"

Alzheimer's ran in their family. Zeke's maternal grandmother had suffered from it before her death. At the end, his grandmother didn't recognized anyone and was living in the world of a five-year-old girl. He couldn't bear to think of his mother ending up that way.

"Susan's busy this Sunday, Mom," he said, not sure if lying was the right thing to do. However, confronting his mother with the truth might frighten her. He would have to make an appointment to take her to the doctor next week.

"Oh, that's too bad," his mother said, as she ran water in the sink. "I'm making her favorite."

Zeke tried to remember what that was, but couldn't. Susan was the last serious relationship he'd had. No wonder his mother was worried about him.

Watching his mother at the sink washing dishes, Zeke found himself wishing he could talk to her about his job and the pressures he was under with his crazy work schedule. But their worlds were light years away from one another. His mother had never worked outside the home. His father had dropped out of school after the tenth grade to work at Midland Steel. Zeke was the first person in his entire extended family to go to college. Although his mother was proud of him, she related better to people on *America's Funniest Home Videos* and *Dancing with the Stars*, her favorite TV shows.

Wiping her hands on the sunflower-yellow apron tied around her waist, his mother pulled a foil-covered pan out of the refrigerator and put it on top of the ancient stove. Just two of the four burners worked, and the oven and burners could not be on at the same time because it blew a fuse. He didn't care what she said; he was getting her a new stove.

"Honey, did you eat dinner?" she asked with a frown. "You're too thin. I made lasagna. I'll heat some up for you?"

He looked at his watch. He had so much work to do and he had to be on time for his date tonight. If he was late again, Pamela just might kill him.

"I'd love to stay," he began, "but..." He broke off when he saw the pain in his mother's eyes.

"And garlic bread?" he asked, sitting down at the kitchen table, his mouth watering in anticipation. And when his mother smiled, he felt better than he had in months.

2

The downstairs buzzer to Inez's apartment in the Uptown neighborhood of Chicago, sounded precisely on time. "Howard," Inez Paris said to herself as she made her way to the front door, "why don't you ever use the set of keys I gave you?" She pressed the button to buzz him into the locked lobby, left her front door ajar and hurried back to the bedroom. She stripped off her shorts and a T-shirt, tossed them onto the bed and then pulled out her dress from her closet.

Inez usually suffered from the Murphy's Law of shopping: when she didn't need anything new, she always found the most adorable outfits while browsing; but when she desperately had to find something for a special occasion, she could never find just the right thing. Last month, however, on a whim, she'd gone into Divine's, a second-hand women's clothing store in her neighborhood that she'd walked by countless times, but had never visited. Half-heartedly poking through the racks, she happened upon this vintage prize—a royal blue chiffon dress with a deep V-neck bodice and halter straps that clasped behind her neck with two rhinestone buttons. Inez had tried it on, twirling in front of the full-length mirror, feeling as glamorous and sexy as Marilyn Monroe standing over the subway grate in *The Seven Year Itch*.

She quickly slipped it on and dashed to the bathroom to check her makeup. Peering into the mirror covered with a film as though it were smeared with a permanent layer of Vaseline, she touched up her eye shadow and lipstick. Inez had often thought that her bathroom, which also featured cracked yellow floor tiles, a rust-stained blue sink and a pea green bathtub, had been designed by a deranged Fiesta ware aficionado. Thankfully, this room was the only ugly part of her apartment. The honey-colored oak floors covering the living room, hallway, and bedroom, and the gorgeous built-in hutch with leaded glass windows in the dining room, more than made up for the bathroom. The 1930s design reminded her of the Milwaukee bungalow she'd lived in until her mother's death at thirteen. Inez heard the front door close and a moment later she saw her fiancé appear in the doorway.

"Hi hon, I brought you something," Howard said, producing a dozen long-stemmed red roses from behind his back. Stunned, she fell against the sink, grasping the cold porcelain with her hand to steady herself. There was even a card. She fumbled with the envelope and pulled out the beautiful note that read: "*To my gorgeous bride-to-be, I love you more than you can ever know—H.*"

In the two years she'd dated Dr. Howard Suterman, a podiatrist, the closest he'd come to commenting on her looks was to describe her in a phone call to his mother, which Inez had accidentally overheard, as "a rather attractive woman." He rarely told her he loved her, although she knew that he did. And, he'd never once given her flowers. Howard, until this moment, had been as romantic as an orthopedic shoe.

"Are you feeling okay, Howard?" Inez asked, looking up at her husband-to-be as if seeing him for the first time. His short-cropped hair was silver gray with a few defiant black strands. His gold-framed, wire-rimmed glasses slightly magnified his intelligent hazel eyes, and a slight paunch hung like a lip over his belted trousers. He looked close to his age—he would be fifty in three months.

"Of course, never better," he said, patting his soft tummy. "I'm getting married to the most gorgeous woman in the world in just a few days. How could I not feel fabulous?"

Inez had never heard Howard utter the words "fabulous" or "gorgeous" before. Come to think of it, he never used superlatives about anything, not even at his happiest—while delivering lectures at

26

nursing homes and assisted living centers about proper shoe fit and foot care, something he did for free in his spare time. Over half of his podiatry practice was devoted to treating the corns, calluses, bunions, and gnarled hammer and claw toes of senior citizens. Through his lectures and scores of medical articles he'd authored, he'd become something of a champion for the deformed feet of the elderly. He never seemed to lose interest in the subject of feet, especially old ones. And they loved him for it. Howard was always bringing over the homemade pies, cakes, and cookies baked by his patients who constituted a sort of "Dr. Howard" fan club.

"You look astonishingly ravishing tonight," he said, bending down to nuzzle her neck with an enthusiasm that caused her to drop the roses to the floor.

Flowers, a card, and three over-the-top compliments in less than sixty seconds—Inez couldn't have been more surprised had Howard appeared wearing a leopard print thong while playing a ukulele. Howard was strictly a white briefs man whose musical preferences were limited to soft jazz and classical. And he was not a nuzzler. What in the world had gotten into him?

"I'm going downstairs while you get ready," Howard said, as he bent to pick up her bouquet. He handed Inez the roses and then took a monogrammed handkerchief from his pocket, dabbing at the corners of his eyes. "I'm starting to tear up."

"Wait," said Inez as Howard headed toward the front door. Putting the flowers in the bathroom sink, she scooped up Beso, plopped him onto the bathroom floor and closed the door. Inez guided Howard to an open living room window.

Howard was allergic to cats, one of the many "flaws" her sister Rachel had pointed out to Inez and happily documented with a flurry of magazine articles about people who dumped their allergic lovers for their pets. But, at least Howard had tried, Inez reasoned. He shared an office building with a dermatologist who'd prescribed several different kinds of medications, but all of them made Howard feel nauseous or break out in a rash.

Rachel just didn't understand Howard like she did—his unfailing kindness and support were more important to Inez than anything else, even Beso. After their wedding on Saturday, Beso would be permanently moving to Rachel's apartment. Although giving him up had been a very painful decision, at least Inez wouldn't have to give Beso away to a stranger or worse, back to the Humane Society where at ten-years-old his chances of being adopted were small.

"I'm meeting Rachel later tonight for a drink," Inez said. "Will you come with me? Please."

Howard peered out the window.

"Howard, did you hear what I said?"

"What?" he said, turning away from the window as abruptly as if she had caught him doing something illegal. "I was just checking on my car."

Howard believed Inez's neighborhood wasn't safe. But she'd lived in Uptown for a decade and loved its little treasures and international flavor—Pakistani, Chinese and Vietnamese grocery stores, local artists displaying their work in funky coffee shops. In her apartment building alone Inez had neighbors from Tanzania, Ethiopia, Rwanda, India, Cambodia, and the Philippines. Best of all, she lived just two blocks from Lake Michigan where she spent hours each summer reading, riding her bike along the path, or just people watching. She would miss living here, she realized with a small ache.

"Rachel doesn't like me," Howard said matter-of-factly, "and I have to pick up my mother tomorrow morning. Her flight gets in early."

Howard's mother was flying in from Florida for the wedding on Saturday. Inez's stomach churned at the thought of seeing Margaret Suterman again—their last visit together had been a disaster.

"I want you and Rachel to like each other," Inez said, knowing that she had a better chance of bringing permanent peace to the Middle East. At this point, she would be satisfied if they could simply exchange a civil word or two. It was heart-wrenching to watch the way they avoided one another, as though they were from separate universes.

"Hmm?" Howard said, turning away from the window once again.

Inez tried not to be annoyed, but during the last six months or so she'd noticed that Howard was often distracted when they talked. She'd frequently catch him staring off into space in the middle of a conversation. When they first started dating, Howard had paid attention to her with such intensity, soaking in her every word, Inez thought she'd found "the missing link"—a man who excelled at listening and made her feel like the center of his life.

Maybe it was the flowers or the little flame of hope burning in her chest that Howard was changing into the romantic man she'd always wanted, or the fact that their wedding was just six days away that prompted Inez to throw her arms around Howard's neck and give him such a passionate, soul-flipping kiss that for some moments afterwards neither of them spoke. Now, as she often found herself doing, she searched his face for some sort of response. It was a kind face, as open and unassuming as a toddler's, but the reaction she'd hoped for wasn't there.

"What was that for?" he asked with a blank look accompanied by mild confusion.

Inez shrugged. She had always been more or less restrained around Howard, not because he prevented her from expressing her true personality, but because he was incapable of bringing it out of her.

Howard patted her cheek. "I'll wait for you in the car," he said, and then looking at his watch added, "We need to hurry to get to Oceanique on time. I'm afraid they might give away our reservation." He took hold of her hands with his perfect doctor's hands—always warm and dry—and gave her a quick kiss on the cheek.

"Okay, I'll be down in five minutes," Inez replied, feeling a mixture of comfort and disappointment. He was the same old Howard after all.

Serena, what was the purpose of sending the Jehovah's Witnesses to Zeke's mother's home?

It isn't obvious to you?

No.

It got Zeke out of the office, didn't it? I took this from my eighth novel, Secret Love. When my female protagonist is about to leave her apartment and get on a plane to Australia never to return, but my male protagonist is on his way to her place with an engagement ring, I thought to myself, how can I keep her there until he arrives? Inspiration struck in the form of a pair of Jehovah's Witnesses.

But Inez does not live anywhere near Zeke's mother. In fact, she has never been to Bellwood.

At least I'm doing something, Herodius.

Serena, you are forgetting free will. Zeke cannot be manipulated like a puppet.

I am not manipulating him. Zeke loves his mamma and I knew he would choose her over his job, as any good son would. But now we need to focus on Inez. It's mighty unfortunate that Howard's receptionist gave him Romance for Dummies, and he actually took the time to read it. Our immediate goal should be getting the wedding cancelled or at least postponed. That'll give us some breathing room to get our darling couple together. Now, how are we going to accomplish that?

Patience, Serena.

We don't have time for patience!

Are you aware that the Latin origin of your name means serene and calm?

Not my strong suit. And speaking of names, yours is a real mouthful. How about I call you H?

But that is not my name.

Lord in heaven, this week is going to be longer than a month of Sundays. By the way, H, I read something very interesting in their file. Did you know that Zeke was conceived on the very same day that Inez was born?

Yes.

They are exactly forty weeks, two earth days, three hours and twenty-nine minutes apart in age. I think this means that they're destined to do something great like give birth to the first female President of the United States, or save the Earth from global warming. Or maybe they'll find a cure for cancer? No, I know, they'll write a romance novel and get an enthusiastic review in the New York Times Book Review!

The timing of conception and birth means nothing.

I know quite a few astrologers who would disagree with you on that one H. But they are soul mates, right?

Yes. However, true soul mates sometimes take many lifetimes to find one another.

As a romance novelist I refuse to believe that. We'll get our darling couple together this week if it's the last thing I do with my dying... Well, you know what I mean.

There is no guarantee that we will succeed.

You're a glass half-empty kind of guy, aren't you, H? Good thing I'm here. My family called me Sunshine Serena because I always saw the best side of every situation. So, H, do me a favor and stuff all that nonsense about free will in some musty drawer somewhere because I don't want to hear about it.

3

Zeke Nomad was late. Although he had made every effort to meet Pamela on time, taxicabs prowling the Chicago Loop on a Sunday night were about as plentiful as miracles. Zeke pushed open the restaurant door and was greeted with the whiny refrain of a Mexican Ranchero song as he made his way through the crowd to the copper-rimmed bar.

"Fernando," Zeke shouted, with a wave to the bartender. Fernando lifted his square chin in acknowledgment and flashed a perfect set of white teeth that looked all the more brilliant against his caramel-colored skin.

"Haven't seen you lately, Zeke," Fernando said, as they shook hands. "You used to be my best customer."

"Same old story. Work, work, work."

Fernando made a clicking sound and waved his index finger in the air as if to scold him. "As my grandmother Maria used to say to me, all work and no play…"

"…makes Fernando a dull peasant," Zeke interjected.

"Oh, I guess I told you that one."

Fernando had repeated his grandmother's words of wisdom, which always sounded suspiciously like lines from famous movies, so many times over the years, Zeke felt as though he'd grown up with her in the Mexican pueblo where Fernando was born.

"Your former best customer desperately needs two of your Don Julio specials," Zeke said.

"Ah," said Fernando, "you're meeting a woman."

"Yes, but even your magic elixir can't help me in that department. I'm afraid I'm hopeless."

"No one is hopeless, besides you must like her," said Fernando. "Don Julio Real es muy caro."

Yes, it was expensive tequila and also his favorite. He usually reserved it for special occasions, but tonight he hoped it might pacify Pamela who, when he'd called her from the cab, conveyed her fury as clearly as if she'd slapped him.

Zeke responded with a shrug. "We've only been dating a few months."

"Doesn't take that long to know, amigo."

Zeke knew Fernando was right. With Pamela, there had been no thunderbolts or signs that she was the one. They shared a few pleasant evenings a week with pleasant dinners and pleasant sex—but Zeke had no intention of settling for pleasant. He would never admit this to anyone, but he supposed he was a romantic at heart. Perhaps it was a curse that befell anyone whose parents had fallen in love at first sight? He'd always thought it would happen the same way for him, and it had, only once. But that was many years ago when he'd been young—and foolish enough to let her slip through his fingers.

Fernando slid two salt-rimmed margarita glasses across the bar. Zeke took hold of the thin glass stems and raised them high above the crowd, as he wedged his body around the little cliques crowding around the bar tables.

Pamela sat on a high stool at a small round table next to the window. The red and green neon sign hanging outside, cast her face in a sickly glow, marring her otherwise flawless skin. Zeke slipped up behind her and planted a kiss on her cheek. She gave a small jump in response.

"Oh, hi," she said, in a flat voice. The laughter that normally played about her mouth was gone; her eyes were two blue marbles, cold and hard.

"I'm really sorry I'm late, Pamela, I should've left work earlier," Zeke said, as he took the stool opposite hers and pushed a margarita toward her. "I hope you like this."

Zeke wanted to explain to her that what had really delayed him was his mother. Somehow, the time had gotten away from him while having dinner with her. What could compare to a home-cooked meal infused with a mother's love, he thought with a smile, picturing his mother's happy face. But before he could explain, Pamela shot him an angry glance.

"What are you so happy about?" she said and then lifted the glass to her lips. Upon taking a small sip, she scrunched up her face like a baby tasting a new vegetable and abruptly plopped the glass down, spilling some of the precious liquid onto the table. "That's way too strong."

"Would you like something else? I could ask the bartender to…"

"No, don't bother," Pamela replied, in an irritated tone. "This bar gives me the creeps. Three guys tried to pick me up while I waited for you."

He had no doubt she was telling the truth. Pamela had the type of looks that should come with a whiplash warning. With her long, straight, bleached-blonde locks, a toned curvy body, and perfectly symmetrical features, she was a knock-out. He certainly found her attractive, but in a detached way, as if he were flipping through a magazine or catching a made-for-TV movie featuring a beautiful woman. There was nothing unique or special about her looks.

Zeke lifted the rim of the glass to his mouth. The fresh citrus juice mixed with the rich, velvety tequila combined into a most intoxicating beverage, one that mere mortals did not deserve. Zeke loved Rico's Restaurante not only for its margaritas, but also its atmosphere, which reminded him of his trip to Mexico five years ago. With its ochre walls covered with Day of the Dead figures, brightly colored painted clay masks, and hand-woven rugs, Zeke almost felt as though he was in San Miguel de Allende, his favorite town in Mexico. As he savored his drink, Zeke signaled the waitress.

"This isn't an excuse for being late, but Pamela, you know this is a big week for me," Zeke said, in the understatement of the century. It wasn't just a big week, it was the week. It was difficult to believe that all of his hard work over the last eight years would come down to a simple vote on Friday morning, he thought, as a ripple of nervousness made his stomach clench.

"This is a big week for me too," Pamela said, blinking quickly, her black mascara-laden lashes flashing up and down like a pair of jumping millipedes.

Zeke scanned his memory over their last few conversations. He couldn't remember anything she had said that would explain why this week was anything out of the ordinary for her.

"Oh, that's just perfect," said Pamela. "First, you're thirty-four minutes late and then you forget that Muffy is getting spayed on Thursday."

Muffy was Pamela's "baby," a three-pound teacup poodle with the lungs of a lion. The ball of gray fluff, which yipped defiantly whenever Zeke knocked on her door, was under the delusional belief that it was a real dog.

"Right Muffy, I'm sure she'll be fine," said Zeke.

The waitress appeared at their table with a basket of chips and salsa and Zeke ordered guacamole.

"No, he really doesn't want anything," said Pamela to the waitress, who briefly knotted her eyes in confusion and then walked away.

Zeke was flabbergasted. "Why did you say that?"

"I don't want to hurt your feelings, but…" She trailed off staring at his midriff.

Zeke glanced down at the roll of blubber around his torso. Margarita salt was sprinkled over it like a bad case of dandruff. Sure he'd noticed his pants getting tighter, but until this moment, he'd blindly clung to his self-image as a six-foot-tall jock with well-toned abs. He was only thirty-three. Could his metabolism already be on the decline? No, Zeke knew it was his usual diet, which wasn't fit for a lab rat. And, he hadn't worked out in at least six months. With a twinge of guilt, he calculated how much money he'd spent on the health club membership he wasn't using. Although his father had been gone for over a decade, these mental gymnastics were automatic. Zeke could still hear his father's booming voice, commanding enough to part the Red Sea: "You think you're Rockefeller or something?"

"I'll start working out again, next week," Zeke said, brushing away the salt. He must have put on twenty pounds. Then Zeke remembered the tux hanging in the back of his closet, which he needed for Saturday night. Hopefully, it would still fit.

"Are you coming over tonight?" asked Pamela.

"I'd like to, but I can't," said Zeke. "Tomorrow is that golf game I told you about."

He'd have to get up at the inhuman hour of five for his seven o'clock tee time. Even squirrels didn't get up as early—only golf fanatics were always eager to spend hours chasing a little white ball around a pesticide-saturated turf.

"How could a stupid game be more important than me?" Pamela asked, with a pout.

"It's not more important, Pamela," Zeke replied, "but I've been trying to get an invitation to this game for years."

Last week, Stu Miller, the managing partner at his law firm, had invited Zeke to join his regular Monday morning foursome at the Bog Hills Country Club, known among the associates at his firm as the "Monday Morning Club." It was no coincidence that Zeke had received the highly-coveted invitation the same week he was up for partnership.

"But we haven't spent a night together in over a week," Pamela whined. "All you do lately is work."

"I promise to make it up to you next week," Zeke replied, as he tried to ignore his rising anxiety at the prospect of the long morning with Stu Miller. Spending time with his boss was typically about as pleasant as a root canal, but Miller wielded the power necessary to steer votes for or against him on Friday.

"Is this what I can expect when we get married?" Pamela asked, crossing her arms over her chest.

Zeke's mind scrambled to find the right words as his fight or flight instincts kicked into high gear.

"You're already taking me for granted," Pamela continued,

brushing a platinum blonde hair from her face. "It's a reasonable question. I need to weigh my options here."

"Pamela, we've never discussed marriage," he said evenly, although his heart was slamming against his ribcage. "We've only been dating a short time."

"You don't love me anymore," she said, her eyes welling up with tears.

Panic was now galloping through his circulatory system like a herd of stampeding buffalo. "Pamela, I haven't led you on about anything," Zeke continued, as though trying to reason with an illogical child. "I've never told you…"

"Oh, yes you did," she said, brushing the back of her hand across her moist eyes. "You might not have actually said those three little words, but it was obvious you were in love with me from the start."

It suddenly dawned on Zeke that the woman sitting across from him was wacky. The signs had been there from the start, but he'd ignored them. Pamela, who had moved into his condominium building a year ago, had an amazing knack for running into him everywhere—on the elevator, at the lawn chair next to his on the roof deck pool, and at Whole Foods three blocks away. Zeke swore she had implanted a microscopic GPS tracking system inside him, perhaps in one of the many batches of homemade cookies she'd baked for him over the last few months. After the third batch of cookies, he had invited her in for a glass of wine. She'd spotted the invitation to his law firm's annual dinner dance, this year at the Planetarium, tacked to his refrigerator. Pamela exclaimed how much she loved black-tie events and before he knew it, she had invited herself as his date.

Pamela buried her hands in her face. Her sobs began silently, a pantomime of grief that gradually reached a crescendo, until her wails all but drowned out the music.

"I'm breaking up with you, Zeke," she said through her tears.

"You'll meet someone else," Zeke said, hoping this weak cliché would somehow have the power to squelch her tears. But Pamela continued to blubber, oblivious to the stares of the bar patrons. Zeke felt their accusatory gazes. There were few things worse than making a woman cry: financial ruin, death—no, on second thought, death didn't sound so bad at the moment. Although he'd done his best not to lead her on, he had obviously failed. The last thing he wanted to do was to hurt her—or anyone else for that matter.

Pamela stopped weeping and pulled her hands away from her gorgeous face that was now a mass of red blotchy skin and raw eyes.

"What about Saturday night?" she asked.

"What about it?"

"How are we going to handle it, now that we've broken up? It might be…awkward."

The only thing that might be awkward would be scrambling to find a replacement date in less than a week, Zeke thought, wondering what she was talking about.

"I can still handle sitting through dinner with you," she said, "but given how you feel about me, I'm not sure you can handle it."

"You still want to go on Saturday?"

"You're sounding a little hysterical, Zeke, calm down," she said. "Of course I'm going. I bought a new dress, I've got a mani-pedi scheduled, and I'm getting my hair done in an up-do."

"Why would you want to go?" he asked, forcing himself to sound cool as he silently vowed to never again date a woman who lived in his building. How could he have been so foolish?

"You're not going to stand me up now, are you?" she asked, her perfectly-shaped lips pursing in disapproval.

"No," Zeke responded. "Yes. I mean, Pamela, you can't be serious about going. You just broke up with me."

"I had no choice," Pamela replied matter-of-factly. "Any self-respecting woman would have done the same thing under the circumstances."

A vision filled his mind of her bursting out crying during the speech congratulating him along with the other newly-named partners, on the biggest night of his career. She seemed capable of just about anything, he thought, with rising horror.

"You need me there," she said, sliding off her stool.

"Wait. Let me walk you home, Pamela," he said, gently taking hold of her arm.

"It's too late to be a gentleman," she said, shaking off his hand. "See you on Saturday."

Zeke wondered how his life had become so complicated. He finished his and Pamela's margaritas and approached the bar to pay his tab.

Fernando raised his left eyebrow. "I apologize for overestimating you, amigo. You're right. You are hopeless."

"Thanks for the support," Zeke replied. He tossed cash on the bar and said his good-byes.

He stepped outside and took a deep breath of fresh air. As he walked the three blocks to his high-rise condo overlooking the Chicago River, Zeke tried to reassure himself that everything in his life was fine. First, he would figure out how to handle this situation with Pamela. Then, next week he would hit the treadmill, do a few rounds on the heavy bag, a little weight lifting, and before long he would be back to his flat abs and college weight. On Friday, the announcement would be made that he'd been promoted to partner. And then, he would stop working such ridiculous hours. He would start living again and travel abroad—something he missed desperately. And, he would find the right woman, a normal woman.

Soon his life would be perfect, he thought. And then, Zeke tripped and almost fell over a crack on the sidewalk.

4

Inez moved through the crowd at Rico's Restaurante like a breeze through a forest. All over the room heads turned, elbows nudged, and mouths dropped open a bit. Although Inez was not a classic beauty—her eyes were set just a fraction too-wide apart and her nose was slightly off center—there was something about her, an energy she radiated which made everyone, both men and women, want to be around her without quite knowing why.

"Hey baby, you look gorgeous tonight," said a bearded man, tugging on the sleeve of her gauzy white peasant blouse, encircled with a twisted silver metal rope belt that accentuated her trim waist.

"Thanks, I'm ovulating," said Inez, with a warm smile and a wink at the man who shrunk back and mumbled what sounded like an apology. Inez glanced back at her much taller sister following behind her.

"Men," said Rachel with a roll of her eyes.

"*Oye Inez,*" yelled Fernando, with a wave.

Leaning across the bar, Inez and Fernando greeted one another with kisses to both cheeks. "*Te extraño mamacita,*" he said, as though his soul was breaking in two.

"How could you miss me?" Inez asked him with a laugh. "I was just here two weeks ago."

"But it feels like two years, *princesa preciosa.*" He grabbed a lock of her auburn hair and pressed it to his lips. "*Que linda.*"

Fernando was certainly not alone in thinking Inez's hair was beautiful. The color of fall leaves, it tumbled to her shoulders in loose corkscrew curls.

"Rachel and I are going to get a table, Fernando. *Ciao, guapo,*" said Inez with a friendly pat to his cheek.

They navigated their way to the windows and selected an empty table for two.

"Please don't go through with it," Rachel said, the moment they'd settled themselves on their stools.

"You make it sound like I'm contemplating joining a terrorist cell," Inez replied.

"I wish that was all you were doing." Rachel flipped her smooth ebony locks off her shoulders as she fixed Inez with eyes that were impossible to ignore—brilliant huckleberry blue flecked with violet.

No one would guess that Inez and Rachel were sisters. Inez looked just like their mother who shared the same curly auburn hair, jewel-shaped face, and eyes the color of a cinnamon. Rachel, on the other hand, had inherited most of her features from the father she had never known—his height, the same straight black hair and those astonishing eyes that one of Rachel's boyfriends had once compared to Tanzanite gems.

"We're not discussing this anymore," Inez said, putting her palms flat on the table and extending her long, thin fingers out like the petals of an iris.

Reaching inside her purse, Rachel removed a white and gold pack of cigarettes. Tapping one cigarette twice on the table, she flipped it into her mouth and lit it.

Inez sighed as she watched her younger sister go through her familiar routine. She'd tried everything she could think of to get Rachel to stop smoking—arranging for hypnosis, slipping photographs of the black, tar-encrusted lungs of smokers into her purse, clipping out magazine articles about how smoking caused wrinkles—but Rachel couldn't quit. Or rather, wouldn't quit.

The waitress appeared, plopped a bowl of chips and salsa on the table and took their drink orders.

"You aren't in love with him," said Rachel as soon as the waitress was out of earshot. She contorted her lips toward the side of her face and blew out a stream of smoke. "I still can't believe you're going to marry him."

"I do love Howard," Inez told her, "and, I respect and admire him. You know I never felt that way about any of my other boyfriends."

"I respect and admire Ralph Nader, but I wouldn't marry him, even if we were stranded together on a deserted island—even if we were the last man and woman on the planet, and it was up to the two of us to repopulate the earth."

"You wouldn't have to marry him then." Inez was usually amused by the dramatic, highly unrealistic examples Rachel used to make her point. But tonight, Inez was just plain tired. They'd had this same conversation dozens of times before. Inez thought back nine months ago to the night she told Rachel that she and Howard had become engaged. Rachel had practically swallowed her cigarette.

"Dump Dr. Dullard and go out with a man who can get your juices flowing, like Richard Burton or Steven McQueen," Rachel had said. "Real men."

"You're the one who told me to stop dating bad boys," Inez had protested in self-defense. "Besides, Richard and Steve are dead."

But as usual, Rachel, once on a roll, had simply kept gathering speed.

"Maybe you're planning to have one of those fake marriages like in *Green Card*?" she'd suggested. "Of course theirs turned into a real marriage after Andie MacDowell and Gérard Depardieu fell in love. Remember when the INS was taking Gérard away, and they kissed good-bye? They could barely tear themselves apart. Honestly, has Howie ever kissed you like that? Admit it, Inez, the two of you have never made hot, sweaty monkey love."

Whatever that was, no, they certainly hadn't. Before they'd slept together, Inez wondered if Howard's professional interest in feet would extend to the bedroom. One of the teachers from her school dated a man who'd been fired from his job for looking at foot porn on his computer all day—just photos of naked feet, no other body parts. Was Howard like that? Did he have a foot fetish? Would he suck on her toes and lick her heels? Do things with her feet she hadn't imagined in her wildest fantasies? But, as it turned out Howard's sexual interests were completely normal. Too normal.

Sure she and Howard had a few problems with their sex life, but didn't most couples after a while? There were things Inez wanted to try, but they'd settled into a comfortable routine—three, maybe four times a month, a little kissing, fondling, and either the missionary position or Inez on top. And then it was over.

She and Howard were in a bit of a slump, she'd realized. Although she wasn't certain she could call something that had lasted nearly their entire two years together, a slump. Then again, how much could she expect from a forty-nine-year-old man? Lots of men that age lost their sex drive, but only if they'd had one to begin with. Inez often speculated about Howard's sex life with his ex-wife Mary. Only twenty-five when he'd married her, Inez surmised it couldn't have been all bad because the marriage lasted twenty years before Mary had left him for her dentist.

When the waitress brought their margaritas, Inez licked some salt off the rim and then bit into the lime. These were best margaritas in town, she thought, taking her first sip and wishing Howard agreed, but he never touched hard liquor.

"I hardly recognize you anymore, ever since you started dating…" Rachel began, and then made a face as though she smelled something putrid, "…Howie."

The few times Inez and Howard had double-dated with Rachel and her boyfriend, Tom, Rachel treated Howard as though he were an inanimate object.

"I haven't changed," Inez replied.

"Please! It's like you're the walking dead. You used to be so alive and full of passion. Now you're like you're a wild stallion he's broken. In a few years, we'll need to ship you off to the glue factory."

"Are you trying to tell me I'm old and fat?"

"Glue horses are not fat," Rachel told her, stubbing out her cigarette. "They're skeletal and decrepit, and no, you're none of those things. Get that look off your face, Izzy. You're perfect. It's just that you don't do anything anymore."

"I'm still the exact same big sister you love to boss around," said Inez, frowning, because in a way, Rachel had a point. Howard

Suterman was light years away from the kind of man she'd assumed she would end up with. She thought of the twist of fate which had brought them together—a bunion. Howard was the doctor who'd removed it from her right foot three years ago.

"No, you're not the same," Rachel protested. "Inez, what's the real reason you're marrying him?"

This was a question her sister had asked so many times over the last several months, Inez had lost count. Inez exercised a lot of patience when it came to her sister, whose opinions tended to have a steamroller effect on people. But given Rachel's past—a subject they never discussed—Inez gave her far more leeway than she gave anyone else.

"Oh God, there it is again, that gooey-eyed I-want-to-be-a-mommy-look," said Rachel, who at four years younger, had not yet gotten the doom-and-gloom lecture from her gynecologist. "Listen Izzy, go to a sperm bank, have a one-night stand, or get a freebie from one of your buddies—do anything but marry Howard."

Rachel finished her margarita and plunked a tortilla chip in the salsa.

"You know my feelings about being a single mom," Inez told her.

"Well, as Mick Jagger says, we can't always get what we want. I predict if you marry him, within three months you'll be climbing his custom-wainscoted suburban walls, bored out of your skull and begging me to rescue you."

Inez knew that if soul mates actually existed, Howard was not hers. Although he was not the passionate lover she had dreamed of, he treated her as though she were a gift sent from heaven. Her mother had often told her, a strand of kindness was the quality above all others that one should seek in a mate. And Howard certainly had that. Shouldn't that be enough? After all, sex wasn't everything. Their friendship was solid, and they shared the same values. And, he wanted to have children right away, which was important because at thirty-four she was running out of time.

Inez swallowed a mouthful of margarita. The cold hit the center of her forehead like an anvil. Pressing the heel of her hand to her head, she winced her way through the pain, hoping it wasn't the start of another migraine. She was getting them every other week now. She willed herself to make the pain go away because she couldn't let her first graders down by leaving them with a substitute teacher, with just three days of school left before summer vacation.

"Izzy, you look like you're going to puke," Rachel said. "Please, call it off."

"It's too late. Besides, I want to marry Howard."

Rachel squared her narrow shoulders, sitting up straighter than usual. "Inez, this is the last time. I'm begging you, don't go through with this."

Inez heard a tone of finality in her sister's voice that hadn't been there in their previous conversations.

"What do you mean, the last time?" Inez asked, afraid of what Rachel might say. "I was expecting you to tie me up in the vestry or pour wine on my wedding dress."

"I don't know how to tell you this, so I'm just going to say it." Rachel did not meet Inez's eyes. "I'm not going to be there on Saturday."

"What? You can't do this to me!" Hot tears sprang to Inez's eyes, and her throat closed up. "You're my only sister, my maid of honor! Of course you're going to be there."

"I'm sorry Inez. I can't just stand by and watch you ruin your life." And with that, Rachel hopped off her stool, gave her a quick hug and left.

As Inez tried to process what had just happened, another sharp pain shot through her head.

They missed each other by four minutes and thirty-eight seconds. If only Zeke had told Pamela off and ordered that guacamole. Or Rachel should've stopped watchin' From Here to Eternity so she wasn't late meeting Inez. She's seen that movie twenty-nine times already. I thought this was going be easy like the novels I wrote where the words just flowed from my pen like honey dripping from a hive.

I would not have been called in to handle this case if it was going to be easy.

And what am I here for, window dressing? If you could handle this case on your own, I wouldn't be here. Well, what've you got to say for yourself, H?

Zeke and Inez are souls adrift, and it is our job to guide them back to their true paths, assuming they choose to listen. If they ignore our guidance there is nothing we can do. Did you attend the orientation, Serena?

Of course I did. As if I need to learn about the human heart. I should be teaching those classes!

Apparently you missed the lesson on free will.

Here we go again. We need to do something before it's too late. We're down to five earth days! So what's the plan, H?

For now we must watch and observe.

You can watch and observe all you like, H. Looks like I'll have to take matters into my own hands. Luckily, this happens to be my specialty. My romance novels are famous for joining star-crossed lovers and tear-jerking HEAs.

HEAs?

HEA stands for "Happily ever after" of course. You know, it might do you some good to read my books.

Monday

5

Zeke Nomad swung a golf bag out of his BMW Z4 M convertible Roadster, closing the trunk as gently as though it were made of glass. The car gleamed like a ruby in the early morning sunlight. He'd just had it waxed and buffed, not that it needed it since he rarely drove it in the city. In fact, he hardly drove the car at all.

"I see you found your way out here, Nomad," said a high-pitched voice behind him.

Zeke's stomach fell. He turned and instantly forced himself to stifle a laugh at the sight of Wallace Archer, dressed in lime green golf knickers; red, green and blue argyle socks and a golf hat adorned with a white pompon bouncing in the breeze. He looked like an oversized leprechaun, Zeke thought, as he shook Archer's pudgy hand.

Zeke noticed Archer staring at his head with a smirk. Bending down to look in one of his car's side mirrors, he saw the shafts of his dark brown wavy hair jutting out at crazy angles. He'd driven with the top down because he loved the illusion of freedom he felt whenever he drove his little convertible with the wind whipping past. Zeke ran his fingers through his hair, smoothing it back as best he could. The mad scientist look certainly would not make the right impression with the managing partner, Stu Miller, who should be along any moment now.

"Nice car," said Wallace, trailing his hand along the spoiler. "How fast does it accelerate?"

"Zero to sixty in four point nine seconds."

He still couldn't believe that he, Zeke Nomad, from his humble roots in Bellwood, actually owned such a car. It didn't compare to the adventures he'd imagined for himself when he was a teenager bent on becoming an explorer in the world's most wild and dangerous places—trekking across Mongolia on horseback or rafting down the Amazon—but these little jaunts in his sports car would have to satisfy his need for excitement, at least for now.

Sauntering up to the driver's door, Archer leaned down and looked at the dashboard, which for some reason, made Zeke as uncomfortable as if Wallace had just lifted up his girlfriend's skirt to get a look at her panties.

"Thirty-two hundred miles?" he said. "When did you buy this?"

"Two years ago."

Wallace hooted like a hyena. "If you're not going to use this car you should give it to someone who can truly appreciate it. Like me."

Zeke forced a laugh, resisting the impulse to tell Archer that that would happen just as soon as the Green Party elected a President. But then, Zeke felt a bout of recurring guilt, which flared up like the occasional case of heartburn. He knew it wasn't right that such a beautiful and expensive piece of machinery spent ninety-nine percent of its time in the underground parking structure of his building. He really should use it more often—especially since it cost a small fortune. Zeke reached into his khaki's pocket for a handkerchief, wiping a water spot off the rear bumper.

"I think we're paying you associates too much money," Archer said, with a snort at his own pitiful attempt at humor.

His emphasis on the word "associates" reminded Zeke that Wallace Archer had a vote on Friday, and he should do his best to be civil. Wallace Archer had made partner two years ahead of schedule, which was remarkable, not only because no other associate had achieved such a feat, but because Archer had the legal acumen of a kumquat and a diploma from one of the lowest-ranked law schools in the country. Rumor had it that his wealthy father had made a ten-million dollar endowment to his law school to buy him out of his failing grades, so he could be awarded his Juris Doctorate degree. Zeke knew he couldn't hope to compare himself to Archer, who had what Zeke didn't—family money and political connections— precisely the type of attributes which counted at Conley, Dwight & Miller, but would hopefully be waived for Zeke as a reward for all of the hard work he'd put in over the last eight years.

"Where's Joseph Banks?" asked Zeke, wondering what Archer, his least favorite partner, was doing here. Joseph Banks, the firm's only entertainment lawyer, was one of the few partners Zeke liked. He'd been looking forward to having Banks as a buffer for Stu Miller—Zeke had doubts as to whether Stu was an actual flesh and blood human being. "Banks couldn't make it," Archer replied. "Had to fly out to New York to hold some rock star's hand. Stu called me last night and asked if I could fill in. So Nomad, first time here?"

"Sure is," Zeke replied, tensing at the thought of the long morning ahead.

"I didn't know you were much of a golfer," Archer said.

"Actually, you inspired me to take it up," Zeke said smoothly, a little too smoothly, he noted as his stomach fluttered.

His "inspiration" came purely from his desire to make partner. After having bragged for years that he would never set foot on a golf course let alone touch a club, Zeke had taken up the game when he'd learned that Wallace Archer, who'd started at his firm a year after him, was getting regular invitations to the Monday Morning Club. Zeke started with group lessons and hired a pro for private lessons until his skills had become passable enough to casually mention his fondness for golf to Stu Miller in the hallway one day. Zeke had been golfing regularly with a few other partners over the last couple of years, but it was this game, today, with Stu Miller, that counted. A momentary queasiness erupted in Zeke's stomach. "You've sold out, Zeke Nomad," he thought.

"Me? Well, I'm...flattered," Archer replied as his ruddy face puffed up with self-importance. Although he was about Zeke's age, he was already getting jowly. The good life apparently wasn't kind to people whose metabolisms couldn't keep up with the rich food and alcohol-lubricated social gatherings Wallace Archer constantly attended in order to lure new clients into the firm. Wallace, who had a Ph.D. in schmoozing, was a born rainmaker. Real legal work wasn't required for someone with his lucrative connections. He could bring more money into the firm by landing a deep-pocket client in a single golf game than Zeke could with years of putting in thousands of billable hours.

That's not to say that Zeke was unappreciated at Conley, Dwight & Miller. There was always a place in big firms for associates like Zeke who were known as the legal workhorses. Zeke excelled at coming up with just the right legal precedents and brilliant loopholes to get the results their very wealthy clients expected. And on top of that, he'd developed a reputation as a great litigator. But Zeke's efforts were rewarded quietly, with five-figure year-end bonuses, rather than admission to the old boys' club that Wallace Archer had received membership in upon joining the firm.

Along the way to the clubhouse, Archer stopped to shake a dozen hands of men whom Zeke recognized as movers and shakers in state politics. But Archer didn't bother to introduce him, and when greeting a top executive at Boeing, a potential client, he actually turned his thick back on Zeke.

Zeke crossed his arms and waited, more amused than anything else. It was difficult to be offended by a man who was dressed like a jester.

They made their way to the enormous clubhouse situated on a grassy rise. It looked like a sprawling white Southern mansion with its red-tiled roof and welcoming wraparound porch, replete with white Adirondack chairs, all of which were empty this early in the morning during prime tee times. As they entered, Zeke glanced inside the pro shop with its crystal chandeliers, plush carpeting, and tastefully displayed racks of clothing on rich deep-colored mahogany tables and shelves. Making a sharp turn to the left, Archer led the way to the restaurant.

The Nineteenth Hole Bistro patio, enclosed in an atrium, overlooked a pond shaded at either end by two enormous weeping willow trees, which bent over the water like a pair of servants. Two white swans floated over the still water as if on glass. Zeke glanced over the crowd—mostly middle-aged men in polo shirts and khakis. He wondered briefly how many millions of dollars in deals were hammered out each month at this exclusive club. Above the hum of conversation, he heard the melodic laughter of a woman breaking out like a songbird piercing the morning quiet. It was a laugh he'd heard before although he couldn't remember where.

The maître' d led them to a table where Stu Miller sat with the woman who belonged to the laugh, Elise Wyatt. At the sight of her, Zeke inhaled sharply.

Miller stood shaking hands with Archer before turning to greet Zeke by sandwiching his palm between his two hands. Miller, a Harvard man, was on the board of directors of a dozen different charities. The consummate distinguished gentleman with a year-round tan, trim waist, and perfectly graying temples, he was the grandson of one of the founding members of the firm and the leader of the one-hundred eighteen partners who would be deciding his future on Friday morning.

"Good morning, Nomad," Stu Miller said, with a slippery salesman smile. "Ready to tackle our championship course?"

"I've been looking forward to this," Zeke lied.

Zeke knew he was not a great golfer. Even worse, this course had a reputation as one of the toughest in the Midwest and was ranked as one of the top courses in North America. Zeke knew he would be lucky to make par on a single hole.

He looked at Elise Wyatt and all of his thoughts came to a halt. When Elise stood, Zeke swore the restaurant and perhaps all of Chicagoland, fell momentarily silent. Why was he here? Oh yes, a partnership. Friday. Focus, he told himself, but it was difficult. She was breathtaking, even this early in the morning. Her blonde hair, like fine spun silk, curled up at the ends and rested on her thin shoulders. She wore a knee-length navy blue skirt and a light blue long-sleeved cardigan sweater. His eyes took in her petite build and a face pretty enough to frame. She'd be a Barbie doll cliché if she hadn't graduated *magna cum laude* from UCLA law school and have a reputation as one of the savviest negotiators in the real estate department. She was the girl-next-door, the glamorous cool blonde, the woman everyone loved, and he couldn't help thinking that she was invited to have breakfast with the managing partner, and he wasn't. An ominous gong reverberated in Zeke's head.

Archer stood there slack-jawed, staring at Elise as though he'd been struck on the head by a nine iron. But he quickly regained his usual smarmy confidence as he kissed her on both cheeks, European style.

"It's so good to see you, Wallace," she said, as though he was a dear friend while keeping her greeting professional and appropriately distant. If his neon-hued attire at all surprised her, she had the grace not to show it.

"Elise dear, do you know Zeke Nomad?" Stu Miller asked. Zeke took a deep breath in a vain attempt to make his belly disappear.

"Of course," she said, with a smile that hit him like a heat-seeking missile. "I've heard about the incredible way you're handling the Xanadu Pharmaceuticals case. And I believe congratulations are in order?"

Mesmerized by Elise, Zeke found he could not speak. Somewhere in the distant recesses of his brain he wondered why she was congratulating him. Years ago, when he first started at the firm, Zeke had been smitten with Elise Wyatt as were most of the men in his office, married or single. But she was engaged at the time. A few years later, he'd heard she'd broken off her engagement, but whenever they'd crossed paths at firm events she had a serious boyfriend in tow, so he'd never asked her out. Zeke wondered if she was dating anyone now.

"Your trial," she said, "the one you won last month."

"Thank you, but it was just a mock jury trial," Zeke replied, as he concentrated on forcing his mouth to form identifiable words.

"I'm still impressed," she said catching his eyes for just a split second longer than polite conversation would call for. Her smile was so warm and genuine, for a moment, Zeke forgot that technically they were in competition for a partnership slot. There was no such thing as making partner after the eighth year. Those associates who weren't promoted were given their six month's severance pay and had their names removed from the building's security list, before their last elevator ride downstairs.

But every year for the past eight years, two or three associates had been promoted. Three years ago, a record five associates had made it. Up until the slight at not having received an invitation to breakfast, Zeke would've wagered that both he and Elise would be promoted because of today's invitation to the Monday Morning Club. But now, he wasn't so sure.

The waiter came to clear off the table and asked if anyone wanted anything else.

"I could use some java," said Wallace Archer.

"That makes two of us," said Zeke, who had skipped his usual morning double espresso in his rush to be on time.

Stu Miller grimaced as he took his seat. Zeke and Wallace took the remaining chairs, but unfortunately Archer got the seat next to Elise.

"Elise, I heard a rumor about you," said Wallace crossing one thick leg over the other.

"Oh, really?" she said. The sunlight framed her face with a soft glow like a dreamy portrait, giving her the appearance of an ethereal angel. She was certainly attractive, but her beauty was nothing like Pamela's head-turning looks. Whereas Elise had a quiet, sweet loveliness that might inspire sonnets, Pamela's looks would inspire a letter to the *Penthouse Forum*.

The waiter arrived with a silver pot of coffee on a tray. Wallace dumped three packets of sugar and enough cream to clog a mile of arteries into his white china cup. Zeke took his black.

"Yes, a little bird told me you're on the verge of bringing in a new client," said Wallace. His chubby face broke into a broad grin. "A potentially very lucrative client."

"Is this true, Elise?" asked Stu Miller, surprise evident on his face, which had thawed momentarily forming nearly human features.

"I certainly hope so," Elise replied. "A friend of mine opened a gourmet chocolate shop last year in Wicker Park. She has plans to open six more shops in Chicago and a dozen more across the U.S. Her long term plans are for Europe, the Caribbean, and Japan. And, Whole Foods just agreed to carry her product."

Wallace Archer let out a low whistle.

"Elise, you're far too modest. Why didn't you mention this at our breakfast?" asked Stu Miller with a fatherly pat to her hand.

"It's in the very early stages of discussion," she said. "We're meeting on Thursday, I hope to know more then."

"And what about you, Nomad?" taunted Archer.

In his eight years at the firm, Zeke had brought in only one client. Wallace no doubt knew this, but Zeke wasn't about to let Archer make him look like a fool—especially in front of Stu Miller.

"Well, Wally," Zeke began, "after my mock trial win last month, forty-nine plaintiffs in the Xanadu Pharmaceuticals case have settled for seventy-five grand or less, each. Those plaintiffs were originally suing our client for over seventy-five million dollars. And the calls keep coming in."

The silence that followed was interminable. Zeke hoped Elise wouldn't think he was trying to outdo her; he wasn't normally one to brag. He caught Elise's eye across the table. She gave him the slightest of nods as if to say, "Good for you." Wallace Archer on the other hand, had fallen into a mute stupor—no doubt he was trying to do the math without the aid of a team of top accountants.

"I must say, son, that is very impressive," said Stu Miller, with a slap on Zeke's back.

Son? He's doing the back-slapping thing? Happiness surged through his every cell. Buoyed with a sudden spurt of self-confidence, Zeke plunged into the topic which had consumed him for the past eight years.

"So, Stu," he said, trying out Miller's first name, "how many associates are getting the nod this year?"

"The nod?" responded Miller, as if confused.

Archer snorted like a horse. Zeke cleared his throat. "For partnership?"

Miller looked at his watch and stood. "We need to leave now to make our tee time. Make an appointment to see me, Nomad."

Ten minutes later as Zeke took his first swing of the day, he watched his ball veer sharply left and disappear into the rough. He caught Archer wink at Stu Miller. It was going to be a very long morning, indeed.

We've got quite a pickle on our hands. How do you want to work this, H?

Work this? I do not understand, Serena. And what do pickles have to do with this?

If I have to translate every single one of the expressions I use on a regular basis, we are going to be here 'til the end of eternity. Get with the program, H. Now what's our strategy? You got any bright ideas?

Not as of yet.

Heaven help us! I hate to point out the obvious, but we don't have time to dilly dally. It's obvious that little lady Elise has caught Zeke's eye. We need to distract him, pronto.

I disagree.

What did you say, H?

Zeke has forgotten his heart. He needs to remember what it is like to fall in love. Then, his heart will open, and he can find true love.

Do you want Zeke to end up with the wrong woman? We don't have time for such shenanigans! Miracle maker my patooty.

6

Inez woke up alone in her apartment in Chicago. Her heart beat wildly like a Merengue in triple time. Her apartment was utterly still except for the sounds of traffic four stories below and the wailing of a siren coming from St. Michael's Hospital a block away. She glanced around her small bedroom—a hand-sewn patch worked quilt faded with age, covered her double bed. A tall chest of drawers stood off to her left. The wicker rocking chair she curled up in to read before going to bed was illuminated by the slatted rays of sunlight streaming in between the narrow blinds. Frida Kahlo's self-portrait, with her severe mono brow and serious expression, greeted her as it did every morning.

The dream was so fresh and vivid it was as though she had relived the birthday she would never forget, on the eve of the day that Carlos had disappeared from her life. How strange, Inez thought with a shudder, Carlos Luna Delgado de la Madrid hadn't crossed her mind in years. Her heart beats slowed to normal; her lips and skin tingled as though he'd actually touched her. Everything was exactly as it had been when they'd lived together in Spain. Even in the dream Inez had fallen into the grip of his incredible charisma, overcome by feelings of lust and love, mixing with fear and suffocation.

Beso jumped up onto her bed and began rubbing his black furry body against her, purring loudly. Inez pulled him onto her lap and stroked his head between his ears as she thought of Carlos, whom she'd met during her college junior year abroad. She'd moved there to live with him after her college graduation. Everything about their relationship was passionate and intense. During their two years together, her emotions were in a state of perpetual flux, ranging from verbal battles to glorious blissful highs. She and Carlos had never experienced that relaxed easy peace she'd witnessed in other couples. And then, one day, Carlos had simply left, causing a wound so deep she was certain it would never heal. She thought of the note he'd left for her on that horrible morning, nine years ago. *"Inez, I've moved out. Please don't look for me. I can't explain, and I don't expect you to forgive me. You will forget me in time. Carlos."*

It had taken years, but eventually she did forget him, although she'd never forgiven him.

Inez glanced at the clock on her nightstand; she had exactly forty minutes to get ready for work. In the kitchenette she started the coffeemaker and plopped a piece of whole wheat bread in the toaster. After taking a quick shower, she dialed Howard's cell phone to tell him Rachel wasn't coming to their wedding.

"I'm sorry your sister feels this way," Howard said as the sounds of car horns and squealing brakes competed with his soft voice. "But I'm sure she'll come around eventually. You'll see. Everything will be okay."

Howard had given this same advice, hundreds of times, about countless different issues over the course of their two-year courtship. He rarely took a position, believing if he remained neutral, peace would reign forevermore. Howard was a lot like Switzerland.

"I just got to the airport, and I'm running late to pick up Mom," said Howard. "Can I call you later?"

"Sure, I love…"

Click.

Inez dialed Rachel's home number. Despite the joke about it being a woman's prerogative to change her mind, Inez had never known Rachel to do it once she made a decision, but Inez had to try. It rang four times and clicked to her voice mail.

"Hello, this is Bond, James Bond," a very proper male voice announced in a heavy British accent. "Miss Paris and I are on a secret mission for her majesty the queen."

The voice belonged to Clive, one of Rachel's former boyfriends who'd worked at a bank in Chicago, a few years ago. Rachel loved the message so much she'd never changed it, even after she and Clive broke up, and she started dating her current boyfriend, Tom.

"Oh James," Rachel cooed in a sultry voice.

"Miss Paris is—er, indisposed at the moment," Clive clipped as Rachel could be heard giggling in the background.

"Rachel, you better not be screening your calls, I'm...," Inez swallowed hard to force back her tears, "...begging you to reconsider. I need you there on Saturday. Please, you're my sister..."

Inez hung up before she could add that Rachel was all she had left, except for Marilynn, the woman who'd raised Inez and Rachel after their mother died. But Marilynn had been in India for the past three years studying yoga. She didn't know Inez was engaged let alone getting married on Saturday. Inez missed her terribly and would have given anything to fall into Marilynn's comforting arms at that moment.

The sudden shriek of the smoke alarm jolted Inez's thoughts. "Oh no!" she cried, running to the kitchen to find thick black smoke pouring out of the toaster. Grabbing an oven mitt, Inez unplugged the toaster and then flung open her cupboard doors searching for baking soda. Or was it baking powder? She ended up dousing the flames with water. There was a loud sizzle and smoke billowed about her as she tried to wave it away from her face. At least, Inez thought, she had the presence of mind to avert disaster, in the correct order— unplug then add water.

She twisted off the cover to the smoke alarm and removed the battery. In the loud silence that followed, all of her emotions twisted up like a cyclone and burst out of her. With tears streaming down her cheeks, Inez remembered that this was supposed to be the happiest week of her life.

7

Zeke approached Charlie at his usual spot under the Madison brown line "L" stop. Charlie had his White Sox baseball cap pulled low over his forehead, which in the winter months, was replaced by a tight red, green, and yellow Rastafarian knit cap. Zeke had never seen him without a hat and strongly suspected it covered a bald spot.

As Zeke waited for the light to change, he noticed streams of well-dressed commuters walk past Charlie, giving him a wide berth without glancing in his direction, as though Charlie were invisible or homelessness was a communicable disease. Charlie's clothes were encrusted with dirt and he looked older today, although Zeke had no idea what his age was or much of anything else about him. He'd tried many times to picture what Charlie's life was like before he'd become homeless. Had he been married? Did he like gardening? Had he ever held a drooling child on his knee? And how had such an intelligent and well-educated man end up living on the street?

Zeke crossed when the light changed and handed Charlie a double half-caf soy latte and a brown paper bag. Charlie put down his sign, a battered piece of cardboard which read, "*Buddy, can you spare a hedge fund? A dime doesn't go very far these days.*" Flipping his frizzy brown and gray-streaked ponytail off his shoulder, he opened the bag and sniffed.

"Shit, cinnamon," he said. "No blueberry?"

"They're out," shouted Zeke, as the deafening rumble of the "L" train roared into the station over their heads, the squealing of the brakes sounding like a thousand hysterical monkeys. The smell of grease and gears filled the air giving Charlie's corner the ambience of an auto shop.

"You're late," Charlie said, lifting the lid of his drink and sniffing that as well. "I bet they had blueberry two hours ago." Taking a bite of the scone, he scowled, stuffed it back in the bag and pushed it deep inside one of his army coat pockets.

"You're welcome," Zeke said. "I had an early morning client meeting."

"Bullshit," Charlie snorted. "You've never had an early morning client meeting. I may be considered a parasite on society, but I'm not stupid. You were kissing ass on the golf course."

Zeke was impressed, and not for the first time, by Charlie's uncanny ability to know exactly what he'd been up to. The guy was a genius disguised as a bum.

"Working for the man completely demoralizes and de-humanizes people, and you are Exhibit A," Charlie said, tugging on the bill of his cap.

"When I looked in the mirror this morning I seemed pretty human," Zeke replied dispassionately.

He had danced around the verbal ring with Charlie long enough to have gotten used to, and in a strange way, to come to appreciate Charlie's sarcasm. Zeke first noticed Charlie at this spot about five years ago. For a year, Zeke simply tossed a few dollars into his cup as he'd walked past. Then, one day in January when the temperature was in the single digits, Zeke dashed into a coffee shop and bought him a latté. After that Zeke brought him a latté every day, but it was a month before Charlie spoke, and that was to say he was allergic to dairy and would prefer soymilk and too much caffeine bothered him so he preferred a "half-caf." Another two months of half-caf soy lattés went by before Zeke learned his first name. Slowly, they'd developed a relationship Zeke wasn't certain how to describe. They weren't friends exactly, but they were far more than acquaintances since they talked about real things, things that mattered.

"You detest golf," Charlie said.

"I don't love it, but it's a means to an end."

"And your job?" Charlie added, "is that also a means to an end?"

"I like my job, and I earn an okay living," Zeke said, only to instantly feel uncomfortable at his choice of words in the face of Charlie's stark poverty. Granted, Zeke wasn't super wealthy, he could not run out and buy a yacht or a small Caribbean island, but for a single guy from a blue-collar family, he felt as though he'd joined the ranks of those on the Forbes 400 list. His salary had more than tripled to a very healthy six figures, since he'd started at his firm. After he made partner on Friday he'd get another bump in salary, although "the bump" would be more like a small mountain.

"Money gives you freedom," Zeke said, feeling compelled to fill the silence, a frequent conversational necessity since Charlie was a man of few words.

But Zeke's horribly trite words instantly fell flat. He knew he was not trying to validate himself in Charlie's eyes, if that were even possible. So what was he trying to do? Justify the fact that he hadn't had a life in years? It was hard enough to bill the minimum twenty-one hundred hours per year required by the firm, but, for the past three years Zeke had been billing twenty-four hundred grueling hours each year—working evenings, weekends, and vacations—fueled by the certainty that all of his hard work would be rewarded with the brass ring of a partnership. And now, after this morning, it was all in doubt.

"Freedom?" Charlie barked. "You tell me how working eighty or ninety hours a week makes you free. I am free. I choose to be here every day. But you," he said, pointing an index finger with a dirt-encrusted nail at Zeke, "...you are a slave to the corporate monster."

"I'll cut back on my hours once I make partner," said Zeke, knowing he was lying to himself yet again, but it was far easier to twist the truth a bit than to face the uncomfortable feeling surfacing with increasing frequency, that his life had taken a drastically wrong turn years ago.

"You mean *if* you make partner."

"I've got it, Charlie."

"Who was the fourth?" Charlie asked, eyeing him carefully.

"Why do you want to know?"

"It was a woman, right? The *Wall Street Journal* just ran an article about big law firms feeling the pressure to promote more women partners."

Charlie read six newspapers a day and was better informed than Reuters, and yet Zeke could not conceal his surprise at his apparent clairvoyance.

"I don't have a good feeling about your chances," Charlie added.

About half of the new associates hired each year at Zeke's firm were women, but out of its one-hundred eighteen partners, only twenty-seven were women. After a few years at the firm, well before they'd become eligible for partnership, many would quit to find jobs with more reasonable hours or to become full-time mothers. But that didn't explain the dearth of female partners. Most of those who did stick around simply weren't promoted. This year, out of eight associates eligible for partnership, only one was a woman, and that was Elise Wyatt.

"If they bounce you out on your ass, you can always join me," Charlie said. "I don't normally share my spot with anyone, but for you, I'd make an exception."

"That's magnanimous of you, Charlie, but I'm going to get it," Zeke declared, meeting Charlie's intense gray eyes.

"Look on the bright side," Charlie told him cheerfully. "If you're wrong it won't be the end of the world. You might actually get to start living again."

"I'll see you tomorrow," Zeke said, discreetly palming a twenty-dollar bill in Charlie's hand as they shook. "Buy some real food."

"I was thinking of dinner at the Ritz tonight except my Armani suit is at the dry cleaners," Charlie said with a smirk.

Zeke's office building, located just two blocks from the Chicago Board of Trade in the heart of the Chicago Loop, was a five-minute walk from Charlie's corner. Zeke approached the non-descript, all windows and steel, fifty-five-story office tower. Conley, Dwight & Miller, the largest firm in Chicago, occupied the top fifteen floors.

Taking the elevator up to the forty-eighth floor, he walked down the carpeted corridor lined with framed posters from Chicago festivals and famous artists.

"Good morning, Melissa," said Zeke greeting his secretary, a gregarious, slightly plump single mother of two. With a straight bob cut and bangs falling to her natural eyebrows, she appeared as earnest as a nun. "How was your weekend?"

"Good morning, Mr. Nomad," Melissa replied, her round face breaking into an engaging grin. "Great, thanks for asking. And yours?"

"It was fine," Zeke responded. "Well, not really. I was here."

"On the nicest weekend of the year?" Melissa said, with a frown. "What a shame."

"Duty calls. Melissa, would you please schedule an appointment with Stu Miller."

"Certainly. Anything else, Mr. Nomad?"

"No, thank you Melissa."

Zeke hated the firm rule that allowed him to call Melissa by her first name, but prohibited the reverse informality. It was this sort of pretentious bullshit he intended to ignore once he made partner, along with the dress code which required a suit and tie every weekday. Conley, Dwight & Miller didn't believe in business casual. He went to his small office packed tightly with files and boxes and standard issue furniture and opened his laptop. A moment later, Wayne Martin, a second-year associate whom Zeke had been mentoring for the past six months, burst in.

"So is it true the partnership is either going to you or Elise Wyatt?" Wayne demanded.

"Where did you hear that?" Zeke asked, taken aback by the question.

"You know the rumor mill keeps tabs on who's invited to the Monday Morning Club," said Wayne, as he plopped down in the only empty chair. He ran his fingers through a mop of dark curls that matched the dark circles under his eyes.

The rumor mill was at warp speed this morning; the golf game had ended just two hours ago.

"Well?" asked Wayne, leaning forward with anticipation, as if receiving Zeke's response a nano-second earlier would make all the difference.

"The gossipmongers think only one associate is going to make it this year?" asked Zeke, concerned that each one of the five-hundred-plus lawyers at his firm knew something he didn't. But it wouldn't be the first time. Zeke had kept a low profile from day one, only socializing a fraction of the time so he wasn't completely forgotten. He'd always hated small talk and preferred to concentrate his time on work. During the little free time he did have, the last thing Zeke desired was to hang out with his colleagues.

"What do I know? It's all hearsay anyway," said Wayne, who then abruptly switched the subject. "Please tell me I can go with you to your dep on Friday. My mother is convinced I've become a vampire because all I do is work, coming outside only after dark."

Wayne had been smiling less and less over the last few months. Zeke had seen it happen over and over again with the young associates he supervised—the initial rocket blast of enthusiasm, leveling off to a determined resignation, and then the slow spiral down to numb weariness as the countless billable hours transformed their lives into one never-ending workday.

Zeke had a sudden urge to tell the young man to quit, find a normal job, a good woman, and get a life. But he barely knew the guy. "The dep is here, remember?"

Wayne's face fell.

"Let's get to work," said Zeke.

8

The Merlot-colored thick leather walls of the booth extended well above their heads and served to muffle the conversations of other patrons and the constant clinking of glasses and silverware at Morgan's, the most popular steak and seafood restaurant in Chicago. Although the restaurant was rated four stars, and it took weeks to get a reservation, Inez was surprised to see it packed at five in the afternoon.

Inez thought back to when she was nineteen and first exposed to the late-night dinners typical of *los madrileños* in Madrid—and to her first tastes of calamari, chorizo and pig's ear. She smiled at the memory of feeling sophisticated and cosmopolitan for the first time in her life. After returning to the States, whenever possible, she still ate late, after nine or ten, just like the Spaniards. Eating this early seemed tacky, like covering a front yard with pink flamingos and lawn jockeys. But Howard's mother wanted to be back at his home in the suburbs by eight, so she could be in bed by nine. And what Howard's mother wanted, Howard's mother got.

"More wine, Inez?" her fiancé asked, filling her glass and then pouring himself a second, which wasn't like him at all. Inez was distracted by how strangely Howard was acting, but realizing her future mother-in-law was saying something, she turned her attention to Margaret Suterman who was seated directly across from her. Margaret was much thinner than a year ago, Inez noted, her weight loss having honed her already pointed facial features to scalpel sharpness. She probably weighed one hundred pounds and had hair and skin so startlingly white she was almost translucent, like a ghost.

"I thought your sister Rachel would be here tonight?" Howard's mother said.

"Rachel," Inez started to say, but then stopped. A mass of emotions tumbled inside her for the thousandth time that day. Inez knew that boycotting the wedding was Rachel's way of saying, "I love you, sis, and want the best for you" but still, she should be there out of loyalty, if nothing else. Inez was just about to tell Howard's mother the truth, figuring it would be better for her to find out now than on Saturday, when Howard spoke.

"Rachel has the flu, Mom."

Inez's eyes grew wide but she quickly hid her reaction and took a sip of her wine. She'd never known Howard to lie, not even the kind of white lies most people told such as, "No honestly, I had no idea that was a toupee."

"Oh, that's too bad," Margaret said, with genuine concern. "I'm sure she'll be fine by Saturday."

Inez painted a smile on her face and took another sip of her Riesling. At this rate, she would be onto glass number three in no time. Inez told herself to slow down and get through tonight's dinner. But then there was tomorrow night, and the next and…the week stretched out with the wedding on Saturday a distant, barely visible goal.

"Howard tells me this will be your last year of teaching," Margaret said, her incisive blue eyes darting back and forth from her face to Howard's.

Inez blanched. Instinctively, she grabbed Howard's thigh under the tablecloth and squeezed. He, in turn, pried her hand off his leg and brought it up to the table where he held it gently. She and Howard had discussed the possibility of her leaving at the end of this school year, but Inez continued to put off making a final decision. It had been weighing on her, for months now, wrapping its tendrils tighter and tighter around her throat.

"Well actually, I…I mean, we haven't made a decision yet," Inez fumbled, annoyed that this woman made her so nervous. Although

Howard's mother might appear to be fragile enough to snap in two like a wishbone, Inez had learned early on that Margaret Suterman was no one to tangle with.

"Oh!" said Margaret, who cut a quick glance to her son catty-corner across the table. "But dear, it's going to be such a long commute from Howard's home to the…uh, neighborhood your school is in."

"You mean the inner city?" Inez said.

Had those words actually left her mouth she wondered, and decided they must have since Howard's mother looked as though she'd just been bopped on the head by a passing waiter.

Inez's school was on the far south side of Chicago in a "rough neighborhood" as Howard referred to it. The location of her school had always bothered Howard. When they first started dating, he'd done his best to persuade her to change schools. "Why don't you get a job in the suburbs, maybe Wilmette?" he would say. "The public high school here is excellent, and there are several private schools as well."

But Inez had no desire to leave; at least not on the days she loved her job. She taught first grade because those kids had not yet reached the frightening apathy that was striking inner city children at a younger and younger age. Too many of the "older" kids, at just nine and ten, were joining gangs, dealing drugs, and having sex, already apathetic and with little desire to learn.

On bad days, the thought had crossed her mind that perhaps Howard was right. Not only would she more than double her salary if she got a job in the suburbs, but teaching kids from stable homes who'd had a good breakfast each morning would be far easier—also, not nearly as challenging. Inez supposed it sounded corny, and certainly her fellow teachers had accused her of being too idealistic, but there was no comparison to seeing the joy of learning light up the eyes of a student, like Jamal Wilson, who couldn't read more than a handful of words at the beginning of this school year, but now was taking dozens of books out of the library each month. It was for those one or two students a year who did want to learn that Inez stayed at her school.

But recently, Howard, no doubt influenced by his mother, had been suggesting she quit working altogether after the end of this school year. His salary could easily support both of them, he reasoned. But the idea of not working was completely foreign to her, and when she'd asked Howard what she would do all day if she didn't have a job, he'd suggested joining the Wilmette gardening club and the Junior League. And what about the other one hundred waking hours a week, she'd thought, the pampered suburban life sounding like a slow death to her. Inez simply could not picture herself as a lady of leisure living in a two-story, four-bedroom brick colonial in the upper class suburb of Wilmette.

But this wasn't the time or the place to discuss Inez's career. "That's a good point, Margaret," Inez said, hoping to smooth things over with her future mother-in-law.

"And Inez, dear, if you stop working, you could get started immediately on your own family since you'll be an older mother," Margaret said with a pat to Inez's hand.

Did Margaret Suterman actually think that having a job, just nine months out of the year, one which allowed Inez to be home by four in the afternoon, would interfere with their love life?

"I've dreamed about my son marrying a woman willing to devote herself to being a full-time wife and mother," Margaret said with a stony smile on her face as she described a woman that sounded like June Cleaver. "I'm sure you and Howard will reach the right decision about your job."

If she kept working and didn't get pregnant within the next few years, Howard's mother would blame her for choosing a career over motherhood and would never forgive her for taking away her only chance to be a grandmother. And then, Inez would be relegated to the category of Howard's first wife, Mary, barren and forgotten.

The waiter came and cleared away their plates. Inez's crab cakes had been divine, and under different circumstances she would have thoroughly enjoyed them, but Margaret's chatter was beginning to feel like a barrage of shotgun pellets aimed at her most vulnerable parts.

"I'm surprised you haven't moved any of your things to Howard's home yet, Inez," Margaret said.

"I'm giving all of my furniture to Goodwill," Inez told her, thinking again of Beso, who would not be coming with her. "I don't have very much to move."

"We're going to clean out Inez's apartment after the honeymoon, Mom."

"Well Inez, I'm sure you're anxious to settle down," Margaret said.

Suddenly, Inez felt suffocated in their little booth. She needed some air, she realized, as she stood.

"Inez?" Howard asked, "are you all right?"

"I just need to step outside. I'll be fine in a minute."

"I'll go with you," said Howard. "You'll be okay for a few minutes, Mom?"

"Of course, dear," Margaret said. "Take care of your bride."

With his arm around her waist, Howard guided Inez to the door. She'd always liked him like this—so confident, so sure of himself. He had this way of making her feel safe without smothering her. But right now, she would prefer to be alone.

Inez leaned up against the brick wall of the building and took a deep breath.

"What's wrong, Inez?" Howard asked. "You're not getting another migraine, are you?"

"No, I'm fine. Howard, did you tell your mother I'm quitting my job?"

"Well, yes," he said, as he shifted his weight from one foot to the other, reminding Inez of her first graders when she confronted them with not telling the truth.

"So you lied to your mother."

"I don't want to upset her before the wedding."

"I don't know what to say," Inez said, shaking her head. She didn't want to think of Howard as a mama's boy, but he did let his mother run his life far more than she was comfortable with. And now he was lying to her? If he lied to his mother, would he lie to her as well?

"There's no point in upsetting her," he continued, "she's so frail after she broke her hip last year."

Howard's mother was about as frail as a Navy Seal.

"Come on," Howard urged, taking her hand. "Let's go back inside."

Inez didn't budge. "Do you realize we've never made love anywhere but in a bed?"

"What on earth are you talking about?" he asked, pushing his glasses up on his nose with his index finger.

"I just read that seventy percent of Americans have done it in a car," Inez said, reciting the statistic, which sounded surprisingly low. "Well? Why haven't we?"

Howard frowned and appeared to sink deep into thought.

"Your car or mine?" he asked.

"What difference would it make?"

"I have leather seats."

"So?"

"And someone might see us."

"That's kind of the point."

"It is? Listen Inez, can we talk about this later? My mother is waiting."

But Inez didn't want to go back in yet. Slipping her hand out of Howard's, she walked over to the railing and looked down at the Chicago River. The nearly full moon reflected in the water as small yachts and cigarette-shaped speed boats floated by. Inez smiled at the laughter drifting up from the boats. Howard's arms wrapped around her waist, and the weight of his chin settled on her right shoulder. She leaned back into his body, feeling his breathing slow to match her own. If only this moment could last forever, she thought. But a minute later when Howard took her hand, she didn't protest as he led her back inside the restaurant.

"Are you feeling better?" Margaret asked as Inez settled herself back into the booth. "Probably a little wedding jitters, dear."

Inez knew it wasn't that. She wasn't sure if she believed in premonitions, but all day she'd had a feeling that an enormous "Aha!" moment was lurking about in the shadows, waiting for just the right moment to turn her world completely upside-down.

"As much as I loved my beloved Francis," Margaret continued, oblivious to the fact that Inez had not responded, "I remember being so nervous, I couldn't eat anything but crackers and water for weeks before our wedding. I lost seven pounds, and my sainted mother had to take in my wedding dress. She was sewing up until an hour before the ceremony."

Their waiter, dressed in a crisp white long-sleeved jacket and black trousers, appeared at the side of their table with a cart and a bottle inside a silver bucket, along with three champagne flutes. He showed the label to Howard and popped the cork. "Is it to your liking, Mr. Suterman?" the waiter asked as he poured Howard a taste.

Inez inwardly groaned at hearing the typical mispronunciation of Howard's surname; she knew what was coming.

"It's pronounced 'suture-man,'" Howard told him with a hearty laugh. "I'm a doctor. You might say I was destined to go into medicine and sew people up for a living."

The waiter responded with a please-tip-me smile, filled each of their glasses, placed the bucket on their table, and rolled the cart away.

"To my beautiful bride!" said Howard, raising his glass in the air. Was Inez imagining it or was he slurring his words?

He leaned across the table with his glass. Inez, on autopilot, tipped her glass to Margaret's and then watched as he downed a third of it. He'd already had two glasses of Riesling, and now he was chugalugging champagne? But the surprises were not over.

Howard placed a blue velvet rectangular box in front of Inez who stared at it, not moving, until he urged her to open it. Inside the case was one of the most gorgeous diamond tennis bracelets Inez had ever seen. They'd never discussed tennis bracelets. He clasped it around her thin wrist. The diamonds caught the glow from the candle, dazzlingly Inez with their beauty.

Howard seemed to be turning into the romantic, charming man she'd given up any hope of ever having. But Inez knew something wasn't quite right with her fiancé's sudden metamorphosis.

9

On his way back to the office after a quick dinner at a sandwich shop, Zeke stopped to look at the seventy-foot long Chagall Four Seasons mural at the corner of Dearborn and Monroe. Chagall's whimsical figures, floating at odd angles, were like magical characters from a beloved fairytale. Zeke thought of Chagall's magnificent stained glass windows at the Art Institute of Chicago, the sunlight shining through the indigo panes of glass, making the scenes come alive.

Years ago, when Zeke was a member of the museum, he would go to lectures and tours at least twice a month. At first, he'd joined to meet new women. For a few years the Art Institute became his own personal singles club, providing a steady stream of dates with interesting, intelligent women. In between chatting up new potential romances, he'd learned about art and had come to love the museum's collection of Impressionist paintings, the largest outside the Louvre. On rainy or cold weekends, he would walk the galleries and lose himself in Monet's dreamy French harbors and farm fields, Gauguin's doe-eyed Polynesian girls and his favorite painting, *On the Terrace,* by Renoir. He spent so many hours staring at the two sisters in that portrait, he had developed an entire fantasy life around them. It was a classic case of having been switched at birth in the hospital nursery, he'd imagined. Those girls were part of his long-lost "real" family—worldly, sophisticated, and well-educated—the family he'd always yearned for, who understood him perfectly and encouraged his desire to explore the world.

Zeke moved past the mural, soaking in the perfect weather, which felt like a balm after the long, cold winter. The last thing he wanted to do was go back to work, but it was too early to go home, and unfortunately, too late to see Stu Miller, who had no doubt left hours ago. On a normal night, Zeke would just be getting his second wind about now, gearing up for three or four more hours of work. But this week was not a normal week.

Zeke headed for his building and caught a glimpse of a man, inside the revolving doors, who looked exactly like… "Oh shit," he thought, it was Stu Miller. Zeke had a sudden childish urge to jump behind the mural, hoping Stu wouldn't see him. Then, reminding himself that he was a mature adult, of sorts, he stepped forward coming face-to-face with the managing partner.

"Good evening St…Mr. Miller, I hope your secretary gave you the message that I'd like to make an appointment to see…"

"Yes, yes," Stu snapped, cutting him off.

"Are you available tomorrow?"

"Call my secretary in the morning," Stu replied briskly, with all of the warmth and friendliness of a slab of concrete. "Have a good evening."

Zeke wanted to lunge for his arm and say, "But you called me 'son' this morning. You slapped my back. We bonded at The Nineteenth Hole Bistro. Don't you remember?"

It bothered Zeke that he couldn't connect with Stu Miller, because he normally got along well with most people. In high school, he'd not only been part of the smart crowd, but had hung out with the star football and basketball jocks as well. He'd moved easily between the groups, which normally avoided one another like the plague, making friends with all of them. Zeke had dated both the painfully pretty cheerleaders and the average-looking smart girls. High school was the last time Zeke felt as though he'd fit in. Zeke pulled his security pass out of his briefcase and keyed in.

"Hello, Zeke."

The sound of her voice behind him made his heart skip a beat. He turned. A swath of early evening sunlight fell across Elise Wyatt's white blonde hair and beautiful face. It was like being greeted by an angel; he envied the lucky guy who got to wake up next to her every day.

"Twice in one day," Zeke said, wishing he could dazzle her with some brilliant repartee. But a generic greeting was all he could come up with in the moment as seeing her again had shaken his equilibrium—but in a good way; his mood was currently soaring toward the heavens.

When no one else got on the elevator before the doors closed, Zeke felt like the gods were giving him a thumbs up. He'd always entertained a fantasy of getting stuck in an elevator for hours with a woman to whom he could bare his soul. Perhaps someone exactly like Elise? Both of them immediately broke elevator etiquette to face one another.

"Dinner?" Zeke asked, when he noticed her holding the familiar international symbols for an overworked professional—a square white Styrofoam container and a large coffee.

"I've got a big closing at the end of this week," she said, with a nod. "I've got at least four hours of work ahead of me tonight."

"Can you believe it's all going to come down to this week?" he said. "Remember the first day in the office when we had the orientation meeting on the fifty-fifth floor? In some ways, it seems like it happened yesterday, but in other ways it seems like a hundred years ago."

When Elise Wyatt had walked in to that conference room on their first day of work eight years earlier, her beauty had caused a seismic wave of testosterone among the men sitting at the table. Strangely enough, Zeke had completely forgotten about that day until seeing her again this morning. Elise was in the commercial real estate department and Zeke in litigation. The transaction and litigation attorneys so rarely interacted they might as well be working for different law firms. But seeing her now, he couldn't imagine letting Elise slip from his mind again.

"I know exactly what you mean," Elise said. "I feel the same way."

"You do?" Zeke asked, finding it difficult to believe that such a angelic creature shared his thoughts.

"It's not easy billing twenty-one hundred hours a year. I've had to make a lot of sacrifices in my personal life, you know."

"Yeah, me too," said Zeke, wondering what she was talking about. She wasn't wearing a ring, but surely a woman like her was living with someone. At the annual firm dinner dance and holiday parties, she always had the kind of date who looked as though he'd just stepped off the cover of GQ after performing life-saving brain surgery, before donning a Ralph Lauren tux to join Elise for the evening.

"I thought by now..." she began, and then broke off, biting her lower lip.

Zeke waited, riveted by what she would say and by that excruciatingly adorable gesture.

"Well, I thought I'd be married and have a family by now," she said, as a rosy hue colored her cheeks.

Zeke gripped the hand rail, stifling his temptation to drop to his knee and propose on the spot. Call it kismet, chemistry, or luck, he couldn't believe she was echoing his self-same thoughts and feelings.

"What's the matter, Zeke? Are you all right?"

"I just can't believe you're single," he said, staring into her gorgeous green eyes. If he wasn't careful, he might fall into them and never find his way out again.

"That makes two of us, right?" she said, with a coy smile. "By the way, good job putting Wallace Archer in his place this morning. He deserved it."

Zeke wondered if she was flirting or just being her natural, friendly self. The elevator stopped at her floor. He stepped forward to hold the door open for her. As she brushed by his chest, the brief physical contact made his stomach do a cartwheel. She turned to face him.

"I wish you all the luck in the world on Friday," Elise said.

"You too, Elise, but I'm sure we're both going to make it."

A shadow crossed her face. "Have a good night, Zeke."

"Wait, Elise. You know something, don't you?"

She tilted her head and bit her lip.

"I'd like to tell you" she said, "but I don't think I should. I hope you understand, Zeke."

"Of course. Have a good night."

He watched her walk down the hallway as the doors closed on his vision. Zeke slumped against the elevator wall, his heart pounding, although he wasn't sure if it was from being in her presence or his realization that the rumor must be true. Only one associate would be promoted on Friday, and it was obvious from her private breakfast with Stu Miller today that it would be Elise.

Minutes later, Zeke arrived at his office feeling no motivation to work, but Friday's deposition was too important, and he wasn't ready for it. Three years ago, when the head of the litigation department called Zeke into his office to tell him that he had been assigned to the Xanadu Pharmaceuticals case, Zeke was thrilled. It was a sign that the powers-that-be at his firm, trusted him and liked his work. He remembered that he couldn't wait to dive into the case, but the excitement was long gone.

The telephone rang, yanking him out of the morass into which he was sinking. His caller I.D. displayed "private number." It could be a plaintiff who didn't know that Zeke could not talk to him without the permission of his attorney, or a headhunter trying to lure Zeke to a more lucrative position in New York or D.C. Right now, he would be happy to get a call from anyone who could distract him from his thoughts, even a telemarketer. He pushed the speaker button.

"Zeke, she left me!" wailed a voice so clear it sounded as though it were coming from the next office.

"Mike?"

"My world has fallen apart," Mike moaned. Translation: Mike's wife Cybele has left him again.

"Where are you?" Zeke asked, worried Mike might be in Chicago. "You sound so close."

"It's my satellite phone," said Mike. "Next to my Hummer, it's my favorite toy."

"Listen," Zeke said evenly, "your world has not fallen apart. She'll be back in a few days, just like all the other times. And I wish I could talk, but this is a bad week for me. I'll call you this…"

"I know she's in Chicago," Mike said. "I'm coming after her. Can I crash with you?"

Zeke's stomach churned. Mike was married to Zeke's second cousin Cybele. The fact that his best friend from college had married a relative he'd once thought of as a sister, bound them together whether Zeke liked it or not. But ever since marrying Cybele four years ago, Mike had become little more than a blubbering jellyfish, although understandable given that his cousin was a real piece of self-centered work as well as a pathological liar. But Zeke had given Mike fair warning about his cousin, which his friend had chosen to ignore by diving into marriage just four months after they'd met.

"Why don't you let me try to find her," Zeke suggested, praying Mike would agree.

"I'm coming," said Mike.

"Don't come. I'll find her. I promise."

"You said you were busy."

Just before Mike hung up, Zeke heard, "Last call for flight number 209 to Chicago, boarding at gate 12."

10

nez tossed her keys and purse onto the coffee table and bent down to greet Beso. It was early. Normally, she wouldn't go to bed for at least three more hours, but she was exhausted from the emotional and mental gymnastics of dealing with Howard's mother. She decided to read another chapter of the Spanish version of Isabel Allende's *Zorro: A novel* and then go to bed. She took off her dress, put on her terry cloth robe and walked into the bathroom. Just as she was about to wash off her make-up she heard a noise from the other room and froze. She'd been so distracted with Howard, she probably forgot to lock her door. And damn those tenants who let strangers walk in with them into the locked lobby downstairs or buzzed people they didn't know into the building. Tiny daggers of fear traveled through her body as she debated what to do, but before she could move, he was in the doorway. She inhaled sharply at the sight of the man she hadn't seen in nearly a decade.

He had changed very little except for a few added wrinkles at the corners of his black eyes. His thick chestnut hair still flopped over his forehead, giving him an innocent, boyish look he did not deserve. His half grin was just as appealing. And his usual five o'clock shadow enhanced rather than detracted from his raw good looks.

"Hello, *querida*. I've missed you," said Carlos Luna Delgado de la Madrid.

He simply stood there, with total self-assurance, as if his testosterone had given him permission to walk uninvited into her apartment and back into her life. She stood before him for a moment, staring into those coal black eyes that gave nothing away. And then, Inez's heart began beating like crazy as she reached up with her right hand and slapped him with all of her strength.

The sound of the slap hung in the air, broken only seconds later by Beso meowing, as he meandered between their four legs. Inez had never hit anyone before in her life, and her initial response was surprise at how much her hand hurt. She reached down to pick up Beso, holding all fifteen pounds of him, close to her chest, like a shield.

"What are you doing here?" Inez demanded, her red curly locks fanning out over her shoulders like a bonfire.

Despite the slap, he stood there utterly unruffled, with the complete confidence of a man who was used to women of all ages, races, and marital statuses being swept away by his charms.

"You're still as beautiful and as difficult as I remember," Carlos said, rubbing the red hand imprint on his cheek. Carlos never answered a direct question.

"You deserved it," she said.

"You're right, I did," he said, with an arrogance which made her want to slap him again. And then, as if he could read her thoughts he said, "Would you like to try again, Inez?"

She was about to respond when the downstairs buzzer sounded. Inez put Beso on the floor and strolled past Carlos, willing herself to walk slowly. By some miracle, Inez hoped it would be Rachel, who'd come to say she'd made a mistake about Saturday and had changed her mind. But now, Inez needed her help with Carlos. Rachel had never met him, but that hadn't stopped her from hating Carlos enough for all women ever wronged by a man in the history of time. After Inez had returned from Spain fresh from their break-up, Rachel used to say, "That bastard better never show his face here or he'll wish he'd been born a eunuch." Inez could count on Rachel to get rid of him. She'd never hated him the way Rachel had. Then again, she'd never hated anyone.

As Inez waited by the door, she turned to look at Carlos to make certain she hadn't imagined his appearance in her apartment.

She'd never expected to see him again. After what he'd done, she didn't think he'd have the *cojones* to ever face her.

"Am I supposed to believe you just happened to be in the neighborhood and dropped in to say hello?" Inez asked, shaking her head in disbelief. She was determined not to get pulled in by his charisma, but was at a loss for words. Having a casual chit-chat with a man who used to be the love of her life didn't seem quite appropriate.

A knock at the door pulled her attention away. She opened it to a pimply-faced young man holding two-dozen long-stemmed yellow roses.

"Flowers for Inez Paris," he said.

"Do you normally make deliveries this late?" Inez asked, her mind whirling in a dozen different directions.

"No, but I got paid extra to make sure you got these tonight," he replied.

Before Inez could get to her wallet to give him a tip, Carlos handed him a twenty-dollar bill. For a moment she was angry, but then she thought, so what? He could try all he wanted to ingratiate himself back into her life—it wasn't going to work.

"Are these from you?" asked Inez, as she carried the flowers to the kitchen sink.

"There's only one way to find out." Carlos leaned against the doorjamb as he held Beso, stroking the white halo-like circle on the top of his head. At his touch, Beso's ears cocked back in feline ecstasy, and his purring was loud enough to be heard across the street. Animals had always loved Carlos, but she would've hoped Beso had better taste.

She put the roses in a vase, placing it on the coffee table next to the red roses Howard had given her earlier that evening. It looked like a hospital room in here. The tantalizing card was just at her fingertips, but Inez didn't want to open it in front of Carlos who she was certain could still read her thoughts.

"Well, what are you waiting for?" he teased. They'd always spoken English to one another and had fallen back into that pattern. Carlos spoke nearly perfect English, with just the slightest lilt.

She tore open the envelope, astonished at the message: "*Each day I love you more and more. You are my world—H.*" Howard again? Had he been brainwashed by some militant sect of romance fanatics? But with the unexpected appearance of the first love of her life, the Howard file in her brain was currently unavailable.

"A secret admirer perhaps?" asked Carlos, with a broad smile, showing off his perfectly white, straight teeth. "I haven't forgotten that purple irises are your favorite. Roses are okay for other women, for ordinary women. But not for someone like you, *querida.*"

She put her hands on her hips and scowled. It was just like him not to notice her engagement ring—a breathtaking two point three carat, emerald cut, E color, S/1 clarity. Astronauts orbiting the Earth could see her rock from outer space, but apparently not Mr. Blasé from just eight feet away. Of course, other men had never been a threat to him.

"How've you been, *querida?*" he asked.

"That's all you have to say all these years?" Inez replied, her voice rising in spite of her efforts to remain cool. "This is the most ridiculous conversation I've ever had," she said, flipping her hair off her shoulders with a toss of her head. She willed herself to calm down, but it was nearly impossible to ignore the look in his eyes, the one he used to give her when he wanted to make love. She caught him staring at her cleavage, or where cleavage would be if she had any. She pulled the sides of her robe tight together.

"Why are you looking away, *querida?*" he asked, in a low voice, which used to make her feel as though he were caressing her breasts with a feather.

"You still haven't answered my question," she said, in control again. "What are you doing here?"

Carlos bent over and placed Beso on the floor. He took a step in her direction. Inez stood her ground. He had changed very little, but it didn't seem possible that at one time she'd been wildly in love with him. Although he had once hurt her deeply, the pain was only a distant memory. Until dreaming about him this morning, she hadn't thought of him in years. This was all so surreal.

"I'm here to ask for your forgiveness," he said.

"Now you want my forgiveness, after nine years without a word," she said, crossing her arms over her chest. "Please. What are you really doing here, Carlos?"

"I want you to be my wife and the mother of my children."

Her heart stopped. Those were the exact words she'd so desperately wanted to hear when they'd lived together in Spain. For an instant, she remembered how deeply she had wanted him then. She steeled herself; she would never go down that road again.

"Too late," Inez said. "You had your chance. You knew I wanted to get married, but you couldn't do it."

"I'm not the man you knew in Madrid," Carlos responded, his eyes were moist with tears like two polished onyx stones. "I wasn't ready, Inez. We were just kids then."

"You were a kid. A real man wouldn't just disappear one day."

Carlos winced. His eyes melted with shame and remorse, but it had no effect on her. Carlos had always been able to emote at the drop of a *sombrero*. What a waste that he'd never done any professional acting.

"What I did to you was unforgivable," he said. "If I could change the past I would, but I've done the only thing I could do, I've changed myself. Give me another chance, *querida*."

Inez could practically hear the orchestra music swell to a crescendo. What bullshit.

"I want you to leave," she said, "now."

"I've thought about you every day since then," he continued, as if she hadn't spoken. "I've never stopped loving you."

"It's too little, too late," Inez said, opening the door.

"I know you don't feel that way," he said, moving toward her and coming to a stop in front of her. She could smell his scent—primordial and pungent, like the smell of sex. She wished he would leave, but he just stood there staring into her eyes. And then, he lightly caressed her cheek with his finger, sending a lightning bolt through her from her loins to her throat.

Carlos, leave now," she said, in an even voice. "Have a nice trip back to Spain."

Smiling, he sauntered out the door as though he were pleased that she was kicking him out. She slammed the door shut.

"What an arrogant ass," she said, trying to ignore her southern hemisphere that started a dance she thought she had long ago forgotten.

Tell me you did not do this, H.

I simply put the thought into Carlos's mind that he should get on an airplane to Chicago now, instead of waiting until next month to visit Inez, which he had been planning to do.

What in the blazes are you yammering about?

Call it creating a hunch, a feeling, intuition—it does not always work, but when does, as you can see, it is quite powerful. It worked wonders with Dick Kowalski.

Do you have even a scintilla of understanding of human emotions? Bringing Carlos back into her life is a recipe for disaster! I know all about men like Carlos—hell, I wrote the books. This man is straight out of my thirty-fourth novel, Enticing Rogue. He's an enticing rogue, Herodius! Men like him are nearly impossible to resist if you are afflicted with a predilection for bad boys like our darling Inez is. This is like dropping a debutante into the middle of a drunken bachelor party and hoping the little lady can escape with her virtue intact.

Let me tell you a story, Serena. Once upon a time...

That is a terrible way to start a story.

Let me finish, please. Many centuries ago, I was presented with a very similar situation. Little Flower was engaged to a farmer—a good man, but not the right man for her. One day, as she was collecting herbs in the forest, I arranged for her ex-lover, a soldier, who was, as you call it, an enticing rogue, to find her in the forest. Little Flower rekindled her relationship with the soldier...

Rekindled? Don't gloss over the details H.

Please Serena, let me tell this in my own way. Little Flower soon discovered that the soldier could not be faithful to her. But because Little Flower now remembered her heart, she was able to gain perspective about her fiancé, the farmer, and see that he was wrong for her. Shortly after that she met her soul mate—the master builder—and they fell in love and married.

Are you telling me that Zeke is the master builder?

Exactly.

Well, that's just a lovely little story—it almost brought tears to my eyes. Except for the fact that we're not dealing with a village with a couple hundred people and a few goats. There are millions of people in Chicago which makes things a heck of a lot more complicated. We've got to get these two together immediately! And don't tell me again to be patient!

11

The cab turned into the circular drive of Zeke's forty-story condominium building in the heart of River North, also known as the gallery district of Chicago. He entered the white marbled lobby and greeted Steve, the night doorman.

"You're home early tonight," Steve replied, looking up from his *Sports Illustrated* magazine.

"Yeah, I've got a friend…" Zeke began.

"Mike-my-life-is-falling-apart?" Steve hooked his thumb in a vertical direction. "He got here about twenty minutes ago."

Zeke forgot that Mike and Steve met on Mike's last visit a few months ago. Mike had camped out at Steve's desk one night while Zeke was working late and relayed his entire tumultuous history with his wife Cybele, in excruciating detail, to poor Steve, a captive stranger.

"I hope this time he spared you his latest tale of woe," Zeke said, apologetically.

Steve nodded. "He barely said hello. I've got to say he looks really bad."

"You haven't seen Pamela, have you?" Zeke asked, half-dreading that she might pop out from behind one of the potted palms in the lobby. He still didn't know what he was going to do about Saturday night, but he'd decided that going stag to the firm dinner dance would be far safer than showing up with crazy Pamela.

"Trouble in paradise?" asked Steve, with a smirk.

Steve, who was about the same age as Zeke and also single, often shared love life tales. At first, Steve was jealous when Zeke started dating Pamela. But when Zeke began to tell him about her stalker tendencies, Steve's jealousy had done a one-eighty, and he advised Zeke to dump her, before she went off the deep end.

"If she asks about me tell her I died," said Zeke. "No, better yet, don't tell her anything. You haven't seen me, alright?"

"I warned you my friend," said Steve, "that chick is nuts. What a shame. The body of a goddess wasted on a bunny boiler."

Zeke braced himself as he rode the elevator to his floor. Spending time with Mike when his marriage was on the rocks was like running a marathon over hot coals, barefoot. Zeke found Mike stretched out, full-length, on the brown leather sofa, holding a tumbler on his stomach. An open bottle of Zeke's twenty-one-year-old Glenlivet scotch and the TV remote sat on the glass coffee table in front of him.

"Hi Mike, I'm home," said Zeke, trying his best to sound cheery.

Mike didn't move. Apparently, he was riveted to the infomercial on bikini waxing magnified to hideous detail on the sixty-inch high-definition screen. Scenes from the commercial flickered on the scotch bottle and coffee table, forming distorted psychedelic images of the woman's crotch.

Steve was not exaggerating. Mike looked worse than Zeke had ever seen him—far more haggard than after one of their many college late-night binges. He was at least ten pounds lighter than the last time he'd seen him, hadn't shaved in days, and didn't have his usual tan. His eyes were so bloodshot he looked like one of the zombies from his last movie. But even in this pitiable state, Zeke knew many women would probably do a double-take if they saw Mike's chiseled handsome features that had graced many *People* and *Entertainment Weekly* covers over the years.

"You look like shit," said Zeke, picking up the remote and pushing the mute button. It was astounding to see how much Mike had changed since they were assigned as freshman dorm roommates at DePaul University. Back then, Mike had had a new girl every week. But when Mike met Cybele, he'd fallen into a yawning crevasse and had yet to hit bottom. The "love stallion"—Mike's college nickname, which Zeke had spent endless hours ribbing him about—had become a lovesick barnacle.

"And you look like a beached whale," Mike said, looking at him through half-opened eyes. "You're really letting yourself go."

"Work."

"How long are you going to cling to that sorry-ass excuse for not having a life?" Mike snapped, sitting up long enough to down what was left of his scotch and refilling his glass.

Zeke didn't want to argue with him. All he wanted was to get the obligatory sob story about Cybele's latest reason for leaving in as little time as possible, catch some of the World Cup soccer playoffs, and go to bed.

"Have you talked to her?" asked Zeke. "Have you tried calling her?"

No response.

Zeke was furious, but only had himself to blame for having introduced the two of them. Four years ago when Zeke flew out to L.A. on a business trip, he'd promised his mother that he would spend time with his second cousin Cybele, who had moved to Los Angeles a year earlier. She'd given up her successful modeling career to try out the clichéd Hollywood dream of becoming a star. Zeke's mistake was inviting Mike to join them for dinner because he hadn't wanted to deal with his psycho cousin on his own. As fate would have it, Mike had fallen head over heels in love. Cybele had been love-struck as well—with Mike's Hollywood connections that could launch her from ex-model to movie star. Zeke begged his best friend not to marry her, but it was like trying to reason with a bull in heat.

"Why did she leave?" Zeke asked, just barely stopping himself from adding the words, "this time."

Mike shrugged. Zeke hated his passive-aggressive routine more than his whining. Mike was acting like a child—in this case a total brat. Zeke pulled his cell phone from his jacket pocket and scrolled through his mailbox.

"Don't bother," Mike told him. "It's really over this time."

Ignoring him, Zeke pressed Charlotte's number on his speed dial.

Charlotte was Cybele's older sister who lived in Wheaton, a western suburb of Chicago. It was Cybele's hideout-away-from-home. Whenever Cybele left Mike she would flee to Charlotte's, although finding her after that was a little like trying to pin down a fugitive, since she spent most of her visits club-hopping. Although Zeke and his second cousins had been like siblings growing up, they'd lost touch as adults. The only time Zeke and Charlotte talked was to try and patch things up between the lovebirds every few months. After a couple of minutes of chit-chat, Zeke flipped his phone shut.

"She's already left to go out tonight, but Charlotte told me where's she's going," Zeke told the unmoving figure on his couch.

Mike put the tumbler to his lips and jerked his head back to catch the last drop.

"I'm going to bed," said Zeke.

Mike suddenly sprang to life. "No, wait! Tell me where she is!"

Zeke saw the desperation in Mike's eyes and couldn't help but feel disgusted. "Club Caliente. Okay, now I'm going to bed."

Mike shot up from the couch and grabbed Zeke's arm. "You have to go with me, buddy."

"No, I don't. I've got a deposition this week that I've…"

"She won't talk to me. She'll talk to you."

Zeke cursed silently. He wished he could say no, but he couldn't let his friend down. "Fine. Let's go."

"Don't you want to put something else on?" Mike asked, with a Rodeo Drive snicker at Zeke's rumpled suit.

"Do you want to go or not?" Zeke asked. How the hell had he let himself get involved in Mike's chaotic love life, again?

They rode the elevator to the lobby in silence.

"She's calling me a one-hit wonder," Mike said, as they walked to the club. "Can you believe it?"

Mike looked stricken when Zeke shrugged. Mike has always had a healthy self-image, but when *Daunted*, a screenplay he'd written in his spare time during college, had won a contest and ended up being sold to Paramount, his ego had expanded to the size of the Milky Way. Ignoring everyone's advice to finish his last semester of his senior year, Mike dropped out and moved to L.A., where he promptly dove into the Hollywood scene that included a dozen parties a week, invitations to the Oscars each year, and any starlet he wanted.

Daunted, a drama about a family that lived completely off the grid with no social security numbers, no credit cards, mortgages, or taxes, had won Best Picture and earned Mike an Oscar for Best Original Screenplay. He'd become an instant millionaire and a Hollywood golden boy. For the next few years, Mike didn't write a word; he was content to simply coast along on his reputation until he realized fame in Hollywood lasted about as long as a bout of the flu. When it was obvious people were starting to forget him, Mike became desperate to get back into the limelight. After a year of self-proclaimed writer's block, he'd starting writing the kind of flicks that appealed primarily to teenage boys where every character was a walking cliché, and all the jokes were about sex, boogers, or getting plastered. In the last few years, he'd stooped to writing gory horror flicks.

"You're writing crap," Zeke said. "Your heart isn't in these brainless movies. You should go back to dramas like *Daunted*."

"I make a good living," Mike replied, which was true even though every movie he'd written since *Daunted* had been a box office failure.

"Money isn't everything," said Zeke, remembering he'd given the exact same justification to Charlie that very morning. "Look at how unhappy you are."

Mike fixed Zeke with his ebony eyes. "I guess that makes two of us."

"My life is fine," said Zeke. "You don't see me running out to L.A. every few months, whining on your couch."

"That's because you don't have a life," Mike said bitterly. "You work ninety hours a week and your love life is a joke. You hook up with a woman for a few months, and then it's the long Saharan desert stretch until the next one comes along. When are you going to grow up and get a real relationship?"

Zeke's stomach lurched. His friend's life might be a complete disaster, but his own was far from perfect.

"You know," Mike continued, "sometimes I'm sorry I ever entered *Daunted* into that contest. Even my own wife doesn't respect me. I guess I can't blame her. Most mornings I hate to look at myself in the mirror."

Reaching the front door to Club Caliente they showed the doorman their ID's and paid the cover charge. The moment Zeke walked in he felt a tingle of electricity. Three nights a week you could find the best Latin music and best salsa dancers in town here. Well, at least that had been the schedule when he'd been a regular at this club. The huge rectangular dance floor was crammed with couples grinding to a bachata, a sexy dance from the Dominican Republic. Zeke looked around the warehouse-sized room. There were the same dark-paneled walls and maroon drapes hanging to the floor with black leather couches lining the wall opposite the bar. The slow moving ceiling fans did nothing to cool off the sticky dancers in a room as muggy as a greenhouse. Zeke recognized Papi, the Puerto Rican D.J. on the stage with Maria, the salsa instructor who gave free beginner lessons before the real dancing began. Nothing had changed, thought Zeke, with a smile.

"When was the last time you were here?" Mike shouted over the music.

"Years ago," Zeke replied, wondering where the time had gone. He just remembered that the main reason he'd ultimately decided to buy his condo was because Club Caliente and Acapulco, two of the best salsa clubs in town, were within walking distance.

And then, as memories have a way of doing, either coming upon us gently like a lover's caress or as forcefully as a stealth uppercut, Zeke thought of the night he met the only woman he had ever felt destined to be with. That night at Grant Park was so long ago, but he'd never forgotten Inez. For years, every time he'd gone out salsa dancing, he'd looked for her, certain he would see her again, but he never had. To this day, he regretted not getting her address or phone number or at least her last name.

Ever since that night he'd been comparing this strange certainty that he and Inez belonged together—with every woman he'd dated—none of whom had come close to engendering the same feelings; not even with Susan from law school had he felt that way.

"You go to the bar," Zeke told Mike. "I'll walk around and see if Cybele is here. And order a mineral water. You've had enough to drink."

As Zeke made his way around the dance floor, his heart beat faster at the thought that Inez could be at Club Caliente tonight. But then, logic overrode his hopes. She was probably married with kids by now or was in South America like she'd planned.

After circling the dance floor three times, he situated himself near the ladies room hoping to find Cybele. A dozen scantily dressed women wearing everything from sequined halter tops to low-riding cropped pants tight enough to show off every curve, strolled in and out. Zeke found himself swimming in an exotic sea of gorgeous women—all of whom loved to dance.

He squeezed his way through the crowd until he reached the edge of the dance floor. As his right foot tapped in time to the clave beat, he watched the dancing couples spinning, dipping, twirling, heads whipping, hips undulating, and feet flying in patterns of magic, making the room come alive.

It was all coming back to him—the passionate, sexy dancing and the intense rhythmic music that moved his soul like no other music ever had. His mood soared. He was just about to ask the brunette standing beside him if she wanted to dance when the song ended and the D.J. put on a Cha Cha Cha, bringing everything to an abrupt halt. He loved listening to a Cha Cha Cha, but the dance moved far too slowly for him, unlike salsa that moved at the speed of light. Zeke took one more swing around the dance floor before giving up and joining Mike at the upper bar.

"Cybele isn't here."

"It's early," Mike slurred.

"Not for me, Mike. Let's go."

Just then Zeke felt a tug on his sleeve. A stunning petite Latina, wearing a black scooped-neck dress looked up at him. She looked so familiar, Zeke guessed that he had danced with her when he used to be a regular here.

"Would you like to dance?" she asked.

All of his confidence from a few minutes earlier instantly vaporized when he saw her low-heeled strappy silver shoes. The low-heels signaled she was a serious dancer and he was so out of practice, there was an excellent chance he might crush her dainty feet.

"I'd love to, but I've got to get my friend home," he said, tipping his head in the direction of Mike.

The minute she turned away, Zeke was seized with regret. He knew he should've said yes.

"How extravagant you are, throwing away women like that," Mike said. His mouth sounded as though it was stuffed with cotton, and he was embracing his glass of Scotch as though it were his only friend in the world. "Some day they may be scarce."

Quoting lines from *Casablanca* was a game they'd played for years, ever since they'd discovered one day, while getting high in their dorm room, that for each of them, *Casablanca* was their favorite movie of all time. At least, until *Daunted* came out.

"Are you coming with me?" Zeke asked, gruffly. He was in no mood for their adolescent game.

"No. I'm going to get very drunk," Mike replied. "You go home and get your beauty sleep for your fucking job."

"Suit yourself," Zeke thought. Then he saw how miserable Mike looked and although any compassion he might have had for him had long since disappeared, leaving something half-way between pity and indifference. He knew their friendship was dying, and that made him sadder than he could have imagined.

12

Inez followed her sister Rachel into Club Caliente with barely a glance at the crowd. A blast of salsa music hit her as they passed by the speakers and, for a moment, the familiar rhythm transported Inez to her past when salsa was her whole life.

At six feet tall, Rachel towered giraffe-like over men and women alike as she loped gracefully through the mass of people surrounding the dance floor to the upper bar, the only place in the club far enough away from the music so they could talk.

"What do you want to drink?" Rachel asked Inez as they hiked themselves up onto adjacent stools. Rachel wore a pair of faded designer jeans, big silver hoop earrings, and a white scoop tank top with three-quarter length sleeves. The outfit was simple but as always, she managed to look chic and elegant with just the slightest hipster edge.

"Water, I guess," Inez replied, lost in her own thoughts. She'd lost her maid of honor, her fiancé had morphed into a montage from *Love Story*, and the man who used to be the love of her life had just popped out of a bottle like a genie, granting Inez her two most-cherished wishes. And it was only Monday.

"Thanks for coming, Rachel," Inez said. She needed to talk to someone after Carlos had left, but she wasn't ready to tell Howard about him, at least not until she figured out how she felt about Carlos's unexpected reappearance.

"You left me a dozen messages," said Rachel.

"Four or five. Okay, maybe eight."

"You're my sister, and I'll always love you," Rachel paused and then added, "even if you want to ruin your life by marrying the wrong man."

Inez sighed. She could always count on Rachel to tell her what she was doing wrong. Inez unscrewed the cap from her bottled water.

"Wow! Nice bracelet," said Rachel, as she reached across Inez's body to touch the diamond-studded bangle.

"It's from Howard."

"Not your Howard," Rachel said, raising one perfectly-plucked eyebrow. "All right, enough about him. Let's get to your most recent problem, Don Juan. I hope you told Carlos to go back to the old country to ruin someone else's life."

"I slapped him," Inez said. She was still amazed she'd actually done that. An incredible anger had welled up inside of her at the sight of him, so the slap was more of a reflex than a conscious decision. But still, it felt good.

"You slapped that rat?" said Rachel, with a nod of approval. But a second later she frowned. "No, actually that was a bad move. Men like him are just encouraged by rejection. He'll be back."

Inez pictured the pleased smirk on Carlos's face after the slap, as though it was exactly what he'd expected, even hoped for. He actually seemed to enjoy it. The bastard. "I know, that's the problem."

"What's the problem?" asked Rachel, with a disapproving tone. "You're not seriously considering his marriage proposal, are you?"

"No, of course not, it's just that—remember what you said about needing a man who got my juices flowing? Well, I guess he kind of turned on the faucet."

Intense passion and chemistry had never been there with Howard. She had convinced herself she could live without it, or that someday it might magically blossom like an English garden in the desert. She'd purposely ignored what she'd known in her heart of hearts—passion was either there from the start or not at all—it wasn't something that could be artificially manufactured like a laboratory diamond. The question was, could their marriage survive without it? And could she?

"Does this mean you're dumping Howie?" Rachel asked hopefully.

Inez shook her head. "Something is going on with him. He's not his usual self. Listen Rach, have you changed your mind about coming on Saturday?"

Rachel fixed Inez with her stormy ocean-blue eyes. "That's a rhetorical question, right?"

"I don't know why you can't see Howard's good points?" Inez protested. "There are so many of them."

"I'll ask you for the last time, are you in love with him?"

Inez looked down at the bar and fiddled with her bracelet. She loved him, but was no longer sure if she was in love with him. Still, people got married for all kinds of other reasons, although she couldn't think of a single one at the moment.

Inez had often wondered what day-to-day life was really like for people with dull marriages. While living a carefree life dating her string of salsa boyfriends, she used to eavesdrop on the conversations among the married teachers at her school. Their talk sounded like canned jokes on a sitcom. With the fascination of those drawn to scenes of disaster from a safe distance, Inez discovered she could not get enough of their banter that usually went something like this:

"The whole damned house could burn down around Fred, and he would still have his fat ass in his barcalounger glued to the idiot box," said Therese, a woman about Inez's age.

"You think that's bad," rejoined Carol, who was in her early forties, "my husband golfs so much, I never see him on the weekends. Our kids refer to him as our part-time boarder."

"Well Sam seems to think I'm his maid. I'm always picking up after him," added Sylvia, a pretty African-American woman who'd only been married three years.

Inez felt a mixture of pity and revulsion for her colleagues and vowed that she would never succumb to their dismal fates. But, over the past several months, she had grown increasingly worried. Were all relationships doomed to lose their passion? Were husbands and wives destined to become little more than roommates, exchanging a few words over breakfast and dinner, with an occasional romp in bed?

Was she better off being single as her colleagues told her so many times—those same co-workers who'd gushed with congratulations when she told them she had become engaged? Or had those couples simply settled for someone less than their ideal partner, which would explain their unhappiness?

"Hey, that guy at the end of the bar looks familiar," Rachel said. "See him? The one who looks like he's blubbering into his drink. I think he's famous."

"You think everyone's famous," Inez grumbled. Inez believed Rachel's fascination with rich and famous people was because at one time Rachel was on the verge of becoming rich and famous herself. But then, Rachel had her downfall—all the things Rachel refused to discuss from her past. Even their surname was a painful reminder for Rachel because that was where her life had changed, in Paris, the City of Light. "Can we get back to my life?"

"My life. Stop being so dramatic, Izzy," said Rachel, the queen of drama.

"It's simple. Carlos is a self-centered egomaniac who's incapable of true love. Have you asked him what he's doing here? Isn't it a little suspicious that he reappears after so long without a word? Is he still working as a fashion photographer surrounded by beautiful temptations every day? Do you want to live with that again?"

"I'm not going to end up with Carlos," said Inez, at the same time remembering that electric shock he'd sent through her body with barely a touch.

"Carlos is a cad who will cheat on you as soon as you let him out of your sight. I give him about a week."

"Carlos never cheated on me."

Rachel looked at Inez as though she'd just announced her plan to join the French Foreign Legion. "He disappears one day into thin air without an explanation," Rachel said. "He wasn't running off to a monastery. Inez, you need to face the truth."

"You're guessing at the truth," said Inez, wondering why she was defending a man who had caused her so much pain. After he'd left her in Madrid, she spent agonizing months wondering where he went and why he left her. She never wanted to admit there might have been another woman, although it was the only explanation which made any sense.

"Even if he didn't leave you for someone else or cheat on you, you deserve better than some guy who leaves you a lame note explaining nothing, after two years of living together," said Rachel. "You guys were practically engaged!"

"That's why I'm going to marry a good man, Howard."

"I hate to play pop psychologist, but it's obvious what's going on in here," said Rachel, pointing to Inez's temple. "Think, woman! Carlos was just the first in a long string of bad boys. It's obvious you were purposely choosing those losers knowing they'd leave you or cheat on you."

"That's insane, why would I do that?"

"Our father abandoned us."

Inez's last clear memory of her father was the time when she'd been jumping up and down on her parents' bed at the age of four. Her feet had gotten caught in the covers and she'd fallen nose first into the solid oak headboard. He'd cradled her in his arms on the way to the hospital, holding a cold compress to her face and murmuring her favorite bedtime story to comfort her. She remembered how her father had held her during the many hours she'd spent in the emergency room, while being examined and x-rayed.

For the next two months, while Inez was branded with a purple and scarlet band around her eyes, her father called her his little "raccoon." After she'd healed, the doctor advised her parents to have her nose re-broken and properly set, but her father couldn't bear the thought of putting her through that pain. A short time later, her mother told her he'd gone away on a long trip, and Inez never saw him again. And here she was, three decades later, with what she liked to think of as her last link to him, her slightly askew nose.

Rachel was still speaking. "Isn't it blazingly obvious to you that Carlos and Howard are complete opposites? Carlos breaks your heart so you go to the other extreme with Howard, who's as likely to cheat on you as your dust mop."

"That's a good thing. Marrying Howard is the right thing to do," Inez replied, with a firmness she did not feel.

"Are you afraid of being alone? Is that it, Inez? You're stronger than this."

Maybe she was afraid of being alone? She had certainly never thought of herself as the kind of woman who had to have a man, although she's always had a boyfriend, except for a few months after returning from Spain.

"So how was dinner?" asked Rachel, changing the subject without warning.

"Howard's mother is anxious for me to settle down."

"If you get any more settled down you'll be in a coma," Rachel said and then, brightening, exclaimed, "I have an idea! Imagine you are enormously fat and hideously ugly. Okay?"

"Should we add halitosis and body odor too?" suggested Inez, knowing it was easier simply to go along with Rachel's preposterous extended metaphors than to resist.

"Yes, excellent!" Rachel continued, clearly in her element. "And imagine not a single man on the planet is interested in you, and never has been, and never will be. Even the ugly, cheap ones don't want to date you because you're also a complete bitch. You will never, ever get married."

"Am I still a virgin?" asked Inez with a smile, as she found herself being drawn in to Rachel's little game. Despite how silly, bossy, and difficult her younger sister could be, Inez truly loved her.

"Technically yes, unless you count battery-operated toys," said Rachel. "Okay, got the picture? Now, ask yourself, what do you want to do with your life?"

"You mean besides slashing my wrists?"

"Come on. I'm being serious."

"It's difficult to tell at times," Inez said, but before she could respond, Rachel slapped her hand on the bar.

"That's it!" Rachel exclaimed, "the guy at the end of the bar, he wrote the screenplay for *Daunted*. He won an Oscar, but it sure looks like he's taken a nose-dive. I loved that movie. Remember the part where Angela is just about to kill herself with sleeping pills, but then she sees Ramon behind her and they fall into each other's arms and make love?"

It was just like Rachel to plunge into a completely tangential subject when Inez was in the midst of a crisis. But then, Rachel has always thrived on movie plots and celebrity scandals. She had subscriptions to *People*, *Us*, and *Star*.

"By the way," asked Rachel, "why did you pick Club Caliente to meet? You haven't been here in years."

"I don't know," said Inez. "The name just popped into my head before I called you. I had a really strong feeling I should come here tonight. But we can leave now if you want."

"You don't want to dance?" Rachel teased. "You used to be obsessed with salsa. And aren't those your dance shoes on your feet?"

Before Inez could respond, she felt a tap on her shoulder. There stood a tall African-American man wearing a white Guayabera Cuban shirt with embroidery running down both sides of the front, like two racing stripes.

"Inez?" he said with a broad grin. "Is that you?"

Sliding off the stool, Inez threw her arms around his neck.

"Calvin," she cried, "it's so good to see you!" The musky scent of his cologne reminded her of the many blissful hours she had spent dancing in his arms.

Calvin had been one of her favorite dance partners when she was a regular in the Chicago salsa scene. Although they'd shared awesome salsa chemistry, she and Calvin had always kept things platonic. Like many serious dancers, Inez had learned the hard way that mixing great dancing with romance was usually akin to mixing fire and gasoline—it might start with an incredible explosion, but quickly petered out.

Calvin looked down at her with an appreciative glance. Her outfit was hardly salsa-worthy—a pair of low cut jeans and a black halter top. She used to get much more dressed up for her nights out.

"You look fantastic," he told her. "Where have you been?"

"I've been…" she started, but wasn't sure how to finish.

"It doesn't matter," he said, taking her hand. "Let's dance."

"You two have fun," Rachel said. "I've got to get up early."

"Thanks for coming tonight, Rachel," Inez whispered in her ear. As Inez gave her a quick hug she added, "even though you can be a total pain in the ass."

"Me?" cried Rachel, in mock surprise.

Inez beamed as she let Calvin lead her to the dance floor.

Look at that glow on Inez's face. She's just spilling over with pure joy. I always wanted to try salsa dancing. It's such a sexy, romantic dance. But my husband Stan was into monster truck rallies, and not much else.

And you married him knowing that?

I thought I loved him, at least for the first few years. I made some poor choices in my last life. Hopefully, I won't be so foolish in the next one. After Stan and I divorced, I never re-married. I had plenty of offers mind you, but I was looking for the real thing the second time around. I guess that's why I turned to writing romance novels. It satisfied a need in me I couldn't find in my own life.

Do not be concerned, Serena. You are a young soul. You will meet your soul mate when the time is right.

Young soul? And I suppose that means you're an old soul?

I had two-thousand-four-hundred and fifty-nine lifetimes on Earth.

And you're still as thick as molasses in January, if you ask me. Okay, now back to our case. They missed each other by just three earth minutes this time. I can't believe Zeke didn't say yes to that lovely Latin lady who asked him to dance. I picked the most gorgeous woman in the club. Has that man gone blind?

Zeke is focused on his job.

Well I know that; it's as obvious as my sister Lena's frozen face after a Botox treatment. So how do we get him unfocused?

--

Why are you looking at me like that, H?

Because you do not want to hear what I have been telling you.

Go ahead.

Zeke is exercising his free will to ignore our guidance. All we can do is to keep trying to get through to him and Inez, but we cannot force anything.

I knew you were going to say that, H.

Tuesday

13

Haunted throughout the night by nightmares and snippets of strange dreams, Inez barely slept. She gave up around five a.m. and was now on her third cup of coffee. She cupped her favorite Windy City mug to warm her hands, inhaling the nutty aroma of the rich Sumatran roast and took a sip, hoping it would work its caffeine magic on her sleep-deprived mind. With her legs crisscrossed, she leaned back against her headboard. Until this moment she never before noticed the jagged crack dividing the white plaster ceiling down the middle like a surgery scar—kind of like how her life felt at the moment, as though it were coming apart at the seams.

Inez has always thought of dreams as free entertainment—the more bizarre, the better—but the ones she had last night were too stressful to be amusing. In one dream, she was kissing Howard, but when they pulled apart it was Carlos's face she saw. Carlos was smiling at her, but then he'd turned into her father as he waved good-bye from their home in Milwaukee in his red Mustang convertible, never to return. In another dream, she was back in the tiny apartment she'd shared with Carlos in Madrid. They were laughing and drinking cheap Rioja, but in a flash she was at the symphony with Howard, who was loudly lecturing her about the dangers of salsa dancing without the use of proper orthotics inside her dance shoes.

She made her way to the kitchen for more coffee, the oak floor feeling cool against the soles of her bare feet. Catching something out of the corner of her eye, she saw a flat rectangular-shaped object slip under the front door. It must be her mail from Ingrid Paros who lived just down the hallway. Inez Paris was constantly getting Ingrid's letters and bills and Ingrid hers. They'd worked out this system to simply slide the incorrectly delivered mail under one another's doors.

Inez picked up a postcard with a photo of the Taj Mahal.

"Marilynn!" She flipped it over, her eyes darting to the neat signature she hadn't seen since her last postcard six months ago. "Thank goodness she's still alive!"

Three years had gone by with only sporadic phone calls, cut off after a minute or two, and the occasional postcard like this one, explaining nothing about what Marilynn was doing or whether she was ever coming home. Before Marilynn had left for India, Inez offered to open a free e-mail account for her, and show her the basics. But Marilynn, who was normally eager to learn anything new, refused to give it a try.

"I don't believe in them," Marilynn had said.

"Well computers certainly believe in you," Inez had replied. "They monitor everything we do."

"Honey, Big Brother is fine for most people, but not for us 'Daunters'," Marilynn had responded, referring to a minor revolution sparked by the movie *Daunted*.

After the movie had won eleven Oscars, thousands of people across North America dubbed themselves "Daunters"—vowing to escape from the prying eyes of the government just like the main characters in the movie. The *New York Times* had run a lengthy article about the trend in their Sunday magazine. Marilynn, like her fellow "Daunters," paid cash for everything, didn't file taxes, and refused to do anything the government could track. Marilynn had never owned a car, earned her income from cash-only jobs, and was given her bungalow, on the northwest side of Chicago by a friend, but kept the title in Inez's name. Marilynn was probably the only person at City Hall each year, bringing a grocery bag filled with twenties, fifties and hundreds to pay her real estate taxes.

Inez read the short message on the back of the card. Her heart lurched in her chest. She tried to read it again, but her hands were trembling so hard the words had blurred. Marilynn has always had an incredible gift for predicting the future—a sixth sense, but to the tenth power. This postcard seemed beyond even Marilynn, unless while in India she had discovered a pay phone on direct-dial to heaven. Inez re-read the message: *"Remember, marriage is like a dance. Make sure you pick the right partner. Love Marilynn."*

But Marilynn had no idea Inez was getting married or was engaged! She'd never even heard about Howard. Then again, Inez knew better than to dismiss outright anything Marilynn said, no matter how outrageous it might sound.

"Signs come," Marilynn has always said, "usually in threes." Marilynn believed there were no accidents or coincidences in life and that the universe was constantly sending us messages—not black cats crossing ones' path, she wasn't superstitious, but the kind of things so many people brushed off. Like those nudges and feelings indicating something was a bad decision, even though everyone around you was urging you to go for it. Or those synchronistic events like having the friend you just thought of for the first time in ages, suddenly give you a call. Or asking a question and seconds later seeing the answer on a bumper sticker. Marilynn lived her life by tuning in to the invisible guidance she swore that she received for everything from finding a new job to making major life decisions, like her announcement three years ago that she was going to India, a country she'd never mentioned before.

First, a good friend had taken Marilynn to a new Indian restaurant for her sixty-seventh birthday. The next day, she met an Indian woman from Hyderabad while shopping at Costco's who invited Marilynn over for a traditional Indian dinner. The third event was the last day of that same week. Marilynn received a phone call that turned out to have been a wrong number from a young man calling from Agra, India, who was trying to reach his cousin in Chicago. Marilynn and the man ended up talking for two hours, and by the end of the conversation, he invited her to stay with him in Agra. Marilynn packed up, rented out her house, and left for India five weeks later. That was three years ago.

Inez realized the postcard was still in her trembling hands. She wanted to trust this message from Marilynn, but how could she? The ringing of the phone interrupted her thoughts. Inez groaned when she recognized the number on her caller I.D.

"Good morning, Jennifer," Inez said, forcing her voice to sound bright.

"Inez, I know you don't want to talk to me," said Jennifer, "but it's sweet that you try."

Inez had never thought of using a wedding planner, but Howard's mother insisted on hiring Jennifer. Having Jennifer on board turned out to have side benefits Inez would not have expected; chiefly, the fact that Jennifer had done most of the preparation for her wedding. In the last few months, Jennifer had taken to calling Margaret Suterman in Florida to work out most of the details for the wedding. Inez didn't feel guilty about her lack of participation in her own wedding because she wanted to elope on a beach in Hawaii. Howard also wanted to elope, but his mother had balked. It was ridiculous to think they were going through this elaborate and expensive ritual just to make one person happy.

"I can't get a hold of Margaret," said Jennifer. "I need the final head count for the caterer by five today."

"I'll call you after school," Inez replied.

"You promise?" asked Jennifer, with much doubt in her voice.

"Promise."

"And don't forget to pick up your dress tomorrow."

Inez didn't reply.

"You forgot, didn't you?" said Jennifer. "Wow. You are definitely the first bride I've ever worked with who forgot her own wedding dress. If I didn't know any better, I'd say you didn't want to get married, Inez."

14

Zeke waved his hand over the compact disc player hanging on his bedroom wall. The glass doors silently slid open. He placed a Héctor Lavoe CD on the disc drive; he hadn't listened to "La Voz" in ages, and what a voice Lavoe had had. The Puerto Rican salsa legend had not merely sung songs; he immortalized them. Listening to him sing was, Zeke thought, to imagine how God painted spectacular sunsets across the horizon.

The music quickly worked its way to Zeke's feet. He stepped in place on the first beat and then broke on the second beat, dancing into his walk-in closet to select a slate grey suit, white dress shirt and a red silk tie, and out again to toss them onto his bed. And then, caught up in the music, he twirled an imaginary dance partner with his right hand held high in the air. "Damn, I should've danced with her," he thought, picturing again the beautiful Latina from Club Caliente last night.

How had he let go of his passion? In the past, he couldn't get enough of salsa—only his work schedule stopped him from becoming a salsa junkie—the men and women who would spend four, five, and even six nights a week dancing. Zeke thought back to when he put all of his free time into salsa and club-sponsored dance contests with his partner, Yvonne, a physical therapist, who could spin like a tornado and whip her thick, waist-length black hair with a flip of her head to accentuate her sexy footwork.

He and Yvonne placed in a few contests, but never won. But that was never the point—preparing for the contests with hours of practice in a rented dance studio and choreographing their own moves were among Zeke's happiest memories. But then, when the Xanadu Pharmaceuticals case was assigned to him, he no longer had time to practice. Yvonne moved on to a more dedicated partner, and his usual three nights a week of dancing dwindled to two and then one. Before long, months would go by without a visit to his favorite clubs. And then around three years ago, he'd stopped going altogether.

And when he stopped dancing, he stopped looking for Inez. If he did see her again, and by some miracle she was still single, so much time had passed since their first meeting, that it was possible he wouldn't feel the same way he had on the night they'd met—that belief which seemed to have materialized from the ether that she was his soul mate. Inez's face appeared in his mind, but a moment later it was replaced with Elise Wyatt's face. His heart quickened at the thought that he might see Elise at work today.

As he entered his marble-covered master bathroom he saw Mike lying naked on the floor, face down, with vomit covering the tile and the toilet seat. The room reeked of booze and of cigarette smoke. Zeke grimaced in disgust and felt ill. He backed out of the room, took a deep breath of clean air and forced the bile from his empty stomach back down. He grabbed Mike under his arms and dragged him across the living room to the guest bedroom.

"Cybele," Mike muttered as he briefly came to, "why don't you love me anymore?"

"She never loved you, you lovesick dope," Zeke said, but Mike had already lapsed back into his scotch-induced coma.

Zeke hoisted him onto the bed. His right leg lolled over the side like a dead limb. Zeke tossed a sheet over him. He was tired of dealing with his friend's domestic crises. Cybele threatened divorce and hopped on a plane to Chicago. Mike came chasing after her. They made up a few days later and then flew back out to L.A., only to repeat the cycle, in another four months or so.

After cleaning up the mess in the bathroom, Zeke took a quick shower, dressed, and made himself a double espresso. He stepped out onto his balcony. A warm soft breeze stroked his face and the earthy smell of the Chicago River rose up to greet him.

"Cybele," he heard Mike call out, followed by a groan.

Cybele. It was hard to believe that the woman who'd appeared on the cover of the Sports Illustrated swimsuit edition seven years ago, clad in a bikini the width of a fingernail, used to be a gangly tomboy with tangled blonde hair, a dash of freckles across the bridge of her nose, and a shy smile. It was more difficult to fathom that Zeke once thought of her and her sister Charlotte like his own sisters. The three of them had grown up together in Bellwood, just a block apart, and a quick sprint down the alley and through the chain link fences surrounding their backyards. Cybele and Charlotte lived with their parents—Zeke's mother's first cousin and his wife. The three of them played together after school every day, going back and forth between their two homes for snacks, watching TV, playing board games and enjoying family dinners.

About the time Cybele began wearing a bra and make-up, she started lying. Little white lies at first, but they quickly escalated in frequency and seriousness until she couldn't be trusted to tell the truth about her own name. Her first arrest for stealing a pair of jeans from a department store was a shock. By the time she turned fifteen, Cybele was constantly in and out of juvenile detention for stealing, smoking marijuana, and running away from home.

But fate was on Cybele's side. She was "discovered" at sixteen while on a high school field trip to the Field Museum of Chicago by a modeling scout, who told her she looked just like a Botticelli angel. She straightened out and enjoyed a highly successful modeling career, gracing the covers of fashion magazines across the United States and Europe. For a short time—about a month—she even achieved the level of fame enjoyed by that handful of stars, musicians, and models known only by their first names. But then, five years ago, she decided she was sick of modeling. With all of the deliberation one normally puts into a sneeze, she decided to become a major Hollywood star, oblivious to the fact that her skills as a pathological liar did not translate to having acting talent. For all of her facility with lying, it never come across on the screen, where she appeared as animated as a department store mannequin.

The doorbell interrupted Zeke's thoughts. Looking through the peephole, Zeke instantly turned his back to the door in a panic. A plan to escape flashed through his mind—he could parachute over his balcony to the riverbank many stories below. Then he could steal a powerboat, at knifepoint if necessary, make his get-away down the river though downtown Chicago and out to the freedom of Lake Michigan where he could make his way to…

The bell sounded again. "You are no James Bond," he chided himself, "and you have only yourself to blame for this."

He swung open the door to Pamela.

"Hi, Zeke!" she exclaimed, with an amazing amount of enthusiasm given her sullen mood on Sunday night. "Good thing I caught you before you left for work."

"Why is that, Pamela?" Zeke asked, wishing he'd taken the immature way out by pretending not to be home.

"I made you cookies," she said, handing him a metal tin covered with kittens playing with a ball of yarn. "Oatmeal raisin, your favorite, right?"

"You shouldn't have," said Zeke, meaning exactly that.

"They might be stale," she said. "I made them Sunday afternoon, before you broke up with me."

"You broke up with me," said Zeke, who tried to remain calm despite his rising anxiety.

"That's just like you lawyers," she said, "always twisting the facts."

Zeke could think of a dozen responses, but there was no point in arguing with a woman who possessed the logic of a common house fly.

"What time are you coming by on Saturday?" she asked.

"Pamela, I've given this a lot of thought. I'm sorry, but you can't go to my office function. I'll pay you back for your…"

Pamela's lower lip pushed out as her creamy white skin reddened like a lobster in a pot. She looked just like a toddler on the verge of a massive tantrum.

"How about six o'clock?" he said, hating himself for being so weak.

"Fine," she said, her face seamlessly transforming back to her usual perfectly made-up mask. "See you Saturday night."

He might have to join the witness protection program to escape from her, he realized, with a sick feeling.

15

At the sight of Carlos leaning against a black convertible Ferrari, Inez's heart catapulted to her windpipe and she felt her nipples harden. How maddening. Her body reacted exactly the way it always had around him, although her mind and heart were over him. Despite the fact that she wouldn't be the least bit upset to see him flattened by a wayward meteorite at this moment, her reflexive physical reaction to him, regrettably, was still very much alive.

"I thought you'd like a ride to work," he said, with a languorous ease as if he showed up at her curb every morning like her chauffeur.

"I told you, I never want to see you again," she said, wanting to scrape that self-satisfied look off his infuriatingly handsome face with a scouring pad.

"I know you didn't mean that, *querida.*"

"I do mean it," Inez said, turning away from him as she began making her way toward her "L" station. "*Adios* Carlos."

A moment later she heard his footsteps behind her and then, he was at her side. She quickened her pace and focused on maintaining her attention straight ahead, but it wasn't easy. Certainly, she was curious about him, but she wasn't about to let Carlos manipulate his way back into her emotions. Or anywhere else for that matter.

"Let me give you a ride," he said.

"This isn't a safe neighborhood," she said, "you'd better get back to your fancy sports car before it disappears."

"It's just a rental."

They walked the next two blocks in silence as she wondered where he got the money to rent a car like that. When they were together in Madrid, they were barely able to cover their rent and food on their meager salaries.

When they reached the station, Inez put her CTA card into the slot and pushed the metal bar with her torso, walking through the turnstile. A few moments later her train rumbled into the station. Packed as usual with early morning commuters, Inez found a spot standing next to the door. Just before the doors slid shut, Carlos stepped inside the far door of the same car.

Standing about ten feet apart, with a solid mass of people between them, Inez wanted to turn around to face away from him, but she couldn't move a muscle with the crush of commuters surrounding her. The train pulled out of the station.

As was typical on the morning commute, very few people were talking. Most were listening to I-Pods, reading the paper, or blankly staring out the window.

"I still love you, Inez," Carlos said, as if they were alone, his voice loud and clear.

Inez felt herself flush. Whenever he'd said those words to her in Madrid, he always looked away after saying them. But now, his eyes bore into her with such intensity, they could burn a hole through her and the wall of the train.

"We can get a home here, in Chicago, if you like," he said, "we can live anywhere you want."

Inez was torn between curiosity at what Carlos would say next and embarrassment that he was saying such things in public.

"We can get married here," he added.

She had no intention of encouraging him by responding, but the words burst out of her before she could stop them. "I stopped loving you the day you left that note."

"You still love me, I know you better than anyone Inez," he said, his black eyes catching her own for a long moment. "*Te siento tu pasión en el fundo del alma.*"

I can feel your passion in the depths of my soul. Yeah, right, she thought, flicking her eyes away. He always switched to Spanish when he wanted to sound profound, but she knew he was just repeating the lyrics from a flamenco song.

Everyone in the vicinity was staring at her. They were waiting for her response, she realized. When Carlos spoke again, all of the heads turned toward him. A live soap opera certainly beat the usual dull morning commute.

"You were right last night," he said, switching back to English with that slight European lilt, which used to make her melt. "A real man wouldn't have left you. I will never leave you again."

"You're lying," said Inez.

"I agree with you, honey," said a heavyset woman with frizzy nectarine-colored hair standing next to Inez. "You can see it in his eyes. This one's definitely a liar."

The train stopped. As people streamed out of the exit door, Carlos moved closer.

"What can I do to convince you I'm telling the truth?" he said when the train pulled away from the station.

"Don't bother," said Inez, holding up her left hand and wiggling her ring finger at him. "I'm getting married on Saturday."

"Nice ring," said another woman with a gold nose ring and hair so black it looked as though it was doused in motor oil. "What does your fiancé do?"

"He's a doctor," Inez said as she suddenly grasped that she never told people what kind of doctor Howard was, unless they pressed for more information. Was she embarrassed that Howard was a podiatrist? Perhaps she was, she realized, with a vague sense of unease.

"You got two men?" said a thin woman wearing a sad smile and a hair net. "Life sure ain't fair. I wish my life was half that complicated, I'll take one of 'em off your hands."

"We belong together," said Carlos.

"Go back to Spain."

"Lady, if you don't want him, I'll take him," said another spectator, a mere wisp of a woman with stringy brown hair who stared at Carlos like a starving dog at steak tartare.

After the next stop, Carlos wedged his way next to her. She could smell him. She used to joke that his scent should be bottled and sold—it was such a perfect combination of freshly washed skin, pine needles on a forest floor, and a musky animal scent she used to find irresistible. He smelled just as she remembered, but now his scent felt suffocating.

"We're coming to my stop," said Inez, in a low clear voice. "If you follow me off, I promise, I'll have you arrested."

For once he looked shocked. She wasn't sure that anything could rock his boat—he'd always been so cool in the face of any tumult. When they used to argue, he was always so damned laid-back. She felt victorious, but an instant later, he was once again the languid Latin lover who was used to getting everything he wanted from a woman.

"I understand, you need more time," he said, with a nod.

Inez fumed as she got off the train and walked purposefully toward the exit, but her heart and head were pounding.

16

Zeke was reading the *Chicago Tribune* when a something caused him to look out the train window at the State Street "L" stop where the brown, purple, green, orange and pink lines came together. Throngs of commuters, each in a determined hurry, streamed by his window in a hundred different directions. At first, her face didn't register. It couldn't be her. But then, a second of incredulity stretched into infinity. It was her!

Zeke sprang from his seat so quickly, the woman on the aisle seat next to him gave a cry of fright.

"Sorry," Zeke said, trying to calm her with an apologetic look. "I need to get off here."

"Where's the fire?" she mumbled.

He lifted his briefcase high above her, trying to brush past her knees that were wedged tight against the seat in front of her. People were pouring onto the train. He knew the doors would close in seconds. He forced his way into the aisle pushing her knees aside.

"Ow!" she exclaimed, and then muttered, "asshole."

Zeke forced his way into a space that didn't exist, stepping on something that felt like a foot.

"Hey, watch it," snarled a tall, red-faced man.

Zeke squeezed and nudged and pushed and reached the doors just as they snapped shut in his face. With his right hand flat against the window, he watched as Inez disappeared into the crowd, her red curly locks pulled up into a ponytail bouncing in time with each step.

His heart plummeted. How many times had he missed her at this stop? How many times had he been so engrossed in reading the paper or doing work, he hadn't looked out the window? Did it mean anything that he saw her today after having thought of her last night for the first time in years?

Zeke wanted to believe in miracles, but lately, life seemed like nothing more than a game where he and everyone else were helplessly buffeted about, like tiny balls in a gigantic pinball machine. Years ago during college, Zeke believed in Albert Einstein's famous quote about there being two ways to live life: one was as though nothing was a miracle; the other was as though everything was a miracle. Back then, he'd believed that anything was possible as long as he put his thoughts, intentions, and actions in the direction of his dreams. But over the years, the drudgery of daily life had masked the magic that could be found in everyday life, like the tiny miracle that had caused him to look out the window, at precisely the right moment. If he'd waited just a second or two longer, he would've missed seeing Inez today.

He took the train to his stop, dashed inside the coffee shop and found Charlie.

"What's up with you?" asked Charlie, taking his coffee drink from Zeke. "You look like you've seen a ghost."

"I just saw someone I haven't seen in a long time," Zeke replied.

"You'll see her again."

"What?"

"Only a woman could've had such an effect on you," said Charlie. He paused, his lined face relaxed into a thoughtful repose. "I was married once."

Zeke's attention went on high alert. This was the first piece of personal information Charlie had ever volunteered.

"It was good," Charlie continued in a soft voice Zeke had never heard him use before. "Better than good, like a slice of warm cherry pie just out of the oven. She was my home."

Charlie stopped speaking.

"No! Keep talking!" Zeke wanted to shout. The silence lengthened. Asking Charlie a direct question would be futile—Zeke had a better chance of learning the identities of the CIA's top undercover agents by placing a phone call to the Director.

"But then it all turned to crap," Charlie growled, with a dismissive wave.

Zeke pulled Pamela's tin of cookies from his briefcase and lifting the lid, offered some to Charlie.

"Where's my scone?" he asked

"They were out of blueberry," said Zeke. "These are homemade."

He leaned in, sniffed and scowled. Charlie was very picky about his baked goods.

"I guess that's a 'no'," said Zeke, thinking Charlie was too skinny. Zeke gave him enough money to eat three decent meals a day, but it was none of his business what Charlie chose to do with the money, so he'd never asked. He just hoped Charlie was spending his nights in a safe place. Zeke had just read another story about a homeless man sleeping in a park in Boston, who was set on fire by two teenagers. It made Zeke sick to think about it.

"Have you talked to your boss yet?" asked Charlie.

"I'm going to see Miller today."

"You could sound a little more enthusiastic, but then again, you know my theory. You don't really want this."

"I've been working for this for eight years," Zeke replied, thinking it was likely Charlie had once been part of the corporate world he scorned so bitterly. "Of course I want it."

"You sure 'bout that?" asked Charlie, crossing his arms in front of his narrow chest.

Zeke had been wrapped up in his job for so long, it was nearly impossible to imagine his life without it, but a small flicker of doubt nagged at his brain. The truth was, Zeke felt uneasy and lost—as if he had once had a map pinpointing precisely the path he should follow, but having lost the map, he had wandered so far off course, he had no clue as to which direction he should head next.

"All of my hard work over the years will speak for itself at Friday morning's meeting," said Zeke, pushing his doubts away. "I'll get the promotion."

Charlie grunted. Zeke said his goodbyes and went to his office building. Minutes later, he greeted his secretary, Melissa.

"I brought these," Zeke said, pulling the tin of cookies from his briefcase.

"Homemade cookies!" Melissa exclaimed. "Did you make these, Mr. Nomad?"

"No, they're from…a neighbor."

"Thank you. I'll put these out for everyone to share."

Zeke knew they'd be gone in less than an hour. His co-workers attacked any item of food brought to the office like a pack of starving wolverines.

"Wayne Martin was here at seven to see you," she said. "Would you like me to call him and tell him you're here?"

"Yes, please, and could you also call Stu Miller's secretary to make another appointment for today."

A ripple of nervousness shot through him, but he was compelled to follow through despite the curious tacit message he'd received from Elise last night. His interest in learning how many associates would make partner this year was overpowering.

Did you see that? They missed each other at the subway station. We were so close this time.

Carlos slowed Inez enough to delay her usual schedule, which allowed Zeke to see her today.

And your point is?

Now Zeke knows that Inez is still in Chicago. So you see, it was a good thing Carlos came this week instead of waiting until next month.

Are you saying that when you tweaked Carlos to come to Chicago you knew Zeke would be on that train and Inez would be strolling across that platform at the exact right moment for him to see her?

No, that was a fortunate occurrence. Humans are far too unpredictable to plan for anything like that.

I'm trying to get a handle on your game plan here, H. I still say you opened a nest of angry hornets bringing that scalawag back into her life. She's weakening. I recognize the signs. In my younger days before I married Stan, I got involved with too many snakes like Carlos. If it were up to me I'd have the whole lot of them shot at dawn without a last wish.

Inez is beginning to remember her heart. The only way to make her see that is by showing her Howard's opposite. Hopefully, Carlos will show his true self, and Inez will realize that he cannot be trusted.

Hopefully? You brought Carlos here hoping that he'll show his true colors? The man is going to be licking her boots this week and be on his best behavior. Did you think about that, H?

Of course I did.

You are impossible! If she ends up in the arms of that cad, I don't think I can ever forgive you. And don't give me any of that master builder malarkey again. We need to be practical. How do we get Zeke and Inez face-to-face?

You are too impatient, Serena.

Wait a minute. You closed those doors on the train a couple seconds early so Zeke couldn't get off. Am I right?

Yes, you are correct. But the reason I did that is because the human heart is a delicate thing...

I know the human heart better than anyone alive or.... Anyway, whose side are you on, H? I just don't understand what you're doing, it seems to be precisely the opposite of what we want to accomplish.

Everything will become clear in time, Serena.

Time is what we don't have!

17

Inez pulled off her ponytail holder, smoothed back her unruly locks, and raked her fingers through her curls. She leaned closer to the mirror hanging on the wall of the teacher's lounge, wiped away a stray smudge of mascara, and smoothed out the wrinkles on her knee-length navy blue linen skirt. Luckily, she'd taken the time last night to iron her long-sleeved, white blouse, since she was running a few minutes late today, thanks to Carlos.

She hated dressing so conservatively, but the principal, Nancy White, a Baptist from Georgia, wanted to set an example for the students. To make up for her schoolmarm look, she'd spent an entire paycheck on matching lacy bras and panties. Amazing how something so simple that no one except Howard ever saw, gave her such a mental boost.

Instead of angering Nancy by defying the dress code, Inez decided years ago it was smarter to save her battles for the things that really mattered. She could still see Nancy's shocked face from a few years ago, when Inez had protested the purchase of a new refrigerator for the teacher's lounge—the old one still worked perfectly well—and demanded that the money be used to buy wall-sized world maps for each of the classrooms. It was only when Inez had persuaded a majority of the teachers to agree with her that Nancy agreed.

The bell sounded like a fire alarm, and Inez hurried down the hallway to her classroom. Just outside the door was a distinguished white-haired man standing so straight he could double as a yardstick.

"Major Turner," said Inez. She reached out to shake his hand, and the Major gripped her own with such force, she muffled a small cry of pain. "I'm Inez Paris. Thank you for coming today."

He pulled up the sleeve of his dark-blue uniform, peering at his watch as if it had just been court-martialed. "We're two minutes late," he clipped, "shall we get started?"

"Of course," said Inez, opening the classroom door and wondering who had chosen Mr. Warm and Fuzzy to speak to a bunch of first-graders. As they entered, the room instantly fell silent.

Inez's classroom was an explosion of colors—finger paintings covered one wall, the doors of the cloakroom at the back of the room had nature posters from famous U.S. National Park sites such as Mount Rushmore and Old Faithful, and a world map was tacked next to the blackboard at the front of the classroom. On the shelf next to the windows were two aquariums—a freshwater fish tank and a tank holding Jésus and Sox—two African Dwarf frogs the children took turns feeding.

"Good morning, children," said Inez.

"Good morning, Miss Paris," her students replied, their sing-song voices fluttering up to the white-tiled ceiling like butterflies.

"Please say good morning to Major Turner, everyone."

The children greeted him in unison.

"What are we celebrating today?" Inez asked them.

A dozen hands shot in the air. Inez called on a boy who was missing more teeth than remained in his mouth.

"Flag Day," he said.

"That's right, Roberto," said Inez, responding to his infectious gummy smile with her own. "Major Turner is here to tell us about Flag Day and show us the correct way to fold a flag."

Each year, the second to last day of school was reserved for a celebration of Flag Day, a week early because it fell the week after school let out for the summer. Inez didn't see the importance of this holiday, but Principal Nancy White believed it was vital to instill some patriotism into their students, whose parents came from all over the globe—Laos, Cambodia, Mexico, Central America, and as far away as the Philippines.

Major Turner stepped to the front of the classroom. "Can anyone tell me how many stars are on the flag?" he began. The medals on his chest flashed under the florescent lights. Inez knew her students would be far more interested in learning about his medals than how to fold an American flag, but she didn't get the sense Major Turner would be willing to deviate from his agenda.

Inez took a seat behind her desk, and her thoughts instantly turned to Carlos. Damn him for coming back into her life, she thought. Why now? Why this week of all weeks? Why ever? Her thoughts traveled back to the two years she and Carlos had lived together in Madrid. She tried to remember what their day-to-day life was like, but the picture wouldn't form. The feelings had come back though—unease, the extreme highs and low lows, and the intense passion. Their sex life was…

No. She wouldn't think about that. She and Howard loved one another and would have a good life together. Howard was her peace of mind. Like a warm comforter on a cold night, she could always count on him to be there for her. She would never have to worry about Howard cheating on her or coming home hours late without so much as a phone call, or ripping off her clothes and taking her wherever they happened to be at the moment—elevators, stairwells, a bathroom at the Prado Museum, even in...

"Miss Paris?"

She looked up at Major Turner. "You look flushed," he whispered. "Are you feeling all right?"

"Yes, of course," said Inez, embarrassment hot on her face.

"I'm through with my presentation."

Inez instructed her students to take out their red, white and blue construction paper, glue, and scissors to make their own flags. He saluted and stepped out into the hallway with Inez following.

"Well Miss Paris," he said, "I really must commend you."

"For what?"

"Your students are surprisingly well-behaved," he said, with a thin smile. "Quite frankly, I was expecting the worst."

Inez crossed her arms in front of her chest. "What do you mean?"

"You know what I mean," he said, "an inner city Chicago school, kids whose parents are druggies, criminals, and…"

Inez glared at him.

"I didn't mean any offense," he continued, "it's just that with these…uh, underprivileged children, they don't receive a proper upbringing, and don't have the opportunities our kind of people have."

Our kind of people?

"Thank you for your time, Major," she said, with a curt nod. She turned and left him standing as stupefied as if every soldier under his command had simultaneously deserted.

Inez hated all of the P.C. labels applied to her students: "high need," "underserved," "low-achieving." In her opinion that was a large part of the problem—people lowered their expectations for these kids so the children unconsciously learned to do as little as possible to get by. Eventually, they gave up and became exactly what people had labeled them from the start.

She entered her classroom where the children were engrossed in cutting paper. Inez stopped at Odilia's desk. Her family had come to Chicago from Guatemala just a few months ago. Odilia, at seven, was learning English rapidly, but was painfully shy and so withdrawn, she seemed nearly invisible. Sometimes, Inez spoke to her in Spanish to make her feel more at ease.

"Why aren't you using these?" Inez asked her, noticing Odilia was tearing strips of paper to make the stripes for her flag, rather than using the pair of children's scissors on her desk.

"I don't know how," said Odilia so quietly, Inez had to lean down to hear her.

Inez showed her how to grasp the scissors and then watched Odilia use them to cut a jagged strip of blue construction paper.

"That's good, Odilia," said Inez. The child, normally as serious as an adult, smiled broadly, tugging at Inez's heart.

Ever since Inez's first Spanish class in high school, when she'd fallen in love with the language and the Latin culture, she decided she would have two biological children and then adopt a third child from Central or South America, just like this little girl. But Howard was against any adoption because years ago a distant relative had adopted a girl from China who'd turned out to be schizophrenic.

It wasn't like Howard to be so firm about any subject, and it wasn't like her to cave in on something this important. Not that she hadn't tried to win him over. Inez had given him dozens of examples of successful adoptions, gathering every story she'd heard and showing him happy photos on adoption websites. But he wouldn't budge.

A few months ago, Inez agreed they would have two children of their own and leave it at that. But, she continued to secretly hope that once they'd had a biological child and Howard learned the joys of fatherhood, his usual generous, good-hearted nature would expand, and he might change his mind. But the thought that she'd compromised still bothered her, especially today. Why had she ever agreed to give in on something this important? That wasn't like her at all. Suddenly, Inez couldn't dream of giving up the future she'd always pictured for herself. She would bring this up with Howard again. He wouldn't be pleased, but this was too important to leave to chance.

18

Damn, these are good," said Wayne Martin, as he entered Zeke's office munching enthusiastically on one of Pamela's cookies. Wayne dropped into the chair opposite Zeke's desk. He popped the last bite into his mouth and brushed his hands together, dropping crumbs onto the yellow legal pad in his lap. "Better than my mother's oatmeal cookies, and she holds the title as the best baker this side of the Mississippi."

Suddenly, Zeke was struck with an image of Wayne and Pamela together, as a happy couple. In spite of the old adage—that there was someone for everyone—it was difficult to imagine Pamela making any man anything but insane. Zeke was not one to conjure visions or premonitions, but the picture in his mind was so clear and vivid, it was as though he held a snapshot of the two of them in his hand.

"Do you have a date for Saturday night?" asked Zeke.

One side of Wayne's mouth turned up into a half-grin as his bright blue eyes began laughing. "I'm touched Zeke, but you're not really my type." Wayne guffawed at his own joke, slapping his thigh. "I'm going stag with a couple of the guys in my class. Why do you ask?"

Anything Zeke might say would make him sound like a New Ager channeling love matches from the astral plane. "No reason, let's get to work."

Zeke's cramped office resembled a storage room. Files and boxes were everywhere, each one representing months of his life. Banker's boxes were stacked on the chair next to Wayne. Brown accordion files teetered in two mini towers on top of the mahogany filing cabinet, and piles of files covered the space heater behind Zeke. Still more surrounded his desk, and were lined up against the wall like small campfires.

Zeke went to the four boxes containing Joseph Pulaski's medical records, chronologically organized for the previous ten years. He lifted the box with the oldest records onto his desk, and pushed it toward Wayne, who put it on the floor at his feet. Wayne grabbed one of the manila folders inside and began flipping through it. Joseph Pulaski, like thousands of other plaintiffs, had filed suit against Xanadu Pharmaceuticals after its former wonder drug, Firmrod, was recalled by the Food and Drug Administration.

"Anything unusual about this dep?" asked Wayne, a veteran of five depositions thus far in his young career, all of which he'd watched from the sidelines.

"Pulaski's claiming the usual, that Firmrod didn't work and he suffered muscle pain in his legs and joints," Zeke replied, "but he is also one of our stroke cases. He alleges that three months after taking Firmrod, he suffered a stroke leaving him partially paralyzed on his right side."

When Firmrod, which was supposed to do exactly as the name implied—help men achieve and maintain erections—had gone on the market six years ago, Xanadu Pharmaceutical's gross profits increased by fifteen percent. But a year later, reports started appearing around the country of men having strokes after taking the drug, which prompted a full-blown study by M.I.T. researchers, who were able to demonstrate a link between Firmrod and strokes.

Xanadu's scientists found legitimate flaws with the M.I.T. study and highlighted the lack of conclusive evidence. However, an eager beaver reporter at the *New York Times* had picked up the story and quoted one of the M.I.T. researchers as saying the science behind their conclusion—that Firmrod caused strokes—was absolutely sound. Similar articles had run in the *Los Angeles Times* and *Washington Post*. Finally, under mounting public pressure, the FDA ordered a recall.

"Hey, did you hear the one about the guy with the hard-on..." Wayne started, but Zeke cut him off.

"I'm sure I have, Wayne."

Many jokes had been passed among the lawyers and paralegals working on the case about limp dicks and penis pumps—jokes Zeke had never found to be funny. He'd always considered the humor juvenile, but which on the surface sounded sophisticated coming from the mouths of men wearing custom-made suits.

"Is Parnell going to be at the dep?" Wayne asked.

Zeke shook his head. T.J. Parnell was the partner in charge of the Firmrod litigation. But from the start, Parnell had let Zeke handle nearly every stage of the proceedings, as if it were Zeke's case alone. Zeke had proven himself early on in the case during oral arguments when he'd convinced cantankerous old District Court Judge Duffy that the litigation should not be classified as a class action suit. In a major drug lawsuit, this was the equivalent of winning the Super Bowl for the defense. It was much more difficult to fight one raging forest fire than to put out hundreds of individual tiny flames, as Zeke was trying to do with every plaintiff's case.

His second victory happened last month when Zeke's team held a mock jury trial to test the legal strategies they intended to use at the real trial. As luck would have it, T.J. Parnell had to have an emergency appendectomy the night after giving his opening statement. Zeke, who was supposed to have second-chaired the trial—keeping a seat warm while handing Parnell the right documents at the right time—was forced to take over. Although it wasn't a genuine trial, the client had spent so much money to hold the test trial, everyone had treated it as though just as much was at stake. Zeke had never been so nervous in his life, but after questioning his first witness, his tension had disappeared, and he'd fallen into the role of lead trial attorney as if he'd been doing it his entire life. The trial lasted a week. The mock jury was split into two groups, with their deliberations monitored under close circuit camera. Two of the women on the panel commented on how cute Zeke was, wondering if he were single. Naturally, he'd received a lot of teasing, but that was nothing compared to the highlight of Zeke's career when one jury group voted for Xanadu Pharmaceuticals, deciding to award the actor who'd portrayed the stroke plaintiff, nothing. The other jury group had awarded the pretend plaintiff $75,000, a nominal amount.

The firm promptly released the results of the mock trial to the plaintiff's attorneys and since then, Zeke received several calls each week from plaintiff's attorneys who were now anxious to settle after realizing their cases were not as strong as they'd thought. However, Pulaski's attorney hadn't called and several months ago, he had rejected a settlement offer of $50,000, a pittance for the country's largest and oldest drug company.

"So we're looking for any other medical problems that could've caused a stroke, right?" asked Wayne.

"Right," said Zeke, "and for any evidence the plaintiff didn't take Firmrod as prescribed."

Zeke opened a manila folder containing the twenty-page "Plaintiff's Fact Sheet" which Joseph Pulaski, like each of the plaintiffs, had filled out. The PFS gave a detailed account of the plaintiff's educational, work, and medical history. Zeke had already been through the document twice, but went through it again in case he'd missed anything. He had a reputation among the plaintiff's bar in Chicago as an attorney who was always meticulously prepared. But this morning he found it difficult to concentrate. His eyes glazed over the words scrawled on the PFS that looked as though a child had filled it out. Most of the plaintiffs had at least a college degree, and a fair percentage had graduate degrees, but Pulaski was in the minority. According to the information on his PFS, he had dropped out of high school after the tenth grade, just like Zeke's father.

Zeke's heart stopped when he noticed something he'd missed. Joseph Pulaski lived in Bellwood, just two blocks from his mother's home. Zeke felt guilty, but he tried to push it away. Why should he feel guilty? Zeke had worked hard to get where he was—just days away from partnership at one of the most prestigious law firms in the country. But the feeling wouldn't go away. Zeke rose from his chair.

"You want some coffee?" Zeke asked Wayne.

Wayne shook his head without looking up from the file in his lap. He was putting yellow post-it notes on practically every page of the medical records and scribbling furiously on his yellow legal pad. Early on in his career, Zeke had been just as enthusiastic as Wayne. Now he only felt numb.

Melissa buzzed. "Mr. Miller can see you now."

Wayne gave him the thumbs-up sign.

Zeke's stomach lurched. "Well, here goes the last eight years of my life."

19

Inez retrieved her new tennis bracelet from her purse and clasped it to her wrist. She twisted her arm in the shafts of late afternoon sunlight streaming in through the windows of her classroom—the diamonds sparkled and burst into tiny rainbow prisms. The bracelet was elegant, beautiful and so out of the realm of Howard's normal type of gift, he might as well have given her a trip to Mars.

His prior gifts had fallen into three main categories—clothing, books, and gourmet food items. He'd never given her anything blatantly insulting like a vacuum cleaner, but his presents always had a practical side to them. And, up until yesterday, the most romantic gesture he'd ever made was to include a handwritten list of all of the reasons he loved her inside last year's birthday card. Inez would never forget that card: "1) You are fiscally prudent, 2) You are prompt for appointments, 3) You have above average looks and intelligence, 4) You are efficient…" and so on. Inez had never read anything more depressing in her life, but knew it wasn't fair to expect Howard to become something he wasn't. She wanted to enjoy this new ultra-romantic, physically affectionate Howard, but a nagging doubt at the back of her mind told her his gestures were not one hundred percent genuine. Although she'd heard stories of people discovering new things about their spouses after even thirty years of marriage, she was convinced that Howard had already revealed every facet of his personality. But, when she walked out of Martin Luther King Elementary, her fiancé managed to shock her, yet again.

Howard leaned against a lamppost with his arms folded across his chest, wearing mirrored sunglasses and a black leather jacket.

"Howard!" Inez exclaimed, noting how handsome he looked, "what are you doing here?"

He pulled her into his arms and kissed her passionately, murmuring, "Oh my beautiful darling."

"Howard, we're at school," she said, gently pushing him away as she glanced around to see who might be looking. But the street was nearly empty. Inez, as usual, was one of the last teachers to leave for the day. Only a handful of boys were playing basketball on the playground across the street.

"How long have you been here?" she asked him.

"Almost an hour," he said.

"What about your afternoon appointments?" she asked, as she mentally calculated what time he must've left his office on the northwest side of Chicago to get here. It would've taken him at least an hour.

"I canceled them," he said. "Come on, I have a surprise for you."

Howard had never canceled his appointments before or picked her up from work. His personality had done a complete reversal— who in the world was she marrying on Saturday?

As Howard drove northeast, Inez let Howard take her hand, which he released every time he shifted gears. They discussed wedding details, which relatives were coming into town, and the menu for their rehearsal dinner Friday night at Bistro 110, one of Inez's favorite restaurants located just off Michigan Avenue near the famous Chicago landmark, the Water Tower, one of the only undamaged structures standing after the great fire of 1871. All the while they talked, she wondered where they were going, but her imagination simply would not take her beyond their usual haunts— restaurants, bookstores, the symphony, the ballet, and an occasional foreign film.

Howard parked in an underground garage near Millennium Park, popped the trunk of his car and pulled out a wicker basket and a blue blanket. He led her by her hand to Grant Park at the lakefront. Inez had always loved the French design of this park; it reminded her of the many beautiful parks that were everywhere in Paris. A rainbow appeared in the spray of water bubbling up from Buckingham Fountain. Bicycles, people on roller blades, and women pushing baby strollers went by along the path next to Lake Michigan.

Since her college days, Inez had come to this park every year for Chicago Summer Dance. There was something about dancing outside to music from a live band that made everything more alive and intense. But the last time was at least five years ago. Inez made a mental note to get this summer's schedule for the Latin nights.

Howard spread the blanket under a large oak tree and motioned for her to take a seat. He pulled out a bottle of champagne and popped the cork, pouring them each a glass.

"Oh, I almost forgot," he said, reaching into the basket to retrieve yet another culinary treasure. He opened a small white box and offered her a dark-chocolate covered strawberry. Her favorite! The chocolate and berry flavors together were such a divine combination, Inez believed that even the angels in heaven would be happy to taste such perfection.

"Inez, have I told you lately how much I love you?"

You've never told me how much you love me, she thought, when his cell phone rang.

"It's my mother," he said, putting the still-ringing phone back inside of his pocket.

Inez almost choked on her champagne.

"You look surprised, darling," he said, with a bemused smile. "My mother can wait."

Inez had decided earlier today to bring up the delicate topics of adoption and Carlos, but this was hardly the appropriate time. Besides, she couldn't concentrate with Howard acting so strangely. He was so dashing and suave, such a contrast from, well, all the time, especially his very first visit to her apartment after her bunion surgery.

Inez was so used to meeting her new boyfriends through salsa dancing that when Howard offered to check on her at home, a few days after her surgery, she'd assumed his suggestion was part of the normal practice of a podiatrist. Perhaps podiatrists made house calls, she remembered thinking. The last thing on her mind was romance.

From the first moment on she could see that Howard was terribly nervous. He didn't know whether he should stand or sit or what to do with his hands. While admiring her framed poster of the Guernica that she'd brought home from the Prado Museum in Madrid, he tripped backwards over the ottoman her bandaged foot was resting on, falling onto the floor with a loud thump. Howard had turned a shade of red she'd never witnessed before and began hyperventilating. Despite her intense pain, Inez hobbled off to the kitchenette to fetch him a paper bag to breathe into. After he recovered, he presented her with a copy of the Rand McNally Historical Atlas of the World.

"You mentioned you like traveling," he said, before rushing out her door without another word.

Now, she and Howard smiled awkwardly at one another, as if they were on their first date. Inez was used to a lot of silences between them—she always found comfort in the spaces these silences provided. Just his presence was enough for her. But this afternoon's silence was uncomfortable.

"I went salsa dancing last night," Inez said.

"Really?" said Howard, taking a sip of his champagne. "I thought you gave up dancing."

"Why would you think that?" she responded, a bit too harshly. She knew her defensiveness sprang from anger at herself for giving up one of her passions. Howard's response was perfectly logical. She hadn't gone dancing since they'd visited his mother in Coral Gables, Florida last year. On their second night in town, Inez asked Howard to go with her to the Miami clubs after his mother had gone to bed. But he was too tired and told her he didn't think it was safe for her to go alone. She went anyway and had a fantastic time, tumbling in at four in the morning.

Inez paid for it the next morning when even southern Florida's oppressive summer heat couldn't thaw the icy reception she'd received from Margaret, who'd obviously found out about Inez's little unsupervised field trip. Although Margaret never said anything directly to her, Inez overheard her say to Howard, "I think that girl is too wild for you. You need to think seriously about this relationship."

Howard's cell phone rang again. "She can be very persistent at times," he said, sounding slightly annoyed as he peered at the caller display screen. This was the closest Howard had ever come to criticizing his mother.

"I might go dancing again tonight," said Inez. It was a crazy thing to do, just days before her wedding, but a few dances with Calvin last night had brought back everything she loved about salsa. And, when it came to salsa dancing, sanity had never been a consideration. The drug of the dance was already working its way back into her veins. Like a junkie, she had to go back for more.

"Do you want to go with me?" she asked, her voice tentative. On the one hand, she would like nothing more than a spouse who loved to dance as much as she did. On the other hand, she couldn't picture Howard as her salsa partner.

"We don't want a repeat of Miami last year, do we Inez?" Howard said, taking a fatherly tone she didn't like.

"Maybe we could go dancing on our honeymoon?" she said, feeling it was important to push this issue, and truthfully, she wanted to see how much Howard had changed.

Howard frowned. "Sure honey, whatever you want."

The troubled look on his face said it all. One would think she had just suggested naked skydiving over Honolulu.

"It doesn't seem like you want to try salsa," she began, "is…"

Howard's phone sounded again; this time he answered it.

"I'm with Inez, Mom," he said. "Yes, yes, alright, we're leaving now."

He clicked his phone shut and began gathering up their picnic. "We'd better go."

20

Stu Miller sat in a high-backed brown leather chair facing the windows from his corner office, which provided a magnificent view of Millennium Park, the sailboats in Monroe harbor to the east, the Adler Planetarium to the south and Chicago's skyline to the north. He gave the perfect impression of a monarch surveying his kingdom, Zeke thought, as he concentrated on pushing his heart out of his throat and back down into his chest where it belonged.

Zeke took one of the chairs opposite Miller's magnificent black walnut desk, which gleamed under the florescent lights. No computer was in sight, and the only thing on Miller's desk was a telephone, a fresh yellow legal pad, and what looked like a Waterman fountain pen.

He tried to read Miller's expression, but Stu was a master at maintaining a poker face. Zeke leaned back, but his pelvis was situated too far forward on the chair. As his back fell against the chair, his torso extended out, almost as if he were lying down. He quickly righted himself, but it was too late. His physical gymnastics had caught the eye of Miller who frowned.

"Thank you for seeing me, Mr. Miller," Zeke stumbled, "I wanted to talk to you about the partnership, about my chances…" Zeke's mouth turned to sandpaper. He tried to get some saliva flowing, but couldn't swallow.

"Something wrong, Nomad?" asked Miller, without an ounce of warmth. His tan spoke Acapulco, but his demeanor was all Antarctica. Stu turned to the glass pitcher on the credenza behind him, pouring Zeke a glass of water. Zeke drank it down and thanked him.

"More?" asked Miller, holding up the pitcher.

Zeke nodded, holding out his glass like a small child as Miller came around to Zeke's side of the desk and poured another. This wasn't how he'd pictured the meeting going. Stu settled himself back in his chair. As Zeke struggled to think of what to say without sounding like a total buffoon, Miller spoke first.

"What do you think the firm is looking for in a partner?"

"Well, Mr. Miller, I think the firm wants a partner who is smart, ethical, hard-working, and dedicated; a lawyer who is willing to put in the hours necessary to serve the best interests of the client. Someone…" said Zeke, purposely adding a pregnant pause, "…who gets the job done."

Zeke crossed his leg over his knee feeling satisfied that he'd just described himself perfectly.

"Hmm," Miller responded, "Actually, we want a rainmaker."

Alarm bells sounded inside Zeke's head so loudly he was certain everyone on the fifty-fifth floor could hear them. He was definitely not a rainmaker. A trickle of sweat fell down his temple. Zeke knew the trickle would soon turn into a river if he didn't calm himself.

"In your eight years here," Miller said, "how much business have you brought into the firm?"

"Just one client sir, Mike Knight."

When Zeke received his job offer at the firm, just before his law school graduation, the first thing he did was convince Mike, who'd just earned his Oscar the year before, to dump his Hollywood lawyer and retain Zeke's law firm. Zeke was the first associate in his class to bring a client into the firm before he'd actually started working. On his first day in the office, Zeke's supervising partner commented on this coup, telling Zeke that he saw a very bright future for him at Conley, Dwight & Miller. But over the years, the coup had become more like a crass joke.

"Ah yes, Mr. Knight, the famous Oscar-winning screenwriter," said Miller, his hands clasped together under his chin. Zeke could've sworn Stu Miller was smirking, although he couldn't be certain because Miller's chair was turned so that Zeke could only see his profile. "What was the name of the last movie he wrote?"

Zeke cleared his throat. "*The Zombie Attack of the Cheerleading Squad*," he replied with as much dignity as possible.

"Hmm, I missed that one," said Miller.

So had everyone else in North America; it was the worst of Mike's box office disasters.

"Not exactly Oscar material, wouldn't you agree, Nomad?" and then, without waiting for a response, Miller added, "I'm sure you talk to Joe Banks. Mr. Knight is not bringing much money into the firm's coffers these days."

Joseph Banks, who was supposed to have been at yesterday's golf game, was the firm's only entertainment lawyer. He used to work in Hollywood and handled all of Mike's contracts. And it was true. Zeke knew the firm earned very little from Mike's low-budget slasher movies.

"Yes sir, he hasn't had a hit recently," said Zeke. He took a deep breath. He would find out one way or another, it might as well be now. "Mr. Miller, how many associates will be promoted on Friday?"

Miller said nothing and then, as if it were part of some bizarre Chinese water torture, poured himself another glass of water, drop by drop. Stu stared at the glass as though time itself were standing still, before he picked it up and took a sip. The silence went on so long, Zeke wondered if somehow Miller had forgotten he was there. Just as Zeke was considering calling in the paramedics to see if Miller still had a pulse, he spoke, breaking the awful silence.

"Just one. Lean times. We can't be as generous as we've been in past years. The firm needs to tighten its belt if we're going to survive for another one hundred years."

Zeke's heart fell. He'd worked so hard and for so long, and for what? For everything to fall apart because all along Zeke had been playing the wrong game? Yes, every year the firm made rainmakers partners, but in the past, the hard workers like Zeke were promoted as well. How horribly unfair it was that the year Zeke was up for partnership was the year only one lawyer would make it.

Zeke thought of all of the networking opportunities he'd passed up over the years, when he could've been schmoozing with prospective clients. Zeke had done none of the things other associates jumped at—joining bar associations and attending all of their interminably boring meetings and cocktail receptions; becoming members of country clubs and service clubs like the Elks; getting on the boards of the wealthiest charities in town. Zeke had always believed that if he worked hard, he would do all right. One of his father's rules growing up was: "Just keep your nose clean and do a good day's work." How stupid could he have been to actually believe that by following his father's advice and taking up golf at the eleventh hour, would be enough to guarantee his partnership?

"Zeke, what I'm about to tell you is completely confidential," said Miller. "Of course, the official vote is Friday, but I took a casual survey among the partners. I'm afraid the majority are for Elise Wyatt."

Zeke was devastated, but determined not to show it. "I understand, sir. Perhaps I should hand in my resignation now?"

"Hell no, I'm going to pull for you, son," said Miller. "You're a hell of a litigator, and you keep your billables up. You're a shitty golfer and no offense, but with your, um, background, I don't see you bringing any big money clients into our firm anytime soon. But, I believe in rewarding hard work. Everyone is very pleased with the way you're handling the Firmrod case."

"Background." The word lanced Zeke like a sword. He'd never gotten over the humiliation of growing up poor. The vast majority of lawyers at his firm came from middle class or wealthy backgrounds. Zeke had always felt like an impostor. He'd done his best to fit in— buying the right clothes, joining the most expensive health club in Chicago, casually dropping the names of the four-star restaurants he used to regularly frequent before getting so busy, and of course, taking up golf. Zeke made certain to never mention where he'd grown up or the name of his high school.

It hadn't always been this way. Throughout grade school, Zeke was blissfully ignorant of the world outside tiny blue-collar Bellwood, Illinois. Zeke's childhood home was less than a mile from Midway Airport and directly under the flight pattern of dozens of departures per day. As a kid, Zeke dreamed of getting on one of those planes and imagined landing in countries all over the world. His father used to take him to the airport on Saturdays to watch the jets take off. He loved those afternoons with his father, who had little time to spend with him because he worked second shift at Midland Steel and didn't get home until after Zeke went to bed. Like most children, Zeke idolized his father and assumed he was wiser than anyone, including the President of the United States.

Everything changed in high school when Zeke won an all-expenses-paid trip to New York to compete in a National Forensic League tournament. Zeke was the first person in his family to venture outside the Midwest and to fly on one of the airplanes he'd spent his childhood watching. His parents couldn't afford to buy him a new suit, so his mother went to Goodwill and picked out an ill-fitting, out-of-style suit jacket, pants that were too short, and a clip-on tie. Zeke had had no idea what kind of impression his clothes would make. He'd been so excited to go on the trip he barely slept for the week leading up to it.

Zeke's roommate in New York for the weekend-long event was a kid from a wealthy Boston family. Nathaniel the Third's first question for Zeke was to ask what his father did for a living. When Zeke told him, Nathaniel looked horrified and spent the rest of the weekend hanging out with his Brooks Brothers-blazered buddies who pointed at Zeke like a monkey in the zoo, and fell into fits of laughter. It was the first time in his life Zeke experienced the hot shame of poverty.

From that point on, as much as he loved his parents, Zeke never looked at them or his home the same way. He always hated himself for thinking it, but every crack in the wall, every torn or frayed piece of furniture and every misspoken word or grammatically incorrect sentence, caused him enormous embarrassment.

The humiliation had lessened over the years, but still resurfaced every so often, like now. Zeke looked at Stu Miller's well-bred good looks. He could practically smell the money coming off him. Their backgrounds were so different, Zeke might as well have grown up in a slum in Bangladesh.

"I'm assuming you have Friday's deposition under control, Nomad?"

"Absolutely, sir," Zeke replied.

"Good. I'm just curious, how old is this plaintiff?"

"Seventy-three."

Miller shook his head and chuckled. "Imagine, suing our client because he can't get it up for more than a minute. These old geezers should be happy they can get it up at all."

Zeke forced a laugh, but he felt like a jerk.

"I've got some favors I can call in, I hope I'll have good news for you on Friday," Miller said. Their meeting was over. He escorted Zeke to the door.

"Thank you sir," said Zeke, holding his hand out, but Miller slapped him on the back like they were team mates celebrating in the locker room after the big game.

Zeke walked back to the elevators, feeling numb. As much as he wanted this partnership, he wasn't comfortable with Stu Miller arm-twisting for him. It wouldn't be fair to anyone, including Elise Wyatt.

21

Carlos Luna Delgado de la Madrid let his instincts, as honed as those of an alley cat, guide him to Lulu's, a martini bar in Chicago's River West neighborhood. The concierge at The Peninsula Hotel recommended he visit several of the art galleries in this neighborhood. Although his mother had taken him to the Prado museum in Madrid nearly every week as a young boy and instilled in him a strong love of art, he wasn't in the mood this afternoon for admiring beauty—at least not the kind in a gilded frame.

Like thousands of other trendy bars around the world, Lulu's was trying too hard to be the latest, hippest hot spot—featuring bizarre light fixtures, purple velvet leopard-print furniture and large abstract paintings on the walls.

"Well, hello there," the bartender greeted Carlos with a big smile as he took a stool. "Would you like to see our martini list?"

"Do you have a wine list?" he asked.

"Oooh, I love your accent," she said, handing him the list, and then leaning across the bar as she devoured him with her beautiful Asian eyes—the kind he'd always found enticingly exotic. "Where are you from?"

Women had always gravitated to Carlos; it was his greatest blessing and his greatest curse. Ever since he could remember, Carlos preferred to be around females rather than males, probably because he had been raised by women—aunts, cousins, au pairs, his grandmother, and of course, his beloved mother—all doted on him as though he were the center of the universe. As a boy, he would listen to them during afternoons when they gathered on the outdoor terrace, drinking strong coffee and eating homemade cakes. He'd learned how women thought, what they wanted from life and from men. He'd carefully collected that knowledge, like precious gold coins, and had put it to good use ever since.

"Spain, I grew up in Madrid," Carlos said. "I'll have the 2005 Montecillo Gran Reserva."

"I'm sorry we don't serve that by the glass," the bartender replied, flashing her heavily made-up eyes. Two smears of deep purple eye shadow covered her lids and brows like bruises.

"It's one of my favorites," he said. "I'll take a bottle."

As she bent over to retrieve the wine, she jutted her hips in his direction, purposely showing off her backside. She rose and opened the bottle in front of him.

"I have to warn you," she said as she poured him a taste, "this Rioja is a little rambunctious, just like me."

"This is fine," he said, ignoring her attempt at flirtation. She filled his glass.

"So, what's your…" she began, but just then a customer at the end of the bar signaled her. She gave him a little pout and promised to be back as soon as possible. He watched her hips sway in time with her gait, and studied her gorgeous body dispassionately, as though it were on display and out of reach. He was actually bored, he discovered, to his surprise. This game had grown old over the last few years. He had changed, just as he told Inez last night and he was finally ready for a real relationship with a quality woman.

He'd almost come for Inez many times over the years, but knew that without a marriage proposal, he could never win her back. He really did love Inez and had never stopped thinking about her. Well, except perhaps during the time he was with the only other woman he'd loved almost as much as Inez—a model he'd met on one of his shoots. She left him when she caught him cheating. He'd cheated on Inez too, a few times, but was certain she'd never found out. He hadn't consciously chosen to be unfaithful to her. For him, sex was a need; like oxygen, he had to have it.

He wondered whether he should return to Inez's apartment that night or try to make her worry by not showing. It was a game he'd played many times before with other women, but with Inez, he wasn't certain his strategy would work. She'd never played the doormat like the average woman. She just might have the strength to kick him out of her life for good, which he knew was exactly what he deserved. But that was what made this week so exciting. He'd always loved the chase; it was the capture that worried him.

The bartender winked at him as she walked past to the cooler. He smiled back and glanced at himself in the mirror behind the bar, noting his nearly unlined face and full head of hair. Not bad for someone on the verge of forty, he thought.

He poured himself a second glass and then allowed the striking brunette at the end of the bar, who hadn't stopped staring at him since he'd walked in, to catch his eye. Timing was everything when it came to this game. A moment later, she began making her way toward him, exactly as he predicted she would.

"Hi, I'm Nicole," she said, upon reaching his side. The slight distance she put between them heightened the sexual tension.

"Carlos."

"Oh my God, I love your accent, where are you from?"

American women were so pedestrian, he thought, mere carbon copies of one another—except for Inez.

"Spain," he said, sparing himself the effort of going into more detail. "Would you like a glass of wine?"

"Oh, no, I'm a Cosmo girl, you know, like the Sex in the City girls," she said, leaning slightly in his direction and bestowing him with a perfect bird's eye view of her cleavage, which he had to admit was spectacular. Carlos had no idea Chicago had so many beautiful women.

He ordered her drink and when the bartender put it in front of him, she avoided looking at him, obviously miffed.

Nicole bent over to take a sip of her pink drink as the wide-mouthed martini glass remained on the bar. Carlos did his best to suppress a grimace. A Spanish woman would never dream of ordering a bubble gum drink over a divine Rioja and then have the audacity to slurp it.

"I love your shirt," she said, fingering the black-ribbed material at his chest. "Versace, right?"

He nodded, momentarily impressed, but the moment passed quickly.

"I'm a buyer for Neiman Marcus," she said. "Well, that's what I want to be. I'm an intern for them. I'm studying fashion design." And then with a smile, she leaned closer and whispered, "So, do you like them?"

He peered again at her cleavage that looked deep enough for a spelunking expedition.

"I certainly do."

"I just got them, a present from my ex," she said with a giggle. A long moment passed before she spoke again. "What do you do for a living?"

"My family is in the shipping business," he said, not wanting to go in to the details since he could see that Nicole, although sweet, had a sponge for brains.

"So, would you like to go somewhere, maybe?" Nicole asked, twisting a strand of her thick dark hair between her fingers.

American women had some attractive qualities after all, Carlos decided. How refreshing; they just went straight to sex. Carlos threw some cash on the bar and put his arm around Nicole.

As they walked out, he thought of Inez. She hadn't said yes to his proposal, although he was certain he would win her over. He would be faithful to Inez once they got married but now, he needed to take advantage of the little time he had left as a bachelor.

22

Howard pulled to the curb in front of Inez's apartment building. "Are you sure you know where the restaurant is?"

"I'm sure the taxi driver can find it," Inez replied, patiently. At first, it drove her crazy when Howard would double and triple check their plans and remind her to lock her door when she got home, as though she were a child. But she'd grown to appreciate his over-protectiveness, and discovered that she liked the fact that he was always looking out for her.

"I love you, darling," he said, with a pat to her thigh and a kiss on the cheek. "See you at seven-thirty."

Her hand was on the door handle, but she didn't move.

"What is it Inez?"

"We need to talk about adoption."

Howard let out an uncharacteristic exasperated sigh. "I thought we had that all settled."

"I've thought about it some more. I feel very strongly about this."

Howard looked at his watch. "Let's talk about this later when we have more time. Okay?"

Inez reluctantly agreed, they said their goodbyes, and she sprinted up the four flights of her apartment building with the ease of a trained athlete, which was fortunate since her building did not have an elevator. Tonight's dress was a very simple cream sundress with slip straps.

As she searched for her white lace shawl, on impulse, she reached for a cardboard box on the closet shelf and placed it on the red, orange, blue and white IKEA rug on her bedroom floor. Sitting cross-legged beside it, she hesitated before unfolding the flaps—it had been a very long time since she'd searched through its contents.

A black photo album rested on top. She breezed through the first dozen brittle plastic pages. All the photographs were of herself—first as a plump baby, then as a thinner toddler with a mop of unruly red curls, and then as a young girl engulfed by an enormous arm chair, holding baby Rachel. Rachel had fewer baby pictures and was suddenly a school-aged girl with a black pixie cut, holding hands with Inez in front of a Christmas tree, both of them clad in Snoopy pajamas. Pages of the girls blowing out candles on homemade birthday cakes and celebrating other holidays followed, like the picture of her and Rachel sitting on their bicycles decorated with red, white and blue ribbons for a Fourth of July parade.

And there was Inez with her beautiful mother, frozen in time at their kitchen table, the contents of a mixing bowl and bag of chocolate chips waiting for the oven. Her mother's fine nose and high cheekbones were softened by her sweet Mona Lisa grin—not quite a smile—and by her round chin. The photo did not do justice to the arresting jewel-shaped eyes Inez was fortunate to inherit. Inez looked to be about five, which would've made her mother twenty-nine. Looking more closely, she could see her mother was sad. As a child, Inez had often caught her mother crying in the evenings after she was supposed to have been in bed. An image formed in Inez's mind of her mother sitting at the kitchen table with a smoldering cigarette in her fingers, staring at nothing, while silent tears fell down her face. Inez remembered her mother's sadness lasting for the rest of her young life, which ended when she died of uterine cancer when Inez was thirteen. After that she and Rachel had gone to live with Marilynn, her mother's best friend, in Chicago.

Inez pushed the memory away, flipping through the album and enjoying the happier memories of her and Rachel as girls, before their mother had passed away. When she reached the last page of the album, Inez made herself look at the only photograph of her father that she possessed. On the street in front of their two-story

Milwaukee bungalow, her father's hand rested possessively on the hard top of a shiny 1958 model Cadillac. Her father had loved older model cars, but Inez remembered riding in this particular car only once, on a drive into the country to buy fresh eggs from a farm. Her father looked to be in his late twenties. He was dark like Rachel and devastatingly handsome.

Although she was just nine-months-old when their father left them, Rachel always had a burning curiosity about him. When they'd gone to live with Marilynn, Rachel peppered her with questions about why their father left. Marilynn would simply say he hadn't been a happy person, always using the past tense, as though he were dead. As they got older, Marilynn changed "unhappy" to "mentally ill" and told them that because he'd loved Rachel and Inez so much, he decided to leave because he couldn't be a good enough father to them. The story satisfied Inez, who as a child, believed everything Marilynn told them. Inez often fantasized about the day her father would knock on the door and come back to them, after he'd become well again. She was so certain of it, that for years, whenever the doorbell rang at Marilynn's, she would rush to the door expecting it to be him.

But Rachel was not satisfied with Marilynn's explanation. As a teenager, she started searching for him and then, with the advent of the Internet, found him—he had remarried, was living in Canada, and had two sons with his second wife. Inez remembered Rachel holding the piece of paper with their father's address and phone number in her hand. Inez wanted to contact him immediately, but Rachel adamantly refused to get involved. For Rachel it was simple, the unsolved mystery had been solved, and therefore, that chapter of her life was closed.

Ever since that conversation, Inez intended to contact their father, but for some reason, she never followed through. There were so many times over the years she'd picked up the phone and started to dial, but hung up. Knowing he'd left their mother for another woman was painful, although Inez could understand that couples fell out of love. But the hurt of knowing that her father had abandoned her and Rachel never went away—it was always there, a small dull ache in her gut.

Searching further inside the box, she found what she was looking for at the very bottom, a yellowed copy of her Peace Corps application she'd typed on Marilynn's ancient Underwood typewriter, just before her junior year of college. Paging through it, she came to the essay portion about her reasons for wanting to serve as a volunteer. She read her own words, brimming with the burning enthusiasm of youth, as though they were written by a stranger; lofty goals about wanting to wipe-out poverty, written as though she, Inez, could single-handedly accomplish what scores of relief and government agencies had failed to do, for decades.

"I have a double major in International Relations and Spanish because I plan on pursuing a life-long career in the development field," she read. A tingle of excitement shot through her body. Inez hadn't thought of her college dream in years, but now she remembered that living abroad and working in a developing Latin American country was something she'd wanted to do ever since taking her first Spanish class freshman year of high school.

What had ever happened to her dream? And then the answer hit her. Carlos. It was just one month after submitting her application that she'd left for her junior year abroad in Spain, and just a month after that she met Carlos. One year later, right before her college graduation, she'd received the acceptance letter from the Peace Corps informing her that she was assigned to Costa Rica, and her orientation would start in August. She remembered being so torn between wanting to go to Costa Rica and her fear of losing Carlos if she went. She'd ripped up her acceptance letter, never telling him about it.

How could she have ever let a man interfere with her life plans? Even worse, was she about to make the same mistake again?

23

Still reeling from his meeting with Stu Miller, Zeke sat in his office wondering how in the world he ended up as a pharmaceutical attorney—a career he'd never imagined nor intended to have. Basically, he stumbled into pharmaceutical litigation the way one might accidentally stub a toe in the dark. A few months after he started as an associate, there was an opening in the Product Liability and Mass Tort practice area of the Litigation Department. Zeke promptly filled the spot with the intention to stay at the firm for two or three years, pay off his student loans, his mother's mortgage, and buy himself a condo. And, he would have the added bonus of being able to tell everyone he knew that he was a trial attorney, which, thanks to television shows like *The Practice*, sounded so glamorous and exciting. No doubt he'd be racing off to a courtroom everyday, mesmerizing juries with his brilliant arguments, while pointing accusing fingers at bad guys on the witness stand, who would then crumple in humiliation and admit to precisely the point Zeke intended to make.

Reality had set in rather quickly, however. It was three years before Zeke saw the inside of a courtroom, and it looked nothing like the one he'd pictured from *The Verdict* with Paul Newman. The typical federal courtroom was stark, white, and windowless with gleaming florescent lights, much like a sterile doctor's office. And so far his litigation career had amounted to dozens of depositions— often in cramped conference rooms—and the highlight of his career, the mock jury trial last month. He supposed it was fitting, he felt like a mock lawyer with a mock life.

Zeke had accomplished all of his original financial objectives years ago. When precisely had his goal changed to becoming a partner, he wondered, and then he realized he had simply slipped into the role of the hard-working associate who couldn't possibly have any other objective than making partner.

Zeke forced his eyes back to the file on his desk, but his mind refused to focus on the Joseph Pulaski case. He was both worried and bored. Conceptually, the two emotions would seem to be mutually exclusive. But the worry was in Zeke's gut—his stomach and intestines were being swarmed by fire ants. The boredom had settled into his brain. His neurons and synapses had gone on strike long ago to protest the constant exposure to repetitive, uninspiring, and really quite depressing material—men in their fifties, sixties, and seventies whose marriages and lives had collapsed because they could no longer get it up.

As much as he was tired of the Firmrod case, Zeke couldn't believe it might all be coming to an end on Friday. If the unthinkable did happen, he would be given the standard six-month period to find a new job, along with a generous severance package. The firm would very kindly report in its newsletter that Zeke Nomad had left Conley, Dwight & Miller to pursue other opportunities—code words for having been dumped unceremoniously, after eight years and tens of thousands of hours of dedicated service. And then after a few months, he would be just another lawyer who used to have an enviable job working for the biggest, most prestigious law firm in Chicago.

Zeke stood to look out his window. From his forty-eighth-floor vantage point, the commuters hurrying along the sidewalk looked like miniature figures from a dollhouse. At this time of day they were rushing home to their spouses, kids, and pets.

He thought again of Elise, who had been entering his thoughts, on and off, all day long. He wanted to tell her about his meeting with Miller and then, perhaps, she might feel comfortable enough to share what she learned at breakfast yesterday before their golf game. And, he hoped more might come out of their conversation. He preferred to keep his business and personal lives separate, not that there had been throngs of nubile, female attorneys throwing themselves at him. Other associates at the firm had had romances. It wasn't exactly encouraged, but it wasn't discouraged either. But, after Friday, it wouldn't matter because they would no longer be working together.

Zeke dialed Elise's number before he lost his nerve, thrilled when she quickly agreed to dinner. Later, in the elevator on his way to meet her, he was as nervous as if he were a pimply-faced fourteen-year-old with a crush on the new girl at school. He waited in the lobby trying to look relaxed, but was as tense as if he were completely naked.

She came around the corner from the elevator bank. With her blonde hair up in a loose chignon, she had that glamorous movie star look from the glory days of Hollywood. Her lipstick-pink pantsuit had a short jacket that hit her at the waist, making it appear even smaller than it was. Zeke liked that Elise dressed less conservatively than other women at the firm. She was a bit of a maverick amongst the many sheep.

"I'm so glad you called," she said. "It gets lonely eating dinner in my office every night."

"I agree," he said. Zeke reminded himself they were just two colleagues having dinner together, but it had the feel of a date. Or perhaps this was just wishful thinking on his part. They decided on Murphy's Bar and Grill, just down the street.

The sunlight, sharply angled from the many skyscrapers towering over them, was still warm, and the few rays reaching Zeke felt welcome on his skin. They chatted about the beautiful weather and reached Murphy's a minute later. The hostess led them to a booth, and a harried waitress plopped menus on their table, returning a moment later for their orders.

"Elise, I just realized I know almost nothing about you," said Zeke, although he had that odd feeling of having known her for years. "Where are you from?"

"I was born in San Diego, but grew up in Laguna Beach," she said, brushing a stray hair from her cheek. "My family still lives there."

"Are you close to them?"

Elise nodded. "Very. I really miss them, especially Ellen, my baby sister."

The waitress brought a hamburger and fries for Zeke and a Greek salad for Elise. Zeke pushed his plate of fries toward her, but she shook her head.

"A California girl," Zeke said. "I know this is cliché, but do you surf?"

"Surfing is not a cliché in California," she replied with a warm smile. "My whole family surfs, and you're looking at the Western Surfing Association's Hobie championship, girls 17 and under short board, first-place trophy winner."

"Really?" he said, genuinely impressed. He'd only tried surfing once in Hawaii, and had nearly drowned when the first big wave crashed over him.

"It's no big deal, and it was a very long time ago," Elise said with her lovely laugh that reminded him of a wind chime tinkling in the breeze. "My real passion is film. That's what I studied at UCLA during undergrad. I've been trying for years to get a job with a studio as in-house counsel. My last attempt was a few years ago when I applied at Universal Studios."

"It sounds like your whole life is in California."

"Are you trying to get rid of me?" she replied with an unmistakable flirtatious tone.

"Definitely not," Zeke said. Their eyes met and held for a long moment until Zeke looked back down at his plate and took a bite of his burger. He was so out of practice with the rituals leading up to romance. With his last real girlfriend, Susan from law school, they'd just ended up in bed together after meeting at a drunken party and the next thing he knew, two years had gone by.

"How did you end up in law?" he asked Elise, hoping his questions weren't beginning to sound like an interrogation.

"My parents thought becoming a film maker was too impractical. They were paying the bills so to make them happy, I double-majored in Political Science and applied for law school."

Elise looked lost in thought. "I can't believe I've been here eight years."

The exact same thoughts were going through Zeke's mind.

"I met with Stu Miller today," Zeke said, and then related what had transpired.

Elise's mossy green eyes grew wide. "He told me the exact same thing at breakfast yesterday." She lowered her voice to imitate Miller. "The majority of partners are for Zeke Nomad, but I like you Wyatt, I'm going to pull for you."

"He told me I'm a shitty golfer," said Zeke with a smile.

"You are a shitty golfer," said Elise.

Zeke laughed from his belly. "I have a confession to make. I hate golf."

"So do I!" said Elise.

"I was hoping we'd both make partner," said Zeke, "but, I think it's going to be you."

"Oh no, Zeke, I'm sure it's going to be you."

"All the weekends and vacations we gave up," Zeke said.

"What was it for?" Elise looked off into a space containing a past which might have been.

"The money? Just kidding."

Ever since that trip to New York in high school with the debate team, Zeke had developed Godiva chocolate tastes, fantasizing about all of the nice things he would buy for himself and his family someday. But with a Hershey bar budget, it wasn't until he started working at the firm when he could finally indulge. The first year he hadn't saved a dime. The second year he thought about saving money, but hadn't gotten around to it. He visited a financial planner his third year and had forced himself to start investing. But a few months ago, he had looked around his condo at all of the beautiful things he thought he always wanted—plush leather sofas and chairs, recessed wall sconces, track lighting he'd had specially installed, custom-made suits and his hand-picked art collection of hand-woven carpets, paintings and sculptures by largely unknown, but talented Central and South American artists—and it had hit him that these things really didn't make him happy. It was embarrassing to learn at the age of thirty-three that he'd ignored the simple wisdom, "money doesn't make you happy."

"Sometimes, I feel like I gave up the best years of my life," said Zeke.

"Me too."

"I've got an idea. Let's go somewhere warm, a beach, and drink rum. How does Cuba sound? And then we can go to South America."

"Okay, when do we leave?" she asked, with a dreamy smile Zeke recognized as the same one that crossed his face every time he thought about traveling.

They didn't speak for a long moment, both of them lost in the possibilities, but then Zeke remembered how much work he had to do on the Pulaski deposition.

"I'd better get back," he said.

As they returned to their office building Zeke wondered why they couldn't just run away together? Why wasn't life that simple?

Two hours later, Zeke's office phone rang.

"I'm going to Club Caliente," said Mike, "can you meet me in an hour?"

"I've got too much work to do," said Zeke, wishing his friend could see the futility in searching for his wife who obviously did not want to be found.

"I remember a time when you would've done anything for me," said Mike. "I guess those days are over."

"I'm not a marriage counselor, you don't need me there," said Zeke. He pushed away a sudden, very strong feeling he should go to the club tonight. "And you can't guilt me into going."

"Fuck you very much," Mike said, and then hung up.

Zeke slammed down the receiver, the sound reverberating in his quiet office. He wasn't certain with whom he was angrier, Mike for being so weak and needy or himself for not being the kind of friend he should be. Or was it something else? The feeling that he should go to Club Caliente was stronger than it was a moment ago. He forced the urge away, with effort, and returned to work.

Follow your heart, Zeke! What is wrong with that darling man? I am getting mighty frustrated with Zeke. And with Inez.

Why do you think I retired from match-making and requested a transfer to the Department of Flora and Fauna Preservation?

It is so blasted obvious what they should and should not be doing. H, what's your theory about why they can't seem to trust their instincts?

Did you ever do anything as a human that you knew was wrong for you? At times, you hated yourself for doing it, but you kept doing it anyway?

Now that I think about it, I did that all the time. How embarrassing.

Do not be so hard on yourself, Serena. It is quite common. This is how people create most of their problems. They tend to ignore their intuition and let fear rule their lives. Usually, just one small decision sets in motion an entire chain of events that takes a person on an entirely different path than the one he or she was meant to follow.

Like Inez and Zeke not joining the Peace Corps?

Precisely.

They would be married if they'd gone to Costa Rica.

Serena, they could be divorced by now as well.

Divorced? Soul mates don't get divorced.

Soul mates do not always join for an entire lifetime.

Well, in my novels they do. Happily ever after is my motto and as an expert in these matters, I declare that these two are destined for it. That is, if we can get them to focus on what's important and get them in the same room.

24

Two things had saved Inez after her return to Chicago fresh from her break-up with Carlos—Beso and salsa dancing. Just twenty-three at the time, she had a vague memory of meeting Marilynn at O'Hare airport and crumpling into her strong embrace. A week after her return, Rachel visited, finding her curled up in a fetal position on her couch. Yes, she had been a trembling lump of grief and self-pity—and to this day she regretted wasting her precious time mooning over a man like a heart-sick teenager—but Carlos's disappearance after two years of living together, along with his many false promises of marriage and children, had torn a deep gash in her heart.

That day Rachel had dragged Inez to the Humane Society, dubbing the get-Inez-off-the-couch mission "Operation Lassie," because she thought Inez should adopt a dog. But Inez has always been partial to cats—she liked their graceful sleekness and their fluctuations from aloof to affectionate, with just the flick of a tail. Inez was immediately drawn to Beso, who was named Angel for the white halo-like circle on the top of his black head—when he poked his paws out of the cage to touch her fingers, as if he was shaking her hand. She renamed him Beso, "kiss" in Spanish, after the tabby cat belonging to her Spanish home-stay parents in Madrid.

A cute kitten playing with everything from dangling shoelaces to its own shadow made Inez smile for the first time since Carlos had left her. But her heart was still raw and her laughter at Beso's antics often turned into tears.

Marilynn showed up on a second rescue mission one evening, when she told Inez to put on make-up and a nice dress and took her to Club Caliente for a night of salsa dancing. Inez had always loved salsa, ever since Marilynn had first put on a Tito Puente record in her living room and had taught her, at the age of thirteen, the basic steps. Inez hadn't danced at all during the two years with Carlos in Madrid. But after that night, she was able to jettison Carlos from her mind, and the Chicago salsa scene quickly became her whole life outside of work. She went out four, five, sometimes even six nights a week. On nights out, during the rare songs she wasn't asked to dance, she watched the best women on the floor to learn new moves. She took private lessons and practiced for hours. Within a few months, she had become one of the best *salseras* in Chicago.

"I was just hoping to make you forget about Carlos," Marilynn used to tease her, "but I see I've created a salsa addict."

Inez has never understood her intense love for the dance. Was it the rhythmic passionate music, which had power over her like a drug? Was it simply a release of endorphins? Or was it the satisfaction that came with executing challenging footwork and turn patterns with a partner? She'd spent hours analyzing her feelings about the dance, as though it were a scientific formula that could be picked apart and conclusively proven. In the end, she decided it didn't matter exactly what it was about salsa that set her soul on fire.

But all of that was long ago. Inez wondered if anyone would remember her tonight as she walked back into Club Caliente. She couldn't wait to get out onto the dance floor, especially after another stressful dinner with Howard's mother, which was filled with more personal questions and words of friendly advice disguised as orders.

At the top of the stairs looking over the crowded dance floor, she recognized a few people, but it was still early. The true salsa diehards came much later. It would be great to dance with Calvin again, but her favorite nights were dancing with dozens of different partners, each of whom had a different style of leading, which challenged her skills to the maximum. Some could dip her so low her head was just inches from the floor. Others loved to spin her like a top. She took pride in her tight spins, staying in place no matter how many times she was twirled, without getting dizzy or losing her balance. Then there were the partners who enjoyed letting her show off. They would stand in place holding her hands, while she performed magic with her feet—combining moves from salsa and tango so sexy they should be R-rated.

The energy from the dancers was infectious. The pounding rhythmic melody of a Marc Anthony song was luring her to the floor. She couldn't stand still for much longer. Aching to get out there, she moved through the crowd and a moment later her plea to the universe was answered when a slim Asian man with a ponytail and long sideburns, pulled her out onto the dance floor.

The next hour passed in a minute. Inez had forgotten how aerobically demanding the dance was. She needed a break and ordered a bottle of water. As she sipped it, enjoying the endorphins soaring through her body, she scanned the crowd for a familiar face.

"Remember me?" asked a handsome Latino stepping in front of her.

A long moment passed.

"You haven't changed," said Inez.

"I'm happy to see neither have you," he said. "Except for this."

He took hold of her left hand, raised his eyebrow as if in disbelief, and then dropped her hand.

"I'm getting married," said Inez. "And you, Diego? By now you must've gone through most of the women here."

Her words came out more severe than she'd intended. Diego was the first man she dated after Carlos. When she first met Diego he was working as a mortgage lender for a Hispanic community bank in Humboldt Park. He hadn't been a replacement for Carlos, more like a distraction from her Spanish beau who still made regular appearances in her dreams. Their arrangement was exactly what she'd wanted—no emotional strings and a nice warm body to curl up with a few nights a week.

She could've gone on like that for years, but one night, after about six months, she caught Diego coming out of a unisex bathroom at a salsa club with a petite brunette. She ended it instantly, without a scene, although she'd never been certain exactly what "it" was. Certainly not a relationship, unless meeting up at salsa clubs several nights a week and then going home together constituted something meaningful.

Within a week she'd started seeing Juan from Puerto Rico. Next it was Patricio from Chile, Andre from the Ivory Coast, Akio from Japan, and a half-dozen other men who formed her very own rainbow coalition—each of whom could dance salsa like a god. But there were no more Spaniards.

And then one night after another salsa break-up, Rachel had said, "Inez, you've turned into a bad-boy magnet. When are you going to stop dating these salsa guys and let yourself have a real relationship?"

"All guys can be bad boys," Inez replied.

"Inez, you deserve a guy whether he's white, black, brown or purple who's going to treat you decently."

Rachel's words had struck a chord. At the time of that conversation, almost six years had passed since Diego cheated on her; she couldn't remember the last time one of her "salsa boyfriends" had taken her out to dinner or a movie. They all shared as much desire to get tied down as an escaped convict.

But more compelling was the fact that she started noticing babies again. Chicago seemed to be in the midst of a population explosion. They were everywhere—gurgling in carriages at shopping malls, at restaurants, parks, and on the "L". Her passion and love for salsa was overshadowed by her desire to marry and have children. It was time for a change. From that point on she'd vowed to Rachel, "Read my lips, no more bad boys."

And then, luck, fate, or the alignment of the stars had intervened in the form of a bunion. She'd been trying, for over a year, to ignore the pain, but after a night of dancing it got so bad she hobbled to her car in agony, her right big toe swollen to twice its normal size. Even her dance shoes, normally as comfortable as a pair of slippers, couldn't cushion the pressure since salsa required her to dance on the balls of her feet and on her toes. But she'd continued to put off making an appointment, knowing she would have to have surgery and wouldn't be able to dance for months.

Even Marilynn, who shunned conventional medical treatment, urged her to see a podiatrist. "Inez, do you want to find out you've waited too long to get help and that you can never dance again?" Inez couldn't have imagined a worse fate.

During her initial appointment with Howard, the very first question she asked was how soon she could go salsa dancing again. He'd replied in his ultra-professional, modulated voice that it would be at least six months after her surgery before she could dance. Inez resigned herself to taking a break from the salsa scene, looking at it as an opportunity to start dating some nice guys. She never would've imagined that the first nice guy would turn out to be the man standing in front of her that day three years ago—Howard, the antithesis of bad-boy-dom.

"I treated you badly," Diego said, bringing her back to the present, "I should've apologized a long time ago."

First Carlos and now Diego; this must be International Bad-Boy Admission of Guilt Week.

It was nice to hear him say it, but Inez knew she only had herself to blame. She knew exactly what she was getting herself into when she got involved with Diego and her other salsa boyfriends—men who couldn't commit to a cheese sandwich, much less a woman.

"This is your favorite salsa song," he said, "*El Cantante*, right?"

He was obviously mixing her up with some other woman. Her favorite salsa song had always been *Mambo Yo Yo*. But it didn't matter. She nodded, knowing this was an invitation to dance. Diego, if nothing else, was a dancer among dancers. He led her to the floor and when he dipped her, it was like riding the world's best roller coaster. She vowed that she would never again give up one of her passions.

Wednesday

25

Still on a salsa high from last night, Inez bounded down the stairs of her building with high energy, despite having gotten only a few hours of sleep. She had stayed out until three in the morning, having way too much fun to pay attention to the time. She wondered briefly if Carlos showed up at her apartment last night, but then a flash of anger flared. Why should she care? But the uncomfortable truth was, she did care, although for the five blessed hours she spent dancing last night, she hadn't thought of him once.

She pushed open the outer lobby door of her building and froze. As if she had summoned him by her thoughts alone, Carlos was there with his hand on the door of the Ferrari, looking so much like her father it made her heart stop. It was surreal; they could pass for identical twins.

"Good morning, *querida*," he said, going around to the passenger door and opening it. "Your chariot awaits."

Where the hell did he pick up these lines? His grasp of languages had always amazed her. The verbal part of his brain operated exactly like Berlitz software, he could simply download the correct phrase, in whatever language he happened to be speaking at the moment, and voila, he was fluent.

"Leave me alone, Carlos," she said firmly, although today she would love a ride to work, for the last day of school, since she was very late. But she had the strangest feeling she should take the "L" as usual. In fact, the feeling to take the train was so strong, she felt compelled. How bizarre—although she appreciated the convenience of public transportation, she certainly never had had any strong feelings about it.

"We need to talk, Inez."

"We have nothing to talk about," she said.

"I love you, I want to marry you."

This needed to stop, she decided, ignoring her gut that had now raised its persuasion level—to take the train as usual—to the red zone. Convincing herself this would be the perfect opportunity to get Carlos out of her life for good, she went to his car.

He held the door for her with a barely disguised look of victory. She wanted to wipe that confident smile off his face, but losing her cool in front of this master of manipulation would not be wise.

At the stoplight before they turned onto Lake Shore Drive, he handed her a flat white box from Saks Fifth Avenue.

"I don't want this," she said, putting the box aside.

"You don't know what it is," he said in a teasing tone of voice, confident he was targeting one of her greatest weaknesses.

While Inez and Rachel were as different as sky and peaches, one trait they unfortunately shared was an insatiable curiosity about all things unknown. Inez flipped off the lid and pulled out a white silk scarf. With the top down on the car, as soon as they turned onto the Drive, her hair whipping in the wind would become a tangled mess she might straighten out, in a year, if she was lucky. Reluctantly, she wrapped the scarf around her head and put on her faux Fendi sunglasses with purple lenses and brown tortoiseshell frame.

"You look like that movie star—Italian," he said, "ah, yes, Gina Lollobrigida."

"It's over between us," she said, staring straight ahead. "It's been over for a long time."

"Have you told your fiancé about us?"

"Of course," she lied. "He's not concerned about you."

Carlos looked at her for so long she began to panic that he might run them off the road. "I know you better than anyone, *querida,*" he said. "You're lying."

Strong winds gusting from Lake Michigan caused her skirt to fly up to her mid-thigh. She could feel his eyes on her legs as she smoothed her skirt back down to her knees. A thought skated through her mind that she wanted him to caress her thighs. She never should've accepted a ride from him.

"I thought we could have two children of our own," he said, "and then adopt a child from Central or South America."

Her mouth opened in shock. She closed it quickly, but it was too late.

"You thought I forgot about your hopes and dreams?" he said. "I remember every word you've ever told me, Inez. That's how much I love you."

"Having a good memory has nothing to do with love," she snapped, crossing her arms over her chest.

"I will make you so happy. Don't you remember how it was?"

Actually she didn't. She remembered feelings and emotions, but few of the details. Ever since it ended a decade ago, she'd blocked it out, and her efforts had succeeded in creating an amnesiac's black hole of their two years together.

"I'm going back to Madrid on Saturday," he said, "I want you to go with me."

"I'm getting married on Saturday."

He reached into the breast pocket of his brown leather jacket, placing an envelope on her lap—a first-class, one-way British Airways ticket leaving Saturday evening from O'Hare airport. It was the second time that he had given her a one-way ticket to Madrid. The first time, she'd made the mistake of using it instead of going to Costa Rica. She wouldn't make that mistake again.

He pulled up in front of her school. The car was still moving slightly when she alighted. She pulled the scarf off her head and threw it and the ticket back into the car.

"How can I convince you that I've changed?" he asked.

"You can't."

He put the car in gear, turned off the ignition and put his hand on his door handle.

"Don't follow me!" she said, in a low even voice.

She turned and walked into her school, hearing his footsteps behind her. She whirled. "This is over!" The look on her face must've been shocking since that is what she saw in Carlos's face. He returned to his car and drove off.

Inez watched until the car disappeared around the corner, but she wasn't confident he would leave her alone. Men never disappeared when you wanted them to.

26

Zeke caught sight of a woman with curly auburn hair exit the train at the State street stop, and his heart began racing. He couldn't see her face, which was obscured by the mob of commuters surrounding her. Bobbing and weaving his head to get a better look, his hopes soared. A second later, the crowd cleared for a second. It wasn't Inez. A crush of commuters pushed past him as if he were invisible. He glared at his watch as if it were to blame for the forty minutes he'd wasted waiting for Inez today.

He boarded the next train feeling defeated when the doors closed in his face. He grabbed a strap dangling from the ceiling and, as he surfed the rocking train to his stop, he tried to console himself with the fact that in a city of millions, the chances were infinitesimally small that he would see her two days in a row or ever again, for that matter. He felt foolish for showing up today. What sane person would still be thinking about a woman he'd spent just an hour with, nearly thirteen years ago? Most marriages didn't last that long; it was time to move on.

At his stop napkins, stray newspapers and crumbled wads of paper rolled along the sidewalk like tumbleweeds. A strong gust of wind caused a woman's skirt to fly up and she quickly pushed it back down. The Loop was often windy, but that was not the reason Chicago had earned its famous nickname—Chicago was dubbed the Windy City thanks to its longwinded and often less than honest politicians.

Zeke greeted Charlie whose cheekbones angled sharply through his tanned skin, etched by age and hours of standing in the elements each day.

"What happened with Miller?" asked Charlie.

Zeke shared the bad news that just one associate would be promoted on Friday.

Charlie nodded thoughtfully. "No doubt it will be the woman you golfed with on Monday."

As happy as he would be for Elise, it was still difficult for him not to feel sorry for himself. Not in the mood for a verbal sparring match today, Zeke handed Charlie some money and said goodbye. At the office Melissa greeted him, not with her usual smile and cheery hello, but with a look so grim Zeke thought the City must have announced the cancellation of summer this year.

"What's up?" asked Zeke, setting his briefcase on the edge of her desk.

Melissa chewed on her lip. "Oh nothing," she said meaning the opposite.

"Melissa, I promise, I won't shoot the messenger."

She looked around and leaned forward. "I heard Elise Wyatt has the partnership slot locked up. Stu Miller is behind it; he's getting all the votes for her."

"Where did you hear that?" he asked, anguish stabbing at his insides like a hot poker.

"The grapevine."

The administrative executive grapevine was far more reliable than the associate rumor mill. Secretaries were the lifeblood of the firm and knew absolutely everything that was going on. Zeke tried to ignore this latest bit of news, but it was already working its way through his system like a painful poison.

"Don't worry, Melissa, if I don't make it, I'm sure you'll be reassigned to someone great."

"I don't want to be reassigned; you're not like the rest of them."

Zeke managed a smile. "I'll take that as a compliment."

He decided not to think about the vote on Friday as he settled himself behind his desk. If Elise got it, then he would be happy for her. But what would he do with the rest of his life?

As if in answer to his question, he opened his inbox to find his semi-annual e-mail from his college buddy, Kevin Casey. Kevin and Zeke had applied to the Peace Corps at the same time, right after their junior year of college. If Zeke hadn't ripped up his Peace Corps acceptance letter a year later, he and Kevin would've been in the same program in Costa Rica. Kevin stayed after his Peace Corps stint and had "gone native," marrying Maria, a native Tico, and opening a business teaching tourists how to windsurf. Kevin worked, if you could call it that, about four hours a day and spent the rest of the time playing with his kids and making love to his beautiful wife. Zeke read Kevin's e-mail:

"Hey working stiff, it's eighty-five and not a cloud in the sky down here in paradise. I'm chillin' in my hammock with a cold Imperial. Business is good. When the hell are you going to get out of the concrete jungle and come to the real one? Maria and los niños send their love."

Zeke's last visit to Kevin and his family was six years ago. He'd planned another trip three years ago, but then was forced to cancel it when he was assigned to the Xanadu Pharmaceuticals case.

Whether he made partner or not this week, Zeke decided he would go to Costa Rica. The tropical sun, windsurfing, and good company would help him get his head on straight. He could make plans for the future while lying on the beach. Zeke began compiling a mental list that had as its number one, two, and three priorities: traveling, figuring out what he really wanted to do with his life, and finding a woman to share it with, a good woman like Elise Wyatt.

27

As the last bell of the last day of school sounded, giddy children rushed out of the classroom, anxious to embrace summer. Usually, by the time this day arrived, Inez was more than ready for the break and just as excited as her students. She never worked during the summers like many other teachers did, preferring instead to sacrifice a more comfortable lifestyle and nicer apartment for the rewards of having three months off during the best weather of the year. But today, her heart ached when she realized this might be her last day of teaching at this school, or at any school.

The sudden silence that descended after the commotion of children had left the building, pounded against her eardrums. She went to her desk, bending down to the bottom drawer to begin cleaning it out.

"Miss Paris?"

Jamal Wilson, a small boy with a long afro and big ears cast his winning smile on her. What a transformation from the start of the school year when he wouldn't make eye contact with anyone. Last September, Inez did a little investigation and learned that Jamal had never known his father, and his mother was struggling to raise four children on her income as a drug store cashier and cleaning lady. Inez helped Jamal get a library card and had arranged, with his mother's permission, to get him involved with Big Brothers Big Sisters. Attention from a caring adult was all he needed to boost his confidence.

"Did you forget something, Jamal?"

He put a wooden plaque on her desk. "It's from my mother," he said, "she told me to tell you 'thank you.'"

Hot tears welled at the corners of her eyes and her throat constricted. She was immensely touched that Jamal's mother had spent some of her precious money to buy her a gift.

"Please tell your mother I love it."

"I will, Miss Paris."

"And don't forget your reading list," said Inez. "You can get all those books from the library."

"I won't forget!" he said, as excited as if he'd been handed the keys to Toys-R-Us.

The moment Jamal left, her emotions escaped in a rush. She couldn't remember the last time she'd cried this hard. She forced herself to stop blubbering, grabbing a tissue and dabbing her eyes.

"Men. You can't live with 'em and you can't kill 'em," said a husky voice that made Inez think of a blues singer in a smoky lounge.

Principal Nancy White leaned against the doorway with her arms crossed over her ample bosom. Inez knew very little about her except that she was from the south, and years ago her husband had left her for another woman. She'd raised five children on her own, while putting herself through graduate school.

"Is the wedding off?" asked Nancy.

"What? No! Well, I don't know, maybe postponed," said Inez. Postponed? The idea, which had popped into her brain without preamble, seemed to belong to someone else.

"I don't want to pressure you," said Nancy, "but have you made a decision yet about whether you're coming back in the fall?"

"Not yet. I promise I'll let you know in the next two weeks. It's just that my life has become a lot more complicated."

"Could it be the Antonio Banderas look-alike in the fancy black convertible that dropped you off today?"

"You saw that?" Inez asked, slightly mortified.

"Honey, we *all* saw that. I just loved the way you tossed that scarf back at him like he was yesterday's trash. It was better than Jerry Springer."

"He deserved it."

"He looks like he deserved it," Nancy said with a throaty laugh.

She stepped forward and picked up the plaque from Inez's desk, reading it aloud in her sultry voice:

Consult not your fears but your hopes and your dreams. Think not about your frustrations, but about your unfulfilled potential. Concern yourself not with what you tried and failed in, but with what it is still possible for you to do—Pope John XXIII.

Nancy returned the plaque to her desk. "Hmm. Good quote. I might use this to start off the next school year," she said, referring to her intercom address at the beginning of each school day that always included an inspiring quote.

Nancy's face softened.

"Inez, you're one of my best teachers. I hope you come back in the fall. But you need to do what is right for you. Believe me, men are not worth giving up anything for."

Nancy left, and Inez was left with the strong feeling that whatever happened, she would not be back in September. She finished cleaning out her desk and took one long last look around her classroom. She'd had nine great years at this school and although the victories had been small and few, Inez knew she'd truly made a difference.

During her subway ride to the Loop, Inez thought about what Nancy had said. She was obviously embittered from her failed marriage, but there were so many women who felt the same way. But what about companionship and genuine kindness? Howard had given her both of those in spades. Like the time he took Beso to the veterinarian for her, despite his allergies, when she was bedridden with the flu. Beso had vomited all over the leather seats of his new Mercedes, but Howard never complained. Another time, Howard took her to a four-hour production of King Lear because he knew she loved Shakespeare. What she didn't learn until months later, was that he had sat through the very same play with his aunt the night before. Howard wasn't everything she'd wanted in a life partner, but she trusted him completely, and he made her feel safe.

Inez reached her stop at State Street in the heart of the Loop. As she walked a block to her destination, the skyscrapers closed in around her. She thought of the poor souls stuck inside those buildings and shuddered at the thought of working in such a sterile environment—like her friend Melissa who used to be a teacher at her school, but quit several years ago to work as a secretary for a big law firm. Every so often, Inez got an e-mail from her. Melissa said the money was better—she needed it as a single mother—but sitting at a desk all day and dealing with stuffed shirts and monotony of the work was difficult. The only bright spot was that Melissa was assigned to work for a really nice associate who wasn't like the rest of the lawyers at the firm.

Inez entered the store, recalling the day she selected her wedding dress: a simple strapless sheath dress in off-white satin, with a Spanish lace veil that came to her waist. It was the very first dress she had tried on, and she knew it was the one. The sales clerk had tried to persuade her to try on more dresses, but Inez has always prided herself on being a decisive shopper.

Inez made her way through the lingerie department to the wedding dress salon, where the saleswoman, Mrs. Phillips, sat at a small elegant desk painted pale yellow and stenciled with pink roses. Mrs. Phillips, a small mouse of a woman, looked up and upon seeing Inez, let out a squeak, saying she'd be right back. She hurried to the back of the salon disappearing through a door. As Inez waited, a young woman came out of a dressing room wearing a stunning gown that fanned out like a cloud as she twirled for her mother. But it was the look on her face that caused Inez to stare—utter, radiant joy. Now that was one happy bride-to-be.

A small ache stabbed at Inez's heart, and a moment later it froze in place as Mrs. Phillips solemnly approached, carrying her wedding gown like a corpse.

"Oh!" cried Inez. Her beautiful dress had a burn in the shape of an iron, front and center, just below the bodice.

"Ms. Paris, I can't tell you how sorry we are," she said, looking as distressed as if it were her own dress. "The seamstress was just finishing up with your dress this morning when she received a pressing call."

"Apparently more pressing than pressing my dress," said Inez.

Mrs. Phillips gave her a wan smile. "We happen to have your dress in stock at one of our suburban stores. It will be here tomorrow. If you could come back for a fitting in the morning, we will work overtime to have it ready for you by Friday." Mrs. Phillips bit her lip. "Possibly, Saturday morning. Of course we will wave all outstanding charges."

Inez made an appointment, assuring Mrs. Phillips that yet another apology was not necessary.

She left the store, turning her face to the sun that pleasantly warmed her cheeks. Marilynn would say her ruined wedding dress was another sign that she should not marry Howard. Instead of dismissing this thought, Inez's mind latched onto it. A strong feeling bubbled up inside of her, and she suddenly knew with a certainty she could not explain, that she was beginning something much more momentous than the start of her summer vacation. A sea change was about to occur.

Inez felt as light as air, as if a horrible weight had been lifted from her, and the answer as to what she should do came to her as clearly as if she'd received an engraved message from a winged angel.

Did you do this, Serena?

I try to be humble, but yes. Brilliant, wasn't it? Not only did I manage to give Inez a sign that she should not marry Howard, but the seamstress who got fired for ruining Inez's wedding gown will find out tonight that she has won the Mega Millions jackpot, forty-three million dollars! She has six children, and her husband has been out of work for a year. *Isn't that fantastic?* Well, say something, H.

This is merely a small delay tactic that will not accomplish our ultimate goal.

What? Her kids and all of her nieces and nephews will be able to go to college! They can buy a house and a decent car. They can buy a whole fleet of cars. I had no idea we wielded such power!

Serena, we must focus on our case.

I hate to point out the obvious once again, H, but the only thing you've done is to bring Carlos here, and for all I know you're trying to get Zeke and Elise together too. If I didn't know better, I'd say you were trying to sabotage this case. Wait a minute, how do I know you're not trying to do exactly that?

I want Zeke and Inez to be together as much as you do.

All you seem to care about are your plants. If you don't work a miracle in this case, you'll never be called in for another special case. You'll get to prattle around in your garden for the rest of eternity.

I am deeply hurt that you think I could be so selfish as to manipulate the lives of two soul mates for my own ends. Please trust me, Serena.

You've given me no reason to trust you. I'm going to have to report you, Herodius.

28

Instead of preparing for his deposition, Zeke found himself, once again, falling into a reverie about Elise Wyatt. In his mind's eye they had already visited the Art Institute, had dinner at The Signature Room on the 95th floor of the John Hancock building, spent a Saturday night at the Kingston Mines blues club, and had taken in a comedy show at Second City. And that was just during their first week of dating. This afternoon, he pictured them riding their bikes along the eighteen-mile Chicago Lakefront bike path. They would stop at the beach to cool off in the water, bike to a nice grassy spot under some trees for a picnic, and spend the afternoon talking. If he craned his neck just right, he could see the bike path from his office window. He used to go rollerblading on that path every weekend. By himself. He longed to get his free time back, but it was no longer enough. Now, he wanted someone to share it with.

Daydreaming came to Zeke as naturally as breathing. As a kid, he was frequently in trouble with his teachers for inattentiveness during class. They would call on him, but he didn't hear his name because he was busy fighting Indians who were shooting poison darts at him in the Brazilian jungle, or he was searching for a long-lost Mayan temple. When they punished him with a detention, he'd pass the time by continuing his foreign expeditions and, with each one, getting braver and more famous.

Daydreaming was fun, but it would not get him a wonderful woman. Zeke clicked on instant messenger to add Elise's name to his list. Unless the nuances of flirting had changed dramatically over the last few years, he recognized some definite signs that she was interested in him. He typed his first message, read it, and erased it. He did the same with his second, third, and fourth attempts. Frustrated, he thought about what he was truly feeling and hoping she wouldn't think he was being too bold typed: "Elise, I've been thinking about you all day—I would love to see you tonight if you're free. Z."

After his message disappeared into cyberspace, he endured the longest five minutes of his life imagining horrible repercussions—everything from Elise ignoring his message to a senior partner stepping in to her office and reading his personal message on her screen, and seeing his name attached to it. He paced the short length of his office until he heard the blessed ping and rushed to his laptop to read her response:

"Zeke, I haven't enjoyed a conversation as much as ours in a very long time. And yes, I'm free tonight and would love to see you too. E."

They agreed that he would stop at her office at six and signed off. A sharp rap on the door was followed by the entry of Wayne Martin.

"Hey, partner," he said, dropping into a chair.

"We'll see about that," said Zeke.

"I'd vote for you, if I could."

"Thanks, but in this case, the thought doesn't count for shit. So what did you find in the medical records?"

"Joseph Pulaski," said Wayne, flipping to a page on the legal pad he held in his freckled hands. "This poor schmuck doesn't have a prayer. He's sixty pounds overweight, has diabetes, gout, and chronic high blood pressure."

The more serious a plaintiff's health problems, the less likely it could be proven that Firmrod had caused a stroke, which was why so many cases were now getting dismissed or settled for small amounts.

"And take a look at this," Wayne added with a broad grin.

Wayne came around to Zeke's side of the desk with the file opened to a page covered in scrawled almost illegible handwriting, which could only belong to a medical professional. It was a hospital record from four years ago when Joseph Pulaski had suffered his stroke. The admitting nurse had asked Pulaski what medications, if any, he was taking at that time. Pulaski had supplied the names of a dozen medications, but Firmrod was not among them.

"Just another money-grabbing plaintiff who wants our deep-pocket client to pay for his medical bills," said Wayne.

Zeke wasn't so sure about that. He'd learned over the years never to jump to conclusions, and he had his own, very personal reservations about this case. The link between Firmrod and strokes had never been conclusively disproven. The FDA had recalled Firmrod, but opponents argued the drug never should've gone on the market in the first place.

Over the years, Zeke had slowly lost faith in the ability of the FDA to protect the public. A perfect example was Firmrod. The FDA had given this non-life saving drug fast-track approval in just six months, instead of requiring it to go through the more rigorous two-year drug-approval process. Of course, telling a man who can't get an erection that this drug was "non-life saving" would be like trying to convince a heterosexual man that women's breasts had gone out of style.

"Let's see how things go on Friday," Zeke told Wayne.

"You're the boss," said Wayne with a shrug. "I've got one more box of medical records to go through. See you later."

Zeke didn't share this with Wayne or anyone, but he had also lost faith in his client. Years ago, he'd had enormous respect for Xanadu Pharmaceuticals, the oldest and largest drug company in North America, founded in the late nineteenth century by a German immigrant and still headquartered in Oak Park, Illinois. They were one of the good guys. Unlike other drug companies that had been dragged through scandal after scandal, for most of their history Xanadu had stood out as the white knight, the drug manufacturer everyone could trust, famous for inventing medicines to fight Parkinson's disease, HIV, and migraines.

Xanadu had capitalized on their wholesome reputation by creating an unforgettable television commercial Zeke remembered from his college days. The scene opened with Adam and Eve in the Garden of Eden, looking blissful in their idyllic, tropical surroundings. Then, the magnificent resonant voice of James Earl Jones was heard in a voice-over saying: "In Xanadu Pharmaceuticals we trust."

But within the last four years everything had changed. Three of their top-selling drugs had been recalled, including Firmrod. The litigation department at Conley, Dwight & Miller had become one of the busiest in the country. Zeke remembered asking his supervising partner if the recalls would jeopardize the future of Xanadu. He'd looked at Zeke like he was a country bumpkin. "They factor litigation into their manufacturing costs," the partner had said. "They made their money off these drugs long before the recalls. If we do our jobs, Xanadu will be around for another one hundred years and so will our firm."

Zeke picked up the phone and dialed Pulaski's attorney. On all Firmrod cases involving an allegation of stroke, he was authorized to make a maximum settlement offer of $75,000, a small fortune for someone who had worked as a baggage handler at Midway Airport for thirty-five years, as Pulaski had.

"I'll present the offer to him, Zeke," replied Pulaski's attorney, Peter Katzman, "but I doubt he'll take it. He's a crotchety old guy. Last week he told me he wants a quarter of a million dollars."

They hung up, and Zeke realized that he hadn't heard from his mother in two days. He dialed her number.

"How are you doing, Mom?"

"I'm just fine, sweetheart," she said sounding tired. He hoped he hadn't woken her from a nap. "How are your classes?"

A thin stiletto of fear pierced his chest. "What do you mean, Mom?"

"You know, law school."

His throat closed. He mumbled something about everything being fine and promised to visit her soon. That his mother could have Alzheimer's was too horrible to contemplate. He didn't want to picture her slow deterioration, becoming nothing more than a flesh and blood shell, as had happened with his maternal grandmother who had confused Zeke with her deceased son, whenever he had visited her at the nursing home.

He pressed the buzzer on his desk. "Melissa, would you please get Doctor Veda's office on the phone for me. I need to make an appointment for my mother for next week."

"I can make the appointment for you, Mr. Nomad," Melissa replied, "and I was just going to buzz you. Michael Knight is here to see you. And if there's nothing else, I'm going home for the day."

Zeke looked at his watch, only twenty minutes until he met with Elise. He would get rid of Mike as quickly as possible. There was no way he was going to let his friend's drama interfere with the best thing that had happened to him in a long time.

Mike trudged in as though he was dragging a thousand tortured souls behind him. Zeke had found him passed out again that morning, this time on the living room floor. Even during their wildest college binges, he never remembered Mike drinking this much. Mike slumped in the chair and fixed Zeke with a horror flick stare.

"Thanks for showing up last night, buddy."

"Sarcasm is not one of your more attractive qualities," said Zeke.

"And blowing off a friend is not one of yours."

"I was busy."

"You've always got some excuse."

The days when they were best friends, always there for one another, had passed. Where had his fun-loving, smart-assed friend gone?

"Well, was Cybele at Club Caliente?" asked Zeke, hopeful that Mike was here to tell him that he and Cybele were flying back to L.A.

"No," said Mike, "and when I drove out to Charlotte's, she wasn't there either."

"With my car?"

"Don't worry, your fucking Beamer is just fine."

Their friendship, if he could call it that any longer, had deteriorated far more than Zeke realized. He was more worried about his car than this human being, who used to be his best friend. The death of a friendship was sad, but sometimes inevitable. People changed and moved on, but Zeke still felt uneasy.

Mike's head hung like a dead weight attached to his neck. He quickly brushed the back of his hand over his moist eyes. "Cybele never really loved me, she was just using me for her movie career."

"It's about time you figured that out," Zeke wanted to say. Amazing how lust could utterly brainwash a person, until they became convinced that the very person who was wrong for them, was precisely the person they should spend their lives with.

Zeke put a hand on Mike's shoulder. "Come on, go back to the condo and get some more sleep. We'll talk about this later tonight."

Mike got up without protest, but Zeke didn't trust him to go back to the condo on his own. He decided to go downstairs with him to make sure he gave the cabbie his address. The elevator came quickly. Just as Zeke was thinking about how excited he was to see Elise, the elevator lurched and shuddered to a grinding stop between the twelfth and thirteenth floors.

They were stuck.

29

Inez pulled her red 1996 Toyota Celica into the parking spot next to Howard's one-year-old shiny black Mercedes. Rust spots and a large dent in the driver's side door made her car look like a candidate for the junkyard, while Howard's car gleamed in the late afternoon sun like a museum piece. She found the contrast between the two cars comical, but it bothered Howard, who offered to buy her a new car—any make and model she wanted, so frequently, it had become a running joke between them.

In the last six months alone, her car needed a new clutch, brakes, and a radiator, and for the past year, it had been leaking oil like the Exxon Valdez. Howard had reasoned with her that wasting money on repairs, which she could be saving, was foolish. It wasn't that she disagreed with him, but Inez had a special attachment to her car, which she'd bought when she turned twenty-one, with the life insurance money she received from her mother's death. It was silly, she supposed, to be attached to an inanimate object, but that was how she felt. "Never argue with your feelings," Marilynn would say, "they know you better than you know yourself."

But her beloved rust bucket of a car was not her concern at the moment; when she'd left the bridal salon an hour ago, her certainty that canceling the wedding was the right thing to do had lessened with every step. After two years with Howard, Inez wasn't ready to break off their relationship completely. After all, she did love him, and she had invested too much time to end things so suddenly. She just needed some time to think. On the drive to Howard's clinic she'd practiced exactly what she would say to him: "Howard, you know how Marilynn says that signs usually come in threes. Well, I've been bombarded with signs about our wedding. Maybe we should postpone it?"

She steeled herself and walked inside the two-story brick office building surrounded with closely-trimmed evergreen shrubs and perfectly-tended grass. Howard shared the building with three medical doctors, a dentist, a psychiatrist, and a therapist. Another of Howard's favorite jokes was that there were enough degrees in his building to raise the surface temperature of the planet.

Taking the stairs to the second floor, she heard the high-pitched whine of a dental drill. Inez didn't like to disturb Howard at work so she rarely came to his office. Just the fact that she was here would signal a need to talk, rather than a social visit. She came to the heavy wood door with neat gold letters: Howard Suterman, D.P.M., took a breath, and turned the doorknob.

"Why Inez, how nice to see you," said Sarah Conway, Howard's receptionist for the last fifteen years.

Sarah fell somewhere between plump and heavy, but all of her extra weight was perfectly proportioned. In centuries gone by, she would've been considered Rubenesque. She kept her thick chestnut hair shoulder length, but tied back at work, and radiated an interest in people that was evident from her keen memory of the most arcane facts about Howard's patients—like remembering that Mrs. Axford collected antique hatpins, and Mr. Portland's middle daughter was studying political science at Stanford. Inez had always wondered why Sarah was still single at the age of forty.

"You must be so excited about your wedding," said Sarah. "And Maui! What a perfect place for a honeymoon."

Her grin was so infectious, Inez responded with a smile, forgetting for a moment the purpose of her visit.

"Yes, it will be very…nice," said Inez, her smile as false as fool's gold, as the weight of the days ahead—explaining to their friends and relatives what had happened—hit her all at once. She hadn't thought of the million things that would need to be cancelled in the next few days—the caterer, the reception hall, the florist, the honeymoon, the string quartet. Thousands of dollars would be lost. And then there was Howard's mother.

"You're a very lucky woman," said Sarah. "Howard is such a good man."

Inez stopped. Howard was a good man. What was she thinking? Was she potentially losing out on the chance to marry a truly decent, kind man?

"Is Howard free?" asked Inez, feeling as though she might implode if this conversation carried on much longer.

"He's in his office, go right in."

She walked down the hallway convincing herself, once again, that postponing the wedding was the right thing to do. Maybe down the road, in a few months, she would be able to make a definite decision that Howard was the right man for her. She stopped for a moment to look inside the examination room where they'd first met. Inez was amazed, as always, by the delicate threads of life that could lead a person down an utterly unpredictable path, resulting in monumental changes. If she'd never gotten a bunion...

Howard was seated at his desk with his back to her. His starched white shirt collar was turned up at the back of his neck, making her want to reach out and fix it. He was humming a familiar tune she couldn't place. And then she recognized it, The Wedding March. It seemed as if all of the forces of the universe were conspiring against her plan. He was so happy. The last thing she wanted to do was to hurt him.

Howard turned and Inez was in his arms before she could react. He dove for her neck like a seagull swooping at a fish. "Inez, oh my love, you really turn me on," he said, between urgent kisses.

Inez pulled away from Howard and looked into his hazel eyes wide with surprise. He was trying too hard, like he had read these lines in a book and was struggling to copy its practical advice.

"What's wrong, Inez?" he asked. "You're acting so strange."

"I'm acting strange?" Inez exclaimed, her voice rising. "What's going on with you Howard? What is with all the compliments and flowers and the tennis bracelet and the sudden romance?"

"I thought you would like those things," he responded like a child who has just realized his mother didn't like the gift of dandelions he'd given her for her birthday.

"And why haven't you ever gone salsa dancing with me, even once?" Inez blurted, knowing she sounded exactly like the drama queen Rachel had accused her of being. "You know how much I love it. I would think the man who claims to love me would want to share one of my greatest passions in life!"

"I had no idea it was that important to you," said Howard, who took a step back from her. "Yesterday was the first time you'd ever invited me."

"That's because you were always giving me a lecture about how bad it was for my feet."

A silence descended. It might have lasted a moment or a minute, but it was filled with the despair of two people who were supposed to be in love, realizing there might be insurmountable problems.

"Carlos is here."

Howard looked as though he'd been punched. "So, the love of your life has finally reappeared. Perfect timing. What does he want?"

Inez couldn't conceal her surprise. "I've never described him that way."

"You didn't have to, Inez."

It was true she'd never told Howard how she had once felt about Carlos, but it must've been obvious. She felt horrible.

"I'm not going to marry him."

"Is that what he wants?"

She nodded. "I told him this morning to go back to Spain."

"You were with him this morning?"

There was a soft knock at the door.

"Excuse me," said Sarah, "Mrs. Owler is here, Howard."

Howard touched Inez's arm. "Let's talk about this tonight."

"I'm sorry Howard, I…"

"Don't apologize," he said, and gave her arm a quick squeeze.

Inez was left with only with anger at herself for having been so weak.

30

What time is it?" asked Mike.

"Ten minutes after the last time you asked," said Zeke. He stood, stomping on his right foot that had fallen asleep. As the blood rushed back in, hot needles tickled his foot, but he didn't feel like smiling. Other than asking the time, he and Mike hadn't spoken in the two hours since they got stuck. Their only contact from the outside world had been the disembodied voice of the building engineer, who mumbled something about a mechanical failure and had promised to have them out of the elevator an hour ago. Zeke strongly suspected it meant the engineer had no clue what was wrong, and they could very well be trapped for several more hours.

Zeke flipped open his cell phone. Still no signal. He wondered what Elise thought when he hadn't shown up at her office, hoping she was disappointed—at least as disappointed as he was. A sharp pain went through him at the thought that he probably wouldn't see her tonight.

"You're using up all of our air," said Mike. "Sit down."

"And you're stinking it up like a distillery," said Zeke, waving his hand back and forth over his nose. With the air conditioning off, the elevator had grown uncomfortably stuffy. The scotch evaporating from Mike's pores made it worse. And Zeke's mouth was as dry as cotton. He returned to a cross-legged position on the hard floor, across from Mike.

"I should've married Bonnie Marshall," said Mike, apropos of nothing.

"Who?"

"Bonnie, the blonde bombshell from Students for Peace."

"Sorry, I left my Rolodex of your past lovers at home," said Zeke, but his memory automatically scrolled back to their college days. Mike had a reputation as a ladies' man, but was never known as a womanizer. Zeke was never sure how he did it, but after Mike had dumped a woman and moved on to the next, his previous lovers continued to call, flirt, and give him the kind of cutesy gifts that said, "I'm still thinking about you." Mike was naturally charismatic and intelligent, but that had disappeared after Cybele trounced his ego, flattening it like sheet metal.

Zeke should've been jealous of all the attention Mike received. But to Zeke, juggling all of those women was like having a jet-setting job with lucrative stock options—after a few years the stress killed you.

"Bonnie and I dated our second semester of junior year," Mike said, clearly surprised Zeke did not remember her. "We were together five months."

"A record for you."

Mike nodded. "I was really into Bonnie."

Zeke saw a glint in Mike's eyes he hadn't seen in years.

"She was the only woman who ever loved me, for me," said Mike. "She really understood me. And she was gorgeous."

"Now I remember, you dumped her when she wanted you to meet her parents," said Zeke.

Mike stretched out his legs, his knees cracked with two loud pops. "Never should've let that one get away. Do you ever wonder what your life would've been like if you'd done something different?"

"Lately, all the time."

"Like what if I'd gone into teaching and had married Bonnie? I'd probably be living in the suburbs, with two kids and a golden retriever."

"Don't forget the white picket fence."

"It might've been nice. Kind of dull, but nice."

"You were never meant to be a teacher," said Zeke. Mike met his eyes for the first time in days. "You're an incredibly talented writer. You just stopped believing in yourself."

When they were roommates in college and both education majors, Mike was always working on a screenplay—even during finals. Sometimes, he would stay up all night writing because he was so inspired, or driven, or deranged or whatever it was that kept writers going—to finish his story. Zeke knew, even then, that Mike was never going to become a teacher.

"And what about you?" said Mike. "All you ever talked about was the Peace Corps. I never understood why you didn't go."

"I should've gone," said Zeke. He'd given up his dream because of his father. He remembered the dinner at his parents' home, during his sophomore year of college, when he told them about his plans to apply for the Peace Corps.

He pictured his father's face, his lined forehead sloping to a nose that was too thin for his wide Slavic features. On an angled, high cheek-boned face, his nose would've been perfect, but it looked out of place on him—like a lumberjack wearing an ascot. His father was of medium build, but with forty hours of physical labor a week, his body was a solid mass of muscle.

"I want to go somewhere where I can learn Spanish and really make a difference," Zeke had announced, plunging forward despite his trepidation at his father's response. His father had raised one eye from his plate and fixed it on his son like a laser.

"It's only for two years," Zeke had continued, afraid to stop talking before he'd made his case. "I want to go to Central or South America. And then, when I come back, I'll go to law school."

For several moments his father remained silent, but then the eye of the storm quickly passed.

"Where the hell did you come up with such a crazy idea?" his father exploded, the veins in his forehead bulging in fury. "Why do you want to run off to some jungle?"

"I can't explain it, Dad. I just know I have to do this," Zeke replied, knowing this justification was mumbo jumbo to his father.

"I'm worried that if I go to law school first, I'll never get to do this."

"You've got what I never got, an education. This is your chance to make somethin' of yourself."

"I'm not giving up on law school," Zeke said, "just delaying it for a while."

"What I know is hard work," his father said as if Zeke weren't there. "You get a good job, pay your bills, save your money, and keep your nose clean."

"And then what?" Zeke remembered wondering. Live for the weekends? For a couple of weeks of vacation each year? For retirement? The only vacation they'd ever taken together as a family was a five-day trip to the Wisconsin Dells. Other than bowling and refurbishing the Airstream trailer sitting in their backyard, waiting until his father's retirement for the trip across America his parents had been planning for years, his father never did anything on the weekends except read the paper, watch TV, and sleep.

"Making money isn't everything," Zeke had said to him.

"You want to struggle your whole life like me?" his father snapped, "be poor as a church mouse?"

"Dad, the Peace Corps is something I need to do. I'd really like your blessing."

"You're a grown man, son," his father said. "You can make your own life, but you won't get my blessing. Not for somethin' this foolish."

Defying his father, Zeke applied for the Peace Corps a year later, receiving his acceptance letter to Costa Rica just before his father's retirement party. But at that party, his father announced to everyone that Zeke was not only graduating with honors from Northwestern, but was going to law school that fall at the University of Chicago. The tears in his father's eyes as he'd made the announcement shocked Zeke. His father had never been able to tell him to his face how proud he was of his accomplishments.

For the next month, Zeke tried to work up the courage to tell his father he intended to go to Costa Rica and defer his law school acceptance. But just a few days before his parents were to leave on their cross-country trip, his father died of a heart attack. The day of his funeral, Zeke ripped up his Peace Corps acceptance letter.

"Face it, Mr. Corporate Attorney, you sold out." Mike said, shaking his head. "We both sold out. We were going to save the world, remember?"

For a moment, Zeke was back on campus. It was January, and the wind chill had fallen to ten below zero. He and Mike had stood outside for hours asking students to sign a petition to be sent to the Chicago Mayor's office to allocate money in the city's budget for the homeless. Zeke was oblivious to the cold, thinking only of the people who lived on the streets and had no homes.

"We swore we'd never become part of the establishment," said Mike, "part of them."

"Now we are them," said Zeke remembering feeling as though he was really making a difference in college. He hadn't felt that way in a very long time.

"Hey," said Mike, "'Them' would make a good title for a horror movie."

"No wonder you haven't written a decent screenplay since Daunted," said Zeke with a smile. "Besides, I think that one is already taken."

He and Mike hadn't really talked like this since he married Cybele. Zeke missed their friendship, but something stopped him from telling Mike. Was he getting emotional or simply drunk on the fumes from Mike's horrid breath?

"I found out I've only got a fifty-fifty chance of making partner," said Zeke. "If I don't make it on Friday, I've wasted eight years of my life."

"Not a total waste," said Mike. "You paid off your mother's house and bought yourself a nice condo."

"I don't know what happened," said Zeke. "I was only going to stay here for a few years. I was supposed to be married and have a family by now."

"So get married," said Mike. "Chicago is full of women."

Inez appeared in Zeke's mind. Seeing her again at the "L" station yesterday had to mean something. But he'd only spent an hour with her, and it was such a long time ago. People changed. Elise Wyatt was right here—so intelligent, so beautiful, and so real.

"I intend to change that," said Zeke, "there is someone."

"Good. Have you two done the nasty…?"

"Not yet."

"What the hell are you waiting for?"

"Just getting out of this box, buddy."

A surge of positive feelings swept through Zeke. He would ask Elise out on a real date, not one of those grab-dinner-and-go-back-to-work substitutes. He was tired of playing it safe. Enough of sticking his toe in the water to test the temperature, it was time to dive in.

31

Inez could not stop picturing the pain on Howard's face that afternoon. Up until the past six months or so, their relationship had flowed like molasses, sweet and slow, with no surprises. There had been no flies in the ointment either. When they'd first started dating, Inez went through something like withdrawal as she waited for Howard to stand her up with some transparent excuse or do something insensitive to make her angry. She held her breath for months, expecting their first argument with every plan they made. Slowly, it dawned on her how dysfunctional her prior relationships had been—filled with broken promises and cheating. Inez had put up with it, convincing herself for years that she didn't want anything more. But with Howard, she'd come to realize that she had only hurt herself by allowing her salsa boyfriends to treat her so poorly.

In many ways, Howard had been a revelation to her—a man who was kind, caring and a great listener. Well, at least he used to be. Early on in their relationship he was interested in everything she had to say. "Tell me more," he would say to her after she'd finished a story about her kids at school, or living in Madrid, or stories from her childhood in Milwaukee. They rarely ran out of things to talk about and had interesting discussions about art, politics, books, and the quirks of people they knew. Howard loved telling her stories about his patients and the doctors in his building. Like Dr. Spear, a psychologist who specialized in couples counseling. What most of his patients didn't know was that he'd been divorced six times and was about to marry lucky number seven. Then there was Mrs. Frankl, a seventy-eight-year-old widow and hypochondriac who came to see Howard with the regularity of the New Moon, each time with a new imagined foot ailment. Howard's receptionist Sarah was convinced that Mrs. Frankl was secretly in love with Howard.

Whenever the thought arose that something might be missing with Howard, Inez dismissed it and congratulated herself for breaking her bad-boy streak. It hadn't occurred to Inez, until recently, that a hybrid might exist—a man who treated her as well as Howard, but also provided the passion and excitement of Carlos.

A knock at her apartment door startled her out of her thoughts. Speaking of bad boys she thought, as she looked through the peephole.

"Go away!"

"You can't avoid me forever, *querida*," said Carlos.

She had to end this now. She opened the door and he held out a bouquet of deep purple irises. Her favorite flowers always made her happy, but now she couldn't stand the sight of them. She crossed her arms.

"I'd like to take you dinner," he said.

"I am getting married on Saturday. It is over between us."

"You can't love him because you're still in love with me."

Inez was disgusted by his utter arrogance, but irritatingly drawn to him at the same time. Like a conditioned reflex, her heart drummed, her saliva disappeared, and the faucet in her loins automatically switched to the on position.

"You're really getting annoying," she said, moving to the opposite side of the living room.

"I never annoyed you when we were together," he said. "This must be some proof that I've changed."

"I've changed," she said. "I'm not the blind girl I was in Madrid who overlooked all of your faults."

"And I'm no longer the self-centered man who is afraid of commitment."

She didn't want to ask the questions that had been swirling around in her mind since he'd shown up two days ago. Asking questions would lead to getting answers. And that might lead to things she did not want to think about. But the first question burst out of her before she could stop herself.

"How did you know I wasn't married?" Inez asked.

He shrugged. "I didn't. I knew I had to come, no matter what. You might say I was compelled to come. I wanted to apologize for leaving things the way I did. You deserved better."

"But why now?" she asked, but was really thinking: "Why this week of all weeks."

"The realization of one's own mortality is a profound…"

Neither of them had moved from their spots a dozen feet away from one another, but she could feel him as clearly as though he was caressing her face.

"Cut the bullshit, Carlos!"

He looked mildly surprised and then amused. "I don't know. I just had a very strong feeling I should come to see you now, instead of waiting until next month, as I had originally planned."

She'd never heard him talk this way before. She'd told him about Marilynn's New Age philosophies, but he'd never expressed an opinion about them. Through trial and error Inez had learned to trust her intuition over the years—not that she always followed it. But Carlos had always put more trust in another part of his anatomy.

"Why did you leave me? Who was she?"

"Do you want the truth?"

She nodded; her heart and stomach flipped in anticipation of his answer.

"There was no one else. I got scared. I had promised you so many times that we would get married, I knew I had to follow through. I wasn't ready, and it wasn't fair to make you wait any longer."

"You expect me to believe you had my welfare at heart? That's why you moved out without a word?"

"It was part of the reason. I do love you, Inez, I always have."

"Did you ever cheat on me?"

"Never," he replied in firm voice meeting her eyes with no hesitation.

It was impossible to see truth in them. In fact, there was nothing there but a dark void. If she ever had the courage to enter it, Inez would no doubt find a maze of passageways with locked rooms holding more secrets. She broke off their gaze.

"There is something I haven't told you," Carlos said.

There were no doubt a million things he hadn't told her.

"My father died last month."

That explained the Ferrari. Carlos, an only child, was now a multi-millionaire. His father had been a shipping tycoon.

"He died a lonely man," Carlos said, "I don't want to end up like him."

And then Carlos did something she'd never seen him do before, something she thought he was incapable of doing. He began to cry. He covered his face with his free hand. She couldn't hear anything, but his shoulders shook. She'd built up so much distrust for this man over the years, her first thought was that he was putting on an act.

"I'm sorry," he said a minute later, wiping away what were no doubt crocodile tears. "You know how much my father meant to me."

A memory of his father flashed in her mind—very distinguished, very charming, and very much a womanizer. Every time they'd had dinner with him, he was with a different woman, usually two decades younger. An older, wiser Inez would've seen a disturbing pattern and have been very concerned about how much Carlos always tried to emulate him.

"I'm ready to be a father and a husband. Inez, you are the only woman I want. Marry me."

"Trust is the most important thing in a marriage," said Inez. "Without that there is nothing. I could never trust you again."

"Just before my mother died, she asked me to promise her that I would marry a good woman and be faithful to her. I made that promise, and I intend to keep it. I'm not my father, Inez."

211

"Promises can be broken."

His black eyes narrowed dangerously. "Not to my mother."

It was so hot in her apartment, Inez's forehead beaded in perspiration. She walked to the open door and waved toward it, avoiding looking at him. But the sexual pull between them was so strong, it had changed the air in the room.

"I never want to see you again. Go!"

For a moment, nothing happened. But then, she saw his hand with her peripheral vision and then felt his touch when he wiped a bead of sweat from her forehead with his index finger and then put it in his mouth, sucking hard. She met his eyes. He dropped the flowers. As he leaned in to kiss her, she knew she should stop this, but she couldn't move. Just before his mouth reached hers, she heard a movement behind her. She turned her face away and was greeted by an beatific vision. Standing in the doorway was a bald woman dressed in white flowing robes to her ankles. Her feet were clad in simple leather sandals and dozens of thin silver bracelets jangled softly on her thick wrists. Her beautiful, unlined face glowed from within.

"Well," said Marilynn, "I got here just in time."

I want you to know, Herodius that I'm only here because I've been ordered to work with you.

Serena, I am so happy you changed your mind and have come back to help me.

You got a screw lose or something, H? I'm here under duress. I reported you because I don't like your methods, but the higher-ups say I should trust you, that you're the Miracle Maker; that you know what you're doing, blah, blah, blah.

Free will is a universal principle. You cannot fool me. I know you chose to return here, Serena.

Okay, you're right, but I only did it for Zeke and Inez. I can't abandon them, and I see things have only gotten worse.

At least Carlos has good taste, Irises are my favorite. There is nothing more beautiful than a mountain meadow blanketed with Arctic Irises in the springtime.

Will you stop with the flowers already! This is serious, Inez is falling for Carlos.

Yes, she is.

And Zeke is getting all gooey-eyed over Elise. Nice girl and all, but she's the wrong nice girl.

Also true.

Wait a minute; I think I see your plan, but it could easily backfire.

That is a risk we must take, wouldn't you agree, Serena?

There must be a better way, but at the moment I can't think of a thing. So maybe my elevator move wasn't such a good idea after all?

That is correct. Finally, Serena, you are beginning to understand that these temporary diversions will not magically bring Zeke and Inez together. We must focus on their hearts, or nothing will change.

Now don't insult me, H. You are speaking to an internationally acclaimed romance novelist. I'm an expert in this field. All I think about are people's hearts!

I know Serena, which is why I would like to work with you.

You would?

Yes. Do you think we can coordinate our efforts?

Well, I suppose; but no more tweaking unless you run it by me first.

I would appreciate the same courtesy.

Agreed. Now, what's our plan?

32

Most boys dream about becoming astronauts or explorers or professional baseball players when they grow up, but ever since he could remember, Howard Suterman had wanted to become a podiatrist. One might say he was called to his career, which he chose after his grandmother had foot surgery to remove a ganglion cyst that had been pressing on a nerve. It seemed a miracle to ten-year-old Howard that just weeks after her surgery she was walking normally again, without any pain. He'd decided that he too would perform such miracles someday.

The fact that some people found amusement in his profession had always bothered him. But people who didn't respect podiatry medicine wouldn't be laughing if they suffered from a bunion or a corn—humorous-sounding conditions capable of causing crippling pain.

For years he'd heard the taunts that he wasn't a "real" doctor because he'd attended the Dr. William M. Scholl College of Podiatric Medicine instead of a "real" medical school. But he had to study for three years to get his degree followed by a one-year surgical residence—nearly as much study as an M.D. And, it took serious dedication to memorize the thirty-eight bones in the foot, connected by an intricate web of muscles, tendons, ligaments, and joints. The foot was one of the most complex parts of the body. Why didn't more people realize that?

Over the years, Howard had learned to ignore the negativity by heading it off with his own humor and focusing on the fact that he'd helped thousands of people over the years, young and old. But it was his elderly patients he took a particular interest in. So many of them lived alone, spending their time watching television or being shuffled off to bingo games or the other empty activities organized to fill up endless days at their assisted living centers and nursing homes. What could be more honorable than alleviating the suffering of these dear souls?

He took pride in giving the best care possible to his patients, but today, he had been barely able to concentrate on Mrs. Owler's hammertoes and gout. In fact, he was having problems keeping a grip on his steering wheel. His shaking hands were wet with sweat. As was normal at this time of the day, the Eden's expressway was a parking lot. Speed up. Stop. Speed up. Stop. He tried to concentrate on his driving, but his thoughts were consumed with Inez.

Howard never imagined he could get a woman as incredible as Inez. Not only was she beautiful and intelligent, but she touched his heart in places that his first wife, Mary, could not. He had thought his heart was permanently scarred through disinterest and ridicule. He had no illusions about himself. He was a middle-aged foot doctor who liked the finer things in life—the opera, symphony, ballet, dinners at nice restaurants, and quiet evenings at home with a good book. Their relationship might not be passionate or exciting, but Howard didn't believe that was a necessary requirement for a good relationship. Theirs was a bond of calm peacefulness, companionship, mutual respect, and shared interests. And that was enough for him.

But recently, he'd come to suspect that perhaps it was not enough for Inez. When they first started dated, Inez told him about her relationship with Carlos and their constant arguments. He couldn't understand how such tumult could be pleasant or appealing to anyone. But it was obvious Inez had loved Carlos deeply and very differently than the way she loved him.

And now their relationship was in trouble. A deep pain churned in his stomach. He'd never seen Inez act the way she had today. He'd known for months that things were not quite right between the two of them, and worse, it was his fault. He just couldn't concentrate when she was talking sometimes. It wasn't that he didn't want to listen to her, but lately everything was disjointed and out of sync between the two of them.

Several months ago, Howard set out to improve their relationship, but figuring out the mysteries of romance and the opposite sex had always been daunting for him. In frustration, he'd turned to his receptionist, Sarah Conway. Sarah was such a good listener and so helpful. Months ago she brought Romance for Dummies to the office for him, but he hadn't taken the time to read it until last week. He was trying his best to implement suggestions from the book, but his efforts had backfired. In retrospect, he supposed that bombarding Inez all at once, was not a wise plan.

Just then, a car cut in front of Howard. He slammed on his brakes, just missing the other driver's fender by the width of an Achilles tendon. His heart raced as adrenaline flooded his system. The other driver whipped him the finger, but Howard did nothing in response. His heartbeats slowed to normal.

When he finished with Mrs. Owler today, he wanted to tell Sarah about his argument with Inez, but she'd already left for the day. He couldn't tell his mother about it because he knew what she would say. "I told you that girl is too wild for you, Howard." His mother was being sweet to Inez this week, but whenever she wasn't around his mother pestered him, continually asking him if he was certain that marrying her was the right thing to do.

Howard knew part of it was jealousy. His mother was angry and hurt because after he met Inez, he stopped seeking her guidance for the first time in his life. He used to talk to his mother on the phone almost every day asking for her opinion on everything from what type of blender to buy to which stocks he should invest in. "Mama's boy," that was what his first wife, Mary, had called him, every time he picked up the phone to call his mother.

The cell phone on the passenger seat chimed with the opening notes of the Pachelbel Canon in D. "Speak of the devil," said Howard. He let it go to voice mail; he couldn't talk to his mother now.

Howard would never forget the first time he saw Inez in his office on the examination table, wearing faded jeans and a royal blue silk blouse that set off her gorgeous auburn hair. He'd never been the type to be smitten by looks and did not believe in love at first sight, but there was something about Inez, some indescribable quality that made it difficult for him to maintain his usual professional demeanor. When he held her foot in his hands, he was scarcely able to find the words to tell her how bunions were formed let alone give his recommendation on surgery.

A few days after the surgery he'd surprised himself by going to her apartment. Inez had inspired him to be bold for the first time in his life. He was so nervous he'd tripped over the ottoman, making a fool out of himself. It had taken all of his courage to call her up several months later, after their professional relationship had ended, and ask her out.

He glanced in the rearview mirror displeased with his reflection. He was divorced, almost fifty, and had no children. He didn't even own a plant. Losing Inez would be like losing everything. He couldn't let that happen. He would plan something else to please her. A surprise. According to Romance for Dummies, women loved surprises.

He would make things right with Inez, somehow, someway.

33

Zeke tried not to stare at Elise Wyatt, but he found himself helplessly drawn to her. The candlelight from the centerpiece on their table danced across her face, enhancing her delicate features into an enticing mix of sensuality and beauty.

"Do you often stand up dates on the flimsy pretense of getting stuck in an elevator?" Elise asked, and then bent her head to take a sip of her margarita.

Zeke watched as she wrapped her kissable lips around the straw and found himself envying the straw.

"Any man who would do such a dastardly deed should be tarred and feathered," replied Zeke.

"Drawn and quartered."

"Shot at dawn without a last wish."

They locked eyes. He wanted their banter to last forever. He wanted to whisk her away to some tropical locale for adventure and romance. He wanted her to be the one.

"You must've thought the worst when I didn't show up at your office at six," said Zeke.

Zeke and Mike were rescued from their stuffy prison by the fire department finally, after three hours. Zeke went straight to her office, relieved to see Elise was still at work. She quickly agreed to have a drink with him at Rico's Restaurante.

"I assumed you had a good excuse," she said with a smile. "I can tell you're not the kind of man to break promises."

A well of happiness filled his chest. It had been so long since a woman he liked had shown the same amount of interest in him. He often wondered why it was so easy for some people, the ones who partnered up in their twenties with little more effort than falling into bed together, when it had been so difficult for him to find that elusive chemistry with a woman, with just the right combination of personality quirks, shared values, mutual respect, and attraction, as well as the right timing.

"I usually don't go out on weeknights," said Elise. "Especially since I have an early breakfast meeting with my friend tomorrow, the one who has the plan for the chocolate shops I mentioned the other day."

"Good luck with that, Elise," said Zeke. Never before in his career had Zeke had a meal—or even a snack—with a prospective client. Elise deserved this partnership. Actually, they both deserved it; the circumstances couldn't be more unfair this year.

"These margaritas are fantastic," Elise said, "is there a secret ingredient?"

Zeke had been trying to pry it out of the bartender for years, but Fernando kept it guarded like a password to his bank account.

"If I told you I'd have to kill you," said Zeke, with a wink, "and believe me that is the last thing I'd like to do."

Her left hand was on the table. He ached to reach for it but feared he might scare her off. With Pamela, he hadn't thought twice about getting physically involved. But with Elise there was real potential. He didn't want to blow it by moving too quickly.

"So where did we leave off at dinner yesterday? Oh yes, we are running away together."

"To Cuba and South America," she agreed, with a nod.

"We've got to try salsa dancing in Havana."

"Oh no, I'm a terrible dancer."

"I don't believe you," Zeke replied quickly, trying to ignore the instant disappointment he felt.

"I'm serious," she said, fixing him with a lawyerly gaze like the one he used while deposing witnesses. "I once maimed someone while dancing."

"This is a story I've got to hear."

"It was at my sister's wedding. I was dancing with this guy at the end of the night. He wasn't wearing shoes. I'd warned him but he spun me four times. I lost my balance and my three inch spike heel went into the top of his foot."

"Ouch."

"Three broken bones."

"So dancing may not be your thing," said Zeke. "What is besides surfing and film-making?"

"Oh no, it's my turn to find out about you, Mr. Nomad. I'm curious, where did this wanderlust of yours spring from?"

Zeke's parents had never left the Midwest so his love of travel didn't come from them. But he remembered clearly when Raiders of the Lost Ark came to the theatres when he was eleven. His father had taken him to see the movie as a special treat for his birthday. After that, his focus instantly changed from sports to becoming an explorer.

"I guess you could say I was kind of a nerd as a kid," Zeke said. "I'd go to the library everyday and get new travel books and read National Geographic magazines cover to cover."

Zeke the Geek. That was his nickname in junior high and high school when he'd immersed himself in books, in particular, stories of brave explorers who had taken Zeke on adventures that his buddies, who were into softball and girls, couldn't have imagined. Mrs. Kohl, the ancient librarian, was more than happy to help Zeke dig out dozens of musty, dust-covered books about Panama, Columbia, Peru, Mongolia, and the other countries he planned to explore one day.

"I was kind of a nerd myself," said Elise.

"I find that impossible to believe."

"No, really, my sister used to make fun of me because I've always loved aquariums. I had one when I was a kid and would spend hours watching my fish."

Zeke had forgotten what it was like to be with a woman he could really talk to. Susan had practiced more subtle manipulation, than ever really listening to him. In retrospect, it was easy to pinpoint the day he should've ended that relationship. It was during their final year of law school when Zeke learned he'd gotten his dream job at the

Legal Assistance Foundation. Zeke remembered rushing home to tell her, assuming she would be as thrilled as he was.

"What does the job pay?" was Susan's response.

"It doesn't matter," he'd said to her. "And you know what these public interest jobs pay."

"It does matter, Zeke. If I get the clerking job I want, we won't have any money."

"We'll manage."

She'd put her arms around him. "Honey," she cooed, "with your grades you'd have no problem getting a job at a big firm. Why don't you interview with a few, just for practice?"

"That's not me. I would never be happy at some big law firm."

She'd removed her arms from him, and switched tactics like a martial arts expert going from Karate to a left hook.

"It's your upbringing Zeke, isn't it?"

"What's that supposed to mean?"

"You know what I mean. You grew up poor so you have this guilt complex about making money."

He remembered feeling betrayed. Susan was the first girlfriend he had let into his life so completely—including sharing his guilt over being embarrassed by his uneducated parents.

"Thanks for the psychoanalysis, Susan, but this has nothing to do with money, it's about wanting my life to stand for something."

"Honey, I thought you loved me," she whined in her little girl voice that she always used to go in for the kill. "Do it for our future."

The next day, he'd signed up for campus interviews with five big firms, including Conley, Dwight & Miller. Having been raised in a very traditional family—where the man was the breadwinner with a moral obligation to support his wife—had, no doubt, played a big part in his fateful decision.

Zeke noticed Elise staring at him intently.

"You're a million miles away," said Elise.

"Actually, not that far," said Zeke who started telling Elise about growing up in Bellwood and his father's death after working his whole life at the steel mill. If it wasn't for his high school social studies teacher, Mr. Holden, who had encouraged Zeke to go out for the debate team and apply for college scholarships, he might never have gotten out of Bellwood.

"I told my parents I was going to college instead of the other way around," Zeke said, remembering his astonishment at being awarded a full scholarship including room and board to Northwestern University.

"Your parents must have been so proud of you, Zeke," she said, touching the top of his hand which shot a spark through his body.

"You're the first person at work I've ever told about my family and where I grew up."

"That means a lot to me."

My mother will love her. Just as soon as Zeke straightened out her health issue, he would take Elise to meet her.

"You know," Zeke said, "after Friday, one way or another, we won't be working together. But I want to see you again, whatever happens."

"Good. Me too."

34

"Y ou didn't recognize me."

"Well, you do look a little…" Inez broke off, not wishing to hurt Marilynn's feelings although this was unlikely. Other people's opinions had never mattered much to her.

"Crazy? Weird? Gone off the deep end?" suggested Marilynn, with a laugh that filled her whole body. "Go ahead, say it."

"Um, different," said Inez, who was thinking exactly along those lines. Three years ago at O'Hare airport when she'd seen Marilynn off to India, they'd shared the same outrageously curly auburn shoulder-length hair, although Marilynn had streaks of gray woven through hers, which she refused to disguise with dye. Her now gleaming bald head would take some getting used to.

A hint of Carlos's sandalwood-scented cologne still hung in the air, all that was left after his abrupt departure upon Marilynn's arrival. Marilynn dropped her canvas duffle bag on the floor, plopped down on the futon, and bent over to remove her leather sandals. She rubbed her bare feet.

"You're staring at my head, Inez," said Marilynn, as she plunked her feet on the coffee table with a thud. "You've seen women with shaved heads before, haven't you? There's that actress who never seems to age, what's her name?"

"Demi Moore," mumbled Inez, "but…"

"But what?"

"Your beautiful hair!" Inez unconsciously twirled a finger through the ends of her reddish-brown locks. She mourned the loss of every centimeter whenever she went to the hairdresser for a trim.

Marilynn flipped her hand in the air as if losing her gorgeous mane that had taken decades to grow could be replaced in the wink of an eye.

"Lice," said Marilynn. "Nasty little devils. I didn't have a choice; I had to shave everything. " She waggled her eyebrows.

Inez burst out laughing. She'd forgotten how much fun it was to be around the woman she thought of as a second mother.

"You have more questions, I see. Go ahead, ask."

"Are you a Hare Krishna?" Inez blurted, and then remembered she could speak freely with Marilynn about anything.

"I was studying with them for a while," said Marilynn. "Beautiful people, very peaceful, and I agree with many of their philosophies. But they're just a little too out there for me."

Too out there for Marilynn must be some distant, as yet undiscovered galaxy. Marilynn always seemed larger than life and so different from anyone Inez had ever met. Growing up as a teenager, Inez decided she wanted to be exactly like Marilynn— adventurous and absolutely oblivious to society's mores. Inez was startled to see how conservative her lifestyle and aspirations had become.

"So why are you dressed that way?" Inez asked, looking at her white robes.

"All of my luggage was stolen the night before I left India," Marilynn replied. "I left the Krishnas six months ago, but I kept the robes to sleep in. They're super comfy. This was the only thing I had left to wear on the plane."

Inez, overwhelmed with happiness that Marilynn was back, was frozen to her spot by the door, afraid if she moved that she would discover this was only a dream.

Beso sauntered in and began rubbing up against the futon and purring loudly. Marilynn picked him and put him on her ample lap. Beso's purring sounded like a buzz saw.

"I've always loved this cat," said Marilynn stroking his fur. Marilynn leaned her head, as smooth as an egg, back onto the cushion.

She hadn't aged at all. If anything, her face looked younger. Inez couldn't see a single wrinkle and wondered how that could be? Marilynn had turned seventy-three on her last birthday in India.

"So what's going on with you, honey?" asked Marilynn. "You look like you've been dragged through a mine field."

"You could say that."

"Well, I'm back for good. We've got plenty of time to catch up."

"Not really," said Inez, as she held out her left hand. "The wedding is on Saturday, and I don't know anymore if I want to get married." There, she'd actually said the words out loud, and the universe had not imploded. Inez noted that Marilynn did not look surprised, and then she remembered the postcard.

"I got your postcard yesterday, and you're already here."

"Sweetheart, didn't you look at the postmark? I sent that four months ago."

Inez went to her kitchenette, took the postcard off her refrigerator and returned to the living room. The postmark was so smudged, it was illegible. She reread the message aloud: "*Remember, marriage is like a dance, make sure you pick the right partner.*"

"But how did you know?" Inez asked. "The message is so perfect, the timing so uncanny, how…?"

"Inez, there is an entire universe out there that your average Westerner knows nothing about. I've learned things that would curl the Pope's toes," said Marilynn, who let out a hoot. Marilynn patted the empty spot beside her on the futon. Inez plopped down next to her.

"You've been gone for so long without a word except a couple of phone calls and a few postcards," Inez said. "Why did you come back now?"

"I had to come back," said Marilynn, "to warn you."

Her words sounded ominous. Inez thought again of Howard's sad face that afternoon when they'd said good-bye. "I think ending it might be the right thing, but I just don't know if I can do it."

"You are so much stronger than you give yourself credit for, honey."

"But I don't want to hurt him."

"Well, he'll be in pain for a while, and what man wouldn't be losing you?" said Marilynn. She stroked Inez's hair, just like when she was a young girl. Inez snuggled closer to her.

"But it's better than being with someone who's wrong for you."

"So you knew about Howard. But how is that possible?"

"Who's Howard?"

Inez pulled away from Marilynn with undisguised shock. "My fiancé."

"Oh," Marilynn said, with a flip of her hand. "I sent that postcard because of Carlos. He wants to marry you, right?"

"Yes," said Inez, "but how could you know Carlos was coming back?"

"Carlos was always coming back," said Marilynn. "The two of you have unfinished business. And, I had your astrology chart done in India. This is your critical week."

That was the understatement of the year. Marilynn had always known things normal people couldn't possibly know. When Inez was fourteen and came home from school two hours late, she lied to Marilynn saying she'd been at the library. But Marilynn said she knew that Inez was with her friends at the shopping mall, which was true. Inez had been more ashamed than astounded. Like many children, Inez didn't question Marilynn's mysterious ability to see things. But adulthood had changed Inez.

"Carlos sure skedaddled out of here in a hurry," said Marilynn. The moment Marilynn appeared, Carlos left without an excuse and barely a good-bye.

"I think he's afraid of you." Inez giggled thinking that Marilynn must be one of the only women on the planet to hold such a coveted position. Then she grew serious again. "He says he's changed, but I don't believe him. But…well, he's being so persistent."

"There are lessons you need to learn in this lifetime, and only you can decide what is right for you," said Marilynn. "But if you were to ask me, I'd tell you that marrying Carlos would be a disaster."

"How do you know?" asked Inez. "You only met him once, well twice if you count tonight."

The first time Marilynn met Carlos was in Spain. Within two weeks of her graduation from the University of Illinois, Inez was back in Madrid, living with Carlos. Six months later, Marilynn came to visit Inez for a week. The two of them went out for tapas and sangria one night without him.

"Honey, your man is beautiful," Marilynn had said. "I don't know how you drag yourself away from that body in the mornings. But Inez honey, mark my words, that man will cause you nothing but misery."

Of course, Inez had ignored Marilynn's advice. Twenty-two at the time, Inez was certain she knew what was best for her. The next two years she'd spent in Madrid with Carlos were amazing, at least in her memories. Inez ignored the nagging feeling that she'd suppressed the unpleasant memories.

"Have you heard of Vedic Astrology?" asked Marilynn.

"You mean like my horoscope?"

"Not really, I won't go in to a long explanation, but I had your chart done four months ago by the best Vedic Astrologer in the world. Think of it as a kind of forecasting system for avoiding future problems."

"That's when you sent the postcard."

"Right. But I knew it wouldn't be enough so here I am in the flesh. All one hundred ninety-two pounds of me."

Marilynn looked to be about thirty pounds thinner than when she'd left, but she was always been the kind of person who never looked fat, no matter how much she weighed.

"So some guy I never met on the other side of the planet thinks I'll be unhappy if I end up with a man he's also never met?" said Inez, her doubt obvious.

"It's a little more complicated than that, but yes, that's the gist of it."

"You want me to believe all this?"

"You need to decide for yourself what to believe."

Inez leaned on Marilynn's shoulder that was big enough to double as a pillow.

"So nothing about Howard from your Indian swami?" Inez

asked, wishing she could regress to her childhood when most decisions were made for her. "Yesterday I was certain that cancelling the wedding was the right thing, but now I'm not so certain."

"We could go see a Vedic astrologer here in Chicago to ask about Howard," Marilynn suggested, "but the decision is really simple, you just need to choose love over fear."

"I do love Howard."

"Do you?" asked Marilynn gently, "or are you running away from your fears of being alone and not having children?"

"I'm so exhausted; can we talk about this tomorrow?"

"Sure thing."

Inez pulled Marilynn into a tight hug. "I'm so happy you're back. I missed you so much."

"I missed you too, honey."

Thursday

35

Except for the radio playing at the security guard's desk, Zeke's office building was dim and eerily quiet. He was not normally an early riser. Getting up to an alarm had always felt like an assault to Zeke's system. An hour ago when the buzzer had sounded—as though a battalion of soldiers had invaded his bedroom—Zeke practically had gone into cardiac arrest. But he had to set his alarm to buzzer-mode because music, the sounds of the ocean, or a radio announcer's voice never woke him. If Zeke could live his ideal life, he would never wake to an alarm again and sleep until noon.

"Good morning," said the security guard, pushing forward a register book for Zeke to sign. "You lawyers sure must love your jobs to work such long hours."

Zeke wasn't sure why he was compelled to rush back to a job he might not have in twenty-four hours. But winging it, the few times he'd done it, had always made him feel uncomfortable. He wanted to be as prepared for tomorrow's deposition, just as he had for all of the others he'd handled—especially since it could be his last.

As much as he tried to resign himself to the fact that he might be forced to leave his job, he couldn't do it. The truth was he wanted to make partner. He wanted, no he needed some justification for working so damned hard over the last eight years, and when he left the firm, he wanted it to be on his terms.

"I've got two months, twenty-one days, and one hour to retirement," said the security guard, whose nametag read Frank. "Been looking forward to it for almost thirty years."

"Good for you, Frank," said Zeke, as he signed the register.

Frank had to be close to sixty-five if he was about to retire, but his blotchy red face and bulbous nose didn't match his full head of slick, jet-black hair that looked suspiciously like a toupee. Frank leaned forward to turn down the volume on the sleek silver radio on his desk, giving Zeke a view of the top of his head. Yup, thought Zeke, definitely a rug.

"I hope you don't think this is too personal," said Frank, "but I've seen your name on the building employee list for years and have always wondered what nationality Nomad is?"

Zeke had heard comments about his unusual name his entire life. Usually, it was a positive comment on its uniqueness and then the subject was dropped. But the bored security guard clearly wanted an explanation.

"My mother was a Madicksky and my father's name was Noman," Zeke explained. He'd often found humor in the fact that two people with the most unfortunate surnames imaginable, had met and fallen in love. "When they got married, they'd decided to combine their names and came up with Nomad."

"Middle name?" asked Frank.

Zeke shook his head. For his Catholic confirmation he'd chosen the name Elmo, not because Saint Elmo had meant anything to Zeke, but for one reason only—he thought it would be cool for his initials to be ZEN. In law school, he considered legally changing his name to add Elmo, but had never followed through.

"Is Zeke short for Ezekiel or is Zeke your real name?" Frank persisted, with his interrogation.

"Zeke is my real name."

"Really? It's pretty unusual to give a child a nickname…"

Zeke, losing his patience with nosy, opinionated Frank, cut him off. "My parents are international trend setters who've never followed the crowd."

Frank was just about to say something when Zeke claimed he had an early morning meeting. Stepping onto the elevator brought back everything from last night. Would the gears grind to a halt? Would he be stuck for another three interminable hours? But the elevator sailed smoothly to Elise's floor, gliding to a perfect stop, the doors opening as usual.

His pace quickened as he approached her office, but then he remembered she was at her breakfast meeting. Her office was the same size as his, but on the opposite side of the building with a far less appealing view of the southwest Loop. Other than a globe-shaped paperweight and three framed photographs, her office looked as though it had never been occupied. Zeke didn't want to snoop, but he bent down to study the pictures, which might provide another window into her life.

A younger Elise was leaning her head against an older woman's shoulder. Their smiles and perfectly straight noses were identical, but other than that they were opposites—Elise blonde and fair while the other woman was olive-skinned with dark chestnut hair. In a second photo, Elise had her arms wrapped around a mammoth-sized black, curly-haired dog in front of a Christmas tree so perfectly decorated with red bows and royal blue ornaments, it might have been plucked from a magazine and set down behind her as a backdrop. The third photo was a studio portrait shot of Elise with what must be her parents and sister. Elise's sister shared the same smile and hair, but with her round face and too-long chin, she didn't have Elise's elegant, fine features. Her parents looked nothing like he'd imagined. He guessed they were in their mid-fifties. They could be ageless, hip college professors who smoked pot with their students or new-moneyed people who didn't flaunt their wealth, but it was obvious they had it because they were always going on exotic vacations and buying things like boutique wineries. Her family looked like the kind of easy-going people who were just as comfortable playing beach volleyball and barbequing as attending black-tie fundraisers. Zeke chided himself for imagining that he liked them based solely on a photograph.

He wrote Elise a note thanking her for last night and propped it next to her phone. As he returned to his office, thoughts of Elise faded quickly at the prospect of catching up on his work. Twenty minutes later, Wayne Martin walked in.

"Good morning, Mr. Partner," said Wayne. "I bring offerings of sugar-laden delicacies." He held out a box of donuts and Zeke selected one with chocolate frosting and jimmies. Wayne took a seat and began munching on a glazed donut. "Did you see the notes I prepared? I put post-it notes next to everything in Pulaski's medical records that will help us."

"Yeah, good job, Wayne."

"It looks solid to me, I can't see how this guy can make a case," said Wayne in an unsure voice, looking for confirmation from Zeke. But, there was no guarantee what a real jury would do with a real stroke victim. The best advice Zeke had ever received was, "Prepare for your case as though you were representing the other side, and then formulate your strategy from that perspective."

"Let me look over your notes, and we'll talk later today," said Zeke.

Wayne left, and an hour later Zeke's phone rang. Before looking at the caller ID, he hoped it was Elise, but was disappointed to see his own home number staring back at him.

"Back at work so soon?" Mike slurred.

"Where did you go last night?" asked Zeke, who was only mildly concerned to see that Mike hadn't returned to the condo when Zeke left that morning.

"Out and about. I need your help, buddy," said Mike, sounding as though he were talking underwater. "Cybele didn't go back to Charlotte's last night. That's two nights in a row."

"Cybele can take care of herself."

"She might be dead."

Dead. Hmm, thought Zeke. Instead of being upset by that remote possibility, Zeke momentarily allowed himself to fantasize about never having to deal with either his second cousin or Mike again. Amazing that all of the warmth he'd felt for his friend in the elevator last night had disappeared so quickly.

"Or, what if she…" Zeke stopped his sentence.

"What?" asked Mike. "What if she decided to disappear and leave me for good? Go ahead be a man. Say it."

"You're drunk."

"So what," Mike replied in a flat, dead voice and then added, "Zeke, it was nice knowing you."

A chill ran through Zeke. Maybe Mike was just being overly dramatic as usual, but something told Zeke that wasn't the case.

"What are you talking about, Mike?"

"Good-bye, Zeke," he said in a hollow voice and then hung up.

A feeling of dread swept its way into Zeke's bone marrow. The fear clutched at his breast and his throat. The certainty that he should return to his condo immediately to check on Mike would not leave his mind, until Zeke convinced himself he was being silly. Mike was just playing for sympathy. Zeke had too much work to do to and would deal with him later.

36

M orning honey," Marilynn said, her voice floating from the kitchenette. She walked into the living room wearing an enormous smile, already dressed and with her duffle bag at the door. "I made us some coffee."

She settled herself on the futon, cupping a steaming mug in her hands. Like a Buddha she sat cross-legged with her robes draped over her legs, the early morning sun cast rays across her radiant face that wore an expression as tranquil as a still pond.

"You're leaving?" Inez said, surprised to hear a childish whine in her voice. "Already?"

"I'm not leaving Chicago, sweetheart," said Marilynn. "I'm just going back to my home."

"Can't you stay with me for a few more days?"

"And then what? Move in with you and Howard? Tuck the two of you into bed every night?"

Not necessary. Howard's mother had already taken that job.

"Honey, I've been gone for three years. I'm anxious to get back to my own space. Communal living was hard on these old bones."

"You're not old," said Inez. And it was true. Marilynn had the vitality of the average thirty-year-old and didn't look a day over fifty. After years of closely observing her, Inez believed she had discovered the source of Marilynn's fountain of youth—intense curiosity and a constant desire to learn and try new things. And, more importantly, lack of fear. Inez could not think of a single time Marilynn had shown fear about anything. "I was just hoping we could hang out today…and talk."

"About your wedding?"

Inez nodded.

"This is where you will find the answer to all of your questions," said Marilynn, pointing to her own heart.

"Are you coming to dinner tonight?" asked Inez, wondering how Howard's family would react to her. She smiled in anticipation of Margaret's reaction.

"Wouldn't miss it," said Marilynn.

Inez drank a quick cup of coffee, and they left together. As they stepped outside her building, Inez was relieved to see that Carlos was nowhere in sight. Hopefully, Marilynn had scared him off for good, although Inez knew that was hoping for too much.

"Would you like a ride, Marilynn?"

"No, thanks," said Marilynn. "I'm looking forward to taking the "L." I should have no trouble getting a seat, maybe even an entire car to myself. Too bad I don't have any finger cymbals."

Inez laughed and watched Marilynn's white robes flow like a sail behind her as she briskly set off for the station. Inez drove downtown, finding an empty parking space just three blocks from the bridal store. Just as she was about to enter the shop, she felt a hand on her bicep. She whirled and there was Carlos, but for a moment, she was so stunned to see him in a place she hadn't expected, her brain didn't immediately register the fact that he must have followed her here. It was bad enough that he was showing up at her apartment building nearly every day, but now he was stalking her as well?

"How nice to run into you," he said.

They blocked the middle of the sidewalk as tourists wearing Windy City T-shirts and business people streamed by them on both sides like water flowing around a boulder in a river.

"I'm on my way to get my wedding dress." Inez turned her back to him.

"I almost came back for you, four years ago," he said, his voice soft. "I'd like to explain. If you don't want to see me after this, I promise I will go back to Madrid and never contact you again."

As much as she didn't want to, she slowly turned to face him. Carlos's usual egotistical mask was gone; his face was naked and as legible as her own handwriting. A mixture of fear and pain shadowed his handsome features. He was unrecognizable; Inez couldn't help but stare.

"Six years ago," he said, "I fell in love with a woman, a model. I'd met her on a *Vogue* shoot."

The news that Carlos had fallen in love during their years apart had no effect on Inez. He'd no doubt fallen in and out of love so many times over the course of his life, it had become nothing more than a habit for him, like flossing after meals.

"I cheated on her, and when she found out, she left me," he said. "I learned a very painful lesson, Inez. I waited until now to come to you, when I was ready to commit to you fully. I will never cheat on you."

"How admirable, Carlos, welcome to adulthood," Inez snapped, tired of his platitudes.

"You know I love you."

"You haven't the faintest clue what love is all about."

Inez entered the store without looking back. She sprinted up the escalator instead of waiting for the elevator, and crossed the floor to the bridal department where Mrs. Phillips greeted her. As they headed to the fitting room, Inez sensed him behind her.

"Inez, please wait," he pleaded.

Mrs. Phillips stopped and extended her tiny hand to Carlos. "You must be Miss Paris's fiancé, it's so nice to meet you."

"We're meant to be together," Carlos said, ignoring the clerk.

Inez acted as if Carlos were invisible. "Mrs. Phillips, can we get started, please?"

Mrs. Phillips didn't move as her eyes darted back and forth between Inez and Carlos. Inez moved toward the fitting room, but Carlos took hold of her right elbow. Inez instantly shook off his hand.

"It's over between us," Inez said. "Can't you understand, I'm getting married to another man."

Silence had fallen over the bridal salon, which a moment earlier, was filled with excited voices of brides-to-be and their mothers and maids of honor. Inez could feel a dozen pairs of eyes on her.

Before she knew what was happening, Carlos's mouth was on hers. She gave in—angry, thrilled, furious, embarrassed, and starved for this kiss that satisfied a need she'd buried for years. When he released her, it was like coming out of a long dark tunnel into the light.

"I knew it," he said, back to his usual arrogance, "you do still love me." And with those words, he left, leaving behind a silence so profound Inez did hear a pin drop.

When Inez's heart regained its normal rhythms she turned to Mrs. Phillips who looked as if she had just seen a gaggle of gargoyles fly by.

"Well then, shall we get started on the fitting?" said Inez.

37

s the morning wore on, Zeke lost count of how many times he'd called his home telephone and Mike's cell phone. Mike, no doubt, was refusing to take his calls or had passed out again. Or maybe he'd driven out to Charlotte's and left his cell phone at home? Or perhaps something horrible had happened? In the span of less than a minute, Zeke's mild concern over Mike's welfare had escalated to acute dread. Zeke dialed Charlotte.

"Hey cousin, how's it going?" she said. Zeke heard the laugh track of a sitcom in the background. Charlotte joined in. Her levity seemed an affront to Zeke's fear until he remembered he hadn't yet told her why he was calling.

"Have you seen Mike or Cybele?"

"Do you ever watch The Golden Girls?" asked Charlotte, as if in a trance. "I just love Sophia. Do you remember the episode...?"

"I'm worried about Mike," Zeke interrupted. "I have a feeling something bad has happened."

"Our favorite couple has probably made up and they're on their way back to L.A.," Charlotte said, and then she erupted into laughter once again.

"So you haven't seen them today?"

"Zeke, what has gotten in to you?" Charlotte asked. "You've never worried about them before."

That was true. Although he'd felt pity for Mike in the past, he was never anxious or concerned for him. And as for Cybele, who might look like an ethereal angel with her white blonde hair and a face so beautiful it could make a grown man cry, she was as devious as a forked-tongued serpent.

Zeke had hundreds of memories of Cybele's deceitfulness to choose from, but the one that stood out was the time when she suddenly had a lot of money—or what passed for a lot of money for a teenager who didn't have a job or an allowance. She started treating them to movies, bought herself new clothes, and surprised Zeke with a new baseball glove. At first, she refused to tell him where she was getting the money. But pride at her own guile burst out of her, bragging about stealing money from patients at Columbia Hospital where her probation officer had set her up as a "volunteer" candy striper. "Those old fogies are sleeping all the time," he remembered Cybele laughing. "It's like stealing candy from a baby. Hey, get it? The candy striper is stealing candy."

Zeke told her to stop and threatened to turn her in, but when her probation officer called Zeke, he'd lied for her claiming he had given Cybele the money. He'd always felt guilty about the whole thing, and over the years, the guilt had turned into anger at himself for covering up for her.

But Mike was particularly vulnerable this week, as helpless and blind as a mewling kitten. Zeke hung up with Charlotte and turned to look out his office window for guidance, but his thoughts raced in a dozen different directions, none of them the least bit comforting.

"I got your note," a sweet voice, interrupted a moment later.

Zeke thoughts came to a screeching halt at the sight of Elise in his office doorway. He gazed at her soft beauty and, in that suspended moment, he fell a little harder for her.

"I had a wonderful time last night," said Zeke.

"Me too. I was wondering if you're free for lunch?"

I'm free for the rest of my life, was the thought that skirted through his brain. "Elise, I would love nothing more than to take you to lunch."

Her smile brightened.

"But, there's something I have to do. Can I call you later?"

"Of course," she said, quickly covering her obvious disappointment. On an impulse he kissed her cheek that was as soft as a flower petal. He put his hand on her arm and gave it a quick squeeze. A few minutes later he hailed a cab outside his building.

On the way to his condo, Zeke's dread multiplied. He silently willed the cab driver to go faster; the blackness of his fears consumed him as the taxi crawled through the mid-day traffic. When they finally reached his building, Zeke pushed open the lobby door and ran to the elevators. His heart punched at his chest as he imagined the elevator moving half as slow as normal. The door to his condo was ajar. He stepped inside as if he were an intruder.

At first, nothing looked amiss. In fact, it looked neater than he remembered leaving it that morning. He was here so infrequently during the day, he almost didn't recognize his space, which looked so much larger and homier in the daylight. And then he saw a bare foot hanging off the arm of the leather sofa. Zeke rushed over and saw Mike lying face down. Mike appeared to be sleeping, but it was a still sleep that mimicked death.

The bottle of scotch on the coffee table did not catch his eye because there had been many bottles there this week, but the prescription vial did. Zeke picked it up. Valium. It was empty. And then he saw the note on the table in Mike's distinctive handwriting, as loopy and neat as a woman's, something Zeke had often teased him about.

The paper shook in Zeke's hand as he read it: "I've made a mess of my life and my marriage. Tell Cybele I've always loved her. And Zeke, find yourself a woman who really loves you and start living again. Don't waste your life like I did."

If he hadn't been terrified that Mike might be dead, he would've found it amusing that Mike's last thoughts were of Zeke's love life. He dialed 9-1-1.

38

Carlos stepped inside St. Sebastian's Catholic Church. It took several moments for his eyes to adjust to the dim church lit only by the deflected sunlight streaming in through the stained glass windows. The sweet pungent scent of incense, old hymnals, and venial and mortal sins confessed under the threat of eternal damnation, reminded him of Iglesia de San Andrés in Madrid, where his mother had taken him as a child, to mass each week.

At the sight of the enormous gold cross behind the altar, Carlos dipped two fingers into the holy water, quickly crossed himself, and genuflected. As he made his way up the center aisle, he saw a handful of parishioners scattered throughout the church, huddled over and kneeling in prayer. Carlos made his way to the stand of votive candles in a small alcove off to the side. The flickering of the tiny flames cast moving shadows over a statue of Mary hanging above him, making it appear as if her pale blue gown were shifting in a breeze that wasn't present. He stuffed a folded twenty-dollar bill in the coin box, lit a candle, and lowered himself to the cushioned kneeler.

Although she had been gone for nearly a quarter of a century, the image of his mother was still vivid in his mind—as clear as if just that morning he had kissed her good-bye on the cheek. Carlos had been with the world's most beautiful women but none, not even Inez, compared to his beloved mother with her obsidian-colored hair held in place by the jeweled hairpieces she'd collected from all over the world. Her complexion was as smooth and luminous as a pearl, and her emerald-green eyes had danced with delight whenever she'd held Carlos in her gaze. Not a day had gone by since her death that he hadn't thought of her.

His mother had always been more like a friend than a parent. She never scolded him, even when he was little and doing something naughty, which was nearly all the time. As he entered his teenage years, it dawned on him that his relationship with his mother wasn't normal. She had breastfed him until he was five. He remembered one day overhearing his mother and grandmother arguing on their terrace when they thought he was inside taking a nap. His grandmother shouted that it was dirty and unnatural to still be suckling Carlito at his age. "You see the way he looks at his au pairs, the way he looks at you," she'd yelled to his cowed mother. "If he turns out like his father it will be your fault!" His mother had immediately stopped breast-feeding him.

No one had ever found out about the many nights she would crawl into bed with him—the nights when his father didn't come home. Those nights she called their "little secret." She had pressed upon Carlos the importance of telling no one about them—especially his father and grandmother. He remembered it happening one or two nights a week. Some part of him knew it wasn't right, but he hadn't wanted it to stop. Nothing sexual ever happened, but to his great shame he would get erections sometimes when she'd hugged him to her body as they curled up together until he fell asleep. She begged him over and over not to become like his father, to be good to the woman he married.

Carlos said a quick Hail Mary for his mother, crossed himself again and rose from the kneeler. A priest with wisps of white hair and a double-chinned, ruddy face with small eyes made smaller by a pair of gold wire-rimmed glasses, stood behind the lectern.

"Excuse me, Father," said Carlos, "would you take my confession?"

"I'm sorry, son," he said, in a harsh east coast accent Carlos could not place, "we only hear confessions on Saturdays."

"This is an emergency, Father," said Carlos. "Please, it won't take long."

The priest raised a white bushy eyebrow and studied Carlos. "Well, I suppose I have time before our five o'clock service." He nodded in the direction of the confessional. The priest stepped inside an elaborately carved walnut door, flanked on either side by red-draped compartments. Carlos pushed the curtain aside and knelt on the *prie-dieu*. A small door slid open, revealing a wooden lattice separating the priest from him. The pretense of an anonymous confession had been shattered, of course, but centuries of formality would not be disturbed.

At first, Carlos couldn't remember what he was supposed to say, but it all came back to him an instant later. He was surprised to see that he'd folded his hands into the praying position; probably a reflex from childhood when he went to Catholic mass twice a week and confession every Saturday.

"Bless me Father for I have sinned. It's been many years since my last confession," said Carlos, in perfect English, which he'd learned in school and as a child from Molly, a British au pair. Molly, a red head covered in freckles, was his first crush. At just five years old, he remembered trying to kiss her. At six he tried to grab her breasts—he missed breast-feeding. At seven, she returned to England and was replaced by Nannette, a French au pair whom Carlos liked even more. Carlos had lost his virginity to his fifth au pair, Gretchen, a buxom blonde from Germany when he was thirteen. His mother had hated the au pairs his father insisted upon hiring. Carlos had been too young at the time to recognize that his mother was probably jealous of them. But thanks to those lovely caretakers, he was fluent in four languages and had become an expert at lovemaking by his eighteenth birthday.

"I did something terrible the other night, Father," Carlos began.

"Go on, son."

It sounded to Carlos as if the priest had lowered his voice several octaves. Perhaps he reserved a special tone of voice for the confessional, inviting sinners to reveal their most private transgressions.

"I proposed to a woman I love."

"Why is that terrible?"

"I don't deserve her Father. I'm not sure I can make her happy."

"Son, this is not an occasion of sin. Many men have insecurities when it comes to their relationships. Is there another issue perhaps? Something…embarrassing?"

Carlos had no idea what the priest was talking about.

"I've counseled many men in this area," the priest continued. "A strong faith and prayer can save a relationship under these circumstances. Of course, the church does not condone premarital sex." He cleared his throat. "I'm assuming…"

"I've had premarital sex, Father." If he had to recount every instance of it, they could very well be in this tiny booth until the end of time.

"Yes, that is a sin, my son, but I'm talking about erectile dysfunction."

"What!" Carlos cried out, and then forced his voice to sound neutral again. "That is definitely not a problem for me."

"Have you ever been unfaithful to a woman you're with?"

"Too many times to count, Father. I am like a magnet for women. I attract them, how do you say, like flies to honey?"

"Bees," said the priest. "So you can't keep women away? Give me an example."

"The night before last after I left my fiancé's apartment, I went to a bar, and two women tried to pick me up. It's a curse, Father."

"Two? In one night? A curse? Do you know how many men would give their right arms for…"

"Father! I came to you for help."

"Sorry, did you resist?"

"Yes, but one of them was so beautiful I almost slept with her," said Carlos. When he and Nicole had left Lulu's bar, they'd kissed in a taxi all the way to her apartment. They gotten as far as the door to her bedroom, both of them half-undressed, when the promise he'd made to his mother on her deathbed flashed in his brain. He claimed an emergency and had left Nicole with her magnificent breasts exposed and so very tempting, standing in shock. It was the first time in his life he'd ever stopped a sexual encounter with a beautiful woman. That was progress of sorts, but it certainly wouldn't win him any fiancé-of-the-year awards.

"I've cheated on every woman I've ever been with, Father. I don't know if I can be faithful after I marry."

"You should seek professional help."

"I did, last year."

"And?"

"My psychologist and I had an affair."

"In fifty years of priesthood, I've never said this to anyone. My advice to you is, don't get married, ever. And, to be on the safe side say twelve Hail Mary's and Our Father's and pray for guidance from the Holy Spirit. God bless you my son."

Carlos and the priest exited the confessional at the same time. Carlos handed the cleric an envelope. "This is for your church."

The priest watched as Carlos walked out into the bright daylight. He looked inside the envelope, stunned to find one thousand dollars in cash. He shook his head and, with a sigh, said: "You can't buy salvation, my son."

39

Zeke clutched the smooth laminated arms of the waiting room chair as he crossed his leg over his knee, and then uncrossed it. It was a busy day at St. Michael's hospital; every chair was filled. Three televisions suspended high above them in the corners of the room carried the drone of a daytime soap opera. But nothing short of an announcement that the apocalypse had begun, heralded by the arrival of the Four Horseman in Daley Plaza could wrench Zeke's attention away from the fear and guilt gripping him. He shifted his weight causing his chair to creak.

"You're as fidgety as my grandson," said the heavyset woman seated next to him. "Do you have ADD?"

"What?" asked Zeke, annoyed to be pulled out of his gloom.

"Some adults have it," she said. The fat on her hips spilled over the open sides of her chair, invading a couple of inches of Zeke's personal space. Under normal circumstances, Zeke would be irritated to find himself pressed up against a stranger, but this fact registered in his brain and was instantly supplanted with thoughts of Mike.

"My brother has it," she continued, "he's been on medication for five years now. It's nothing to be ashamed of."

"I don't have it."

"It's okay if you do, is all I'm saying," said the woman. She opened her shopping bag-sized purse filled with enough food to stock a convenience store. Selecting a large bag of Doritos, she took a handful and tipped the bag to Zeke, who shook his head.

"Who are you waiting for?" she asked, with a mouthful of chips.

Apparently she believed the normal rules of privacy were suspended in a hospital waiting room, or Zeke had drawn the unfortunate lot of being stuck next to the nosiest person here—punishment, he supposed, for being such a shitty friend. The vision of Mike lying on a gurney, pale and motionless, as still as a corpse in a coffin, refused to leave Zeke's mind. And he couldn't stop thinking about what he'd overheard at his condo when one of the paramedics had said to the other, "It doesn't look good." In that moment, Zeke wanted to die himself.

"A friend," he said.

"What's wrong with him?"

"With who?"

"Your friend," she persisted, crunching her way through the bag. Her ranch-flavored breath reached Zeke's nostrils. He felt like he might throw up.

"Excuse me," Zeke said. As he reached the edge of the waiting room where the tan carpeting stopped and the gleaming white hospital floor began, a sandy-haired man who looked like John Denver, took hold of his arm.

"Are you alright?" he asked Zeke.

"I guess so."

"Are you here for Mike Knight?"

Zeke nodded.

"I'm Doctor Gray," he said, and then he paused far too long. Zeke wanted to shake him and demand an update but the doctor smiled.

"He's going to be fine."

All of the pressure and worry of the last few hours flowed out of him like water down a drain.

"You found him just in time," Dr. Gray said, "before he'd lapsed into a coma."

Zeke's relief was short-lived, instantly leeched away by the guilt over putting his job before his friend. What if he'd waited longer? What if he hadn't gone home at all?

"His blood alcohol level was very high," the doctor said, as if

251

giving a lecture. He was no doubt used to dealing with relatives and friends of patients too shell-shocked to speak.

"What's very high?" Zeke asked.

"A .42, more than five times the legal limit for driving. A normal person would be dead, but alcoholics develop a tolerance. I've seen some walk around with a .25 BAC as if they're stone sober."

Alcoholic. Zeke couldn't bring himself to associate that label with his college buddy. An alcoholic was someone who couldn't function, who couldn't get through a day without liquor. An alcoholic was someone who had nothing left to live for. Mike was far worse than he'd imagined. Of course, he was so caught up in his own life, he hadn't been paying attention.

"He'll have to have a psych evaluation, and then we'll be able to determine the next step," said Dr. Gray.

"Can I see him?"

"For a few minutes."

The doctor directed him to a nurse who showed Zeke to Mike's room. The beeping of hospital machines, IV fluids dripping into his veins, and the loud snoring from a shriveled man in the next bed, were the only sounds in the room. Mike had some color back in his cheeks, but his black hair was glued to his forehead with dried sweat. He hadn't shaved in days, and if he weren't in a hospital gown, he might've looked like one of the homeless people Zeke often spotted curled up on park benches and over grates.

Zeke loved and hated his friend at this moment. Then anger welled up inside of him. "You stupid pussy-whipped sap," he thought. "Goddamn you for almost killing yourself over a woman who doesn't give a fuck about you!"

Mike opened one eye startling Zeke. "I'm not dead," he said.

"You came really close," said Zeke, his words sounding like an accusation.

"Cybele, do you know where she is?" he asked, in a thick raspy voice.

"No," Zeke replied. He'd called Charlotte two hours ago from the waiting room to tell her about Mike. There had been no word from Cybele for three days. Charlotte reluctantly agreed to file a missing person's report with the police department, but when she called Zeke back, she reported that the police weren't concerned when they learned a marital spat had precipitated her disappearance. "Happens all the time, ma'am," the jaded cop had told her.

"Will you find her for me? Promise, Zeke?"

The last thing he wanted to do was to get them back together, but Zeke couldn't refuse a man who'd almost died.

"I promise."

"I've really screwed up," Mike said, in a hoarse whisper.

"Don't talk about that now. We're going to get you help. Everything is going to be okay."

Mike closed his eyes again, and in a moment, when his breathing slowed and became heavy, Zeke returned to the nurse's station and learned that Mike could be released as early as Sunday. The nurse handed him a list of in-patient and out-patient residential treatment centers in Chicago. Zeke thanked her and turned to leave, when heard a familiar gruff voice down the hallway.

"Holy cow, that's not Andy's boy is it?" said a man as wide as a semi, swinging his bad leg forward by swiveling his right hip. Zeke would've recognized that gait anywhere. Sid Rosiak grabbed Zeke's outstretched hand, engulfing it with his own enormous, heavily calloused paw and shook it like he was priming a pump. The last time he'd seen Sid was at his father's funeral over ten years ago.

"Mr. Rosiak," said Zeke, greeting his father's co-worker from Midland Steel and bowling partner for two decades. "It's good to see you. What are you doing here?"

"Well, at my age everyone you know starts getting sick. One of the guys from the plant had a heart attack," he said. "How's that fancy law job of yours, Zeke?"

Zeke inwardly winced. Everyone he'd grown up with used terms like "hotshot lawyer" and "big city attorney" as if he'd morphed into an alien having nothing in common with the mortals with whom he'd grown up.

"Fine. How's Tony?" Zeke asked, purposely changing the subject.

"You heard he's married with two little ones and another on the way," Sid said, pride evident on his face.

Zeke was stunned. His childhood friend had vowed he wouldn't marry until he turned fifty. The Tony Rosiak Zeke remembered was always scamming new ways to pick up women. In fact, the last time Zeke talked to him, Tony had bragged about picking up a "looker" at a bar by writing his name and number on the back of a manipulated ATM slip, which made it appear as if his bank account balance was fifty thousand dollars. Tony, who'd dropped out of high school and worked as a school bus driver, probably had $500 in his account, if that.

Tony, married with kids. Unbelievable. Zeke, who always had steady girlfriends would've predicted that he would certainly marry before Tony. But life didn't always turn out the way one planned.

"Have you thought about the softball team this summer?" Sid asked. "Tony's the captain this year."

When had Zeke quit the team? It must've been about six years ago—even before Zeke had allowed the Firmrod case to take over his life. Zeke, Tony, and other school chums would play on Thursday nights at the neighborhood baseball diamond and then head to their favorite local watering hole, Jim's Tap, with fifty-cent tap beers before six, going up to a whopping seventy-five cents until closing time. Zeke used to look forward to those nights that were filled with pool, darts, and male bravado.

"I'll try, Mr. Rosiak," said Zeke. And then a thought came out of nowhere, and he asked the question before thinking it through. "Do you know a Joseph Pulaski?"

"He lives on Tony's block, oh, I don't suppose you know where that is," said Sid kindly, although Zeke felt as though he'd just had his hand slapped for having lost touch with his childhood friend. "Pulaski lives on Lincoln Street, but his house is for sale. He used to keep it up real nice with flowers, and the trim on his house was always painted. But then he got sick, and well, I shouldn't say anything."

Zeke didn't push him. He already felt as though he were rummaging through the man's underwear drawer.

Sid Rosiak lowered his voice. "I heard the bank is foreclosing on his house. And, I gotta tell you, I love my wife, but boy did I envy Pulaski when he married that hairdresser a few years ago. That's why he started taking that Firmurod," he added, with a wink. "Gotta keep the young ones happy, I guess. But then he had that stroke. It's a shame. A guy that age, where's he going to go but a nursing home?"

And I'm going to be the one to put him there, Zeke thought, with a sick feeling.

40

Rachel Paris was naked and rolling on the beach with Tom, her boyfriend of three years. The surf washed over their calves as they made love just as passionately as always. Tom thrust inside of her, hard, the way she loved it. Rachel's nails raked down his back as she was on the verge of coming, coming, oh God…

The sound of the doorbell wrenched Rachel from her delicious dream.

"Shit!" she cried, upon opening her eyes and seeing her bedroom ceiling. The From Here to Eternity dream was her favorite, and she didn't have it nearly as often as she would've liked. The bell rang again.

"Hold on, hold on," she said, as she trudged to the door and flung it open out of annoyance.

Rachel's mouth dropped at the sight of the tall, perfectly proportioned woman whom she hadn't seen in years. Her fire engine red leather mini skirt skimmed the top of her legs that once had been insured by Lloyd's of London as a publicity stunt to launch her movie career.

Rachel was instantly self-conscious in her baggie sweat pants and Rolling Stones T-shirt, feeling like a cowhand who'd been interrupted shoveling manure by the Lady of the Manor.

"I had a feeling you might show up," Rachel said, "come on in."

Cybele Knight glided into her tiny apartment as though she were on a catwalk in a Milan fashion show. Although she'd left the world of modeling years ago, some habits were impossible to break. She pulled a silver cigarette case from her Gucci red leather Bardot handbag and offered one to Rachel. Gauloises Blonde—the same brand they used to smoke in Europe. Rachel leaned in as Cybele lit her cigarette.

"I'm glad to see you haven't given up all of your bad habits, Rachel" Cybele said, in a nasty tone.

The comment stung, but Rachel refused to let Cybele get to her. "Cheers," Rachel replied, raising her cigarette in the air like it was a drink.

Cybele moved across the carpet like a lioness. Her cheeks caved in dangerously as she sucked on her cigarette and then blew out a long stream of smoke. Stopping on the opposite side of the room she gave Rachel an appraising stare. "You haven't lost your looks, Rach."

"I know you didn't drop by after all this time to give me a compliment," Rachel replied, crossing her arms. "What do you want, Cybele?"

"I guess we're getting right to the point," Cybele said with an ugly smirk. "You heard I left, right?"

"I read all about it in People," said Rachel. "What does this have to do with anything?"

"I'm getting to that," Cybele said. "So you must also know I married Mike Knight."

Rachel nodded. When she'd recognized Cybele's husband at Club Caliente the other night, Rachel didn't say anything to Inez about knowing his wife, because Cybele was too intricately involved with the painful past she wished she could pretend had never happened.

"I was the star in my husband's latest flop," Cybele continued.

Rachel, a self-proclaimed movie buff was surprised she didn't know the film. "What was the name of it?"

"The Zombie Attack of the Cheerleading Squad," Cybele replied, with a bitter laugh. "I should've stuck with modeling."

Rachel didn't know how to respond. A small part of her took pleasure in Cybele's career woes. She didn't like that part of herself, but she couldn't help her feelings.

"I never told you, Rach, I was sorry when you left," Cybele said, bringing up the subject Rachel had been hoping to avoid. "You could've made it you know."

Nine years ago, Rachel and Cybele were aspiring models, represented by the same New York modeling agency and sharing an apartment in Paris. Although they'd always moved in separate circles, they gravitated toward one another as the only Midwesterners in a group of girls from all over the world, and had decided to share a small fourth-floor loft near the Latin Quarter.

Rachel couldn't pinpoint the day when her life took a drastically wrong turn. It might've been the first time she smoked marijuana, which had seemed so harmless, nothing more than an experiment tried by tens of thousands of college students each year. But with a party to go to nearly every night of the week, there was always a new drug to try—uppers, mushrooms, cocaine, and then her downfall, heroin. It seemed as though no time at all had passed between the first time she tried it—feeling as though she could fly to the moon—to falling into a perpetual throbbing need for the drug.

At first, she was getting high once or twice a week, then every day. And before long, it was as many times a day as Rachel could get her hands on the stuff. Some of Rachel's modeling friends—not Cybele who'd been too busy concentrating on her own career—had tried to get her help, but Rachel was convinced she wasn't addicted. Then one day, Rachel passed out and didn't wake up until twenty hours later. But that hadn't been just any day. Rachel had missed an assignment which would've launched her career as a supermodel—her face on the cover of Elle. When she should have been at the Eiffel Tower for her big shoot, she was in a rat-infested apartment on the outskirts of Paris, doing an altogether different kind of shoot. Her agency had fired her, and her boyfriend had taken her to his family's home in the country where he helped her go cold turkey. She'd returned to Chicago a month later.

Rachel looked at Cybele as she lit her third cigarette; she supposed she should be jealous. When she hadn't shown up for the Elle cover shoot, Cybele had stepped in as her replacement. It was because of that day—fortuitous or fateful depending upon how one looked at it—that Cybele's career had taken off. But despite her success, Cybele didn't look happy.

"Do you miss modeling?" Rachel asked her.

"No," said Cybele. "It was so boring. You?"

Rachel shook her head. Sometimes, when she picked up a copy of Vogue or Glamour she thought about the life she might've had as a model—dating rock stars, having plenty of money, and traveling the world. But the decision to leave the glitzy, plastic world of modeling was the right one. After she returned to Chicago, Rachel finished college and earned her Master's degree in Social Work. Working as an alcohol and drug counselor at a halfway house for the past five years certainly wasn't glamorous. But her work was real, and it helped her to stay alive. She had a classic addictive personality and needed constant reminders to stay on track, and her job provided the perfect, stark daily reminder of where she could end up if she wasn't careful.

"I saw your husband the other night at a salsa club," Rachel said. "He looked really bad."

Cybele shrugged and pulled another cigarette from her case. "I'm getting a divorce."

"He looked suicidal, Cybele."

"Not my problem anymore," she said, with a conspiratorial grin. "Thank God!"

God was not the one to thank, thought Rachel, who was disgusted with Cybele's indifference. Now she remembered why the two of them had never really become close. Cybele was as heartless as a doorknob.

"I need a place to crash," said Cybele, "just for a night or two. What do you say, Rach, just like old times?"

What old times? Cybele made it sound like they were two giggly teenagers about to have a slumber party.

"Why don't you stay at a hotel? What are you hiding from?"

Cybele looked uncharacteristically embarrassed. "My husband is an alcoholic. He drank away all our money. He's here in Chicago looking for me. I don't want to be found."

"But what about all your money from modeling?"

"Gone. Bad investments, a beach house in Maui, a mansion in

Beverly Hills, you know how it goes. I've got just enough left to get to Europe on Saturday."

"And then?"

"I'm going to meet a friend."

Something about the way Cybele said the word "friend" led Rachel to believe this person, no doubt a man, was much more than that.

"Does he know you're coming?"

"You're assuming it's a he?"

"I don't remember you having any female friends."

"I suppose you're right," said Cybele, pursing her lips smeared with red lipstick. "You were the closest friend I had in Paris, Miss Paris."

"Do I know him, the guy in Europe?" asked Rachel, forcing her voice to sound casual although she was consumed with curiosity. Daunted was one of her all time favorite movies. Michael Knight's career may have gone on the rocks since then, but Rachel could only imagine how incredible it would be to be married to someone so brilliant and so handsome. She couldn't imagine who Cybele would leave him for.

"Haven't you heard that curiosity killed the cat? You haven't changed much," said Cybele. She leaned forward to stub out her fourth cigarette in the ashtray on the coffee table. "You're still alive, Rachel, curiosity hasn't killed you like the cat."

"No," Rachel replied in a flat voice. "It was heroin that almost did that."

"You don't know him. He's someone I met after you left. Listen, can I stay? I was at my sister's place out in the burbs, but she is really becoming a nag."

Rachel was tempted to throw her out. Cybele never helped her when she'd needed it most. Many of Rachel's friends said that Cybele had stolen Rachel's modeling career from her, although Rachel had never viewed it that way. Now she could see what that lifestyle had done to Cybele and felt nothing but pity for her.

"You can sleep on the couch," said Rachel.

41

The meet-the-future-in-laws-before-the-wedding dinner at Howard's two-story brick colonial in the Village of Wilmette, a charming suburb, thirty minutes north of Chicago, was not going well. Other than a polite discussion at the beginning of dinner about places to sightsee in Chicago, held for the benefit of Howard's Uncles Joe and Steve and Steve's son Jim, who had flown in that afternoon from North Carolina and Oregon, the room had fallen silent except for the sounds of silverware clinking against plates and the muffled sounds of chewing. This silence was not the type inspired by the awe one experienced when taking in a majestic scene from nature, but rather the painfully uncomfortable sort, as though someone had just farted.

Marilynn's presence, as solid and reassuring as a mountain, helped to relax Inez's nerves, which had been as taut as a Stradivarius string ever since her encounter with Carlos at the bridal salon. Inez needed to reach out and touch Marilynn's arm periodically for reassurance that she had not disappeared.

"Does everyone here know that mom picked out all of the furnishings for this house?" said Howard, with a nod to his mother who beamed with pride.

"If you ask me it looks like a funeral parlor in here," Marilynn said, in a too-loud whisper to Inez.

Margaret, who had been watching Marilynn all evening as though she might try to pocket some of the silverware, shot her a look filled with venom.

Howard's home was lovely. He had lived on this quaint cobblestone street lined with black wrought iron street lamps, ever since his divorce. The bones of the home were gorgeous. Built in the nineteen-thirties, it had a stunning open staircase, gleaming maple hardwood floors, wainscoting the color of butter and ceilings high enough for a pole vaulting competition. But the natural beauty of the home had been marred, in Inez's opinion, by Margaret Suterman's morbid taste in Victorian furnishings. The gorgeous natural wood of the home had been completely overshadowed by ponderous purple velvet drapes and reddish-brown alder wood furniture festooned with elaborate rose-and-leaf carvings and brass accents. Whenever Inez was here, she felt as though she had somehow fallen through the beveled looking glass into a giant antique doll house.

"Young man," Marilynn said, addressing Howard's pimply sixteen-year-old cousin Jim, sitting across the table from her. "Would you like to ask me something?"

At nearly six feet tall and almost two hundred pounds, Marilynn had the bulk of a linebacker. Add to that her gleaming bald head, both of her wrists adorned with dozens of silver bangles jangling and clinking against the gold-rimmed white china plates and her powerful personality, it was no wonder that everyone at the table had been casting furtive and frequent glances at her.

Jim reddened. He squirmed in his seat looking as awkward as a camel riding a bicycle. Uncle Steve elbowed Jim.

"Well, it's just that…" Jim began haltingly, "I was wondering about your hair or really, no hair at all."

Marilynn slapped her thigh and let out a deep throaty laugh, causing Margaret Suterman to pop out of her chair for a second, her ghostly appearance going from pale to ashen.

"That's an excellent question!" exclaimed Marilynn. "I had to shave my head. Let's just say that India's cheaper hotels have many uninvited guests."

"More wine anyone?" asked Howard. Moving clockwise around the large dining room table, he filled a few glasses.

"What do you plan to do now that you're back home in Chicago, Marilynn?" asked Howard's Aunt Martha, sitting opposite Inez.

The room tensed and relaxed only when the moment passed without another guffaw from Marilynn.

"Thanks to my stay in India, I've found my true calling," said Marilynn. "I'm going to become a stand-up comedienne."

The table filled with confused faces.

"Spirituality and a sense of humor are intricately linked," said Marilynn. "I studied with Swami Sushmajee for two years. We cracked each other up every day."

"I see," said Margaret, whose watery blue eyes had filled with dismay, not seeing at all.

"A funny swami?" said Inez. "That's funny."

"You just gave me a great idea for a joke, thanks honey," said Marilynn with an affectionate pat to Inez's thigh.

"Are you going to take any classes, Marilynn?" asked Howard, who was doing his best to keep the conversation.

"No, I'm just going to get up on stage and go for it."

Inez had no doubt Marilynn intended to follow through with her pronouncement, but she just couldn't picture this bald, seventy-three-year-old woman up on stage cracking one-liners. Then again, maybe she could.

"At first, Swami Sushmajee wouldn't break a smile, but by the end of six months the two of us were laughing so hard we couldn't see straight. We had to meditate in separate rooms but even then, telepathically, we'd crack each other up."

Margaret Suterman clutched her heart looking as though she might expire on the spot. She gave Howard a look that said, "All is doomed," giving Inez the distinct impression that Margaret might not support this wedding after all.

The clock ticked. A dog barked in the neighbor's yard. Margaret dropped her fork, which landed with a loud clank against her plate.

"Inez," Martha said brightly," I never told you this, but the first time I met you I knew you were the perfect woman for my nephew."

Inez had always liked Martha who was Howard's deceased father's younger sister. The frigid blood of Howard's mother did not run in Martha's veins. Martha's personality was warm apple cobbler to Margaret Suterman's frozen fish.

"Why is that, Aunt Martha?" asked Howard, seated to Inez's left. He took hold of Inez's hand and smiled.

"Call it women's intuition," said Martha with a warm smile. Inez shifted in her seat and looked away. Just ten hours after she'd given in so easily to Carlos's kiss, the timing of Martha's well-intentioned sentiment could not have been worse. Guilt gnawed at Inez. Picturing the scene in the bridal salon from the viewpoint of a spectator, she was ashamed for not having had more control. But that had always been the problem with Carlos. She'd never felt in control around him.

"Inez," said Howard's mother, "is Rachel still sick?"

"Rachel sick?" Marilynn blurted, "that girl hasn't been sick a day in her life."

Margaret scrutinized Howard's and Inez's faces, clearly demanding an explanation.

"What did I say?" asked Marilynn.

"Rachel isn't coming on Saturday because she's opposed to our marriage," said Inez, feeling a slight release of pressure now that the truth was out in the open.

"Now that sounds exactly like Rachel," said Marilynn, with a nod.

"But she's your maid of honor!" exclaimed Aunt Martha.

"My sister can be…difficult at times."

"Oh honey," said Martha to Inez, her sweet matronly face filled with concern, "how horrible for you."

Howard's mother rose from her seat at the head of the table, waving Howard off as he stood to help her.

"I'd like to propose a toast to my son and Inez," she said, in a soft voice.

Everyone at the table fell silent as they strained to hear her. She'd broken her hip eight months ago and had been forced to move into an assisted living home. Before her accident, she was out everyday taking walks along the beach and playing golf at her gated community.

But now, she couldn't get around without a walker. Breaking her hip had aged her ten years.

"My son could not have chosen a better woman to spend his life with," said Margaret with a distant expression on her face, as if citing the words by rote. "Inez is like the daughter I never had."

Inez felt all of the eyes of the table upon her, but she couldn't meet any of them. Margaret cast her cold eyes in Inez's direction.

"As a wedding present, I'd like to give you these pearl earrings that have been passed from generation to generation in the Sullivan family, from my great-grandmother who died before I was born, to her daughter and on down, until I was given these by my own dear mother just before I married Howard's father fifty-two years ago. May God rest their souls."

Murmurs of amen were heard around the table. Howard had been raised a Protestant while Inez had been raised with no religion at all, unless Marilynn's New Age spirituality could be considered a religion. Howard wanted their children brought up in the Protestant faith, which was fine with Inez, who had no strong feelings about it one way or another. To her, Protestants were safely neutral, like dry white toast.

Howard's mother used her walker to come around the table behind Inez's chair. She placed a tiny velvet box in front of Inez. Inez sat gripping the sides of her chair staring down at the box as though it contained a ticking bomb. She quickly glanced at Howard, catching his concerned stare. Howard squeezed Inez's right knee—the pause had gone on too long. The room had collectively stopped breathing in anticipation of what might happen next.

Inez turned to her right, hoping to get some guidance from Marilynn who gave her an encouraging nod as if to say, "You can do the right thing, Inez." But Inez couldn't move; every fiber of her being screamed for her to put a stop to the wedding.

Howard reached in front of her and opened the box. Two pearl-studded earrings stared at Inez like crazed eyeballs.

"Listen to your gut," Marilynn seemed to be silently communicating, but how could she do it when it would be embarrassing the nicest man she'd ever known in front of his family?

"Put them on Inez," said Howard.

Inez rose. She met the eyes of every person at the table, finally resting upon the stony face of Margaret Suterman.

"These earrings are lovely, Margaret," Inez said. "But I can't accept them."

Margaret reacted as though she'd been slapped.

"Now," Howard quickly interjected. "She means now. But they'll look beautiful on her on Saturday." Howard seized the velvet box. "I'll hold these for you, honey."

Inez opened her mouth to speak, but the right words refused to exit. She sat back down, defeated and furious with herself for not having the courage to do the right thing. Marilynn patted her thigh, but the gesture only made her feel worse. When had she become so weak and fearful?

42

Zeke kept replaying a horrible scene of finding Mike too late, cold and dead, like switching to a selection on a DVD to view an alternate movie ending. His face must have been easy to read, because the moment he stepped into Elise's office after returning from the hospital, she took hold of his arm and told him they were going for a walk.

"What happened, Zeke?" she asked, as they stepped outside of their building from the cool air conditioning to the muggy June air.

Burdening Elise with the Mike-Cybele-Oscar-winner downfall to alcoholism and attempted suicide saga, this early in the relationship, did not seem like a good idea, but the normal rules no longer appled. And so, as they walked east, Zeke told Elise everything.

They reached Millennium Park and without speaking, chose the nearest bench. The entire twenty-four-acre park had the feel of a playground for aliens—an appropriate setting for the strange twists his life had taken this week. Zeke had a view of the Crown Fountain featuring faces of Chicago citizens projected onto huge LED screens. Each face remained immobile for several seconds and then suddenly burst into a smile. A few moments later, their mouths closed to a pucker as water spurted out into two shallow reflecting pools. The first time Zeke saw it, he freaked out as he watched the giant face of a wrinkled Asian man abruptly grin. Today, Zeke didn't even glance at the screen.

Elise took off her robin's egg blue tailored suit coat and laid it over her lap. The air was hot and humid with no breeze to cool them off.

"I didn't care that he was depressed," said Zeke. "I didn't want him here; I was disgusted with him."

She brushed a few golden hairs off her neck and continued to listen without interrupting. Her eyes did not leave his face.

"He almost died because of me," Zeke said, turning his eyes away from hers to the much safer, more neutral ground of the pavement. "I'm a terrible friend."

"He lived because of you," she said, putting her hand on top of his. "You saved his life."

A group of children ran by, pulling Zeke from his guilt-ridden reverie, but a moment later he plunged back into the darkness.

"Mike was drinking a lot, he was depressed, but all I was thinking about was my promotion. My priorities are all screwed up and have been for years."

"It's easy to blame yourself in hindsight."

"No, it's true, I've changed," said Zeke, realizing that he didn't like the person he'd become.

He told Elise about the first case he'd ever worked on at Conley, Dwight & Miller. He'd been an eager new associate desperate to stand out among the fifteen other new lawyers—including Elise—who'd started at the same time. He would never forget his first day. He was temporarily assigned to a partner in the Insurance Defense department before he moved to his permanent spot on the tort litigation team a few months later. Zeke would never forget the grisly facts of his first real law case. A repairman, just a few years older than Zeke, who was married with two children, had been standing in the basket of a cherry picker working on electrical wires. The worker failed to properly ground himself, and when a live wire had fallen across the worker's body, his right arm and both of his legs had been burned off. The firm's client was the insurance company and Zeke's job was to find legal precedent which showed that due to the contributory negligence of the worker, the insurance company was not liable.

Zeke had gone back to his office feeling sick and thought seriously about walking out the door and never looking back. But he'd convinced himself that this job was exactly what he wanted, even putting a noble spin on it because he had done it for Susan, for their future, a future that never happened.

"Did you ever find out how the case turned out?" asked Elise.

Zeke followed the case all the way through the trial. The jury had awarded the repairman nearly ten million dollars. Zeke was glad, secretly of course, that the plaintiff had won, which should've been a big clue that he was in the wrong job.

"I used to care, but now the only thing that matters is getting the best deal for my client. I put more thought into what tie I'm going to wear in the morning than what kind of person I've become."

"You're a good person, Zeke," Elise said gently. "Stop doubting yourself."

"I'm sorry I'm being so morose. I'm usually not like this."

"I know that," she said, with a kind smile. The way she said it made him feel as though they truly knew one another, even though that wasn't possible after such a short time. But already, Zeke had fallen under the magical spell, which happened at the start of a promising new relationship, when the other person was little more than a stranger, but somehow, seemed closer than friends you've known for years.

"I'll make it up to you. Can I take you to dinner tomorrow night?"

"I'd love to," she quickly replied.

Their eyes met. For a moment, the tropical air made Zeke imagine that the two of them were lying together on a beach, somewhere beautiful like Costa Rica. He leaned in to kiss her as she wrapped her arms around his neck and kissed him back.

Oh no, H! They're falling in love!

Frustration is a human emotion. It would be wise for you to learn how to control yourself, Serena.

The plan is gonna backfire! We've got to do something! Tell me you've got a great trick up your sleeve, something you haven't shown me yet, something that's better than tweaking.

Free will, Serena. I am afraid there is not much we can do at this point.

If this were a romance novel, I could just write Elise out of the story. Wait a minute, why can't we? We can get her that job in California with Universal Studios.

And what would Zeke do then?

He'd follow her. Darn.

There is hope, Serena.

Really? Spill it!

Humans have been known to change their minds from time to time…

--

That was a joke. You were supposed to laugh, but obviously you are not in a humorous mood. Zeke and Elise might fall in love, but could just as easily fall out of love in a few earth months or years.

That's our only hope? A few years! You're giving up, aren't you?

Of course not. I am simply observing at this point. You should do the same. Emotional involvement with our case is a liability, not an asset.

That might work with plants, H, but it doesn't work with people. We are running out of time.

43

Inez was able to catch only stray notes of Beethoven's Moonlight Sonata coming from the CD player, over the soft purr of the car engine. Howard had refused to tell her where they were going after he dropped Marilynn off at her home, only saying it was a surprise. But Inez didn't want any more surprises. She just wanted to talk to Howard—the old Howard.

The light from passing street lamps briefly illuminated his face, the reflection bouncing off the lenses of his glasses. She could see lines of worry grooved across his forehead.

"We're here," said Howard, as he turned into a conservation area. It was after ten o'clock, and no other cars were in sight. The air was still, as if all of the animals living in the forest had fallen quiet to watch them.

"I'm not up for a hike, Howard."

He said nothing as he continued to drive deeper into the gloom. The trees lining the narrow winding paved road were barely visible—mere outlines against the starlight sky. He drove ten minutes before he pulled into a parking lot and shut off the car. He walked to the trunk and pulled out a bed sheet.

"Can you help me put this on the backseat?" he asked.

"What's this?"

"I thought we could, you know, increase those statistics you talked about the other day?"

"You want to have sex? Here? Now?"

"I thought that's what you wanted?"

The sight of him trying to put the sheet over his leather backseat made her want to shake him. Couldn't he see that dinner tonight had been a disaster?

"I'm not in the mood," she said.

"You're always in the mood. What's wrong now?"

"We need to talk," she said, uttering the four words that so often signaled doom for a relationship.

They found a nearby picnic table. Inez perched on top while Howard sat on the bench below. There wasn't enough light to make out his features, but that was a good thing.

"Howard, I've been doing a lot of thinking and…"

"Why do you go to the symphony with me?" Howard asked, cutting her off.

She was surprised by both his question and his interruption—something he'd never done before in their two years together.

"Because you get season tickets every year, and you love the symphony."

Howard knew the names of every member of the symphony and the instruments they played, the way other men kept tabs on the names, plays, and positions of the Chicago Bears.

"That's right," he said, "I love the symphony. But what about you?"

"I enjoy our evenings out."

"Inez, you fall asleep at almost every concert."

Although she liked classical music, Howard was right; it usually put her to sleep. The only part of the evening she truly enjoyed was getting dressed up and trying a new restaurant beforehand. Watching a group of tuxedo-clad men and women in black plucking at their instruments was about as interesting to Inez as watching water evaporate.

"Well, I do it for you," she said.

"I know. And when my mother broke her hip last year you offered to go with me."

"I remember."

"Mary," he said, referring to his first wife, "hated my mother and refused to spend time with her except at holidays. She never would've gone with me."

Howard took hold of her hand. "I know you're not crazy about my mother. And I don't blame you. She can be, well, difficult. Your offer to go to Florida meant more to me than anything."

The offer to go with him had been genuine, but she'd made it out of obligation, thinking that was what a fiancé should do.

"Inez, there's something I need to say." He stroked her hand. Inez held her breath, filled with anxiety and curiosity at facing a fiancé she was no longer sure she knew. The Howard she used to know was a rock of strength when he wasn't tripping over ottomans. But this Howard, the Howard of the last few days, was unrecognizable.

"This is something I've wanted to say for a long time," he began and then paused as he took a deep breath and wiped at something on his cheek. Was he crying? Howard wasn't unemotional, but Inez had never seen him tear up. He tended to recount his feelings as though he were giving directions—exactly the same way he dispensed medical advice.

"Inez, I know you don't love me in the same way I love you. I hope someday that will change, but if it never does, I want you to know it's okay. I can't imagine my life without you."

The words hung in the air—impossible to ignore. She could no longer go on pretending this was an equal relationship—if there was such a thing. Try as she might, she simply could not bring herself to swear to him that she did love him as much as he loved her. More than anything, Inez wished they could rewind everything that had happened this week and go on pretending that everything was okay.

"Our relationship might not be passionate or intense, but there is real love between us," he said.

Inez wasn't certain she knew what love between a man and a woman should feel like. She loved Marilynn and Rachel, but that love was bound by blood and thousands of shared memories. Her love for Howard had always felt more…well, practical.

"I don't think that's enough," Inez replied sadly.

"What else do you want?"

She could hear desperation in his voice, which only made her feel worse.

"I can make this right Inez, I can make you happy."

Seeing Howard in denial was more painful than what she was about to say, but Howard spoke first.

"Why wouldn't you take my mother's earrings tonight, Inez? You embarrassed me in front of my family."

"I'm sorry about that." Inez truly was sorry; she'd made a total mess of things. It would've been better to tell the truth then and there. And now she could no longer wait. "I didn't want to say this in front of your family…"

"Say what?"

"I think we should postpone the wedding."

The momentous words had left her mouth, and for a moment the world seemed exactly the same.

"No," he said with a vehemence that surprised her.

"What do you mean 'no'? We need to discuss this."

"Inez, I love you, and that's all that matters," he said. "I'll take you home now."

Of all of the surprises this week, this was perhaps the most shocking of all. Their strong suit had always been their ability to talk to one another. If that was gone, then truly, they had nothing left.

Friday

44

Pulaski must have some muckety-muck attorney," said Wayne Martin to Zeke as they rode the elevator to the fifty-fifth floor.

"Why do you say that?" asked Zeke.

"Conference Room A," said Wayne. "I've never been in it, but I've heard about it."

The few times Zeke had used conference room A, which was reserved only for partners, was to meet with Xanadu Pharmaceuticals executives to discuss the lawsuit. Their motto when it came to litigation was: "Money is no object." And for that reason, the firm's best client got the firm's very best of everything—including, Zeke supposed, himself, the hotshot associate. With effort he pushed away the thought that the partnership meeting had started a few minutes earlier, and his fate was being decided at this very moment.

"Pulaski's attorney just graduated from law school a year ago," said Zeke. "He's a solo practitioner and, as far as I know, he's never handled a pharmaceutical case."

Wayne got a glint of life in his eyes, and his smile seamlessly transformed his face from cherubic to devilish. "What a fantastic strategy!" said Wayne flashing a thumbs up. "He's going to be intimidated as hell. We should stroll in about fifteen minutes late. That'll have the rookie lawyer and his old fart client scared out of their wits."

Zeke winced. Ever since his conversation with his father's old friend, Sid Rosiak, yesterday, thoughts about Joseph Pulaski kept surfacing. He thought about postponing the deposition to see if a settlement could be reached, but if he didn't make partner, he didn't want this case falling into someone else's hands.

"Let's be professional, Wayne."

Zeke knew Wayne was a good guy, just a little over zealous like most new associates who were always trying to take on more responsibility to escape from tedious legal research, with his sights no doubt already set on a partnership.

Conference room A looked more like a suite at the Four Seasons than a place of business. The deep maroon walls had actual artwork—a Warhol, a Salvador Dali lithograph, and even a Picasso—instead of the framed posters lining the walls of the rest of the office. The carpeting was as soft as a cloud and floor-to-ceiling windows ran the length of two sides of the room, offering spectacular views of the sailboats scattered across Lake Michigan on this gorgeous cloudless day. Along the walls were plush couches and a wet bar at the back of the room completed the look and feel of the old boys' club. At the custom-made, twenty-four-foot long, cherry conference table sat a curvy Filipino woman with curly, black shoulder-length hair. On the floor at her side was a stenograph machine. Zeke introduced himself to her, and they exchanged business cards.

"Sorry I'm late," said a hurried voice behind him. "Which one of you is Zeke Nomad?"

Zeke turned to a man who didn't look old enough to have graduated from college much less law school. He was so tall and thin, he resembled a prehistorically large praying mantis.

"Hi, I'm Peter Katzman," he said grasping Zeke's hand with a cold sweaty palm. "It's nice to finally meet you."

"Nice to meet you as well," said Zeke, and with a wave in Wayne's direction, added, "this is Wayne Martin, an associate who's been assisting me on this case."

Peter and Wayne shook hands. Zeke caught Wayne grimace and wipe his hand on his pant leg.

"Where's your client, Pete?"

"He's coming."

Several long minutes later the plaintiff appeared at the conference room door. Pulaski leaned against his walker breathing heavily and winced when he shifted his weight. As he began moving again, Zeke started toward him, but Katzman grabbed his arm to stop him.

"Trust me," whispered Katzman with a raised eyebrow, "he doesn't want any help."

It was agonizing to watch Pulaski's stiff, crablike progress from the doorway to the table as he dragged his right leg behind him like a dead log. Zeke instantly chastised himself—his personal agony was nothing compared to having actually suffered a stroke that had left Pulaski partially paralyzed. Pulaski's gut hung over his olive pants and jiggled like rubber with each step. Zeke stood so long in the same spot, he felt as though he'd sunk into the carpeting up to his knees. Splotches of perspiration appeared under Pulaski's arms and at the back of his neck. Zeke imagined a stadium full of spectators breaking into applause when Pulaski, at long last, took his seat.

The court reporter administered the oath to Pulaski who agreed to tell the truth. Zeke introduced himself and Wayne to Joseph Pulaski and explained that he would be asking questions; his attorney could object for the record, but he would still need to answer every question. A judge would rule on any objections later, if necessary. Zeke informed Pulaski that every word he said would be taken down by the stenographer, and could be used against him if he testified differently at the trial.

Pulaski focused on his age-spotted hands clasped tight in front of him as if glued together, not making eye contact with anyone in the room. Only the soft sounds of keys being punched on the court reporter's machine, as she caught up, punctured the silence. Zeke had done enough depositions to spot a hostile witness early on. He could feel the anger coming off the plaintiff like a blazing fire.

Zeke began by asking for the usual background information: name, age, address, date of birth, education and prior occupation, each of which Pulaski answered with a gruff, firm response.

Getting through Pulaski's medical history was more tedious, but by patiently reminding him of the answers he'd filled out on the

Plaintiff's Fact Sheet, Zeke was able to establish his long history of health problems—hypertension, diabetes, gout, and the fact that the plaintiff had been at least thirty to sixty pounds overweight for the last ten years. More importantly, Zeke established that Pulaski had suffered from all of those problems—the combination of which certainly could've caused a stroke—well before he'd been prescribed Firmrod.

"Does anyone need a break?" Zeke asked, looking at his watch and seeing that an hour had passed. "No one? All right, let's continue. Mr. Pulaski, why did you first see Doctor Watt about your erectile dysfunction?"

"My second wife made me go," he said. "She's a lot younger than me. Forty-two now."

Zeke managed to hide his surprise, but Wayne Martin's chin dropped to the table with a thud. Zeke elbowed him. "Sorry," Wayne muttered.

"Mr. Pulaski," Zeke continued, "why did you start taking Firmrod?"

Pulaski made eye contact with him for the first time that morning, but it was with only one bloodshot milky brown eye, sunk in a face that might've been handsome thirty years ago, but was now a mass of bulging veins and deep wrinkles cutting through his skin.

"Why the hell do ya think?" Pulaski spat with a scowl.

"Mr. Pulaski, you have to answer the question," said his attorney, Peter Katzman who sat to his left.

"I couldn't get a…" he faltered, "I don't know the fancy word for it. I couldn't get a hard-on. There, you happy?"

"You couldn't get an erection?" said Zeke. "Is that correct?"

"That's what I said," Pulaski growled.

"According to the testimony you've already given, you started taking Firmrod in July of 2008. Did you take it as prescribed?"

"What d'ya mean?"

"Did you ever take more than one pill before having sexual intercourse?"

"No, but that damn drug didn't work," Pulaski said. "I still couldn't, ya know, get it up for more than a few seconds."

"Did it ever work as promised?" Zeke asked.

"No."

"Did you discuss this with your physician?"

"No."

"So you continued taking the drug even though it wasn't working, is that correct?"

"Yeah."

"At what point did you stop taking the drug?"

"When I had my stroke," he said, "when I almost died."

Zeke asked the stenographer to mark the hospital admittance record for the day of Pulaski's stroke as an exhibit, and placed a copy in front of Peter Katzman.

"According to Exhibit 22, Mr. Pulaski," Zeke began, "neither you nor your wife told the hospital staff that you were taking Firmrod. Is that correct?"

"If that's what it says," Pulaski snapped.

"You told them the names of twelve medications you were taking at that time," said Zeke. "Why didn't you tell the hospital staff you were taking Firmrod?"

"I was too busy trying to stay alive that day. I guess me and my wife forgot to mention it."

"But you already testified," Zeke continued, "that Firmrod wasn't working for you. So why would you keep taking it?"

Pulaski cried out like a wounded animal, shocking the room into silence.

"I've lost everything because of that damn medicine," he shouted, shaking his meaty fist in the air. "My wife divorced me, my pension's gone, the bank's taking my house, and I can't hardly move. I got nothun,' nothun' left."

Pulaski buried his face in his hands.

"Let's take a break," Zeke announced, feeling as though he'd been fighting a long war only to find out he was on the wrong side, all along.

"We can't quit now," whispered Wayne Martin, "let's finish this off and nail him to the wall."

A soft knock at the door interrupted them; the fifty-fifth floor receptionist poked her head in. "Excuse me Mr. Nomad, but Mr. Miller would like to see you right away."

Zeke turned to the credenza behind him, poured a glass of water and set it in front of Joseph Pulaski. He walked out of the conference room feeling more ready than ever to face Stu Miller and his future.

45

nez was short on miracles this week, but a tiny throw-away miracle enabled her to find a parking spot on Marilynn Street, just a few doors down from Marilynn's red brick bungalow. The fact that Marilynn lived on Marilynn Street had become a family joke over the years. The joke went that Marilynn was such a famous Chicago personality, the mayor had named this street in her honor. What Marilynn was famous for changed nearly every time the joke was told. In one story, Marilynn had rescued a family trapped in a car that had plunged off the Michigan Avenue Bridge into the Chicago River. Marilynn dove in and had pulled the family to shore, performing life-saving mouth-to-mouth resuscitation on the youngest child. In another story, Marilynn had written a Pulitzer-prize-winning novel about the adventures of two orphaned girls, originally from Milwaukee, who had come to live with their mother's best friend in Chicago after their mother died. Not surprisingly, the girls were named Inez and Rachel.

Growing up, Inez wanted to believe these stories were true. Marilynn had always seemed like a character from a fairytale. When Inez and Rachel had gone to live with Marilynn after their mother died, Inez remembered thinking that she'd entered a movie set like The Wizard of Oz, except that even the Emerald City couldn't compare to Marilynn's home. Everywhere Inez had looked were things she'd never seen before, but eventually learned the names of—sextants, sun dials, lava lamps, Ouija boards, Tarot cards, crystals, jars of unrecognizable things that reminded Inez of her science projects at school, gargoyles, miniature pyramids, beaded curtains instead of doors and the one item she was most intrigued by—an actual crystal ball.

Marilynn must've seen Inez staring at the crystal ball because a minute later Marilynn had emerged from one of the back rooms with a blue bandana tied gypsy-like around her head, a long-sleeved gauzy white top and a patch-worked skirt reaching to her ankles. Inez and Rachel had instantly scooted to the furthest corner of the room, cowering at the sight of Marilynn, who they already thought of as one of the strangest humans they'd ever met. Marilynn grabbed the crystal ball, cleared off one of the tables, put it down, and said in a dramatic voice, "Come closer girls, come closer," with her hands winding around one another like two snakes rising in the air. Marilynn's gypsy impersonation had made Inez laugh for the first time in months. Marilynn had told Inez her fortune and from that moment on, they'd bonded like twins.

Passionate about everything—even the most banal conversations about the weather—she seemed capable of making magic happen by her mere presence. Someone this special, whom Inez loved so intensely, deserved to be publicly recognized with a street named after her.

Inez took the red brick path to Marilynn's home and the door opened before Inez had a chance to ring the bell. They greeted one another with a hug. Marilynn's living room was full of moving boxes that had been pushed to the walls to make room for a hand-woven carpet Marilynn she had received as a gift from a medicine man she'd met in Oaxaca years ago. They sat on the carpet as Marilynn poured herbal tea.

"How are you?" Marilynn asked, handing her the steaming cup.

"I couldn't sleep last night," said Inez.

Inez had spent a fruitless night analyzing her relationships with Carlos and with Howard. The memories of her time with Carlos were more difficult to revisit—not because it was Carlos—but because so much time had passed. It was as if her unconscious had purged her Carlos memory-bank, leaving just a few highlights and a general impression of a rocky road with many valleys, steep hills, and hidden pitfalls. With Howard, it had been like paging through a beloved scrapbook she wasn't ready to put away.

"That's understandable," Marilynn said. "Things didn't go exactly smoothly last night."

"What did you think of Howard?"

Inez tensed in expectation of what Marilynn might say—knowing Marilynn, it could be anything, but at least it would be the truth.

"You two are like peanut butter and jelly."

"So you think we're a good match?"

"Peanut butter and jelly might go together, but they're an awfully boring combination."

A quick rap on the front door was followed by Rachel entering like a miniature tornado. Rachel plopped down on the rug and crossed her legs. She looked at Marilynn's gleaming bald head and rolled her eyes, mumbling something about her looking like Captain Picard.

"What's going on?" Inez asked.

Rachel would sooner grow a mustache than voluntarily spend time with Marilynn. Unlike antagonistic mother-daughter relationships that tended to mellow with age, their battles had only gotten worse. They couldn't be in the same room longer than five minutes without Rachel tearing into Marilynn like an alpha wolf fighting to maintain her position.

"This is an intervention," said Rachel. "You're on the verge of losing it, Izzy."

"Inez," Marilynn intervened in a calm voice, "I think Rachel is trying to say that we love you and want the best for you."

Rachel fixed Marilynn with an icy stare. "What I'm really trying to say," Rachel said, returning her focus to Inez, "is that you need to dump both of your losers and get on with your life."

"Inez needs our support, not sarcasm, Rachel," said Marilynn gently.

"You know what I needed Marilynn, I needed the truth," Rachel cried. "How many times did you lie to us about our father? Is that how you supported us?"

"Rachel, although I loved both of you as if you were my own daughters, I never wanted to be a mother. I did the best I could."

"I would've been better off in an orphanage," spat Rachel.

Inez stood, her eyes filled with tears, and her face was on fire. "That's enough! I'm sick of you two arguing every time we get together."

Inez brushed her hand across her wet eyes. "I'm leaving!"

"Wait Inez, what are you going to do?" asked Rachel. "Are you going to marry Howie?"

"If you really cared about the answer to that question, you wouldn't have gone scheming behind my back to plan this…whatever this is," Inez said, trying to hold back her tears. "And you would've shown up this week, Rachel, when I needed you most."

"When it comes to men you've always been blind," said Rachel. "A little tough love is good for you"

"Rachel, you are a selfish know-it-all bitch!" cried Inez.

The foundations of the house trembled as her words shot out of the walls of the living room. She had never before spoken this way to her sister; the shocked look on Rachel's face said it all. Marilynn, on the other hand, was trying her best to look neutral, but was doing a very poor job of hiding her evident pleasure at Inez's outburst.

"And stop calling him Howie!"

And with that Inez left, slamming the front door behind her.

46

Stu Miller waved Zeke into his office looking as friendly as a hunter zeroing in on its target. Zeke took the same chair he'd sat in just a few days earlier. Miller, in his high-backed chair with his right foot resting on his left knee, studied his fingernails. Zeke purposely shifted in his chair causing it to creak. If Miller pulled the water torture thing again, Zeke thought he just might lose it.

"I suppose you're wondering which associate has been promoted to partner?" said Miller, still focused on the keratin shields at the ends of his fingers as though they were the most fascinating things on the planet.

"I've been in a deposition all morning," said Zeke. "I assumed that was the reason you pulled me out of it."

Miller eyed him without an ounce of warmth, and then like one of the faces on the Crown Fountain at Millennium Park, he abruptly broke into a smile. "I want to congratulate our newest partner."

Stu came around to the other side of the desk and thrust his hand toward Zeke, who stared at it as if it were a poisonous snake. On autopilot, Zeke took hold of Stu's outstretched hand.

"Well, what have you got to say for yourself?" said Stu with a pat to Zeke's back.

"Thank you, Sir, I'm..." Zeke's words trailed off. He was so certain Elise would get the partnership that some part of him was already packing up his office and writing his resignation letter.

"Surprised?" said Stu. "I told you I'd pull for you. I thought you'd have more faith in me. Anyway, welcome to our exclusive club,

Nomad. We expect great things from you. Now, you better get back to that deposition, I understand it's going very well. Good work."

How would Stu Miller know that? Was the conference room bugged? Had all of the partners been listening in, and was that what had tipped the decision in his favor? Zeke dismissed the thought as too John Grisham-like. Stu was no doubt simply expressing his expectations. But the thought clawed at Zeke's mind, refusing to leave.

"How do you know how my deposition is going?" asked Zeke.

Stu winked at Zeke. "Let's just say a little birdie told me. Stop by when you're finished nailing that coffin shut. I'll let you in on a little secret, partner."

Zeke felt sick. A flash of his future fast-forwarded through his mind: Elise would move back to California, she'd already told him that that was her default plan. Zeke's hours wouldn't decrease, in fact, the pressure would build for him as a partner who was not a rainmaker, to do his fair share. The pharmaceutical lawsuits would never end. He would spend the rest of his life doing work contrary to his true values.

And then, from some hidden place deep inside, the strength to do what he should've done a long time ago bubbled to the surface. Zeke looked Stu Miller directly in the eye and smiled.

"Thank you for everything, Mr. Miller," Zeke replied. "But I quit."

Stu's oily smile freeze-dried on his face, revealing an ugly snapshot of a powerful man rendered speechless, for perhaps the first time in his life. Zeke turned on his heel and left.

The theme from Rocky played in his head as happiness flooded through him; he wanted to skip down the hallway. Molecule by molecule the rightness of his choice filled his spirit. Visions of all of the things he intended to do poured into his brain, each one competing for his attention.

But there were a few loose ends he needed to tie up before he could allow himself to fully experience the joy of his newfound freedom—and he needed to move quickly. He entered the first empty conference room he could find and placed his first telephone call.

47

Howard pulled into his usual parking spot, having no memory of the drive to his office. His thoughts were consumed with last night's disastrous dinner and his heart-breaking conversation with Inez at the park. Inez wanted to postpone the wedding. Postpone. When Howard heard her say that, the carefully guarded gates to his heart felt ripped asunder. His refusal to even discuss postponing the wedding was a desperate attempt to ignore it and go through with their wedding as planned. Later, he'd felt guilty about it. They'd always been able to discuss things—that had never been a problem. But by telling Inez she was wrong, and that the love they shared was enough to make a happy marriage, he was only saying what he truly believed. Now, he wasn't so sure.

Howard had just two appointments today, having cleared the afternoon to pick up his tuxedo and run some last minute errands for the wedding. He'd almost called his receptionist Sarah to have her cancel his appointments, but Mr. Jenkins needed to be seen after his surgery last month to repair his degenerated Achilles tendon, and Mrs. Sullivan's removable walking cast was not working out. He couldn't let them down.

Sarah Conway greeted him as always, with a radiant smile as she handed him a mug of steaming coffee with a splash of skim milk and one packet of sugar—just the way he liked it.

Sarah's brow knotted with concern. "I'm guessing last night did not go well? Would you like to talk about it?"

They went to his office where he told her everything, including his fear that perhaps Inez was right—that the best move right now would be to postpone the wedding. Sarah listened without interrupting. When he'd finished, Howard waited with anticipation for her response. He realized how much he'd come to depend upon her thoughtful, sensible advice over the past several months.

He recalled the day she'd first walked into his office, sent from a temporary agency, to fill in for his previous receptionist who'd retired at the age of sixty-two. Sarah was just twenty-five at the time, much thinner, and quite pretty. Howard remembered his wife Mary being jealous of her. She'd told him not to hire Sarah, but he'd ignored Mary's directive—something he'd rarely done. Sarah had proven to be not only a skilled typist with excellent organizational and people skills, but she was professional and above reproach. Besides, Howard would never think of cheating on Mary or getting involved with an employee.

After his divorce, a friendship—limited to office hours—had developed between them. Sarah shared with him her passions for quilting and the symphony. Howard gave Sarah his symphony tickets on the occasions when he wasn't able to use them. She told him about some of the men she'd dated over the years, but none of those relationships had become serious. And then, when he and Inez began having problems, he'd turned to her for advice.

Her face was expressionless. Hope surged that Sarah would urge him to go through with the wedding, that she would see some way to turn things around with Inez. Perhaps it was not too late after all?

"Howard," Sarah began in a calm but firm voice—a voice that conveyed wisdom and understanding, "I think you're selling yourself short."

"What do you mean?"

"I think you're settling for less than what you deserve."

A spark of anger ignited in Howard's chest. This wasn't at all like Sarah, who'd been nothing but supportive of his engagement and who seemed to genuinely like Inez. "Sarah, I can't believe you would insult..."

Sarah rushed to explain, cutting him off. "Howard, I think you may have misinterpreted what I mean. I think Inez is great. I can see why you're in love with her."

Normally, their conversations flowed with an ease that he'd never experienced with any other woman, including Inez. He and Sarah shared the same temperament, and they found humor in the same things. They often spoke in shorthand, understanding what the other was trying to communicate with few words necessary. But now, Howard was confused.

"What I'm trying to say is that you're wonderful too, Howard. You deserve someone who loves you as much as you love Inez."

Howard was stunned. Wonderful? He'd never thought of himself that way. He was not given to false modesty. He knew he was a good man, and an excellent doctor, but he had no delusions about himself. He was an ordinary man with rather ordinary interests. The quality of being wonderful applied to other people—people like Inez.

As if reading Howard's mind, Sarah added: "Howard, I don't think you see even half your good qualities."

Sarah fiddled with the hair clip that held her thick dark hair in a neat bun at the nape of her neck. She cleared her throat and shifted in her seat. "There's something I've never told you."

Sarah paused; in the long moment that followed Howard noticed her smooth unblemished skin, the elegant brooch in the shape of a treble clef pinned to her jacket, her nails cut in neat short squares with a gleam of clear polish. He wondered, for the first time since he'd known her, why she'd never married.

"What is it?"

Sarah took a deep breath. "I've had many other job offers over the years that would've paid me more than you're paying me, with better benefits."

Howard couldn't find his voice. When was the last time he'd given Sarah a raise? Four years ago? Five? He was only beginning to see how much he'd taken for granted her solid, comforting presence and competence over the past fifteen years.

"But I turned them all down," Sarah continued. "Do you know why?"

"Not a clue," mumbled Howard whose cheeks were hot with embarrassment.

Sarah met his eyes in a way she had never done before. Even if Howard had wanted to look away—which he didn't—he was incapable of doing so. She held him firmly in the grip of her intense gaze. "Because working for someone I admire, someone who gives himself so selflessly to his patients, is far more important to me than money."

Sarah slipped out of Howard's office, leaving him alone with his buzzing thoughts that were beginning a journey to places that they'd never dared to visit before.

48

Inez sat on her futon with her arms wrapped around her knees hugged close to her chest as her mind raced in a thousand different directions. She wasn't proud of how she'd let fear rule life and how wishy-washy she'd been. She wasn't much for prayer, but she said a quick prayer now for the strength to do the right thing.

A bolt of clarity was followed by a delicious calm—she wasn't in love with Howard and never had been. Inez almost laughed out loud—half with the sheer relief of having finally realized the obvious as the other half imagined Rachel rolling her eyes and saying, "I told you so."

Inez's thoughts coalesced. At first, she dated Howard because he'd treated her so well. She kept hoping to find the passion with him that she'd had with Carlos, but had only grown to respect Howard and love him for the good person he was. Some part of her had known for a long time that she shouldn't marry Howard, but she'd convinced herself that Howard, the kindest and most selfless man she's ever known, was right for her.

To make the relationship work, she'd slowly adjusted herself to Howard's unhurried pace of life and predictable routines. One by one, she'd given up her passions—salsa dancing, going to parties, foreign travel—all of the things she'd once loved to do. How could she have been so blind? Howard didn't know her—the real Inez—because she'd never shown her true self to him.

For the past several months, she had been focusing on what was wrong with Howard when she should have seen that she had been terribly unfair to him. She was just as wrong for him as he was for her. Howard deserved someone who loved him as much as he loved her. And she deserved someone who truly loved her as well, a man who knew and understood the real Inez. The insight was as clear and strong as if an angel had lovingly whispered these thoughts into her ear.

She got up and grabbed her purse. Just as she was about to leave when she heard a key in the deadbolt, and Howard burst in as if he were being chased by a herd of elephants. His face was red, and he was out of breath. He came directly to her side, clearly on a mission. She'd never seen him this full of life. The irony that her fiancé might have kept his true self hidden from her, as well, hit her.

He took hold of her hand. "Inez, I have to talk to you!"

"I have to talk to you, too."

Just then Carlos strolled in. Howard rose to his feet and stood protectively in front of Inez.

"Who are you?" Howard demanded.

Carlos stepped forward with his hand outstretched. "I'm Carlos Luna Del…"

Howard's fist hitting Carlos's face sounded with a loud thwack. Carlos tumbled backwards and hit the wall as blood spurted from his nose and his lip.

"Stay the hell away from my fiancé," Howard shouted.

Instead of looking angry or shocked, Carlos slowly reached inside his jacket pocket and retrieved a monogrammed handkerchief. He wiped the blood away, as calmly as if getting punched were an everyday occurrence for him.

"Well," Howard said to him, "don't you have anything to say for yourself?"

"Good punch," Carlos replied with a bemused smile, and then turned to Inez. "Inez, I have to talk to you."

Howard stepped in front of Carlos and poked a finger in his chest. Howard had a look on his face that Inez had never seen before—part bulldog, part boxer. A flicker of fear crossed Carlos's face. "Get out," Howard ordered.

Carlos backed out of the room without taking his eyes off Howard who slammed the door shut behind him, instantly relieving the tension in the room.

Howard turned and cradled his right hand. "Ouch."

Inez ran for an ice pack and gave it to Howard. His hand was already discoloring

"Is your hand going to be okay?" asked Inez who was concerned that he might've permanently injured it and could no longer perform surgery.

"It hurt's like hell," said Howard, "but it'll be fine."

They sat together on the futon.

Before she lost her nerve Inez blurted, "I don't think we should get married."

"I agree!" Howard replied, with just a tad too much enthusiasm.

No doubt the shock of what had just happened had rattled Howard's mind.

"Howard," said Inez gently, "do you understand what I just said? I want to cancel our wedding."

"I do too," said Howard. "That's what I came here to tell you."

"You did?"

"Inez," he said, taking hold of her hand, "when you suggested postponing the wedding last night, I couldn't bear the thought of losing you. I kept thinking that if I loved you enough, someday you might love me the same way. But last night I couldn't sleep. I went over my marriage to Mary, and I realized something. I truly loved her too, but it wasn't enough to make my marriage work. I don't want to make the same mistake again. I don't want to marry someone who's settling for me."

"Oh Howard, it's not…"

"It's okay Inez. I know I'm wrong for you."

"I'm wrong for you too. You deserve someone who truly loves you."

"I know I do. We both do."

It seemed impossible to have any bodily fluids left after all of the crying she had done this week, but once again her eyes teared-up.

Although she knew this was the right thing to do, there were many things she would miss about him.

Howard pulled her into his arms. "Everything will be all right, Inez, you'll see."

Well, we have removed one hurdle. What is wrong? I thought you would be happy, Serena.

I feel kind of sorry for Howard, he looked so sad.

Howard chose to have this relationship with Inez and in the process, he has learned a great lesson. He will find true love someday.

I hope I do too. When I go back, I intend to write my own script and find my great love. I can't wait for all the romance—those sweet nothings tickling my ear, staring into my lover's eyes for hours on end, love letters so poetic and beautiful they will make me weep, and yes, lots of flowers. I never had any of that with Stan.

Serena, that is not real love. Real love comes after the honeymoon phase, after you have seen the other person's faults, their ear hair, and varicose veins, their short tempers and selfishness, yet still want to be with them. Real love, when it happens, is extraordinarily special .

For someone who spends most of their time with plants, you seem to know an awful lot about love.

I have been studying the human race ever since my first incarnation in Mesopotamia in 3214 B.C.

Who was your great love, H?

Her name was Cleopatra. She had the most beautiful heart and mind. Her soul sang to me. We were deeply in love, but alas, that was a very long time ago.

Cleopatra! As in ruler of Egypt? Lover of Marc Antony? Wearer of all of those fabulous gowns and headpieces? Well, at least that's how she was portrayed in the film with Elizabeth Taylor.

No, Cleopatra of Pompeii. She was a milk maid. I lost her in the great eruption of Mount Vesuvius.

Oh! You must've been devastated. But how did you survive?

I was away in Rome on a matchmaking errand for the emperor. After I lost her, I chose to never reincarnate again.

Oh! That's so tragic and beautiful. Do you mind if I borrow your story for my next historical novel? I plan on continuing my career as a romance writer in my next life.

I would be honored, Serena.

49

Zeke returned to Conference Room A where the mood was about as jolly as mourners gathered at a funeral parlor.

"I'm sorry for the delay," said Zeke.

Joseph Pulaski looked as if he hadn't moved from his spot at the conference room table. His head hung over the glass of water he hadn't touched. Turning to Pulaski's attorney Zeke said, "Peter, I'd like a few minutes to confer with my associate."

Katzman nodded. Wayne Martin puffed up with importance as he followed Zeke to a nearby empty conference room that Zeke prayed wasn't bugged.

"What happened with Miller?" asked Wayne, as soon as Zeke closed the door. "Did you get it?"

"Yes."

Wayne's mouth fell open and he burst out with his congratulations, slapping Zeke on the back.

"And then I quit."

Wayne's freckles pulsated in astonishment. "You what?"

"Are you happy here, Wayne?"

Wayne looked surprised. "I suppose. What does that have to do with anything?"

"I used to think being happy wasn't important," said Zeke, wondering how he could've been so blind. "But now I know it's not just the most important thing, it's everything. Don't get trapped in the golden handcuffs, Wayne. Think about what you really want from your life. Promise me."

Wayne looked at him curiously for a long moment and then nodded. "I will."

"Good," said Zeke, putting a hand on his shoulder. "Two more things. First, I just got off the phone with our client. We've been authorized to make a $250,000 settlement offer to Pulaski."

"That's not possible!" Wayne exclaimed. "Pulaski doesn't have a case."

"He'll make a sympathetic witness," said Zeke. "Besides, I believe Firmrod caused his stroke."

The realization of what Zeke had done dawned on Wayne's face that was as malleable as silly putty. "If Xanadu ever found out," said Wayne, "you could get disbarred for this."

Zeke supposed he should feel guilty for having highlighted those aspects of Pulaski's case that would be most damning to Xanadu, and advising them to quickly and quietly settle, or risk getting some very bad press and a gargantuan jury verdict in the plaintiff's favor. It certainly could happen; juries were notoriously unpredictable.

"I'll understand if you don't want to make the offer," said Zeke.

"No, I'll do it," said Wayne. "You said there were two things?"

Zeke pulled a slip of paper from his coat pocket. "Since I quit, I don't think it would be wise for me to show up at the firm dinner dance tomorrow night. I'm hoping you'll take my place with my date, Pamela. Here's her number, she's expecting your call."

"What does she look like?" asked Wayne.

Zeke laughed. "Trust me, you won't be disappointed with her looks."

"What are you going to do now?"

Zeke paused and then broke out into a broad smile. "I'm going to start living again."

Zeke went to Elise's floor and practically sprinted to her office.

"Congrat..." he began, as he stepped inside her office, but she wasn't in. He was momentarily disappointed, but then he thought of the date they had planned for tonight with a surge of anticipated pleasure. He left her a note telling her he would call her later.

He spent the next hour packing his personal belongings, and saying good-bye to Melissa, Mike Knight's lawyer Joseph Banks, and a few of the associates he'd worked with over the years. He took one last look around his office, stepped into the elevator and walked out of the building without a backward glance.

Zeke turned his face up to the sun. He wanted to drop to the pavement and kiss it or run through the nearest fountain or hug the first person who came along, but he did none of those things as he made his way to Charlie's usual spot where Zeke found him, holding his sign and sporting his usual scowl. Zeke would miss seeing that scowl each morning. The wisdom and wit Charlie had showered upon him over the years had been a gift. The few dollars he'd passed to Charlie was poor compensation indeed for what Charlie had given him. Zeke opened his mouth to speak, but Charlie spoke first.

"Congratulations."

"For what?" asked Zeke, wondering if Charlie's seemingly endless powers of foresight could include the news that Zeke had quit his job?

"You tell me," he said, "either you made partner, which is what you wanted or you didn't, in which case you're out of the rat race."

For once, Zeke knew something Charlie didn't. "I got the partnership."

Charlie's face was as expressionless as a stone pillar; he looked away down the block.

"And I'm out of the rat race."

Charlie squinted hard at him; confusion filled his face.

Zeke smiled broadly. "I quit, Charlie."

Charlie stared at Zeke, agog with surprise. Zeke had never been able to shock him before. This moment alone had made the last eight years worthwhile. Well, let's not get ridiculous, thought Zeke.

Charlie reached for his hand and cupped it between his two warm hands. "I'm proud of you, Zeke," Charlie said, addressing him by name for the first time since they'd met on this corner four years ago. "Really proud."

50

Elise joked with the waiter as she gave him her dessert order. Her hair was up in a casual twist with wisps of flaxen hair framing her face. Her hairstyle showed off her long, thin neck and the small hollow at the base of her throat that Zeke imagined kissing. And then he'd move to her shoulders as he gently pushed aside the thin straps on her black, low-cut dress and…

"Didn't your mother teach you that staring is rude?" said Elise with a smile.

Zeke snapped out of his trance, blushing furiously.

Elise giggled and took hold of his hand. "It's okay. You make me feel sexy."

"Sexy, stunning, gorgeous, dazzling, lovely," he said, as he kissed the inside of her wrist. "Shall I go on?"

"If you must."

"Intelligent, witty, mesmerizing, charming, and," added Zeke, "now a high-powered partner at the biggest law firm in Chicago."

"Oh please, I'm just sloppy seconds," said Elise. "I wasn't offered the job until you turned it down. You haven't really explained why you did it. Do you feel comfortable sharing your reasons?"

I would feel comfortable sharing my life with you, thought Zeke. But instead of saying that, he forced himself to focus on her question.

"It was the strangest thing, Elise, as I went to Stu Miller's office I had this feeling that everything would be all right. I didn't think about it. The words 'I quit' just came out as though someone else was speaking for me."

"Any regrets?" she asked.

"Absolutely not," he said, wondering if she'd really heard what he'd been trying to tell her this week about how this job was wrong for him from the start. "I should've done it five or six years ago like I'd originally planned."

The waiter brought a white ramekin of crème brulée and placed it in front of Elise along with the bill for Zeke. He slipped his credit card inside and handed it to the waiter.

"This looks delicious," she said, putting some on a spoon. "Would you like to try it?"

Zeke bent forward; she put the spoon in his mouth giving him a come hither look that made it difficult for him to swallow.

"But aren't you a little worried?" she asked, in between ecstatic murmurs of appreciation for her dessert. "What about an income? And the job market isn't that great for lawyers right now."

"I've got money saved," he said, "I'll be fine for a while."

"I can't wait for my first partner meeting," she said. "I'll finally find out what happens behind those closed doors. Maybe they carry on some bizarre ritual involving chanting or reading tea leaves."

"You seem really happy," said Zeke.

"I'm thrilled. I've been working for this for eight years. That's why I'm surprised you gave it up so easily."

A nagging doubt tugged at Zeke. He hadn't given up anything, why didn't she understand?

"But what about your dream to work in film?" he asked.

"Oh that," she said, with a dismissive wave. "Maybe I'll do it someday, but now isn't the right time."

The waiter returned with the credit card receipt for Zeke's signature.

She put down her spoon and smoothed her hand over her flat stomach. "That was absolutely fantastic. How can I possibly thank you for this lovely dinner, Zeke?"

He could think of any number of ways. God, she was beautiful, he thought. His concerns of a moment ago were instantly banished by his libido, but for the first time in a very long time, it was coupled with real feelings.

"Shall we go?" he suggested.

They lived in opposite directions and before he could muster the courage to invite her over, she grabbed his hand and pulled him into a waiting cab. Zeke gave the driver his address, and their mouths and hands found one another. The drive to his condo could've taken thirty seconds or thirty hours. Time had passed into that nebulous zone where it simply didn't have any meaning, until Zeke heard the cab driver's voice and sensed that the car had stopped.

They entered his building, greeting the doorman like chaste acquaintances, and then, when the elevator doors closed upon them, they were like a pair of teenagers discovering the joys of kissing and groping for the first time.

Pulling apart from her when they arrived on his floor was difficult, but Zeke was able to take a deep breath for the first time since they'd left the restaurant. He unlocked the door and waved her inside, debating briefly whether he should do the polite thing by offering to give her a tour. But they instantly latched onto one another as though their lives depended upon it and ended up on Zeke's king-sized bed. Their clothes came off in a jumble of confusion—hands everywhere, and annoying hooks, zippers, and buckles were obstacles conquered as quickly as possible.

She looked into his eyes as she wrapped her legs around his torso. In contrast to the frenzied moments to get to this point, they made love slowly as if they had all the time in the world. Afterwards, Zeke lay on his side stroking her face.

"Elise…" Zeke began, but didn't finish what he wanted to say, which was that he was falling in love with her.

"I think I know what you're thinking," she said, "but let's not talk. How about we do that again?"

Saturday

51

Great torrents of rain assailed Inez as she made her way down Michigan Avenue toward the Peninsula Hotel. Drops of rain the size of marbles ricocheted up from the pavement, as tiny tidal waves of water splashed over the curb at the passing of every car. Lightning flashed in the sky, followed by a crack of thunder so loud, it sounded as if the earth was breaking in two. The weather seemed to be sending her a message of warning that her mission was a dangerous one, and she needed to be careful. Inez pushed aside the urge to turn around and go home.

She breezed past the white marble lion standing sentry outside the hotel—the one where oil sheiks and movie stars stayed, and also, apparently, sons of European shipping tycoons who'd recently inherited millions of dollars. Stepping inside the lobby, she shook out her umbrella, and brushed off the raindrops clinging to her navy blue trench coat—a Christmas gift from Howard. She allowed herself a few moments of melancholy. It was strange that one could be certain of a decision and yet, mourn the loss that resulted from it. The fact that Howard had wanted to end things as well made her feel only slightly better. They'd cried and had wished one another well, hugging for one last time. And then it was over. Two years ended in less time than it took to change a flat tire. Both Rachel and Marilynn had offered to come over after Inez called them with the news that the wedding was off, but she needed to be alone. And she was alone, until Carlos, no doubt with some sixth sense that she'd broken off her engagement, had begun his salvo of attempts to reach her.

Carlos had called her at least two dozen times last night and had shown up at her building. He'd stood outside her door for hours, knocking and trying to coax his way inside with his charms. "Inez, I love you, I want to marry you. You're the only woman for me…" She'd buried herself under her bed pillows, but his words rang in her head like the tinny voice coming from an old time Victrola, until eventually she'd drifted off to sleep.

This morning she'd found the envelope he'd slipped under her door. Inside was a Peninsula Hotel key card and a note in Carlos's handwriting giving her his suite number along with an urgent request for her to come and see him today. Her first impulse was to throw it away. But curiosity soon gripped her in its ugly vise. What could be hiding in his room? Another woman? No, more likely a harem of women. Maybe she would find his little black book? That would be something to see—she could probably donate it to the Musée de Cads. She wouldn't be trespassing—after all she had a *carte blanche* invitation to drop by, from the devil himself.

Inez dripped her way to the reception desk no doubt looking like she'd swam through the sewer, crawled out of a grate and slithered onto the Magnificent Mile. But the pretty young woman behind the desk greeted her as graciously as if she was a perfectly coiffed member of the British Royal family. At Inez's request, she rang Carlos's room, but there was no answer.

"Would you like to leave him a note?" suggested the hotel clerk.

Inez shook her head, thanked her and made her way to the restroom. She stepped in front of the mirror. Not too bad. She combed her hair and reapplied her lipstick.

As she rode the elevator to his floor and approached his room, her heart pounded in anticipation of what she would find and fear of being discovered "accidentally" snooping through his things. She slid the card in the slot and heard a click in time with the blinking of the green light.

His suite, in a word, was magnificent. Twice, perhaps three times the size of her apartment, the extravagant luxury was a shock compared to the way they had lived in Madrid. A grand piano sat in a corner opposite an enormous brick fireplace. In front of the windows was a telescope. She wondered briefly how many hours he'd spent spying on unsuspecting females window shopping below. She meandered past oversized couches and chairs looking comfortable enough to sleep on, and into the bedroom. His open suitcase on the bed was as irresistible as a treasure chest. She poked through the clothes he hadn't unpacked, and under a shirt she found a stack of envelopes tied together with a string of red yarn. She inhaled sharply when she saw that the first one was addressed to her at her apartment in Chicago. Untying the string, she shuffled through the stack seeing that every envelope had her name and address on it. She opened the first letter, dated four years earlier.

"*My dearest Inez, You must be so angry with me, as you have every right to be. I have no excuse for leaving you other than my own fears, arrogance, and immaturity. You are the most incredible woman I've ever met. I think of your kindness, your grace, and your beauty, and it astounds me that I could not see those qualities when we were together. You showered me with love and I cast it aside, not realizing it was the most precious of gifts. I don't yet have the courage to send this to you, but hope someday you will read these words and know I have never stopped loving you. Yours, Carlos.*"

She read the next letter dated three months later. "*Inez darling, I am tormented by your absence from my life. I cannot stop thinking that I have lost you forever and yet, I am powerless, paralyzed by my fears that you will reject me. All my life I have treated women as if they were playthings for my amusement. I am deeply ashamed that I could've treated your love so casually. I dream that someday you will know my thoughts and if you could find it in your heart, you will forgive me. All my love, Carlos.*"

Inez couldn't stop reading. Every letter had different words but they all pointed to the same conclusion. Carlos had not lied to her—he really did love her and had never stopped.

Inside the tenth letter a photograph fell out. There she was, just nineteen years old at a café in Madrid with her American girlfriends Beth and Dee—also on their junior year abroad—on the day that she'd first met Carlos. He had approached their table asking if he could take their picture. The fact that he had kept this photograph all these years surprised her. Carlos was far more sentimental than she would've ever imagined.

Because she was in the midst of re-reading the letters scattered over the bed, she didn't hear him walk in.

"I was going to give those to you before I went back to Spain."

Her heart stopped at the sight of him. She stared at his face that was missing its usual arrogant mask. His high cheekbones looked sharp enough to etch glass, and his Roman nose had a bump on the bridge of it, which looked hand-placed by a sculptor. It was a face she knew well and didn't know at all.

"Are you leaving?"

"Yes, tonight. I wish I could stay but I have an important business meeting in Madrid on Monday morning."

"I should go," she said, rooted to her spot, unable to move. She dismissed the strong urge to leave, knowing that if she left now, she would never see him again.

Carlos didn't hesitate. He took her into his arms. As they fell onto the bed, Inez had a fleeting thought that she should put a stop to this. But the thought vanished as he tore off her clothes, and his mouth and hands found all of the places that he knew better than anyone else.

What are you doing, Serena?

Haven't you ever seen a woman cry before? We've lost both of them.

Ha, ha, ha, he-he, ho-ho-ho, oh my...

How can you find humor at a time like this? You should be ashamed of yourself, H.

This is turning out better than I had hoped for.

You don't have the sense that God gave a goose. Don't you see, our darling couple will never end up together. It's over. We've failed.

No, Serena, now our real work begins.

52

The blueberries smell heavenly," said Elise, who sat perched on a bar stool on the opposite side of Zeke's kitchen counter that extended out and doubled as a table. Her face was propped in the palms of her hands, her elbows resting on the black granite countertop.

"It's my specialty," Zeke replied. He stopped stirring the blueberry compote warming on the stove.

"You're gorgeous," he said, leaning across the counter to stroke the side of her face; he kissed her.

"Even wearing your shorts and your Chicago salsa con…?" she stopped and pulled the shirt away from her body in an attempt to read the letters up-side-down. "What does this say?"

"Salsa congresso," he said. "It's basically an excuse for salsa fanatics to get together in a hotel ballroom and dance for four days straight." The last congresso he'd gone to was five years ago. Getting back into salsa dancing was just the first of many changes he planned to make in his life. "And yes, you look beautiful in my clothes." He raised one eyebrow. "And out of them."

Just then, thunder cracked, rattling the windows. "See," Zeke said, "Even the heavens agree with me."

Returning to the stove, he expertly flipped pancakes sizzling in the pan, and slid them onto a plate, placing it in front of Elise.

"So I'm wondering Miss Partner, how soon can you take some time off?"

"For what?" She stabbed a blueberry with her fork.

"Well, I thought we'd start our travels in Argentina. I've always wanted to learn the tango. How does wine country in Chile sound? Then there's Patagonia. Maybe we could go hiking in the Andes and Easter Island is just a quick plane ride…"

He stopped when he saw the space between her eyebrows knot like an accordion. She went to the living room and sat on the leather sofa.

"What's wrong, Elise?" he asked, sitting next to her. "We don't have to go to South America. There are thousands of places we can explore."

"I'm going to have to work even harder now that I've made partner. I've got to prove myself all over again, especially as a woman."

"But you get six weeks of vacation. You don't have to take it all at once. We could take short trips, a week or two at a time."

"I don't want to tie you down, Zeke."

"You wouldn't tie me down," he said, grasping her hand. "I want to be with you."

"I want to be with you too," she said.

"So what's wrong?" Zeke had been looking for someone like her for so long, he didn't want to lose her now.

"It's not just that the timing is bad," she said, biting her lip. "I guess I was enjoying our conversations so much this week, and well, I exaggerated."

"What are you talking about?"

"My idea of roughing it is a swim-up bar that's run out of piña colada mix at a five-star resort, on American soil. I really admire your adventurous spirit, but it's just not me."

"We could take it slow, start with a nice resort in the Dominican Republic, or I know, Puerto Rico! You don't need a passport for Puerto Rico. And maybe you might be willing to try dancing again—the Merengue is fun and safe…"

Elise put her hand on his face. "I'm not the woman you want me to be. I wish I was, but I'm just not. I really like you, Zeke, but I don't want you to give up your dreams for me."

The disappointment didn't hit immediately, but came over him in little waves of pain with the realization that the woman he'd thought he was falling in love with was a total stranger after all. He'd been blinded by his intense longing to find the right woman— pushing Elise into that spot before finding out whether she actually fit.

"This isn't going to work, is it?" he said, with aching sadness, thinking of all the plans he'd made for them before knowing if she was the right woman.

"At least we gave it the old college try last night," she replied with a wry smile.

Zeke wondered if he would be single for the rest of his life. Was he giving up too easily? "Can we see each other again?"

Elise looked into his eyes and shook her head. "I really like you, Zeke, but I think a clean break is best, don't you?"

"Do you like the blues?"

Elise made a face. "Please don't tell me you bought us tickets to one of those dirty, smoky, blues bars."

Kingston Mines was certainly out. As much as he did not want this to end before it even started, he knew Elise was right.

"You can do anything right now, Zeke. What do you want to do?"

"My biggest regret was ripping up my acceptance letter from the Peace Corps." He thought he was honoring his father's wishes by doing it, but now he knew he should've followed his dream.

"You want to go into the Peace Corps?"

"No, I don't think I can do a two-year commitment and besides, the application process takes at least a year, but, I definitely want to travel."

"It's funny," she said, "I hardly know you, but I'm really going to miss you."

"I'm going to miss you too," he said pulling her close.

53

The grandfather clock in the next room chimed three times as Inez burrowed under what must be one-million thread count Egyptian cotton sheets, stretching her arms and legs in the afterglow of the best sex she'd had in ages. The rain had stopped. Sunshine streamed in through the hotel windows warming her face. And then it hit her—three o'clock; she would have been walking down the aisle at this very moment, Howard waiting for her in his black Armani tux. She should be on Interpol's most wanted list—surely, lying in bed with another man on your wedding day was a crime, somewhere.

"I can't wait to wake up every day next to you like this," said Carlos.

Inez wasn't certain how she felt at this moment. Was it pure lust or her memories of loving him that had allowed her to let down her guard and fall into bed with him? Had anything actually changed? And if it had, could she ever again get to the point of trusting him completely?

"Come with me tonight," he said.

"I'm not ready."

"I'm ready to share my life with you, to make you my wife, and start our family."

"I need time. I came here to end things with you."

That wasn't entirely true. She could've called. Telephones infinitely safer than planting herself inside his hotel bedroom. She might as well have hopped inside the lion's cage at the zoo. So why had she put herself in the most vulnerable position possible? Had she wanted this to happen?

Carlos went to his suitcase and returned to her side of the bed, kneeling down. "Inez, I love you. Will you marry me?"

He proffered a small black velvet box and opened it. She gasped. The single square-cut stone must be four carats. She'd only seen diamonds this big in glass cases surrounded by security guards and the latest high-tech infrared motion detectors. Whoever sold him this ring had probably retired off the commission and was now sipping umbrella drinks on a beach in Fiji. He took the ring out of the box and reached for her hand.

"No!" she said, pulling her hand away.

"Say yes," he said, as persistent as a commissioned salesman.

"I don't accept naked proposals."

He laughed. "I'll get dressed then."

"Carlos, please give me some time. I'm just not ready."

"Alright, querida." He replaced the ring and snapped the box shut. "But you know, I won't stop until you say yes."

It sounded like a threat. She remembered the five months he'd spent pursuing her after they'd first met in Madrid. After their first meeting, he started showing up at that café where she and her girlfriends went after classes every day. He became their unofficial tour guide taking them to museums, churches, parks, and restaurants—teaching them far more about how Madrileños lived than they would've ever learned on their own. The memory of why she'd rebuffed him all those months was vague, but the day she'd finally capitulated was crystal clear. After turning him down for the umpteenth time, he'd said good-bye to her for the last time. As she watched him walk away, she called out to him and accepted his dinner offer. To this day, she wondered how her life would've turned out had she simply let him disappear down the street and out of her life forever.

"I can come back to Chicago next month or you can come to Madrid for a visit, whenever you're ready."

Madrid tugged at her heart like a small child begging to go to the playground. Her memories of living abroad for the first time in her life, and discovering a city that was alive with passion and history, were among the happiest of her life—and the most painful, which explained why she had not gone back since leaving a decade ago. But now the possibility of visiting her beloved adopted city was tantalizing.

"Let me think about it."

"You are being difficult," he said, "but I love that about you." He kissed her mouth, his tongue playfully searching her own. Inez felt a rush of excitement, but he abruptly pulled away from her, looking at the clock on the nightstand. "Mierda. Will you see me off at the airport?"

"Well, I'm very busy…" she said, but when he looked stricken, she gave him a playful smile. "Of course I will."

54

Hours after she'd left, Zeke could still smell Elise's perfume on his clothes, a painful reminder that he was once again, back to square one—utterly alone. He supposed it wasn't surprising that last night he'd truly felt as though he was falling for her. As he sat on his balcony nursing a beer, it was now embarrassingly clear that what he had actually been falling for was the dream of having found the right woman. Being without a partner had been a constant ache, which had dulled over the years—filled with long hours at work—until he'd barely noticed it. But with Elise, all of those desires had been jarred wide awake, once again. He'd leapt head-first off the cliff into the land of happily-ever-afters when he should've stayed on solid ground a while longer.

All was not lost. A vision of the many roads he could take opened up in his mind's eye. He could reach out and touch the whole world, jab his finger at any location and be there in just a few days. The thrill of having his freedom back swelled inside of him as his disappointment ebbed away, bit by bit, until all thoughts of sadness and loneliness were banished, replaced with hope and excitement for his future.

His cell phone buzzed, crawling cockeyed across the small round glass-topped patio table at his side. Zeke answered.

"Zeke, where are you?" asked Mike.

"At home, is everything okay?"

"You've got to go to the airport right now," said Mike, whose voice still sounded raw from having tubes shoved down it two days ago. "Charlotte called me, Cybele is leaving."

Zeke silently cursed. He'd hoped that almost dying for a woman who cared more about how her manicure looked than the welfare of her own husband, would've knocked some sense into him.

"It's a very big airport," said Zeke, wishing he could retract the promise he'd made to Mike at the hospital. What good would it do to chase after someone who did not want to be found?

"I know where she's going."

"Cybele told Charlotte?"

"No, Cybele refused to tell her anything."

"Then how could you possibly know where she's headed?"

"She met this guy a few years before we got married. Whenever we had an argument, she threw him in my face saying he was the only man she'd ever loved. She threatened to leave me for him a dozen times."

That would be just like his cousin to do something so cruel. It wasn't bad enough that she treated Mike like he was something she'd scraped off the gutter—she'd had to add insult to injury as well.

"But she never followed through," said Zeke. Cybele had always been full of idle threats.

"Trust me on this," Mike said. "She's going back to this guy. Carlos something, a photographer she met on one of her shoots when she was a model."

Zeke didn't respond.

"You promised, remember?"

"Fine. Where is she going?"

"Madrid."

With Carlos and Cybele on the same flight, Zeke and Inez will meet at last. Serena, you look upset. What could possibly be wrong now?

This is the absolute worst time for Zeke and Inez to meet!

Well, I have to admit that a roving Mariachi band serenading our lovers on a warm summer's night with a hint of jasmine in the air might have been a bit more romantic than the airport food court, but we cannot always arrange the perfect circumstances.

Herodius, you've been inhaling compost and manure fumes for too long. Don't you understand? If they meet at the airport that's all it's going to be, just a meeting. They will never fall in love!

I do not agree with you.

Never doubt a romance novelist.

It is too late. Everything has been set in motion. There is nothing more we can do.

55

Zeke's heart soared as he entered the international terminal of O'Hare airport. Colorful flags representing nations from around the world, hung like hand-engraved invitations beckoning him to explore each one. The thought of stepping on a plane and landing in a place where the customs, language, food, and people were entirely different was so strong, he entertained the idea of purchasing a ticket for the first flight to any foreign destination he'd never visited before. He passed by the ticket counters for Lufthansa, Japan Airlines, KLM, Air France, and British Airways, practically salivating, as if the world was offering itself up like a stunning gourmet buffet, piled with every delicacy imaginable. The credit cards in his wallet sang a chorus of "pick me, pick me" and "let's go, let's go."

"Soon," he said, patting his wallet.

Finding the nearest computerized departure board, he quickly scanned down to the middle of the alphabet. There was a British Airways flight leaving for Madrid in just three hours. With any luck, Cybele had already passed through security and was far beyond reach. But a promise was a promise. He made his way to the British Airways ticket counter, along the way hearing a half dozen foreign tongues, each exotic word a tease, making the fact that he could not travel today all the more excruciating. He scanned the serpentine queue for a tall blonde, his eyes quickly passing over the dozens of prospective passengers of every shape, age, race and size who did not match his cousin's six-foot good looks.

Zeke moved to the white-tiled food court filled with the smell of frying grease and a dozen depressing chain restaurants. Whenever he traveled, he avoided the food court, instead, planting himself at a front row seat at the gate closest to security. That way he could see hundreds of passengers streaming past as he tried to imagine where each of them was headed and why. He'd fallen into his usual airport game until he remembered why he was here. He made another pass through the food court, this time making a point to look for Cybele, but when he reached the end without spotting her, it struck him that she would probably be at a bar. Turning around, he returned to an airport lounge he'd passed a few minutes earlier.

Zeke entered a golf-themed bar, tacky in the way of lawn ornaments and velvet paintings. Green artificial turf covered the wall behind the bar, criss-crossed golf clubs were everywhere, and golf-ball shaped napkin holders sat on each table. Zeke experienced a moment of pleasure that no matter what his future held, he would never again have to pick up a golf club.

His eyes swept across the bar landing on a man large and furry enough to double as a Yeti, who was rubbing his hairy mitt over his cousin's naked thigh. Sharing adjacent bar stools, she was leaning so far in her admirer's direction, she might as well have been sitting on his lap. Although Cybele hadn't modeled in years, she'd lost none of her looks. Her skirt was so tiny it could double as a bar rag; Zeke suspected that she was doing her *Basic Instinct* move by not wearing any panties. He tapped her on the shoulder.

"Cuz!" she slurred and stumbled off the stool, throwing her arms around him. "Hey everyone, this is my cousin Zeke. I love him!"

She pulled his head toward hers, thrusting her tongue deep inside his mouth. Her hands gripped the back of his head with such force, he felt as though he were attached to a giant squid that was sucking the life out of him. All eyes were on them when she released him.

"She's my second cousin," said Zeke to no one in particular, wondering why he was bothering. "You can legally marry your second cousin in all fifty states."

"He's a lawyer," said a giggling Cybele. "He knows these things.

And so cute, too!" She pinched his butt, causing him to jump.

He grabbed her offending hand and led her to a booth. He ordered two bottled waters and a cup of coffee from the waitress.

Cybele fumbled with her lighter as the cigarette dangling from her mouth dropped onto her lap. "Oops!" She reached for the cigarette pack inside her purse and slid out another, this time successfully lighting it.

The drinks came. He opened one bottle of water and told her to drink it. Just then, he noticed her boarding card sticking out of her purse, but he couldn't read the destination or gate information. Mike might think she was headed for Madrid, but Zeke had his doubts. He reached for it, but she was surprisingly quick given her inebriation. "Ah, ah, ah," she said, wagging her finger at him as if he were a naughty child. "No sneaky-peeky. Hey, I made a joke."

Exasperated with Cybele, Zeke didn't notice when Inez and a handsome, dark-haired man took a booth on the opposite side of the bar.

Serena, I have given your viewpoint some further consideration, and under the circumstances, I agree with you.

What was that, H? I'm not sure I heard you correctly.

You most certainly did hear me, but I will say it again. You are correct, Serena. This would be a most inopportune time for Zeke and Inez to meet.

Hallelujah! Now that you've finally come to your senses, how do we stop them from seeing one another?

I see no options at this point.

That can't be! So there's no hope at all?

There is always hope, Serena. Have faith.

H, I don't intend to sit here on my beautiful behind and do diddly-squat. Wait! I have a brilliant idea! In my fifty-first novel, Distant Shore...

56

Inez watched a tall blonde woman with a pair of legs that seemed to go on forever, kiss a tousled-haired man as though she'd just found her long-lost soul mate after a search spanning decades and thousands of miles. The woman's back was to Inez, but she could see that she had the same kind of model-thin body as Rachel. How ironic Inez thought, that she used to be jealous. But after Rachel became addicted to heroin, she'd never again been jealous. Their lives might appear to be perfect and glamorous, but they had problems just like everyone else—sometimes, much worse.

Carlos hadn't stopped touching her since they left the hotel. All the way to the airport, during the limousine ride, he'd kissed and caressed her as if the transfer of her skin cells to his own body could somehow guarantee that she would accept his marriage proposal sooner rather than later. But if trust could be measured in building blocks, he had yet to set the cornerstone. She was willing to give this relationship another try, but would not make the mistake of giving up anything for him, at least not until she was certain she could trust him.

Carlos reached into his suit coat pocket pulling out his cell phone and placing it on the table along with the black velvet box. He opened the box and pushed it toward her. "At least try it on," said Carlos, opening the box. "Give me something to think about until the next time we see one another."

The light was low in the bar lounge, but the diamond sparkled brightly enough to disorient pilots trying to safely land their planes.

Inez imagined that, at any moment, airport security rushing in and throwing themselves on the rock to prevent a plane crash.

Her ring finger felt naked after she'd returned her engagement ring to Howard last night. Although she loved the ring Howard had given her, never in her wildest imagination had she pictured a ring this magnificent. Only the size of the stone made it gaudy, but the elegant cut of a single stone on a plain platinum band was exactly her style. Well, she supposed just trying it on wouldn't hurt. She felt the weight of it in her palm and slipped it on her finger. She felt his eyes upon her.

"We're not engaged."

"Not yet," he said, wearing the half-smile that could be boyish at times and, at other times, insufferably arrogant.

Across the bar Cybele lit a cigarette and blew smoke rings in the air.

"Cybele, I have something important to tell you."

"If this is about my loser of a husband, I don't want to hear it."

"You'll want to hear this. Mike tried to commit suicide two days ago. He's in the hospital."

Cybele gazed at the smoke rings that looked like lopsided halos.

"He almost died," Zeke continued, annoyed that Cybele wasn't looking at him.

She turned her attention to Zeke, suddenly looking completely sober. "Yeah, I know. Charlotte told me."

Zeke knew Cybele was cold-blooded, but he couldn't believe this, even of her. "Mike loves you, and he needs you. When he woke up, the first thing he asked about was you."

"It's really over this time. I'm going away and filing for divorce from my new country."

Cybele and Mike had always made up, or rather, Cybele would trick Mike into falling for her again. After being a total bitch one minute, she would turn around and shower Mike with love and affection, making him feel like the luckiest man on the planet. Cybele had always been an expert at knowing what made people tick. It came as naturally to her as breathing. In the sixteenth century, she would've been burned at the stake.

Zeke sighed. "Do you have any message for him?"

"Tell him I'm sorry I ever met him. Take care of yourself, Cuz," she said, grabbing her purse, and then she was gone.

Inez watched the blonde woman walk out of the bar. Her face was more stunning than her body. Inez's eyes quickly flicked to Carlos. She was happy to see that he hadn't noticed the woman. When they'd lived together, it used to drive her crazy when he flaunted his appreciation for attractive women right in front of her. That blonde was exactly his type, and he'd had a perfect view of her. Perhaps he had changed, Inez thought, with a small flicker of hope.

"We have time for one drink," Carlos said. "I'll get us some wine."

Carlos went to the bar and a moment later, his cell phone made a sound as though the telephone ring had been swallowed. He had just received a text message. The phone called to her like a friendly spirit begging her to unveil its secrets. She reached for it and stopped. She shouldn't read his message. She had been raised to respect other people's privacy. And trust was the foundation of all good relationships. She'd made a point of following the Golden Rule her entire life. She certainly wouldn't want him reading her mail, or digging through her luggage or… She looked up to make certain he was still at the bar. Flipping open his phone, she pushed the button and quickly read the message.

The floor suddenly opened up. Inez felt herself plunging straight to the center of the earth. Feeling nauseous, she clutched the material on her blouse at her breastbone. How could he do this to her? He lied to her, again! She reread the message: "Can't stop thinking about you. Meet me tonight? My apartment. Nicole."

The vile snake! He was lower than the Ebola virus. Lower than a condemned mass murderer. Lower than the rotting flesh of a dead disfigured pedophile putrefying under the hot sun. All rational thought escaped Inez as she quickly typed a reply text and replaced the phone where he'd left it, just in time.

He placed a glass of red wine in front of her and sat down.

"They didn't have Rioja. I hope you like this Merlot," said the villainous scum as he reached for her hand. She used all of her willpower to not pull away from his scaly clutches. "Are you alright, *querida?*"

"I'm fine, just a little overwhelmed with everything that's happened," she replied sweetly, while thinking, "you two-faced, despicable gangrenous rancid wound on the buttocks of the earth."

"This wine is awful," he said, pushing his glass away.

"I have to use the restroom, honey. I'll be right back."

As Inez made her way to the restroom, Mike Knight's hospital room telephone rang twice, but Zeke snapped his cell phone shut before Mike could answer. What was he thinking? He couldn't tell Mike about his wife leaving him over the telephone. He needed to tell him in person. Zeke rose to leave. As he walked out of the bar, someone brushed past him, knocking into his shoulder. He had read it was possible to feel the emotions of others—especially strong emotions—and if that were true, the woman who had just bumped into him was furious beyond measure. Zeke watched her walk away; what a funny coincidence, she had hair exactly like Inez's.

Inez entered the nearest bathroom, made her way to the sink, and splashed water on her face. As she patted her face dry with a paper towel, Inez felt someone staring at her and turned. It was the blonde model that had been in the bar a few minutes earlier.

"Wow, that's some ring you've got there," the woman said. "It must be worth a fortune."

Inez had completely forgotten about the ring, which was a little astounding given its size and weight, sort of like forgetting that one had a noose around one's neck. "Yeah, you're right," Inez replied, lost in thought.

Both women stared at the gorgeous ring for a long moment, and then, Inez calmly walked to the nearest stall, slipped it off, dropped it in the toilet and flushed, waiting only long enough to make certain it had disappeared forever, far into the bowels of the Chicago sewer system.

Carlos fidgeted in the booth, wondering why Inez was taking so long, but before he could think about looking for her, his cell phone rang. He looked at the unfamiliar number with the Chicago prefix and answered it.

"I just read your reply text," said a woman, through her tears. "You asshole!"

"Who is this?"

"You are fucking freaky, you know that? First we get totally naked, and then you get all religious on me or something and won't sleep with me. And now, I find out you have a disease. You can't come over tonight because you have syphilis! It's men like you who make…"

Carlos closed the phone. A feeling of dread swept through him. He flipped his phone back open and read his most recent incoming and outgoing text messages.

"*Mierda,*" he said, to no one in particular.

Mike was sitting up in his hospital bed eating a sandwich, almost looking like his old self—the pre-Cybele Mike Knight. "This tastes like dog crap," he said, as he tossed the remains of the sandwich back onto the plate and pushed the tray aside. "I need some real food."

"Glad to see you're feeling better," said Zeke.

"Yeah, well, just about anything feels better than getting your stomach pumped."

"I just came from the airport."

"She's gone, isn't she," Mike said, in a flat voice.

Zeke nodded.

"Well, I knew it was really over this time," said Mike. "Before I tried to…before I took the pills and the scotch, I got a call from my accountant. Cybele drained all our bank accounts. Millions are gone."

"You gave her access to your bank accounts!" Zeke wanted to shout. That's like giving a teenaged boy keys to a liquor store that also sells condoms in bulk.

"Did she have any message for me?" asked Mike.

"No," Zeke lied, and then quickly changed the topic. "When are they letting you out?"

"Tomorrow."

"Why don't you stay in Chicago. You can do your alcohol treatment here."

"You mean that?" Mike asked, wide-eyed.

"Of course. Stay as long as you want."

"Thanks Zeke for, you know, for finding me and everything," Mike said. "I wouldn't be here if it wasn't for you."

"I just have one request."

"What's that?"

"Don't ever pull anything that stupid again. You scared the shit out of me."

"I scared the shit out of myself," said Mike, with sheepish grin. "I love you, man."

"I love you too, Mike."

"Carlos? Is it really you?"

Carlos looked up, briefly met her eyes and returned his gaze to his lap. Cybele stared at him; her mind spun wildly like a pinwheel on a stick.

"Hello, Cybele."

"Is that all you have to say to me after all these years?" Cybele looked around the airport departure lounge. "What are you doing here? I thought we were supposed to meet in Madrid."

Carlos didn't respond.

"Can you believe this? We must be on the same flight," said Cybele, a master of observation.

"You should cancel your flight," said Carlos.

"What do you mean?"

"I no longer want you to come to Madrid," said Carlos.

"I left my husband," she continued. "I'll file for divorce from Spain."

"I don't love you anymore," he said. "I'm not sure I ever did."

Cybele was struck dumb—even dumber than usual.

"That's impossible," she sputtered. "Of course you love me."

Cybele reached out to touch Carlos. He removed his hand from her arm.

Tears began streaming down Cybele's cheeks. "I never loved my husband! I always loved you! Even after I caught you with that bitch in our bed!"

"Go Cybele, please."

"Carlos, it's me, Cybele," she said, tears streaming down her face. "Look at me!"

Still staring at his hands in his lap, he said, "I've lost the best woman I've ever known."

And with that Carlos rose, leaving Cybele frozen to her spot.

One Month Later

57

Rollerblading through the Chicago Loop, mid-morning on a weekday, wearing black cargo shorts and a black T-shirt, Zeke expertly weaved in and around wing-tipped businessmen in wing-tipped shoes and women in high heels and then skidded to a quick stop with a combo heel brake and a T-stop. His rollerblading skills had come back to the level of his law school days in just a few weeks. He hadn't spilled a drop of Charlie's soy latté. And there was even one blueberry scone left, although he'd slept in late that morning, as he had every morning over the last month.

There was just one problem. Charlie wasn't at his corner. In his place was a thin, twenty-something African-American man sporting an enormous Afro encircling his head like an aura. Alarm turned to near panic when Zeke saw that the man was holding Charlie's mutual funds sign. Zeke knew life on the streets was rough. This guy could've killed Charlie for something as small as a few dollars.

"Hey," Zeke shouted to the interloper, hoping he looked tough wearing rollerblades. "Where's Charlie?"

The man turned, his face impassive. He looked Zeke over as if to say, "Who the hell are you?" But then he broke into a wide toothy smile. "Where you been, man?"

"What?"

"You Zeke, right?"

Zeke nodded.

The man dug in his pocket and pulled out a crumpled envelope. "Charlie said to give you this when you showed up."

Zeke handed him the coffee and scone and a twenty-dollar bill, and thanked him. He rollerbladed to a bench in the sun and opened the envelope, finding a handwritten note inside.

"Dear Zeke, I've never talked about my past because for a long time I couldn't face it. I was trying to pretend it had never happened. But I want you to know about me, and why I was so hard on you all these years.

At one point, I had it all. I was married to a wonderful woman, had a son, a beautiful home in Atlanta, and wore a fancy suit to work every day, just like you. But I fell into that trap, the trap I saw you getting yourself into. Getting that next promotion and salary raise became all important to me. I ignored my family, my wife left me, and I turned to drugs. I lost everything. I came to Chicago because I didn't know a soul here. Chicago, I thought, was a place I could live out the rest of my life in complete anonymity. And then you came along. When you told me you quit your job, you inspired me to do the thing I'd been avoiding for years. I called my son in Atlanta. I learned I have a daughter-in-law and a grandson. I've moved back home. I'm not certain what the future holds for me, but I'm finally willing to give life another chance.

I hope someday to see you again. You treated me with dignity when I had none to give to myself. Good luck with your future, Zeke. I know you'll make me proud.

Your friend always—Charles Sage."

Later that night, Zeke and Mike maneuvered their way to the bar as salsa music blasted over the hum of the Friday night happy-hour crowd.

"Hey, Fernando," Zeke yelled, interrupting the bartender in the midst of jiggling a cocktail shaker in his hands, while gyrating his hips for a group of ladies who cheered him on as though he was a Chippendale dancer. Fernando finished his show and made his way over to Zeke's end of the bar.

"*Ay, mira,*" he said to Zeke. "You look like a *Papi Chulo*. I almost didn't recognize you."

Zeke laughed, shaking Fernando's hand and introduced Mike.

"What's a Papi Chuhoo…?" asked Mike.

"Chulo," said Zeke. "It's not important."

"It means a hot guy," said Fernando. "Shit, sounds bad in English, like I'm hitting on you or something."

Through rollerblading everyday, salsa dancing a few nights a week and working out at the gym, Zeek had dropped twenty-five pounds and had the kind of tan he hadn't sported since his college days when he and Mike would cut classes to play Frisbee at the lakefront.

"You want one of my world famous margaritas?" asked Fernando.

"We're going to find a table," said Zeke. "Can you send one over?"

"You got it."

"Do you mind if I have a margarita?" Zeke asked Mike when they were seated, realizing he might've been insensitive. After everything Mike had been through in the last month, it was still difficult to think of him as an alcoholic. "I can cancel the order?"

"Don't worry about it, I'll have my usual," said Mike. "I should say my new usual. I'm learning to appreciate sparkling mineral water."

A pretty waitress came to take their orders, and Zeke was happy to see Mike flirt with her. The old Mike was coming back, little by little.

"Are you finally ready to tell me about your screenplay?" asked Zeke.

Mike had been working on a new screenplay every day since he'd been released from the hospital. But he'd refused to tell Zeke anything about it, giving him some mumbo jumbo about disturbing the numinous writer's inspiration that only the fickle writing gods would bestow, only if Saturn aligned with Mars or if the wind stroked a butterfly's wings on Santa Lucia day, but only during Leap years—or something like that.

"Well, all right, but only because you're leaving tomorrow," said Mike, giving Zeke a short synopsis of the story.

The main character, Sam, was an unhappy alcoholic who got so drunk one night, he crashed into a tree and ended up paralyzed from the neck down. Sam, a forty-eight-year-old Pulitzer Prize winning novelist, was severely depressed and no longer wanted to live.

"Can't imagine where you got that idea," Zeke interrupted.

"Let me finish," said Mike, who was clearly enjoying sharing his plot. "Sam meets a twenty-year-old paraplegic who goes to the same physical therapist. Sam is amazed by the positive attitude of the young paraplegic who begs Sam to mentor him because he wants to write a novel. In the end, Sam learns how to be happy again."

"And the young paraplegic's novel?" asked Zeke.

"I don't know yet, I'm thinking it should suck," said Mike, "or, maybe I'll kill off Sam and the novel ends up on the *New York Times* best seller list. The ending can't be too happy."

"I like happy endings," said Zeke. "What does your agent think?"

"He loves it, thinks it's going to be another *Daunted*."

"That's great!"

Mike shrugged. "Whatever happens, it just feels good to be writing something I believe in again."

Their drinks and food came.

"So how long are you going to be gone?" asked Mike, taking a bite of his chicken fajitas.

"I don't know."

"Where are you going?"

"After I step off that plane tomorrow night, it's all up for grabs."

"How can you travel like that?"

"It's the only way to travel," said Zeke. "Now don't forget, you promised to look in on my mother."

"At least once a week."

"Make sure she's taking her medications," said Zeke. "I don't want another scare like I had last month."

Zeke's mother didn't have Alzheimer's after all. There had simply been an imbalance with her medications, which had caused temporary dementia. The doctor explained that it was really quite common. After he'd readjusted the doses and switched one of the brands, she was back to normal.

Mike handed Zeke a stack of documents. Scanning them, Zeke looked up at Mike in surprise. "You filed for divorce?"

"It took me long enough, but now I know that Cybele was more poisonous to me than the scotch. I should've listened to you when you tried to talk me out of marrying her."

Zeke wouldn't have given Mike this much credit for being so strong. Cybele, as unpredictable as ever, had mysteriously cancelled her trip to Madrid last month. She'd spent the last four weeks in Chicago trying to win Mike back. They'd even gone out a couple of times. Zeke had been expecting Mike to announce any day, that he and Cybele were leaving for L.A. yet again.

"I'm really proud of you," said Zeke.

"I'm proud of you. I didn't think you'd have the balls to quit your job."

"Thanks, I think. You're okay, right?"

"I'm good," said Mike. "Don't worry about me. Just enjoy your trip."

"I intend to," said Zeke, feeling a surge of enthusiasm. His life was finally about to start.

58

I nez pushed opened the heavy wooden door, instantly relieved to see that the receptionist's desk was empty. She could only imagine how Sarah Conway would treat her now, after breaking off her engagement to Howard. "Howard is such a good man," she'd said the last time Inez was here. Sarah was right, Howard was a good man, just not the right man for her, and she was not the right woman for him.

Over the last month, Inez had picked up the phone a dozen times to check on him, but had hung up before trying his number, knowing it was too soon. But she couldn't leave for her trip tomorrow until she made certain he was all right. Saying good-bye in person would be difficult, but it was the least she could do. She hoped someday they might be friends.

As she walked down the hallway toward his office, she heard what sounded like murmuring and then the muffled voices of a man and a woman. His door was open. Inez listened outside for a moment, hearing the rustling of clothing. She peeked through the crack of the door jam and almost fell against it in disbelief. Howard and Sarah were kissing and groping one another like two teenaged-lovers.

Inez tiptoed back out of the office with a smile, gently closing the door behind her. She wouldn't have to worry about Howard, after all.

A delicate breeze blew over their outdoor table in Old Town. The clatter of plates and chatter of other diners was like a friendly bon voyage to Inez who felt at peace and utterly content. Here she was with the two people she loved most and was leaving tomorrow to start her new future. A swell of happiness filled her.

"Are you growing your hair back?" Inez asked Marilynn.

Marilynn rubbed the quarter-inch gray stubble on her head as though she was checking to make certain it was still there. "I might shave it off again, I don't like the gray," Marilynn replied. "Besides, I think I need to be bald for my comedy act."

Rachel rolled her eyes and snorted. Inez elbowed her hard under the table.

"Ow!" said Rachel. "I'm here under duress. If you weren't leaving tomorrow I wouldn't be here, Izzy."

"I don't know how long I'm going to be gone," said Inez. "Try and control yourself. It's just one dinner, Rachel."

"Yes, big sis," replied a chastened Rachel.

The waitress cleared away their plates, asked if anyone wanted dessert and, with no takers, plopped the bill on the table. Inez reached for it, but Marilynn put her hand over it.

"Honey, let me," she said, pulling out a wad of cash from her jeans pocket, "you need every cent you've got for your big trip."

"Thanks," Inez said. "Where is your comedy routine?"

"Just up the street at Zanies Comedy Club," said Marilynn. "I had my audition two weeks ago. They loved my swami jokes, and I have my first gig next week!"

"That's great!"

"They even let me sit in the green room," Marilynn continued, as excited as a teenager getting her first job. "And it pays fifty dollars a night!"

"I told you she'd come back from India flakier than a pie crust," whispered Rachel loud enough to be heard by the kitchen staff at the restaurant across the street.

Inez glared at Rachel.

"I'll be a big star by the time you get back, honey," Marilynn continued. "Comedy Central. Vegas. Jay Leno. Maybe I'll have my own show!"

Inez had no doubt it would happen. Marilynn had always been able to create her life exactly the way she wanted it—just like a magician.

"I thought you were a 'Daunter,' Marilynn," Inez said. "Those places aren't going to pay your huge salary in cash."

"They found me," said Marilynn.

"Who found you?"

"The IRS, who else?" Marilynn replied. "I couldn't get my passport for India without giving them my social security number. Can you believe that?"

"Speaking of passports, where are you going, Izzy?" asked Rachel.

"I'll see what happens after I land tomorrow night," replied Inez. "Wherever the wind blows me, I guess."

"You don't know how long you're going to be gone or where you're going?" "How can you travel like that?"

"It's the only way to travel," said Inez. "I've got a one-year leave of absence from school, maybe I'll take the whole year?"

"How are you feeling, honey," asked Marilynn, "about the whole Howard and Carlos…?"

"Fiasco?" interjected Rachel. "Sorry, Izzy. Listen, I know I wasn't very nice about that situation. I want you to know, I will never interfere with your love life again."

Inez raised her left eyebrow.

"Really, you can date anyone, even a convicted felon and I swear I won't say a word," Rachel said, drawing her fingers across her lips like closing a zipper.

"I'm glad to hear that, Rach," said Inez, "although I have my doubts. But anyway, I'm not ready for a relationship right now. I've done a lot of soul searching over the last month. I want to be by myself for a while. I need to figure out what I really want."

"Good for you, honey," said Marilynn, with a pat to her hand.

"I can see now that I lost myself when I was with Carlos," said Inez. "Then, for years I lost myself in salsa dancing. And when I met Howard, I lost myself in…"

"Boredom?" Rachel suggested.

Inez and Marilynn both glared at Rachel who sunk into her seat and mouthed "sorry."

"I don't want to ever let that happen again," said Inez.

"But what about having kids?" asked Rachel.

"I haven't given up my dream of being a mother. I've got time. It's not my first choice, but I'm willing to raise a child on my own, if I have to."

"You're a man magnet," said Rachel. "That's not going to happen. Mark my words, you're going to meet someone before you step off that plane tomorrow night."

The three of them walked out of the restaurant and gathered on the sidewalk in a tight circle, each going in a different direction. Inez hugged Marilynn and then Rachel.

"Take good care of Beso," Inez said to Rachel.

"I will."

They said their good-byes and Inez set off in the direction of the setting sun.

59

A few hours later, Inez, feeling alive, entered Club Caliente as if coming home after a long journey. As she made her way to the stage at the far end of the dance floor, she was stopped by a dozen men and women. She exchanged greetings with all of them with a kiss to both cheeks. A moment later, she was pulled to the floor and didn't stop dancing for the next hour until she took a break and went to the bar.

"Inez!"

Turning to the voice behind her with a salsa glow on her face, Inez saw a man she didn't recognize.

Her auburn curls tumbled over her bare shoulders and her chest rose and fell as she caught her breath. Perspiration glistened at the hollow of her neck and on her forehead. She was the most beautiful woman Zeke had ever seen. He couldn't take his eyes off of her as he tried to cram every nuance of this moment into his memory. His heart pounded against his chest, desperate to escape, as he stifled the urge to take her into his arms.

"How do you know my name?" asked Inez. She tipped her head back as she took a sip of water. Zeke stared at her long thin neck—as perfect and fragile as an angel's wing.

"We met at Grant Park, at Dancing under the Stars thirteen years ago."

"Thirteen years ago? You certainly have a good memory," Inez replied, as she tried to keep the wariness out of her voice. Red flag.

Potential nutcase here. And he didn't look like much of a salsa dancer. He might be one of those guys who stalked salsa clubs just to pick up women.

Thirteen years was nothing if you knew that I'd never forgotten you, Zeke thought. Luckily, he resisted telling her that.

"Would you like to sit down?" Zeke suggested with a wave toward an empty booth.

"Listen I'm not…" Inez stopped. She wanted to dance and had no interest in meeting anyone, but she suddenly felt as though she should talk to this man. He was okay looking, tall enough, with a great body, and kind of cute. But it didn't matter because she wasn't looking.

"I'd love to," she replied, but the words weren't coming from her. She had a disembodied feeling, as though someone else was putting thoughts into her head and speaking for her.

They slid into opposite sides of the booth. An exchange of polite smiles was followed by an uncomfortable silence. This guy had invited her to sit down, and now he couldn't make simple chit-chat. She should've said no.

"So, you know my name. What's yours?" Inez asked, as she tried to think of an excuse to get back out to the dance floor. One of her favorite salsa songs was playing, and it was pure torture to sit through it, especially with Mr. Mute here who, she'd just noticed, was sweating—a lot.

"Zeke Nomad," he said, holding out his hand. As they shook, a prickle of electricity raced through her body. Weird, but she had to admit that their meeting had a bit of a *déjà vu* feeling to it.

"I don't know your last name," Zeke said, warning himself not to blow it. He discreetly wiped a bead of perspiration from his forehead, hoping she hadn't noticed how much he was sweating.

Inez hesitated. Normally, she wouldn't tell a complete stranger her last name, but it felt like the right thing to do. He seemed harmless enough, and there was something about him that was strangely familiar.

In that long moment, seeing the doubt cross her face, Zeke died a thousand deaths. He shouldn't have asked for her last name, he thought, cursing his boldness.

"Paris," she said, breaking the terrible silence.

"Are you going there?" he asked, relieved at least that she hadn't fled from him in fright.

"No, that's my last name."

"Oh, and one of my favorite cities."

"Mine too."

Was it her imagination or were there waves of excited energy flying back and forth across their table? I'm taking a break from men, she mentally reminded herself.

Zeke wondered what he could he say to make this right, but realized that if he tried too hard, he would ruin everything. He didn't want to freak her out, at least not anymore than he already had.

"Do you know how to salsa?" she asked.

"I love it," Zeke responded. "I love the whole Latin culture. I was supposed to go into the Peace Corps, Costa Rica and I...what's the matter? Is something wrong?"

Inez's heart pounded so hard she could scarcely speak. "Me too. What year were you supposed to go?" she asked, afraid to hear his answer.

"2002."

She looked so startled that he impulsively reached across the table to take her hand. Thankfully, she didn't seem to mind or maybe she hadn't noticed? But he had. His whole body was buzzing at the touch of her soft skin.

"I should go," she said. She didn't want this to happen. She'd just gotten out of two relationships that were wrong for her. Another man complicating her life was the last thing she wanted.

Zeke had a horrible flash of watching Inez walk away from him like the last time they'd met. He couldn't let that happen again.

"Inez, wait please," Zeke said. "Just sit here for a few more minutes? I need to tell you something."

Inez wondered what this total stranger—who didn't feel like a stranger at all—would say to her.

He searched for just the right words knowing that if he came on too strong, she would leave, and he'd never have another chance with her.

"Wait," Inez said, interrupting his thoughts, "I do remember you! We danced and talked and then it rained. More like poured."

Relief flooded through Zeke. "So you didn't go into the Peace Corps?"

She shook her head. "But I was supposed to go to Costa Rica too, the same year as you."

Now Zeke was shocked. Peace Corps volunteers going to the same counties always had their training together for six months, before being sent out alone on individual assignments. And since Costa Rica wasn't that big, they definitely would've met and might've ended up working close to one another.

"This is kind of amazing, isn't it?" said Zeke.

Inez nodded and finished her water as Zeke thought about kissing her collarbone.

"Listen, Inez," he said, "this is going to sound nuts, I hope you don't think I'm nuts. Okay, I might be a little, but..." he paused, realizing he was rambling like a lunatic. "I'd love to see you again, except that I'm going on a trip tomorrow and I'm not sure when I'll be back. Can I have your number?"

When Inez shook her head, Zeke felt as though he'd been severed in two. But then Inez laughed, marveling at this avalanche of coincidences.

"I'm going on a trip tomorrow too, and I'm not sure when I'm going to be back either."

They stared into one another's eyes, both thinking the exact same thought. What were the chances they were traveling to the same place? There were almost two-hundred countries in the world, it couldn't be possible.

"Costa Rica," Zeke said, at the same moment Inez said, "Mexico."

"Oh," they responded in unison, both disappointed.

"Inez, can you keep a secret? I'm actually going to Cuba and because it's illegal to go, I'm..."

Inez nodded.

"Oh my God, you too?" Zeke exclaimed. "Let me guess, via Cancun?"

She nodded.

"Smart."

"I need to salsa," Inez said, standing up quickly.

Taking her hand Zeke led her to the dance floor. He twirled her several times, first in one direction and then the other, and managed to dip her on the very last beat of the song. When a Cha Cha Cha came on they returned to their booth. Zeke plunged in with the plan he'd formulated while they were dancing.

"Let's meet in Havana Monday night, at La Bodeguita del Medio for..."

"...a mojito. Ernest Hemingway's favorite hangout," Inez said, finishing his sentence.

Please, please, please say 'yes' he begged her silently while trying to look as nonchalant as though he was discussing the weather with his mailman, a ridiculous hope.

She hesitated. This was exactly what she didn't want, another relationship to take her off the path that she finally knew she needed to follow. Of course, maybe they could start out as friends? For some reason, she knew that Zeke wouldn't pressure her, and, overriding any concern was an undeniable warmth and familiarity she felt with him that she simply could not explain. It was the same way she'd felt with him in Grant Park, on that magical night, so many years ago.

"I really should go," said Inez, as she started to slide out of the booth.

"Wait!" said Zeke. He grabbed a pen from his pocket and scribbled his name and cell phone number on a napkin. "Can I have your number Inez, just in case we miss each other in Cuba?"

Inez looked at Zeke's friendly face and adorable smile.

"Don't worry, I'll be there Monday night," Inez said. "I can already taste that mojito, Zeke."

As Inez walked out of the club, she wanted to run and skip and dance—the wonderful feeling of wild freedom filling her with joy and hope. Inez was on the edge of a precipice, but she could fly without fear of falling. Her life was finally about to start.

Zeke watched her walk away her dress billowed about her and her flaming hair bounced in time with her graceful gait, until she disappeared into the crowd. A peaceful feeling washed over him, confirming what he already knew in his heart, he and Inez were meant to be together. And for the first time, in a long time, he felt no fear.

Well, Serena, our assignment is complete. It was a pleasure working with you.

That's it? H, I have to know what's going to happen.

You really want to know?

Stop teasing me. Spill it!

Wayne Martin and Pamela, Zeke's law firm dinner dance date, are soul mates. And, I am certain you surmised that Sarah, Howard's receptionist, has been in love with him for the past fifteen years. Howard reminds me of Dick Kowalski. Just like Dick, it took Howard long enough to realize that Sarah is the right...

Stop! You know I want to hear about Zeke and Inez. They're going to get married, right?

We cannot see that far into the future.

But they're going to fall in love, right?

Free will, Serena, anything can happen. But if it makes you feel any better, I do know they will see one another in Cuba. What happens after that is up to them. Besides, it is of no consequence.

No consequence? H, it's the whole reason we spent the last five earth weeks agonizing over them!

Inez needs to decide if a relationship is something she wants. She now knows that she can be happy without a partner. That was the life lesson she needed to learn.

What about Zeke? What if she turns him down? He's going to be devastated.

Zeke will be fine whether or not he and Inez end up together.

But they're soul mates and they're meant to be together!

Serena, do you remember reading in their file about the night they met and fell in love at Grant Park?

Of course I do.

Even if they don't end up together in this lifetime, their souls will never forget that night.

Well, I guess that is that. Herodius, any chance you might consider going back?

Oh no, I need to get back to my Rhododendrons immediately.

I'm going back. I'm being sent to Minot, North Dakota. Of all the places on God's green earth...

You could stay, Serena. I have recommended you for a permanent position in this department.

Well butter my biscuit! Are you getting soft on me H?

We make an excellent team, Serena.

And the feeling is mutual. Except for when you drive me crazy, which is most of the time.

What is your decision, Serena?

I appreciate the recommendation, H, but I am aching to find my true love; although the thought that he might be in North Dakota is mighty difficult to fathom.

You will find him. I will look in on you from time to time, especially during blueberry season.

Blueberry season?

Blueberry bushes are another of my specialties.

You're something else, H. I think I'm going to miss you.

I may appear in your dreams from time to time, but you will never think of me during your waking hours.

H, you're too much of a pain in my behind to ever forget. Will we ever work together again?

I will plan on it, Serena.

H, any parting words of advice for me?

Yes, remember that a life lived in fear is a life half-lived.

ACKNOWLEGEMENTS

Thank you to Elaine Baur for her excellent editing skills.

To my sister, Carol, for her amazing ability to catch misspellings, missing words and punctuation errors, even after the manuscript has been scrutinized, with a fine-tooth comb, many times before.

My brother Steve Hornak, Ilene Breitbarth, Monica Alesci-Swinson, and my husband Russ, read earlier versions of this manuscript and their feedback helped to improve this story.

And, of course, thank you to my family and friends, who steadfastly believe in me and encourage me to persevere when I lose faith in myself.

ABOUT THE AUTHOR

JoAnn Hornak was born and raised in Milwaukee, has lived a significant amount of her adult life in Chicago, and currently calls Napa, California home. This is her third novel. She is not yet a *New York Times* or *USA Today* best-selling novelist, but would very much like to be one, someday, soon.

Please visit her website at: www.joannhornak.com